The Journey Begins

CUB
HOUSE

The Wormworld Saga, Volume 1, The Jouney Begins, published 2018 by The Lion Forge, LLC. © 2018 Daniel Lieske/TOKYOPOP GmbH. All rights reserved. LION FORGE™, CUBHOUSE™ and the associated distinctive designs are trademarks of The Lion Forge, LLC. No similarity between any of the names, characters, persons, and/or institutions in this issue with those of any living or dead person or institution is intended and any such similarity which may exist is purely coincidental. Printed in China.

ISBN: 978-1-941302-71-2
Library of Congress Control Number: 2018931085

10 9 8 7 6 5 4 3 2 1

Contents

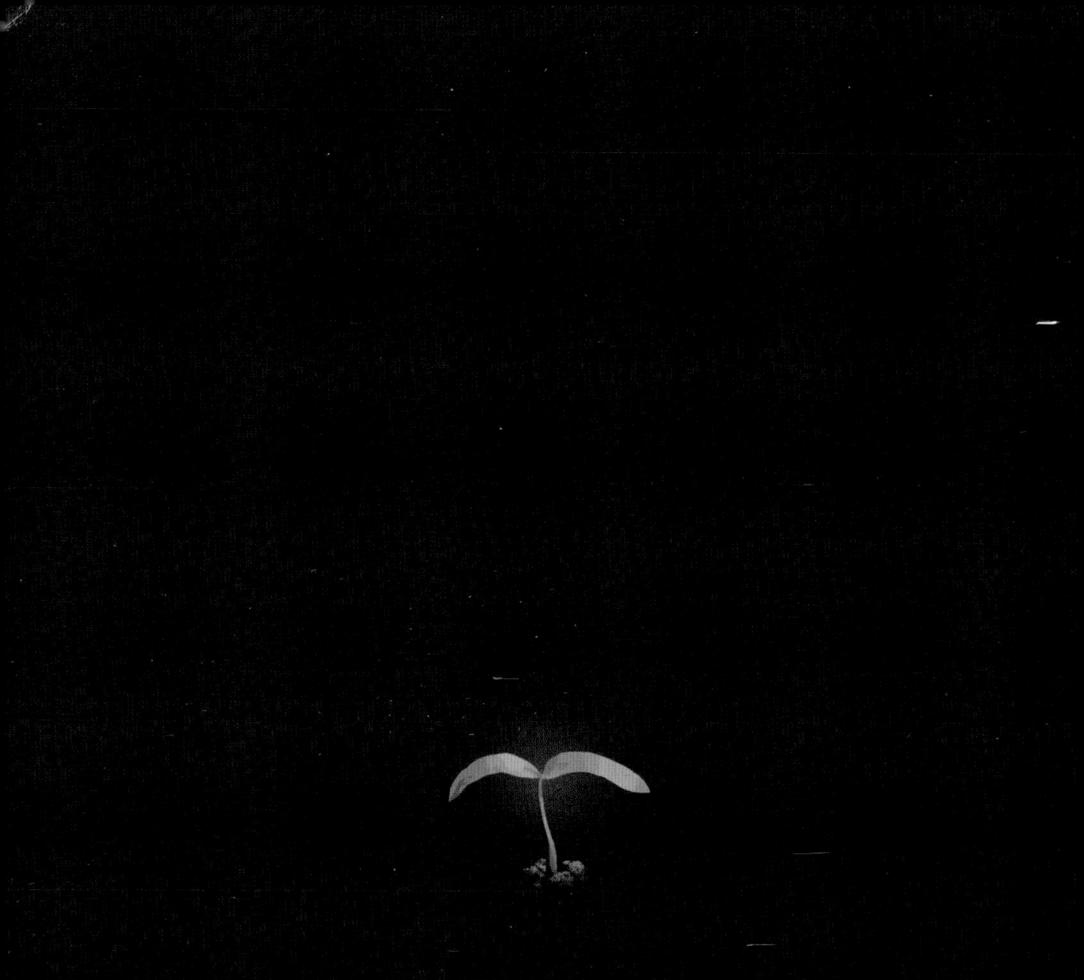

To my wife and the stirring little life inside her.

Chapter 1
The Last Day of School

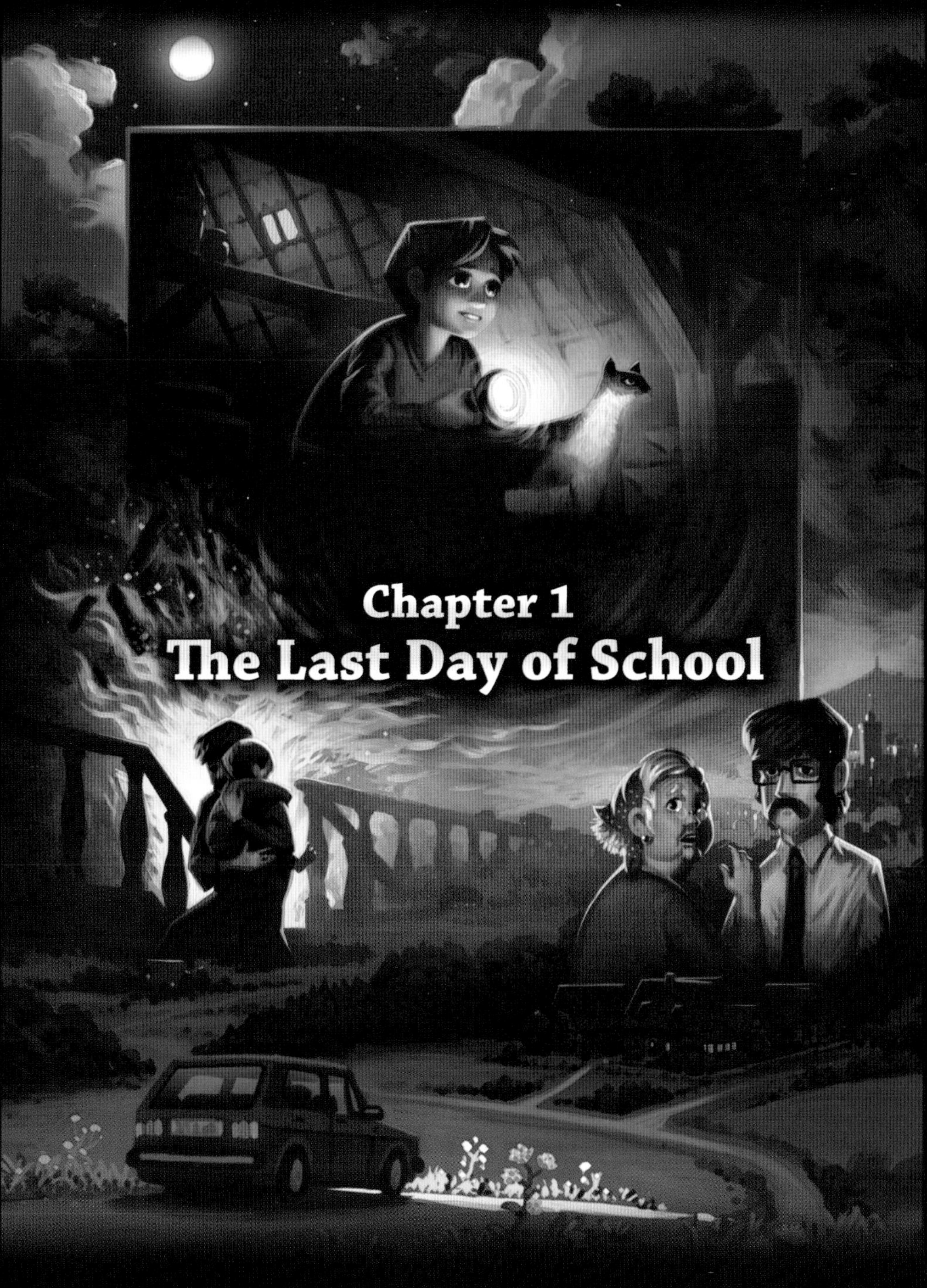

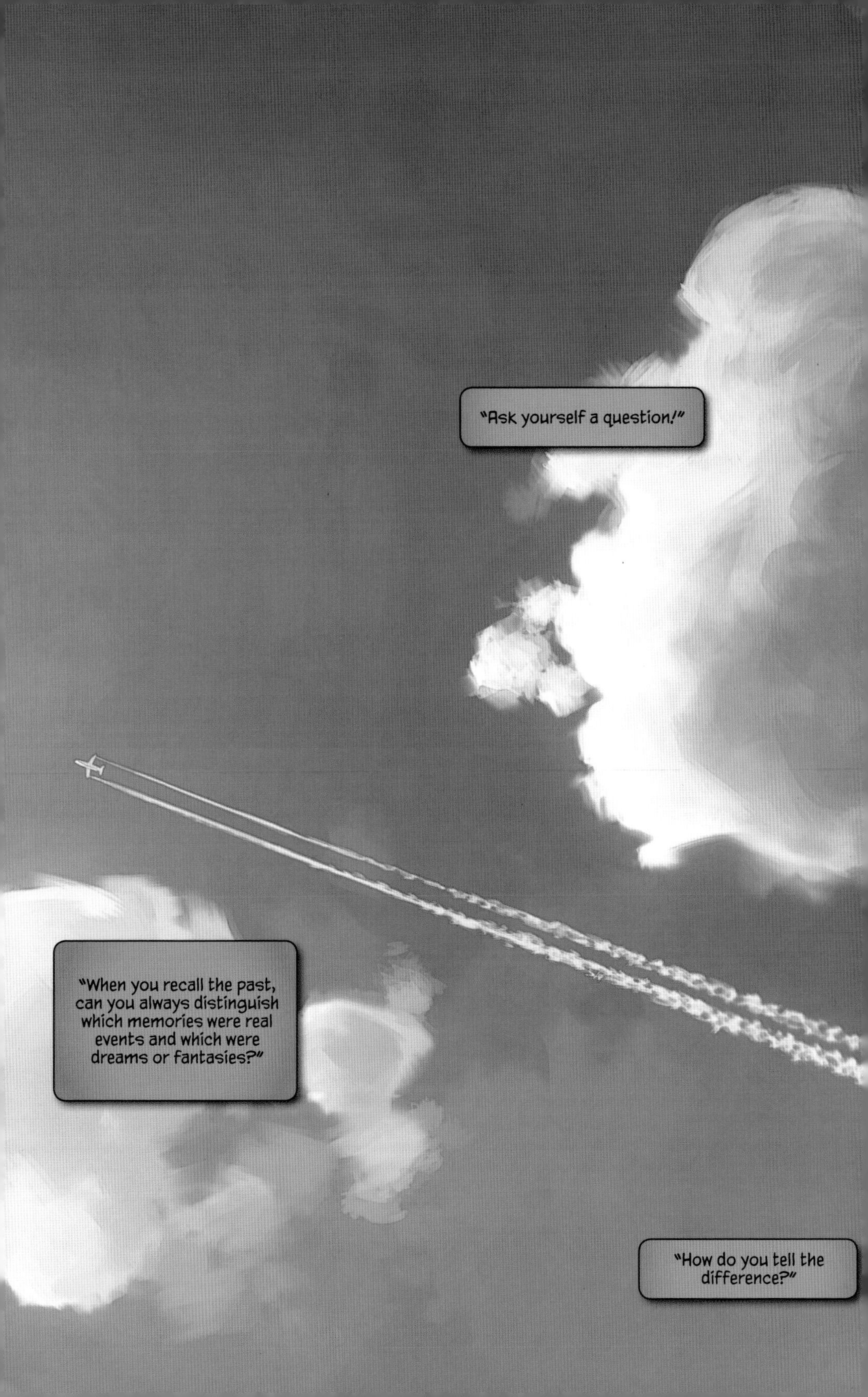
"Ask yourself a question!"
"When you recall the past, can you always distinguish which memories were real events and which were dreams or fantasies?"
"How do you tell the difference?"

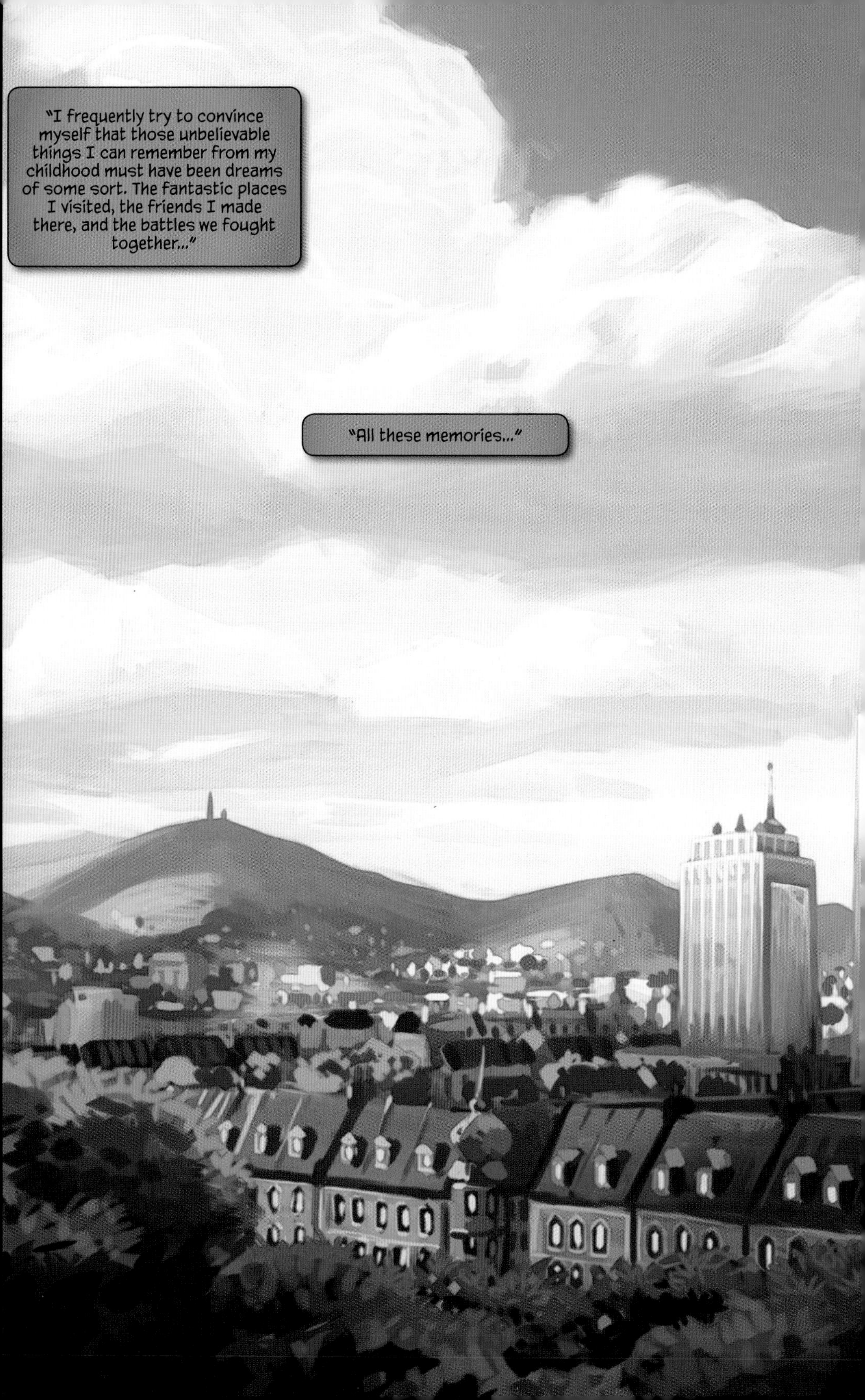
"I frequently try to convince myself that those unbelievable things I can remember from my childhood must have been dreams of some sort. The fantastic places I visited, the friends I made there, and the battles we fought together..."
"All these memories..."

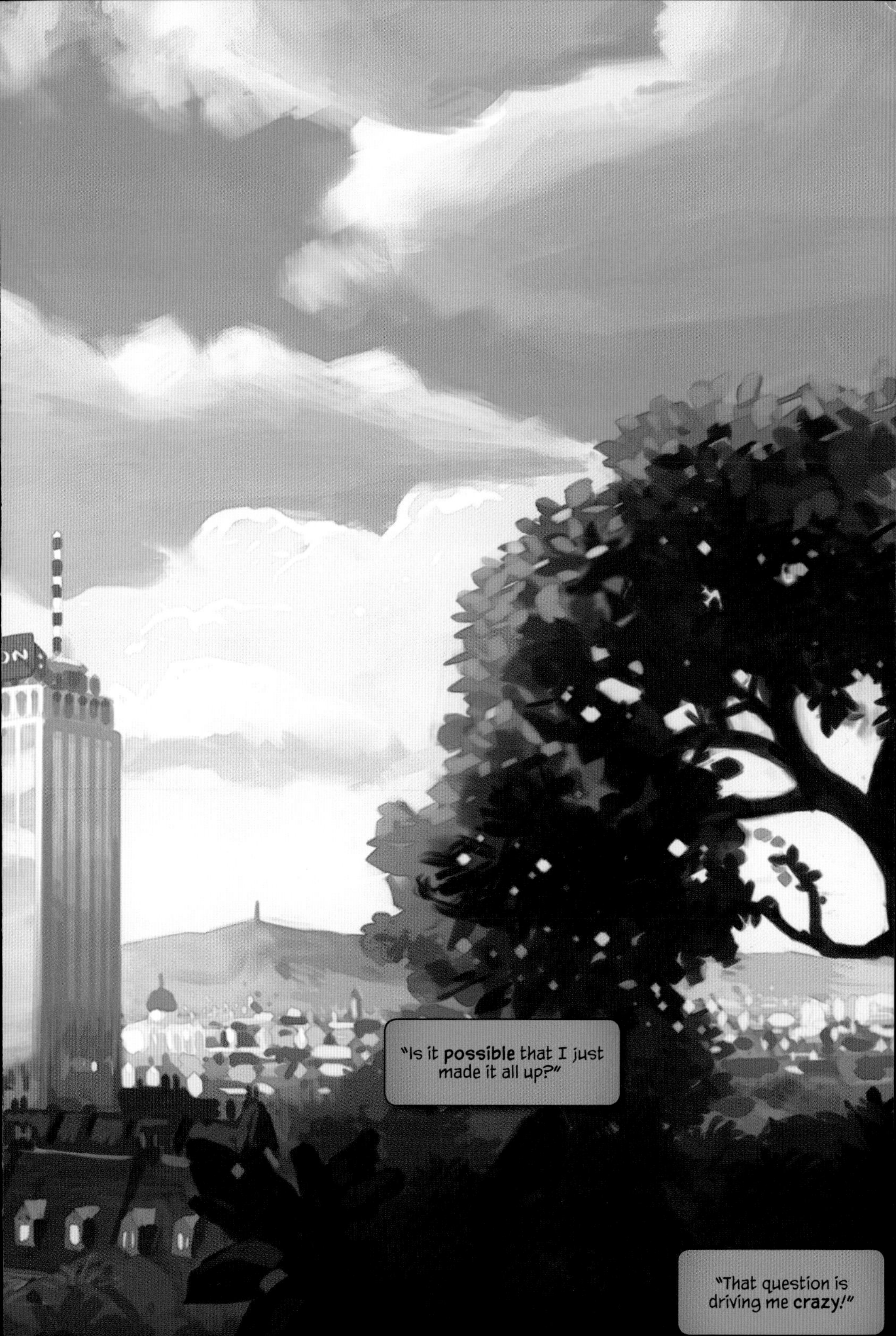
"Is it possible that I just made it all up?"
"That question is driving me crazy!"

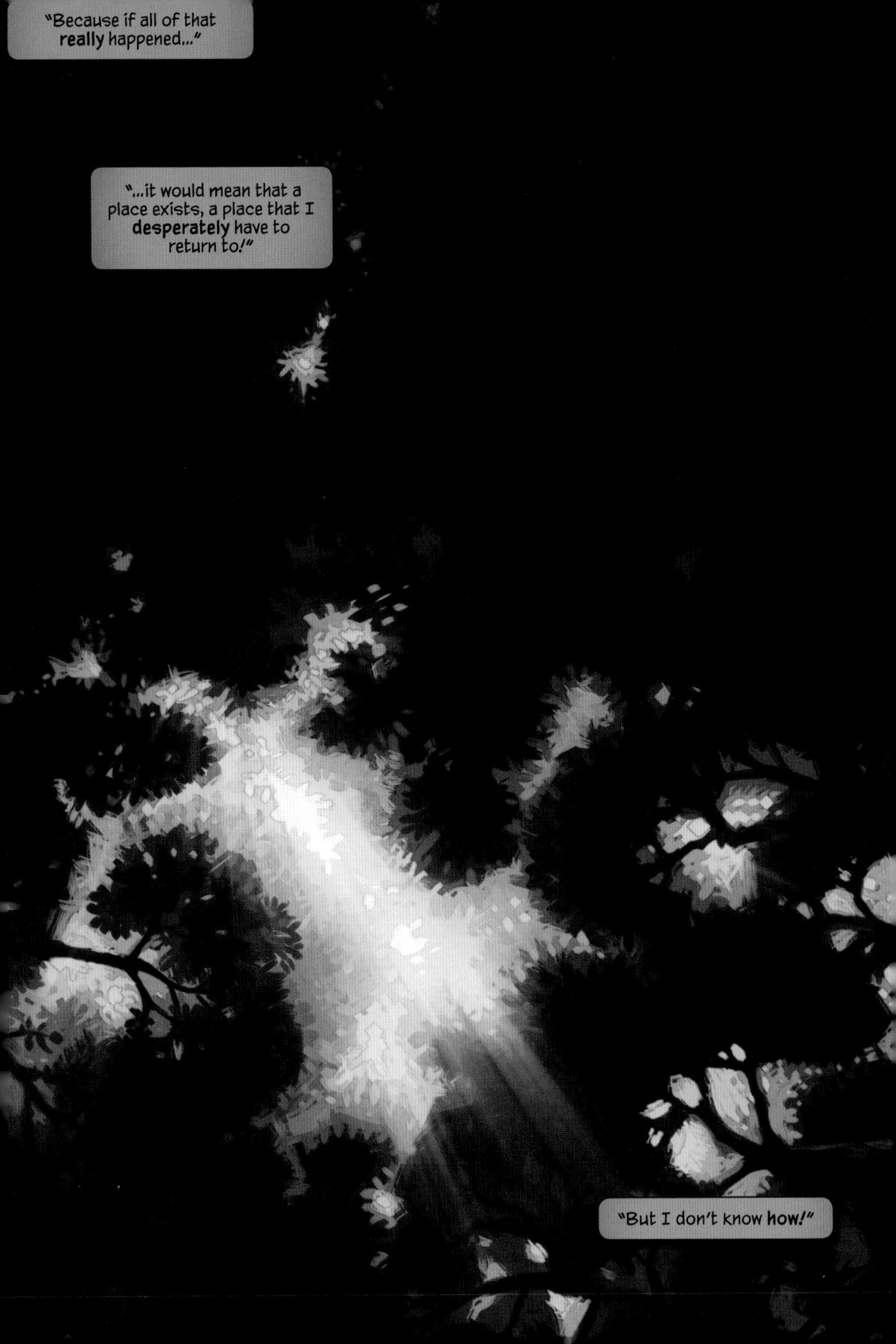
"Because if all of that **really** happened..."
"...it would mean that a place exists, a place that I **desperately** have to return to!"
"But I don't know **how!**"

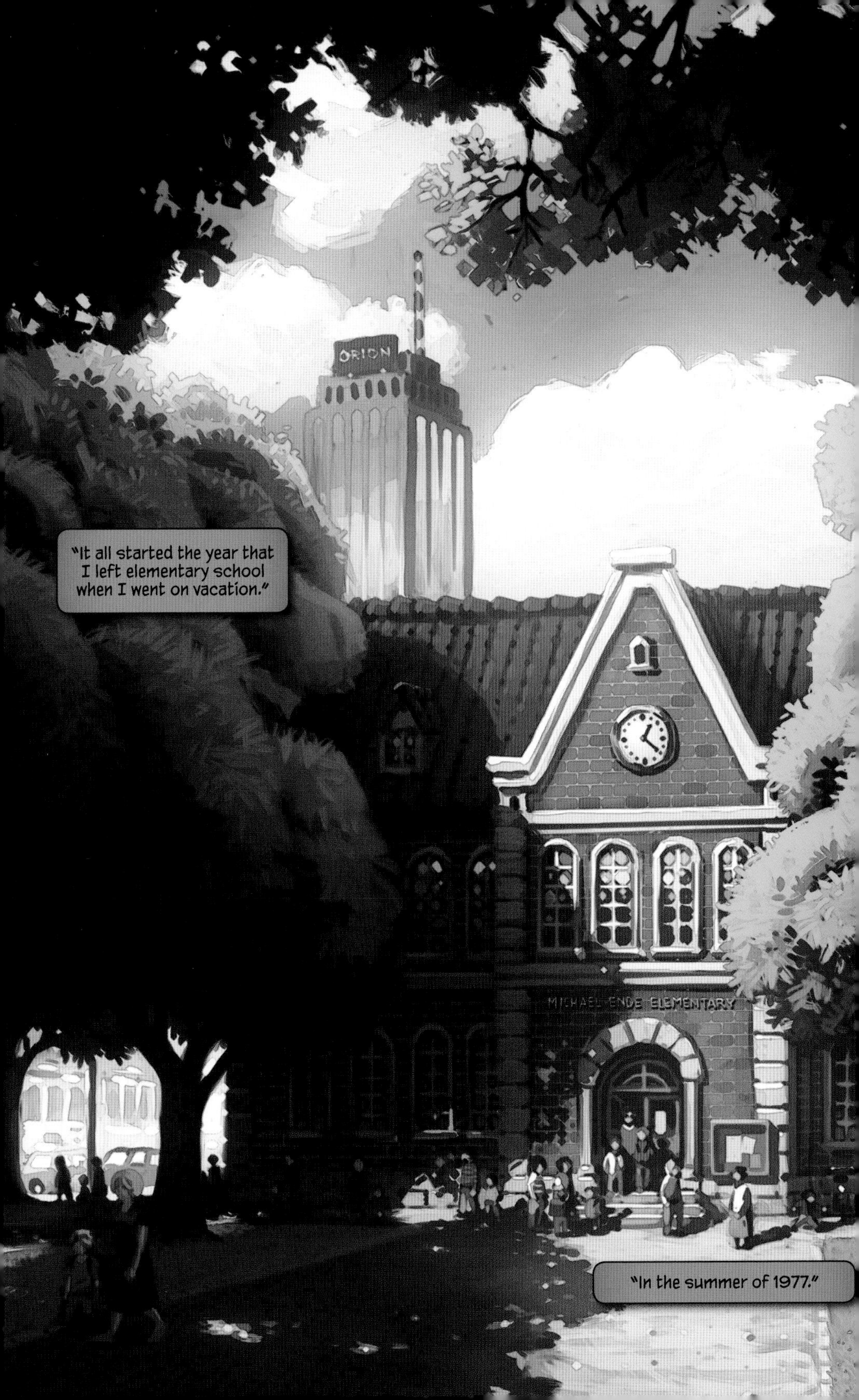
"It all started the year that I left elementary school when I went on vacation."
ORION
MICHAEL ENDE ELEMENTARY
"In the summer of 1977."

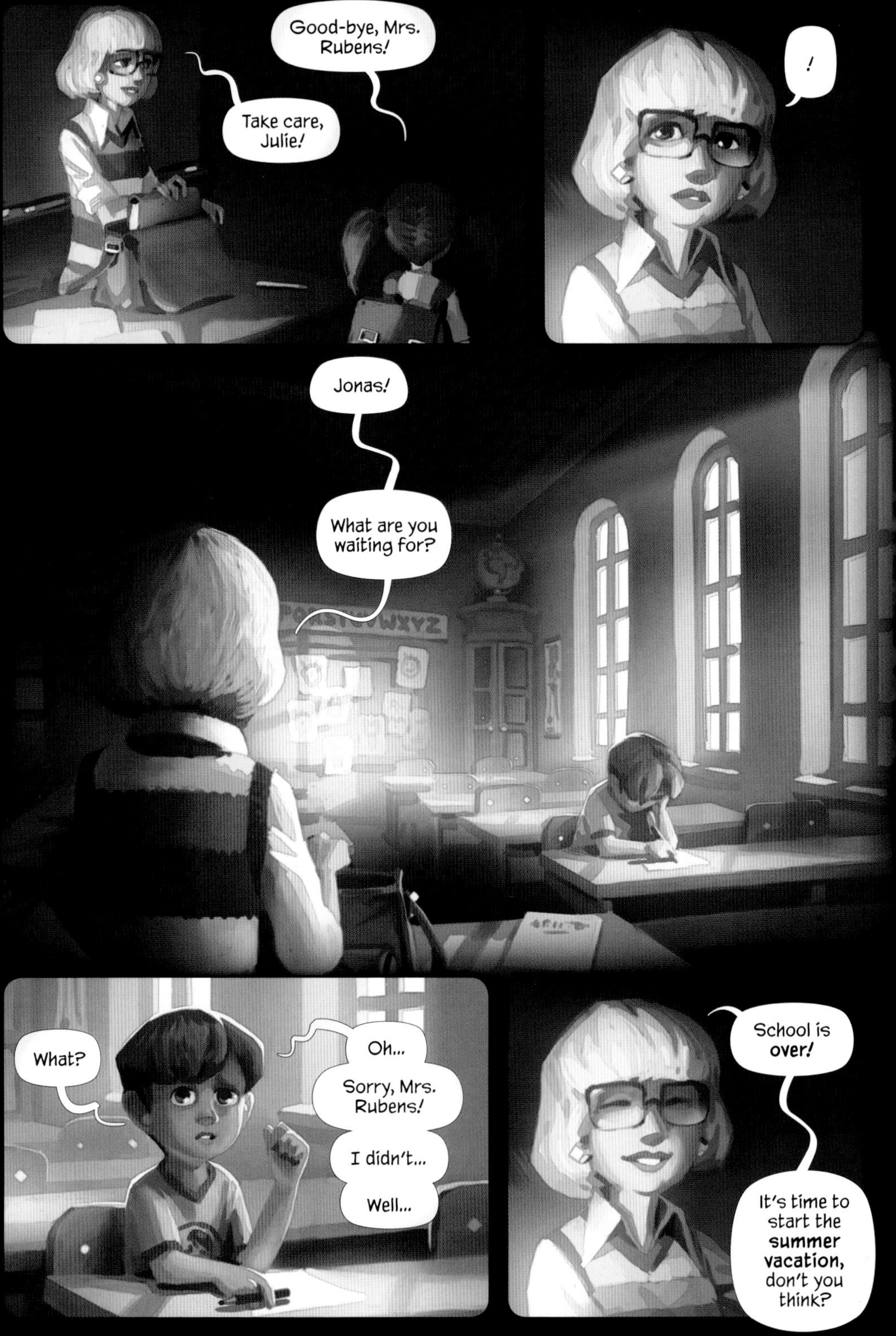
Good-bye, Mrs. Rubens!
Take care, Julie!
!
Jonas!
What are you waiting for?
What?
Oh...
Sorry, Mrs. Rubens!
I didn't...
Well...
School is **over!**
It's time to start the **summer vacation,** don't you think?

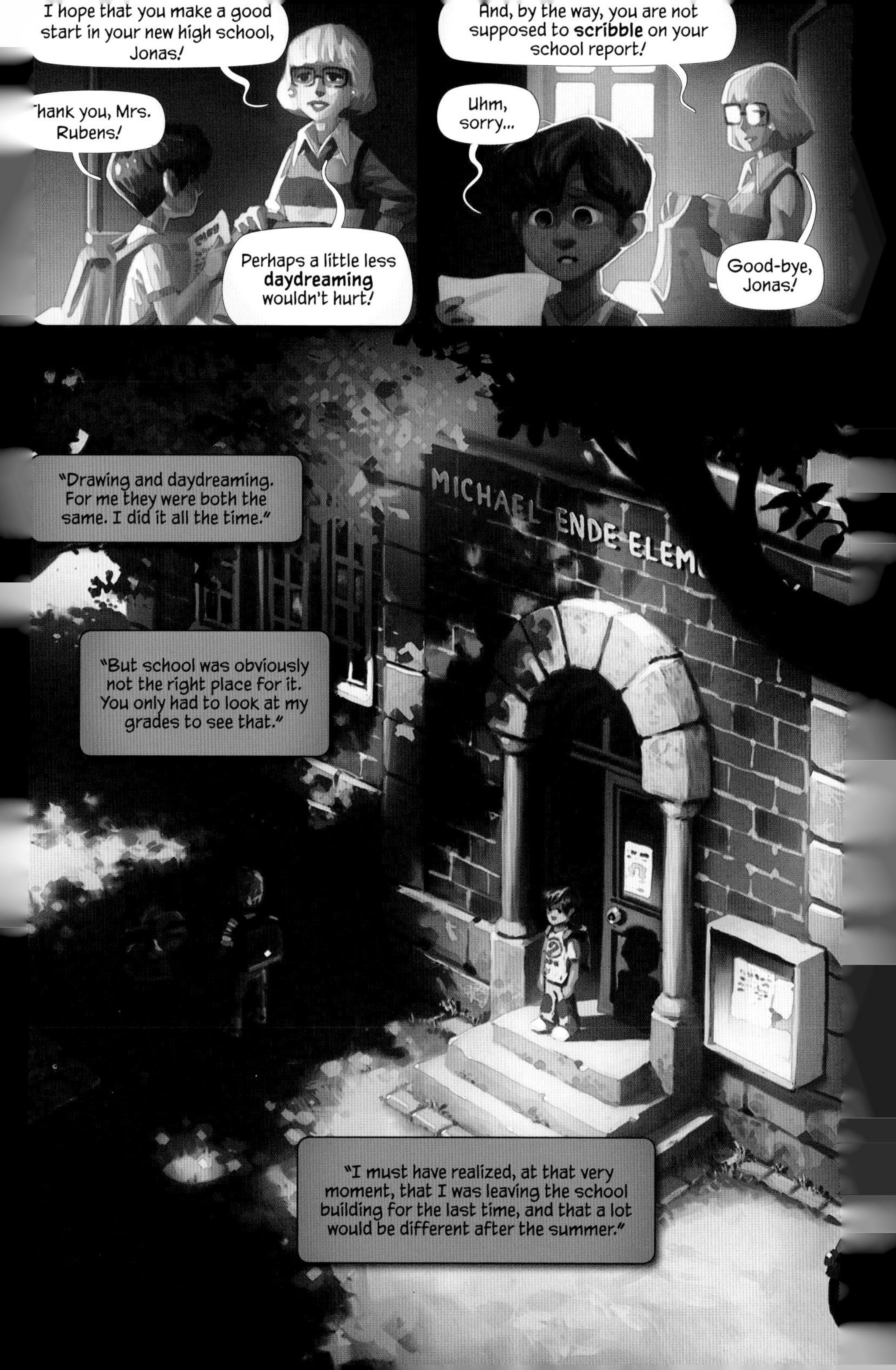

I hope that you make a good start in your new high school, Jonas!
Thank you, Mrs. Rubens!
Perhaps a little less **daydreaming** wouldn't hurt!
And, by the way, you are not supposed to **scribble** on your school report!
Uhm, sorry...
Good-bye, Jonas!
"Drawing and daydreaming. For me they were both the same. I did it all the time."
MICHAEL ENDE ELEM
"But school was obviously not the right place for it. You only had to look at my grades to see that."
"I must have realized, at that very moment, that I was leaving the school building for the last time, and that a lot would be different after the summer."

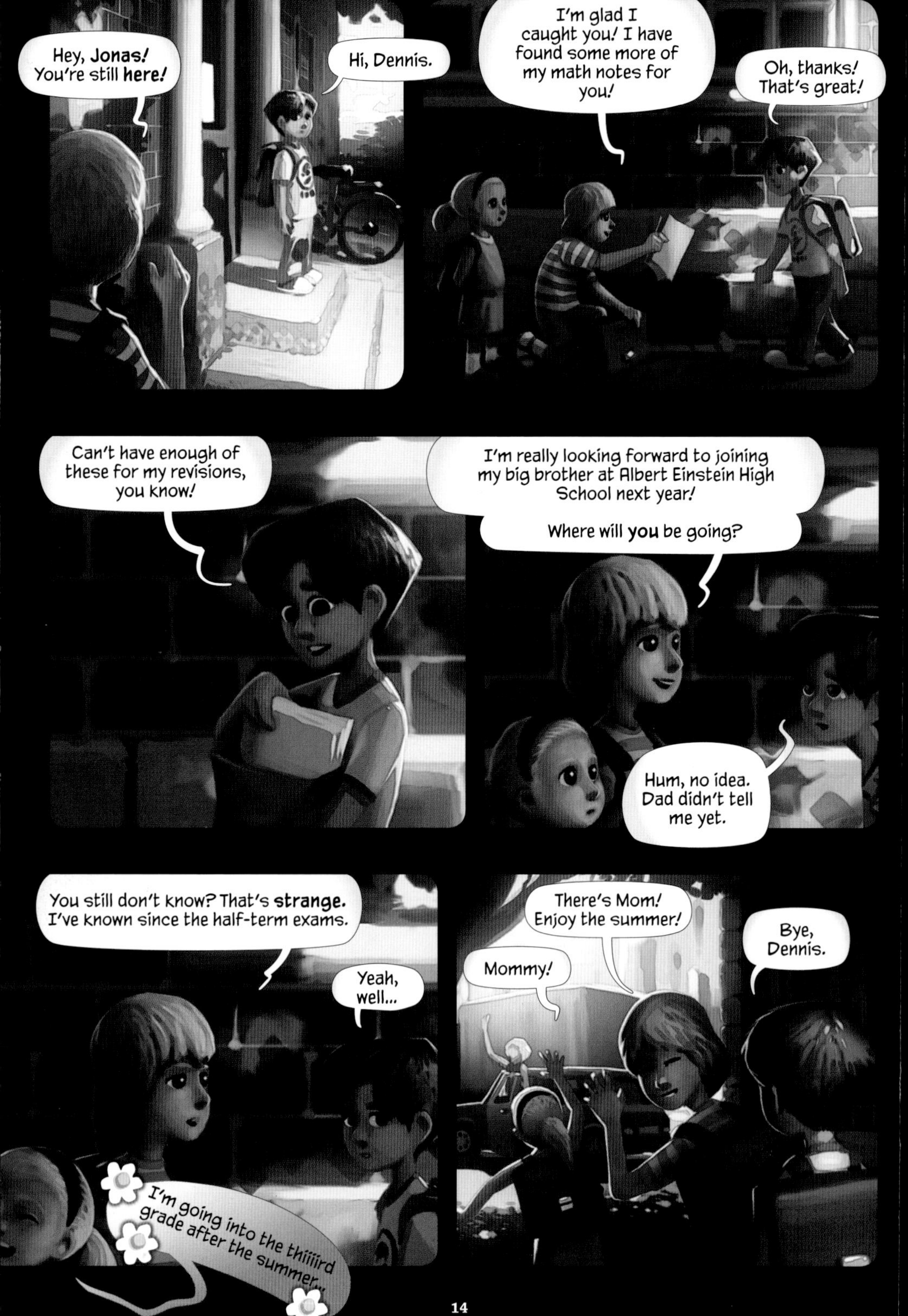
Hey, Jonas! You're still here!
Hi, Dennis.
I'm glad I caught you! I have found some more of my math notes for you!
Oh, thanks! That's great!
Can't have enough of these for my revisions, you know!
I'm really looking forward to joining my big brother at Albert Einstein High School next year!
Where will you be going?
Hum, no idea. Dad didn't tell me yet.
You still don't know? That's strange. I've known since the half-term exams.
Yeah, well...
I'm going into the thiiiird grade after the summer...
There's Mom! Enjoy the summer!
Mommy!
Bye, Dennis.

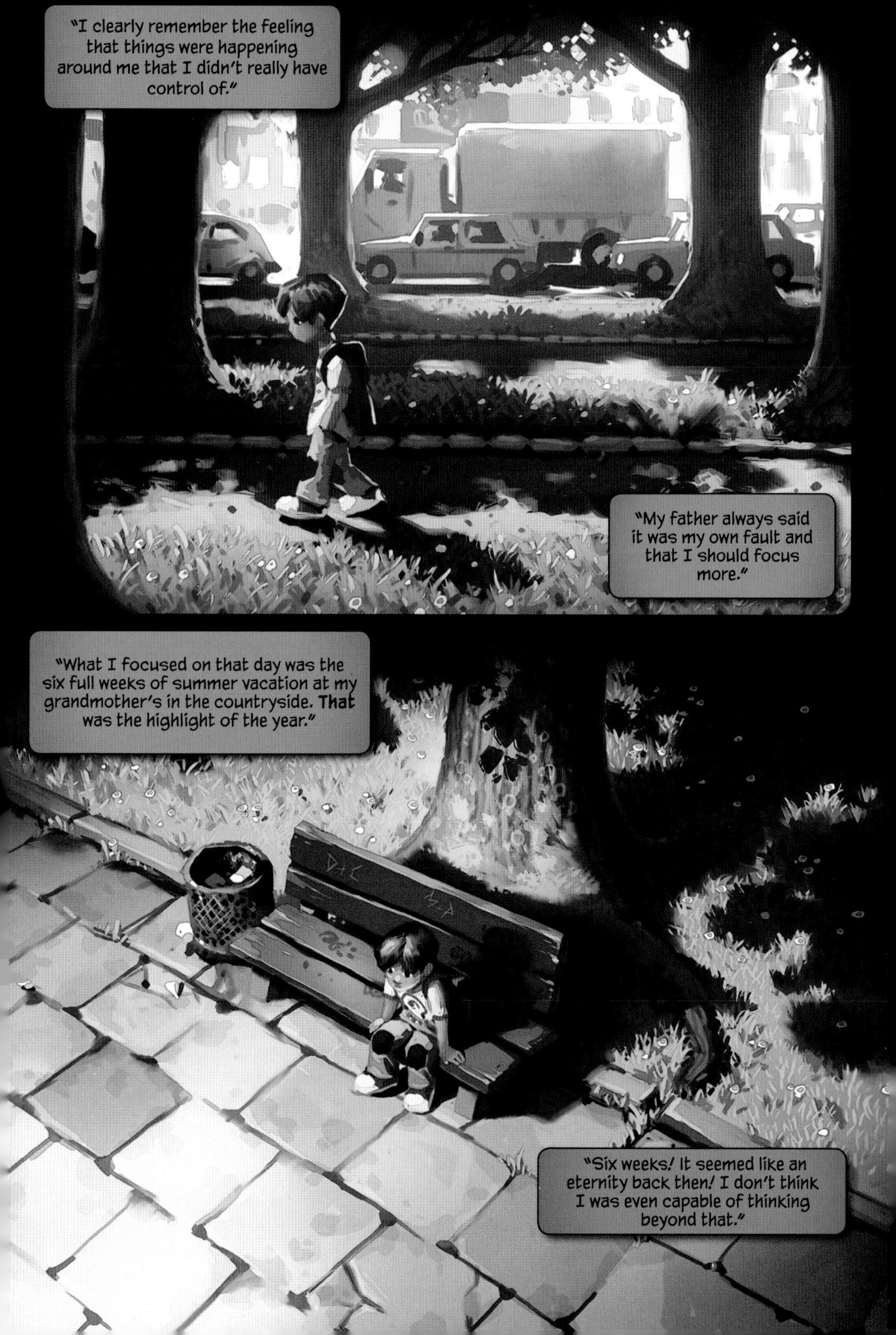
"I clearly remember the feeling that things were happening around me that I didn't really have control of."
"My father always said it was my own fault and that I should focus more."
"What I focused on that day was the six full weeks of summer vacation at my grandmother's in the countryside. That was the highlight of the year."
"Six weeks! It seemed like an eternity back then! I don't think I was even capable of thinking beyond that."

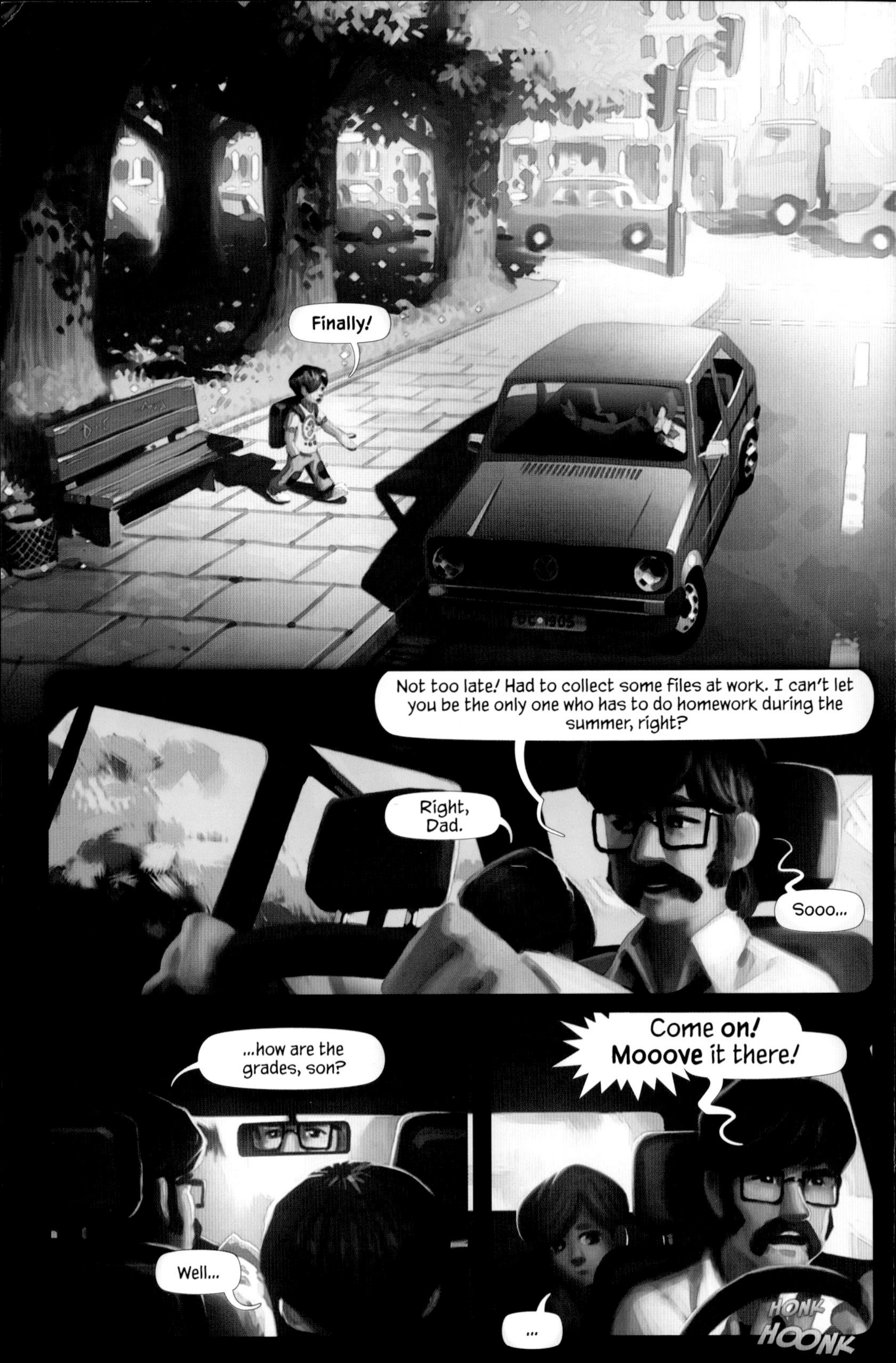
Finally!
Not too late! Had to collect some files at work. I can't let you be the only one who has to do homework during the summer, right?
Right, Dad.
Sooo...
...how are the grades, son?
Well...
Come on! Mooove it there!
...
HONK
HOONK

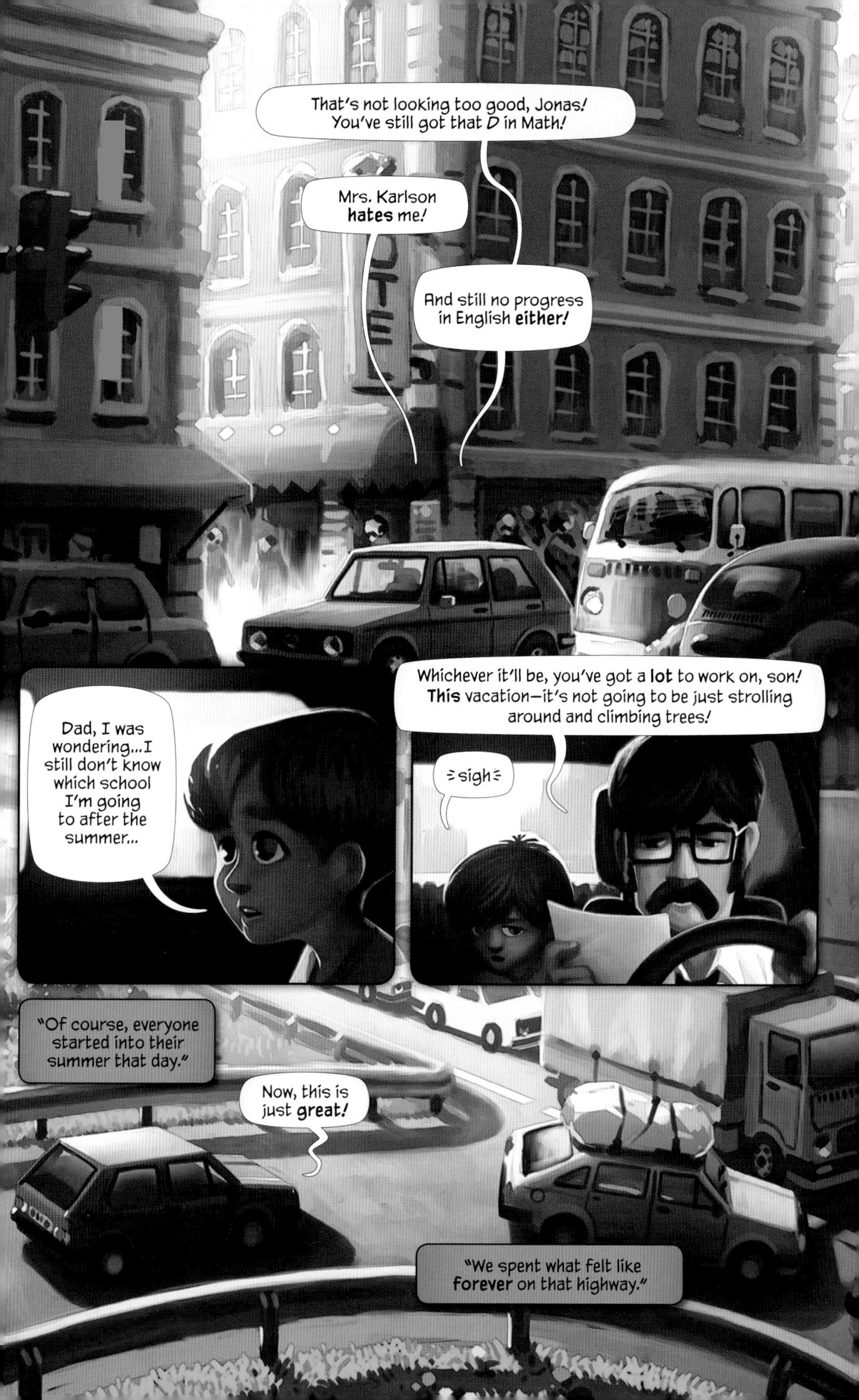
That's not looking too good, Jonas! You've still got that *D* in Math!
Mrs. Karlson **hates** me!
And still no progress in English **either!**
Dad, I was wondering...I still don't know which school I'm going to after the summer...
Whichever it'll be, you've got a **lot** to work on, son! **This** vacation—it's not going to be just strolling around and climbing trees!
sigh
"Of course, everyone started into their summer that day."
Now, this is just **great!**
"We spent what felt like **forever** on that highway."

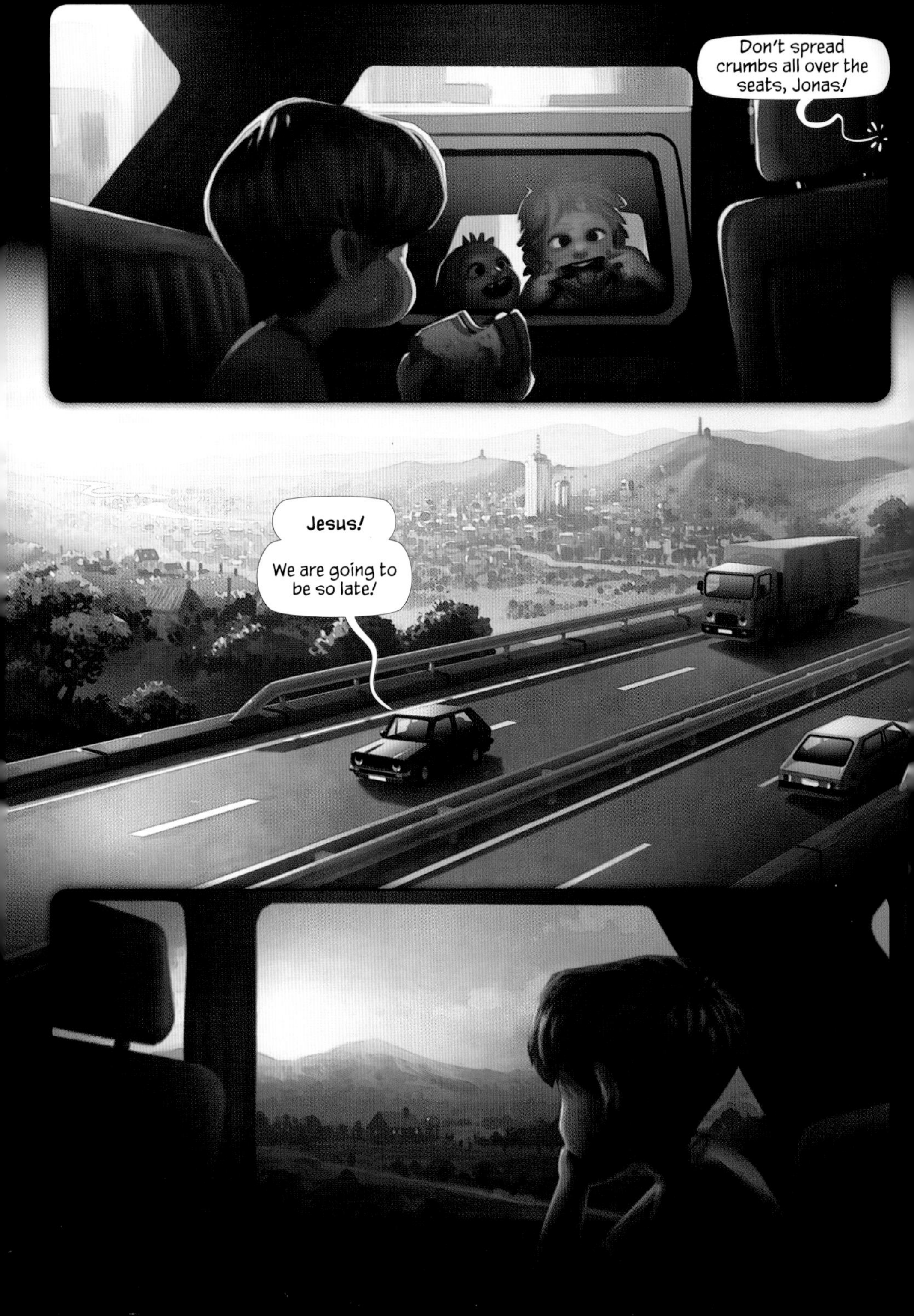
Don't spread crumbs all over the seats, Jonas!
Jesus!
We are going to be so late!

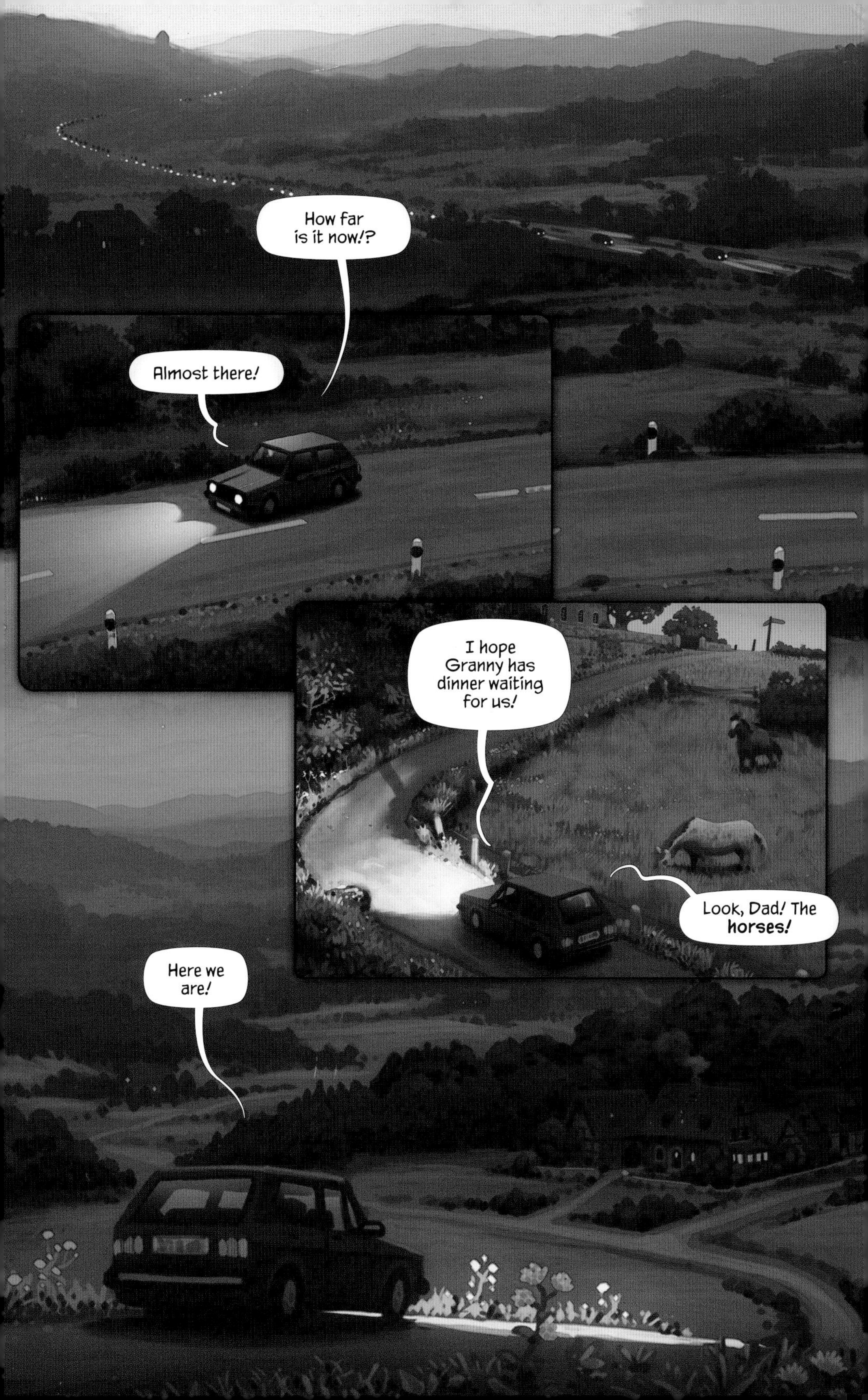
How far is it now!?
Almost there!
I hope Granny has dinner waiting for us!
Look, Dad! The **horses!**
Here we are!

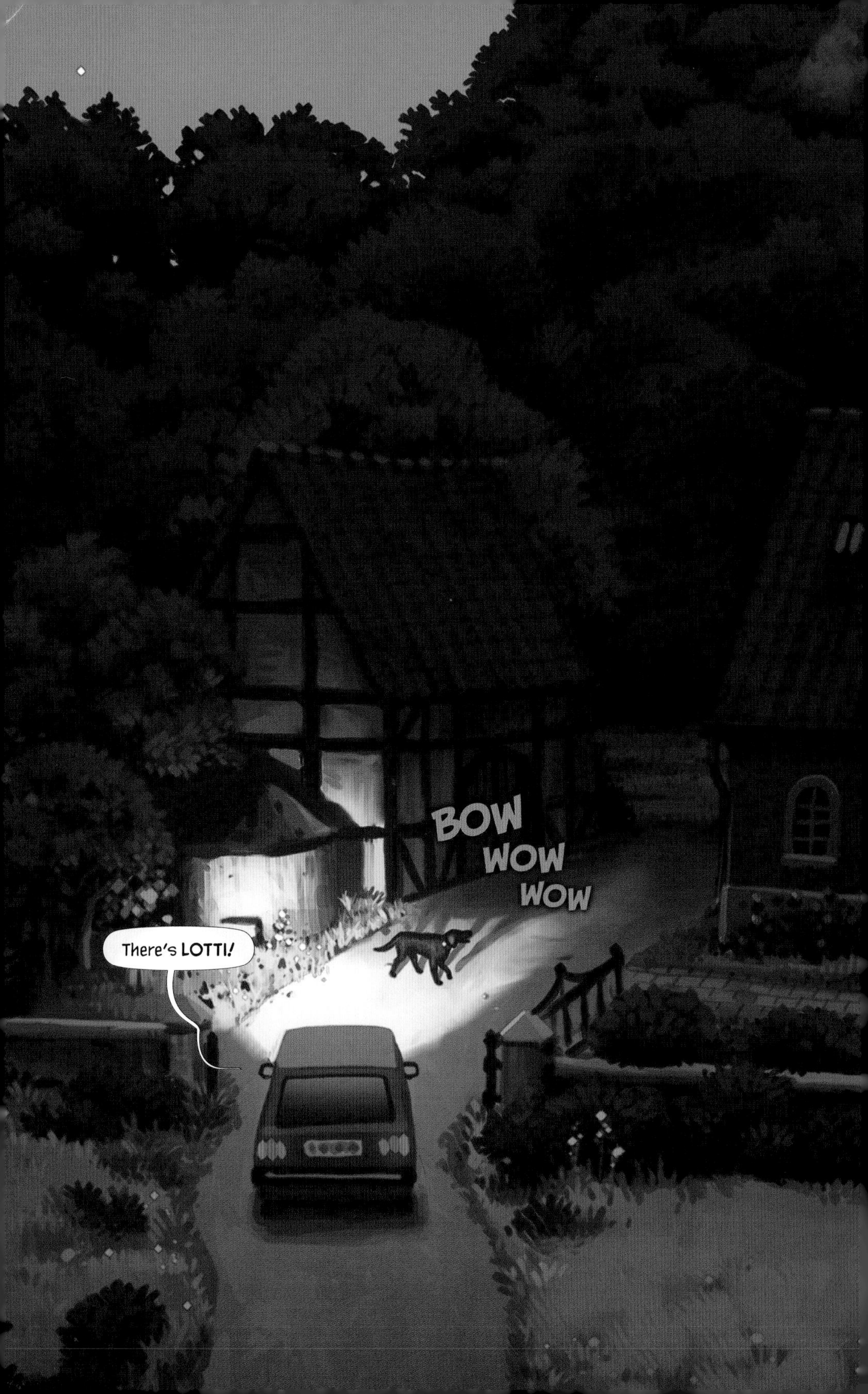
BOW
WOW
WOW
There's LOTTI!

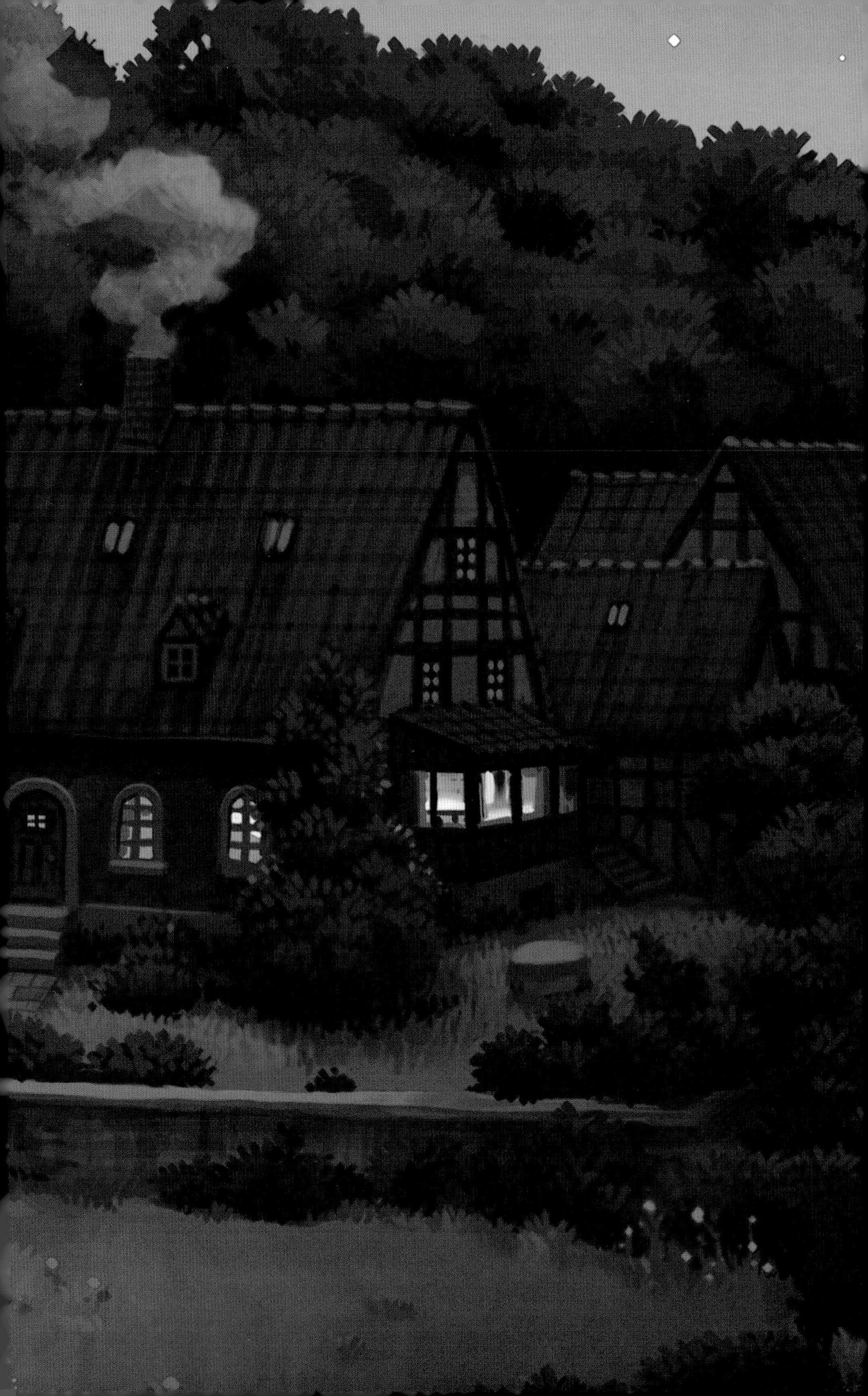

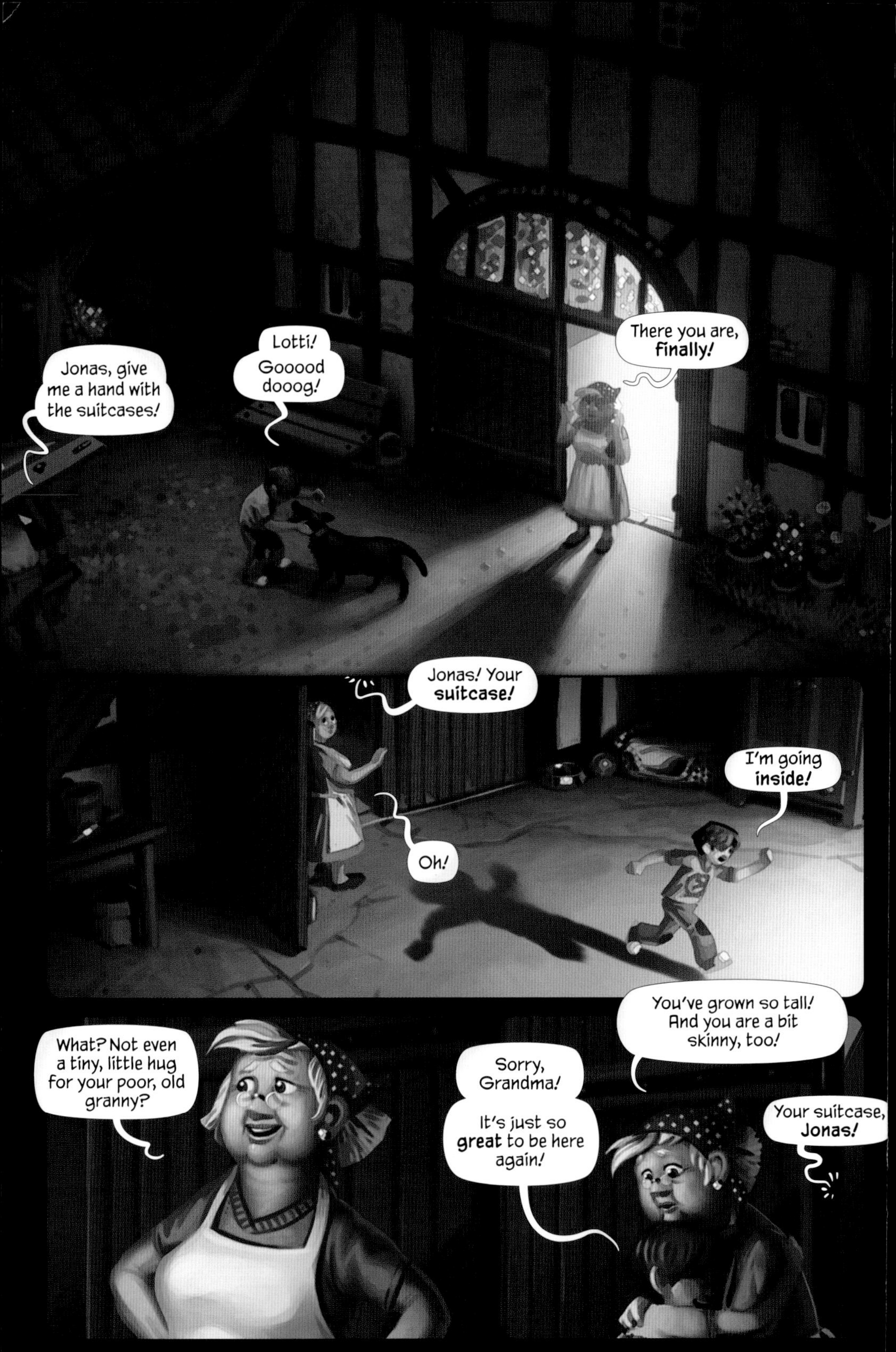
Jonas, give me a hand with the suitcases!
Lotti! Gooood dooog!
There you are, finally!
Jonas! Your suitcase!
Oh!
I'm going inside!
What? Not even a tiny, little hug for your poor, old granny?
Sorry, Grandma!
It's just so great to be here again!
You've grown so tall! And you are a bit skinny, too!
Your suitcase, Jonas!

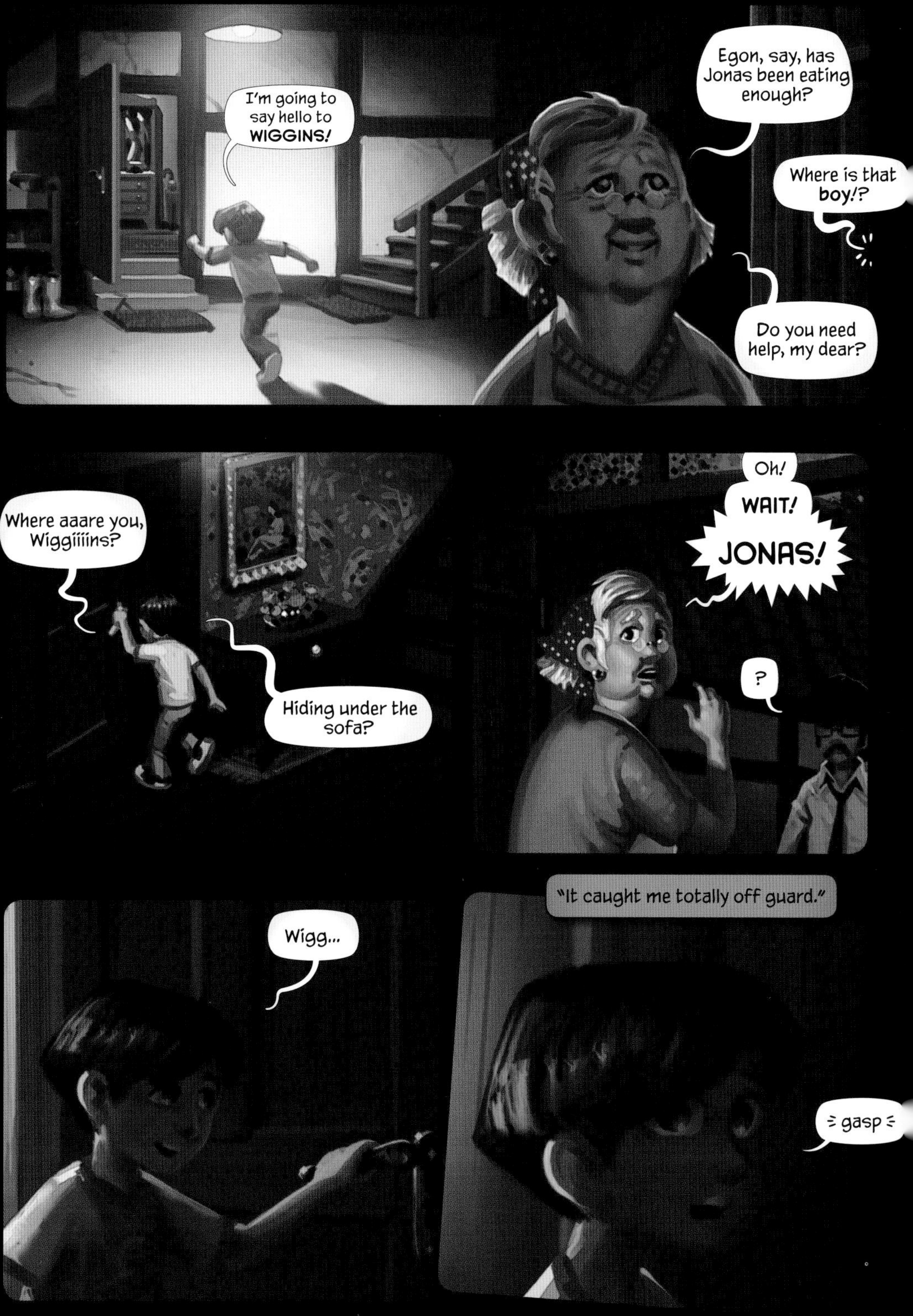
I'm going to say hello to WIGGINS!
Egon, say, has Jonas been eating enough?
Where is that boy!?
Do you need help, my dear?
Where aaare you, Wiggiiiins?
Hiding under the sofa?
Oh!
WAIT!
JONAS!
?
Wigg...
"It caught me totally off guard."
gasp

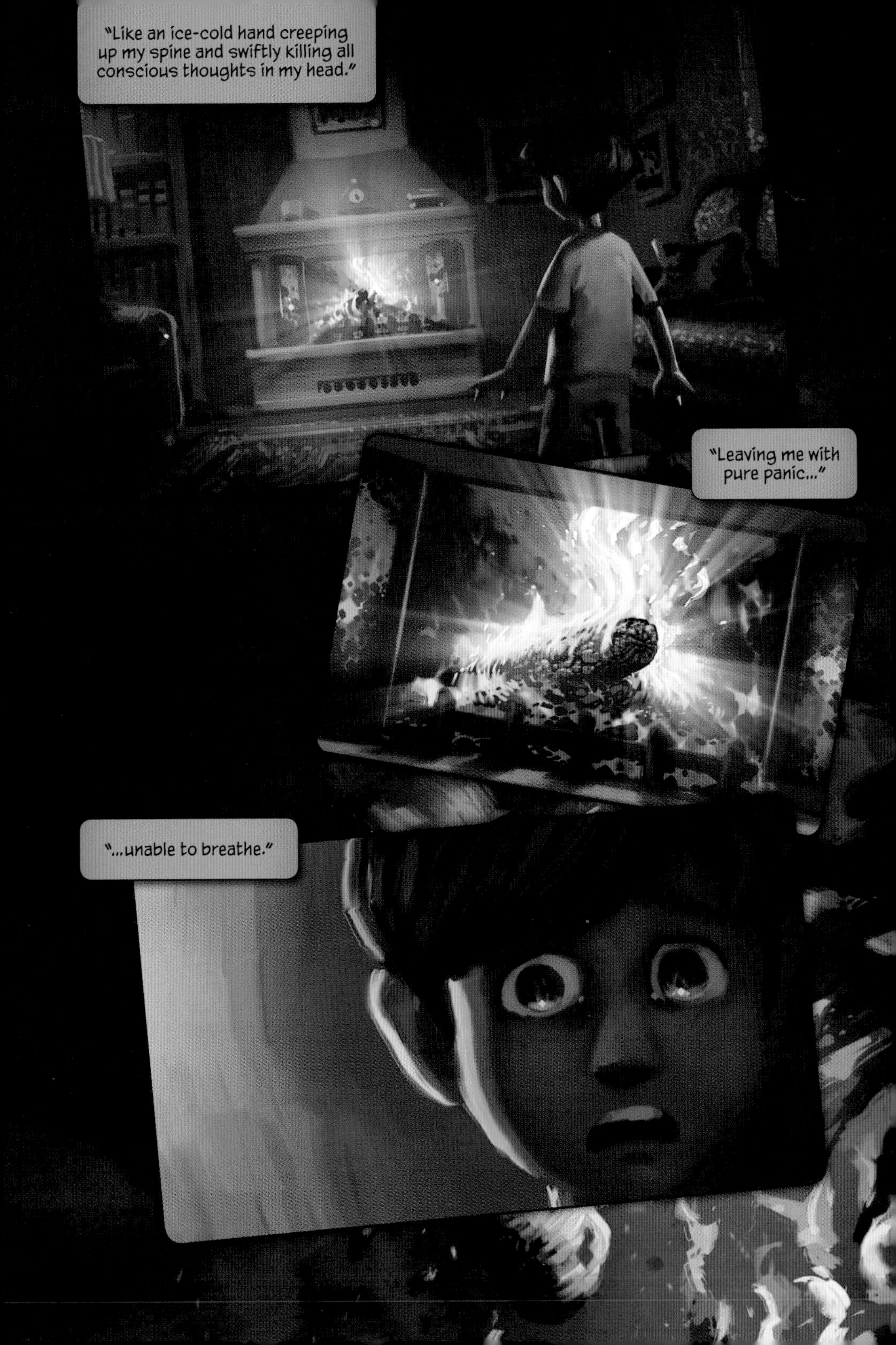
"Like an ice-cold hand creeping up my spine and swiftly killing all conscious thoughts in my head."
"Leaving me with pure panic..."
"...unable to breathe."

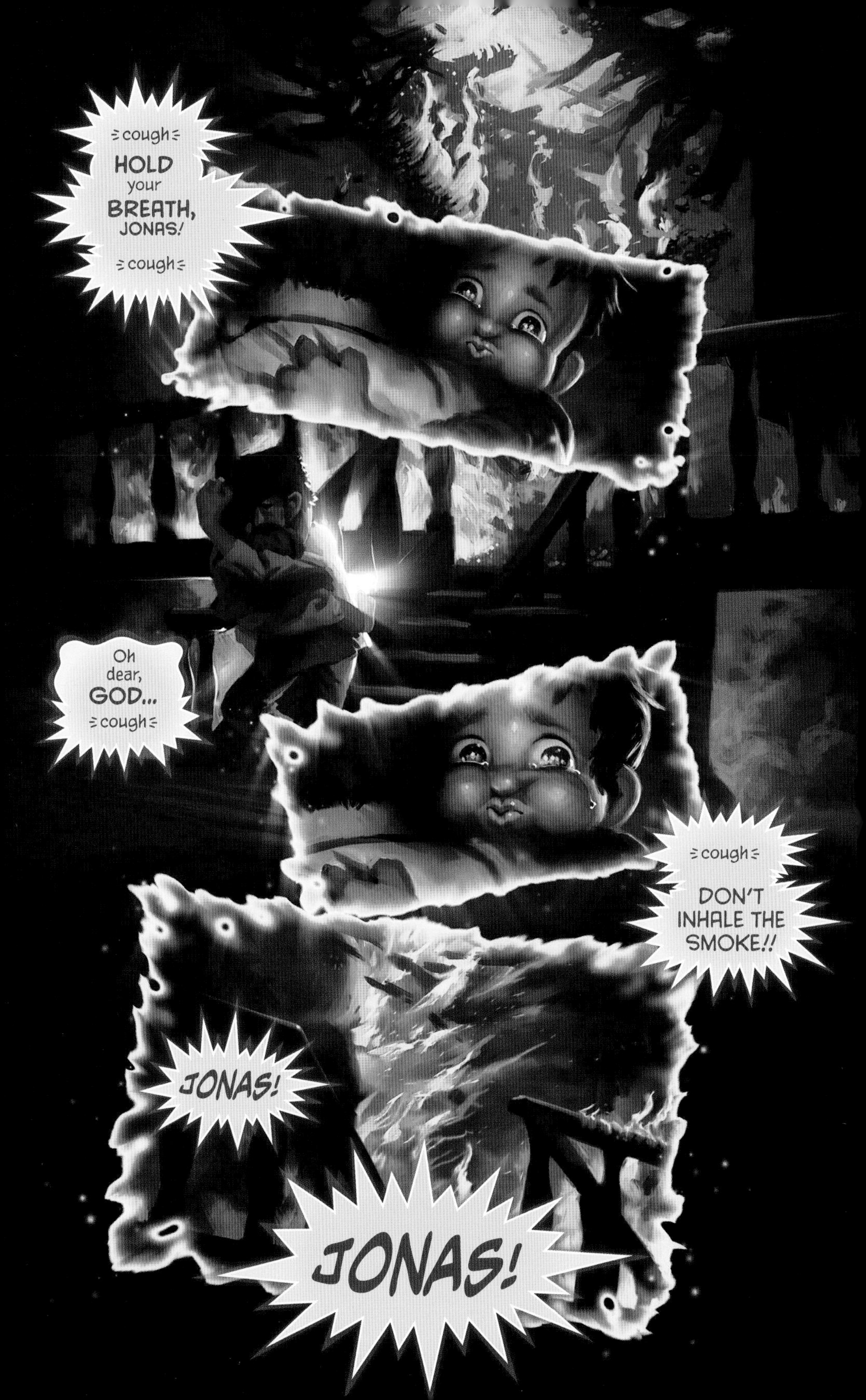

cough
HOLD your BREATH, JONAS!
cough
Oh dear, GOD...
cough
cough
DON'T INHALE THE SMOKE!!
JONAS!
JONAS!

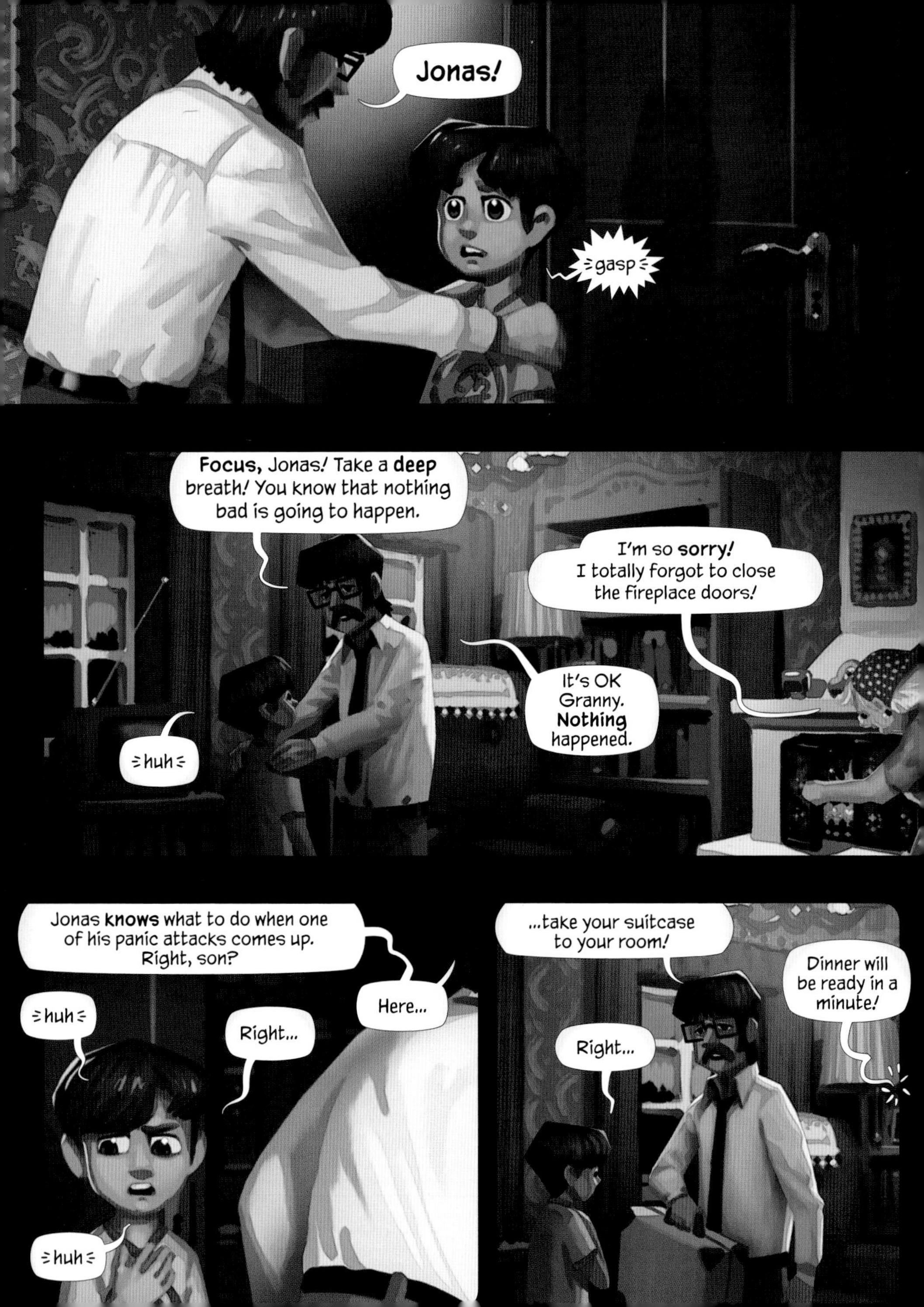

Jonas!
gasp
Focus, Jonas! Take a deep breath! You know that nothing bad is going to happen.
I'm so sorry! I totally forgot to close the fireplace doors!
huh
It's OK Granny. Nothing happened.
Jonas knows what to do when one of his panic attacks comes up. Right, son?
huh
Right...
Here...
huh
...take your suitcase to your room!
Dinner will be ready in a minute!
Right...

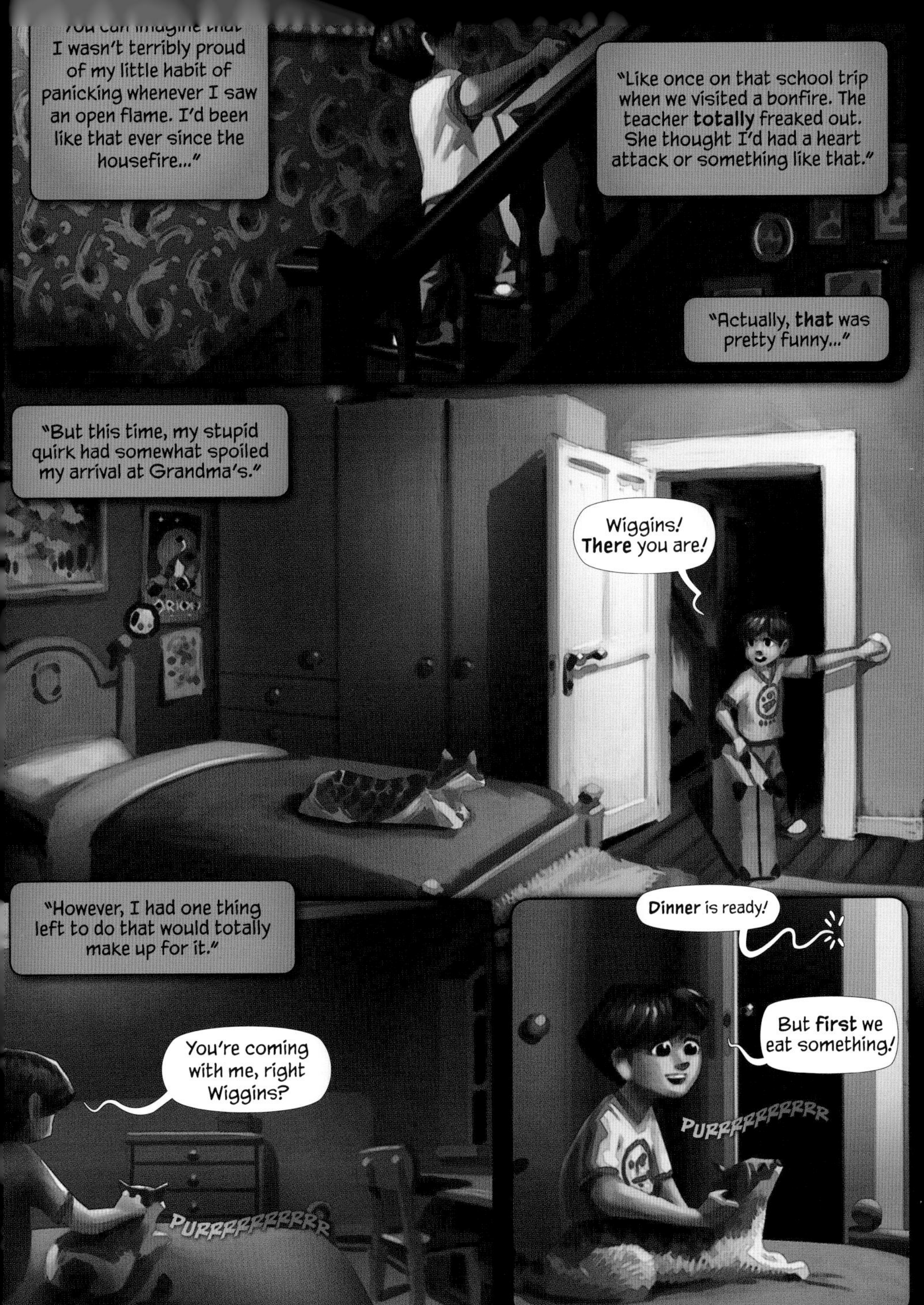
You can imagine that I wasn't terribly proud of my little habit of panicking whenever I saw an open flame. I'd been like that ever since the housefire..."
"Like once on that school trip when we visited a bonfire. The teacher **totally** freaked out. She thought I'd had a heart attack or something like that."
"Actually, **that** was pretty funny..."
"But this time, my stupid quirk had somewhat spoiled my arrival at Grandma's."
Wiggins! **There** you are!
"However, I had one thing left to do that would totally make up for it."
You're coming with me, right Wiggins?
PURRRRRRRRRR
Dinner is ready!
But **first** we eat something!
PURRRRRRRRRR

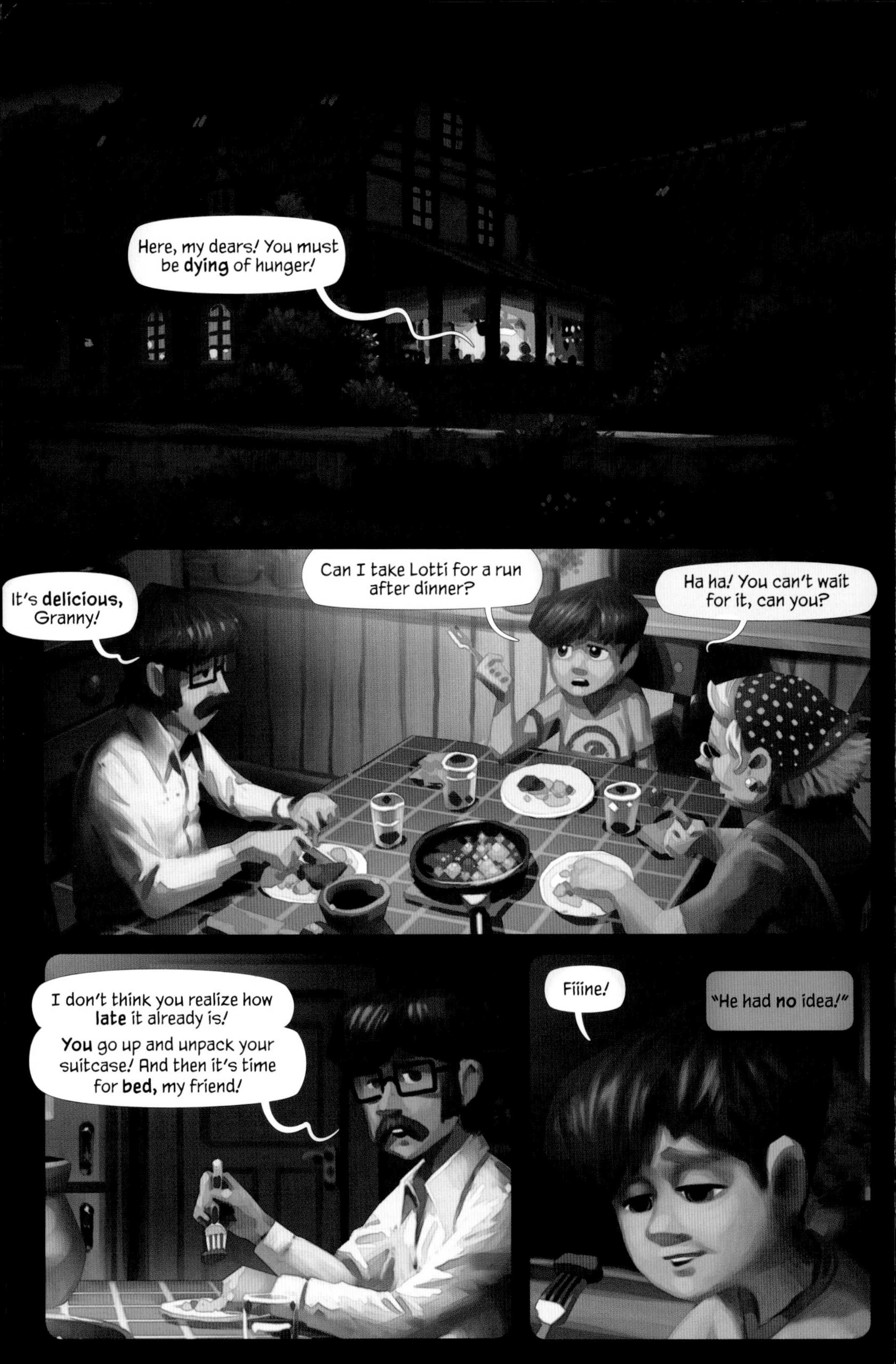
Here, my dears! You must be **dying** of hunger!
It's **delicious,** Granny!
Can I take Lotti for a run after dinner?
Ha ha! You can't wait for it, can you?
I don't think you realize how **late** it already is!
You go up and unpack your suitcase! And then it's time for **bed,** my friend!
Fiiine!
"He had **no** idea!"

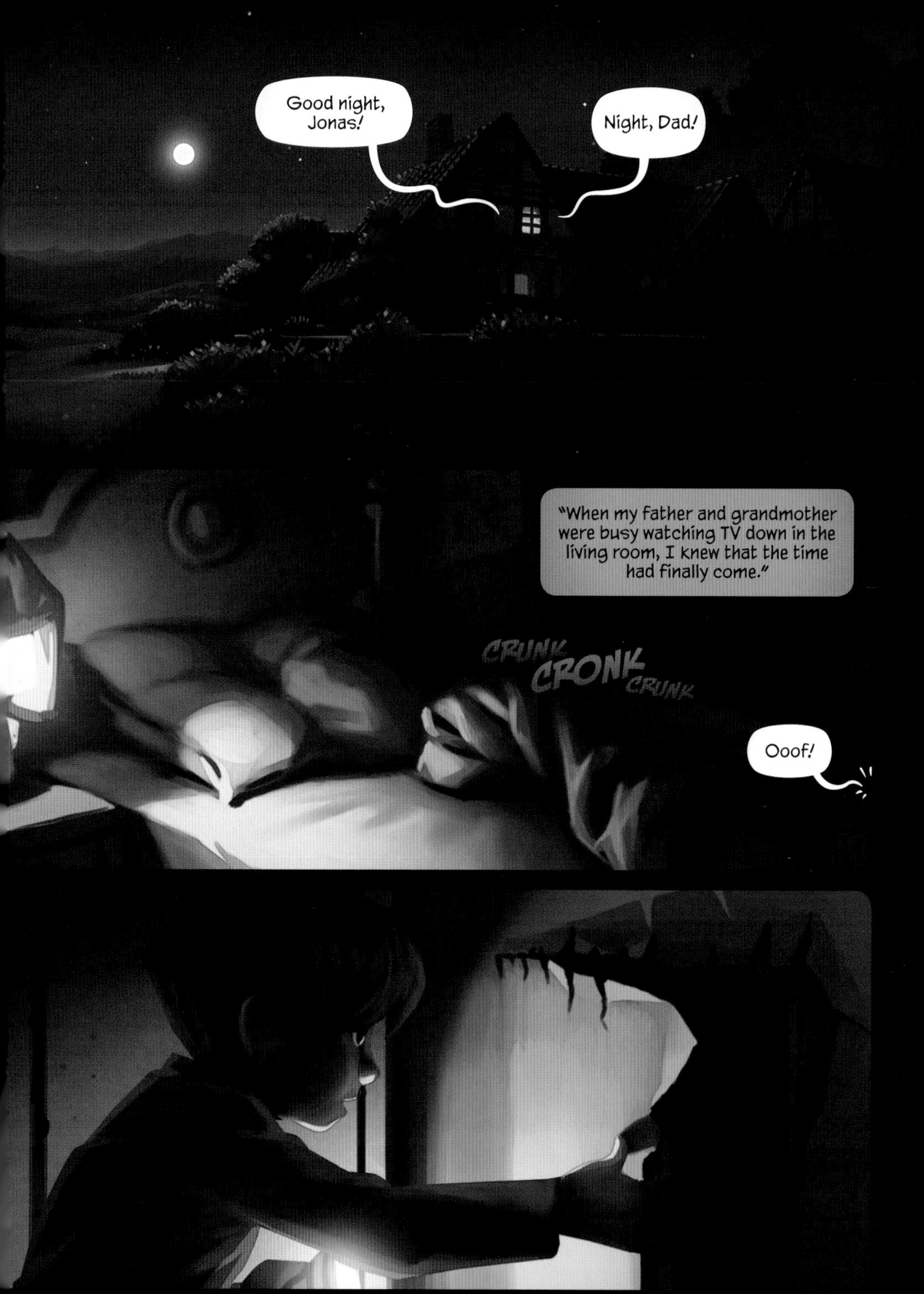

Good night, Jonas!
Night, Dad!
"When my father and grandmother were busy watching TV down in the living room, I knew that the time had finally come."
CRUNK
CRONK
CRUNK
Ooof!

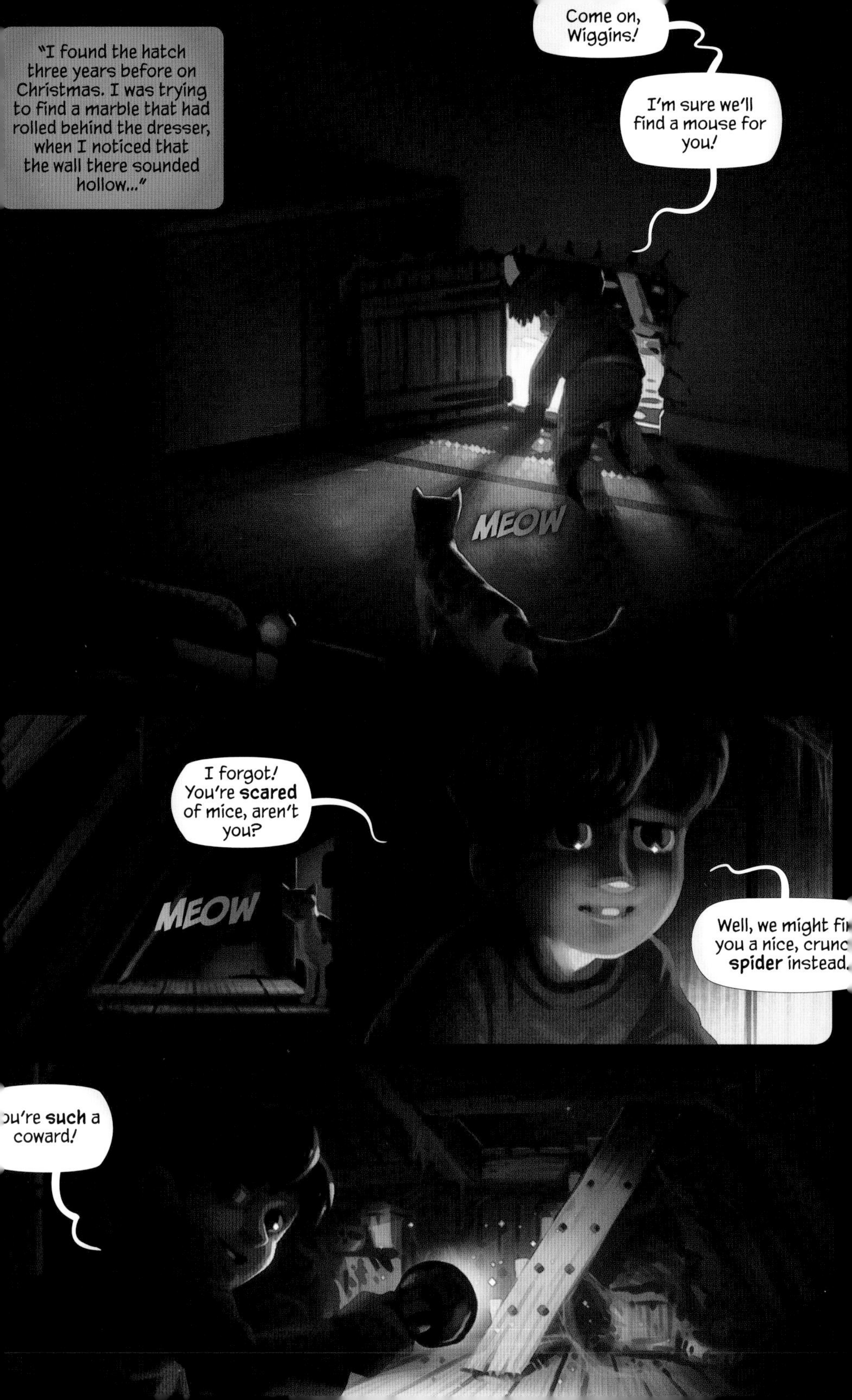
"I found the hatch three years before on Christmas. I was trying to find a marble that had rolled behind the dresser, when I noticed that the wall there sounded hollow..."
Come on, Wiggins!
I'm sure we'll find a mouse for you!
MEOW
I forgot! You're **scared** of mice, aren't you?
MEOW
Well, we might fi
you a nice, crunc
spider instead.
u're **such** a coward!

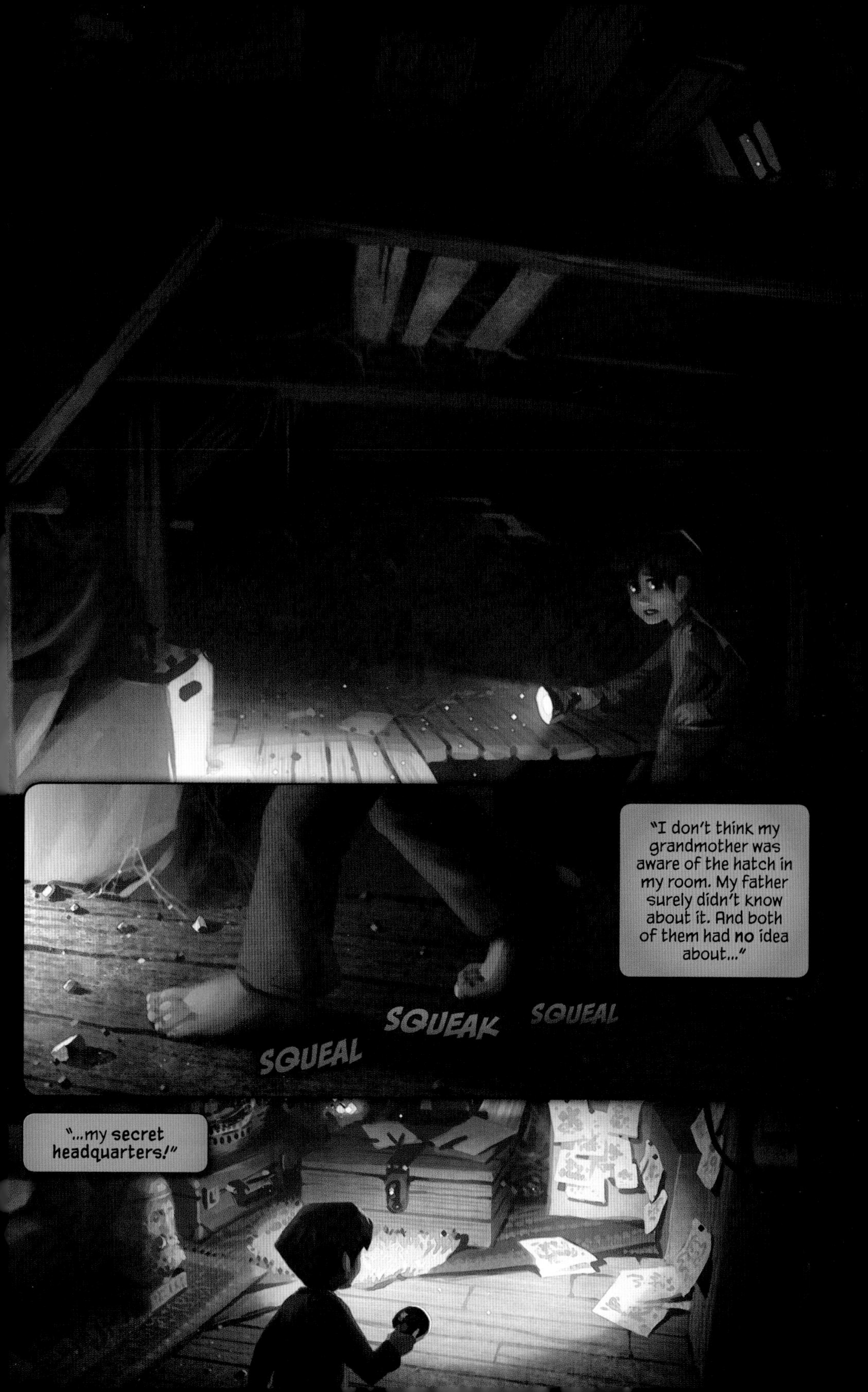

"I don't think my grandmother was aware of the hatch in my room. My father surely didn't know about it. And both of them had **no** idea about..."
SQUEAL
SQUEAK
SQUEAL
"...my secret headquarters!"

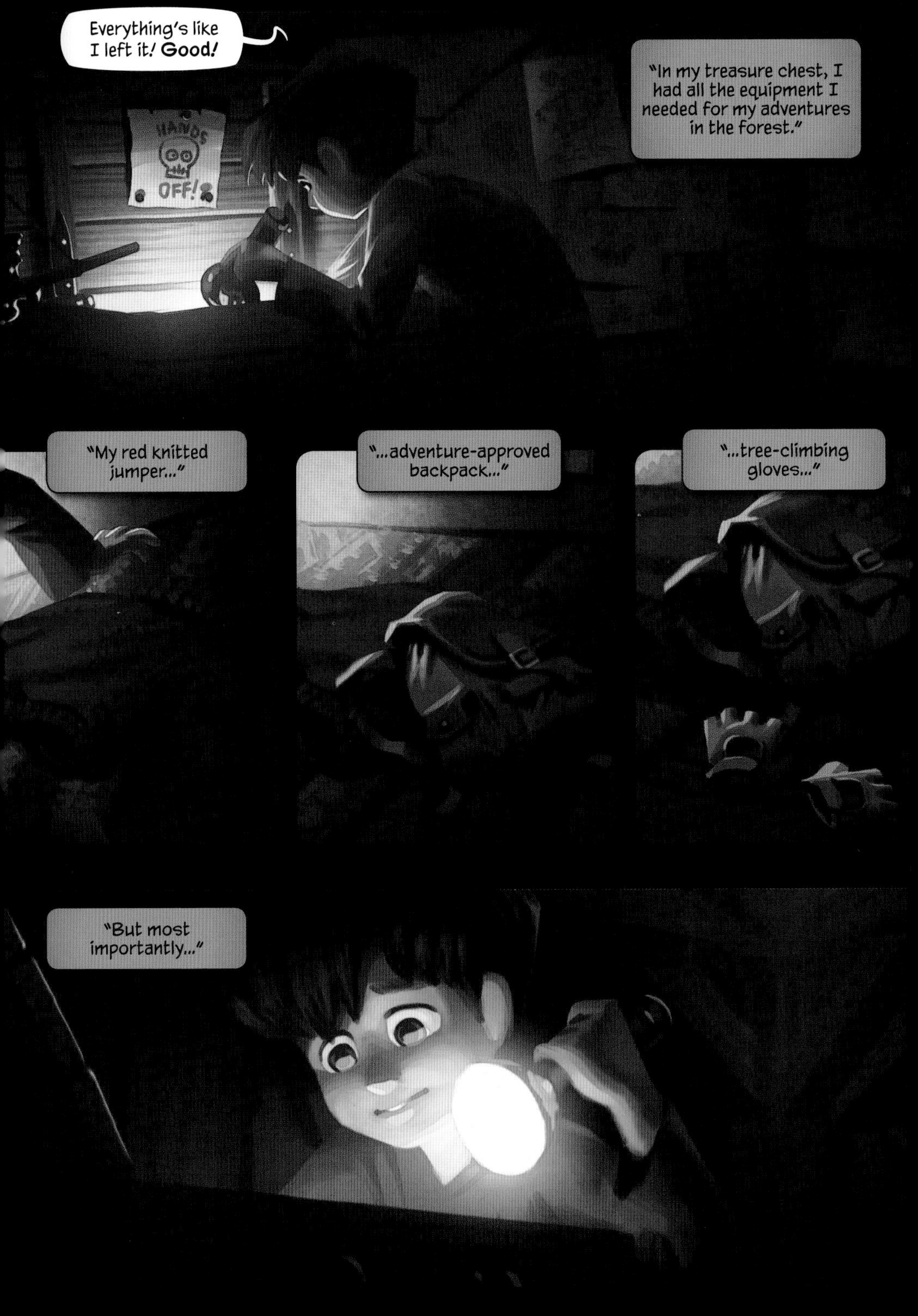

Everything's like I left it! **Good!**
"In my treasure chest, I had all the equipment I needed for my adventures in the forest."
"My red knitted jumper..."
"...adventure-approved backpack..."
"...tree-climbing gloves..."
"But most importantly..."

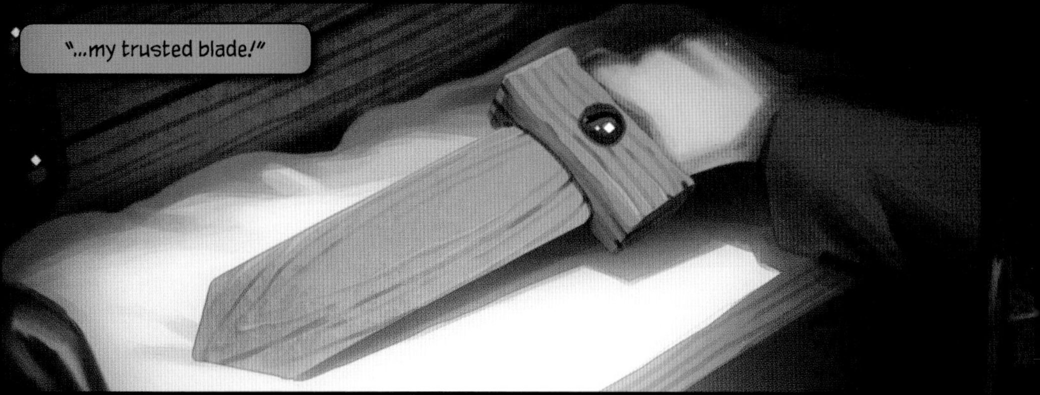
"...my trusted blade!"

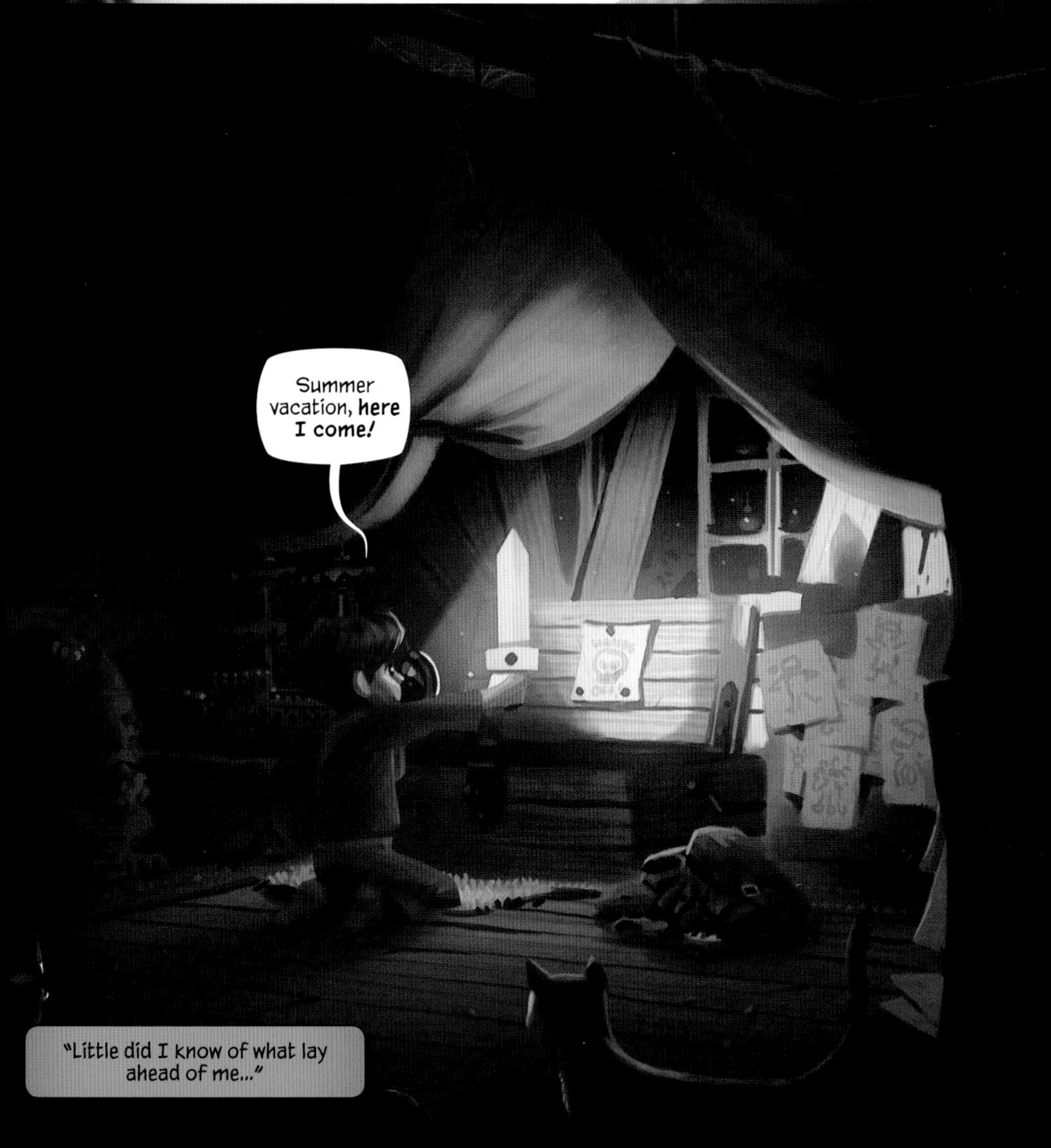
Summer vacation, here I come!
"Little did I know of what lay ahead of me..."

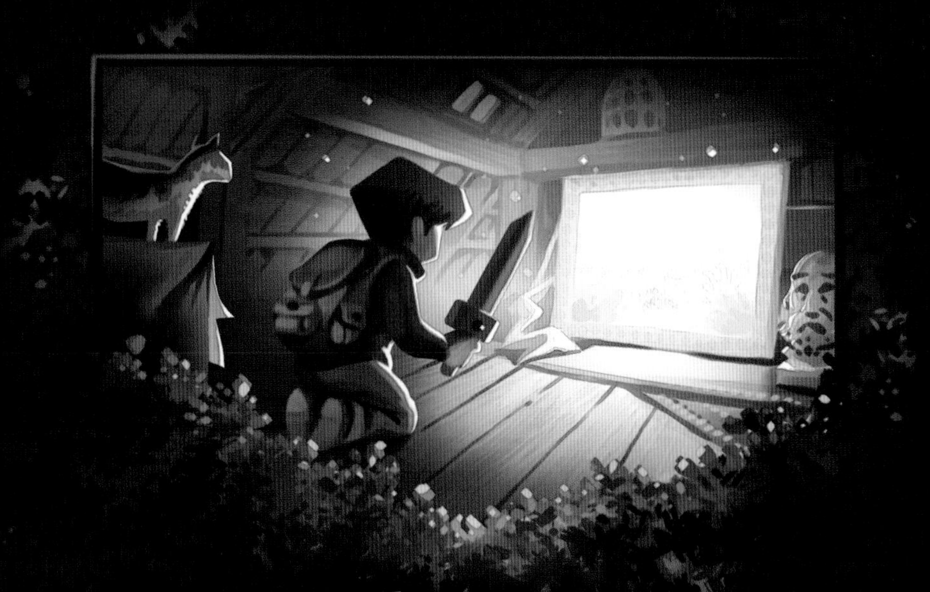

Chapter 2
The Journey Begins

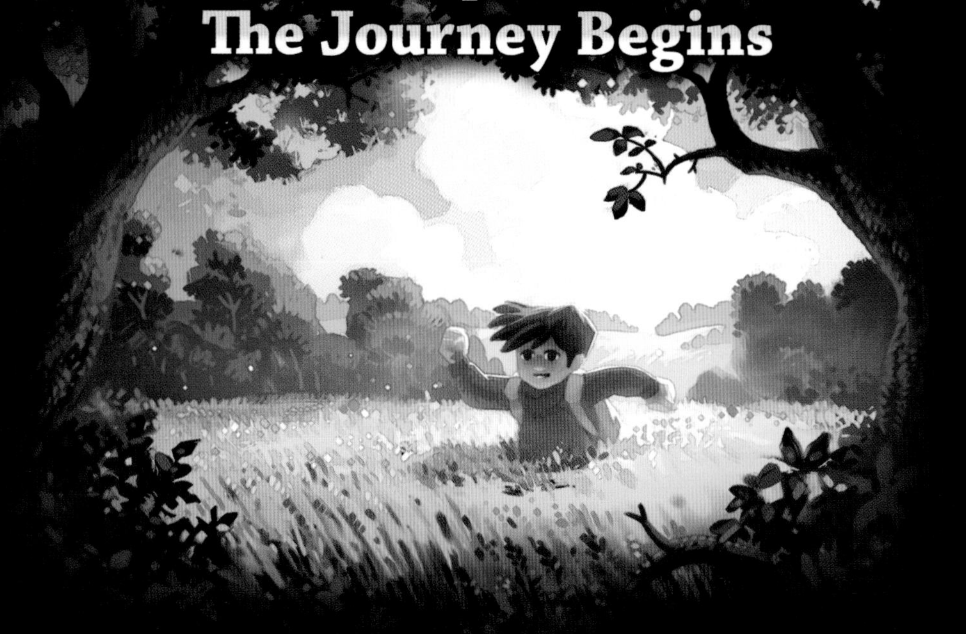

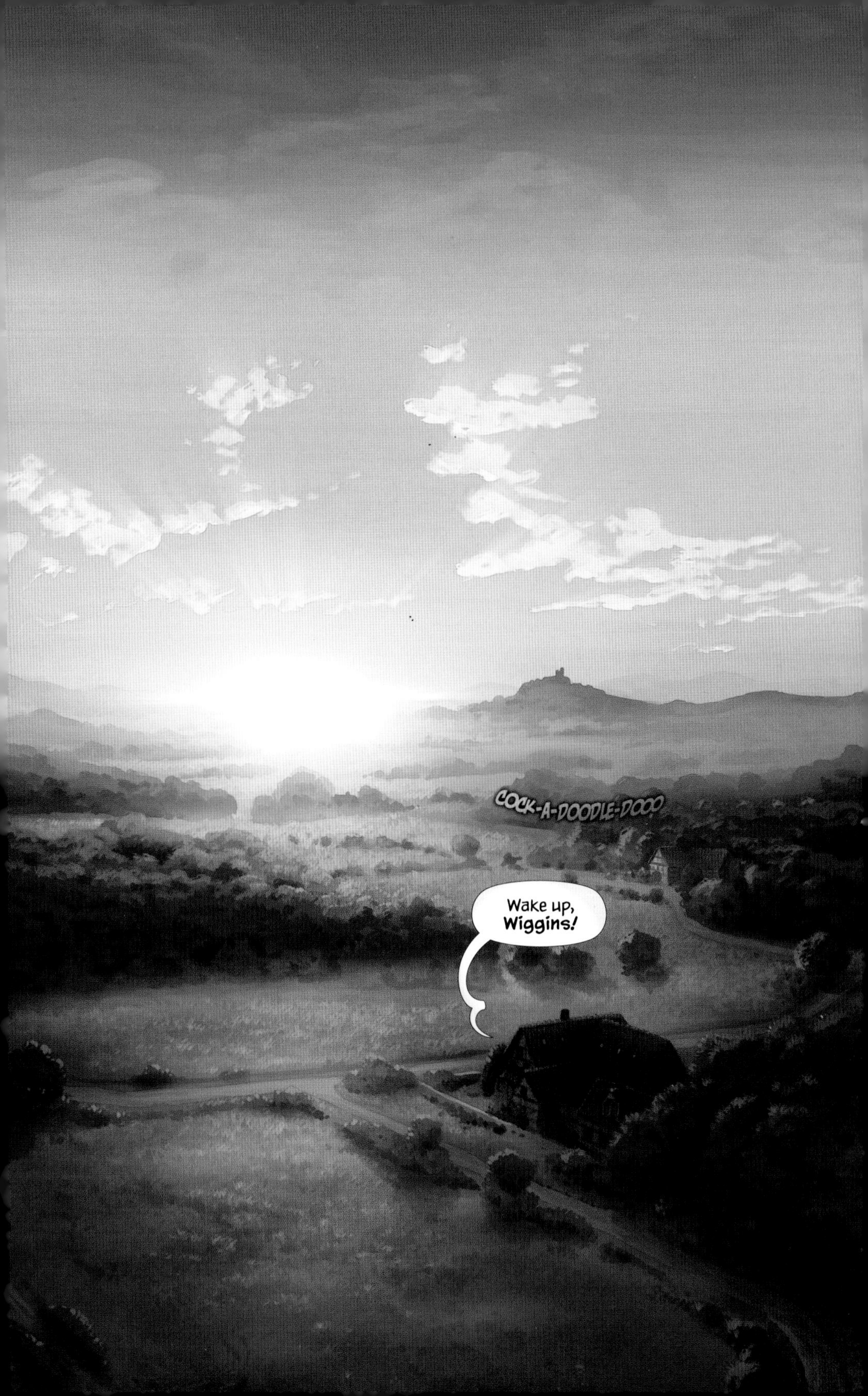
COCK-A-DOODLE-DOOO
Wake up, Wiggins!

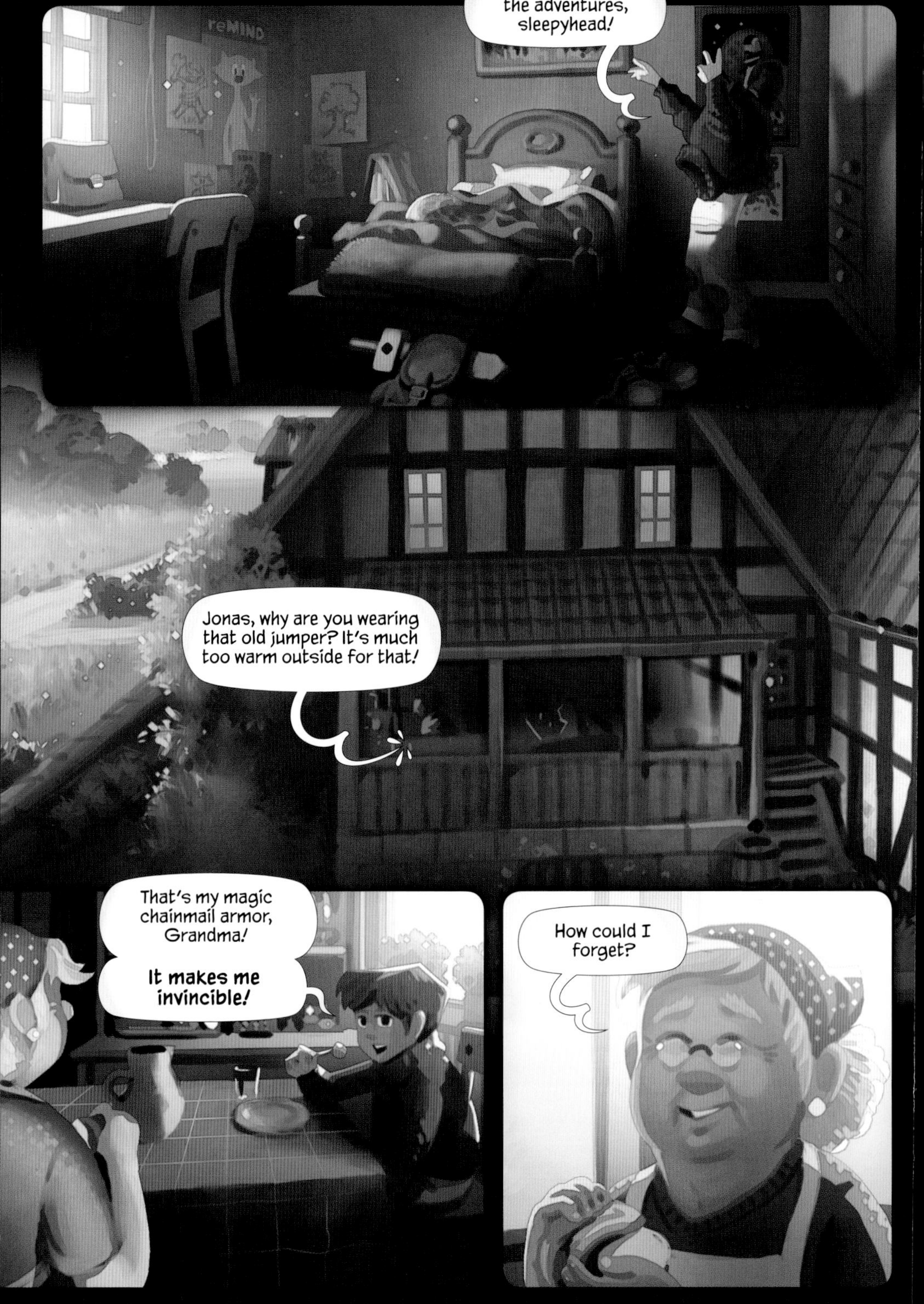
You'll miss all the adventures, sleepyhead!
reMIND
Jonas, why are you wearing that old jumper? It's much too warm outside for that!
That's my magic chainmail armor, Grandma!
It makes me invincible!
How could I forget?

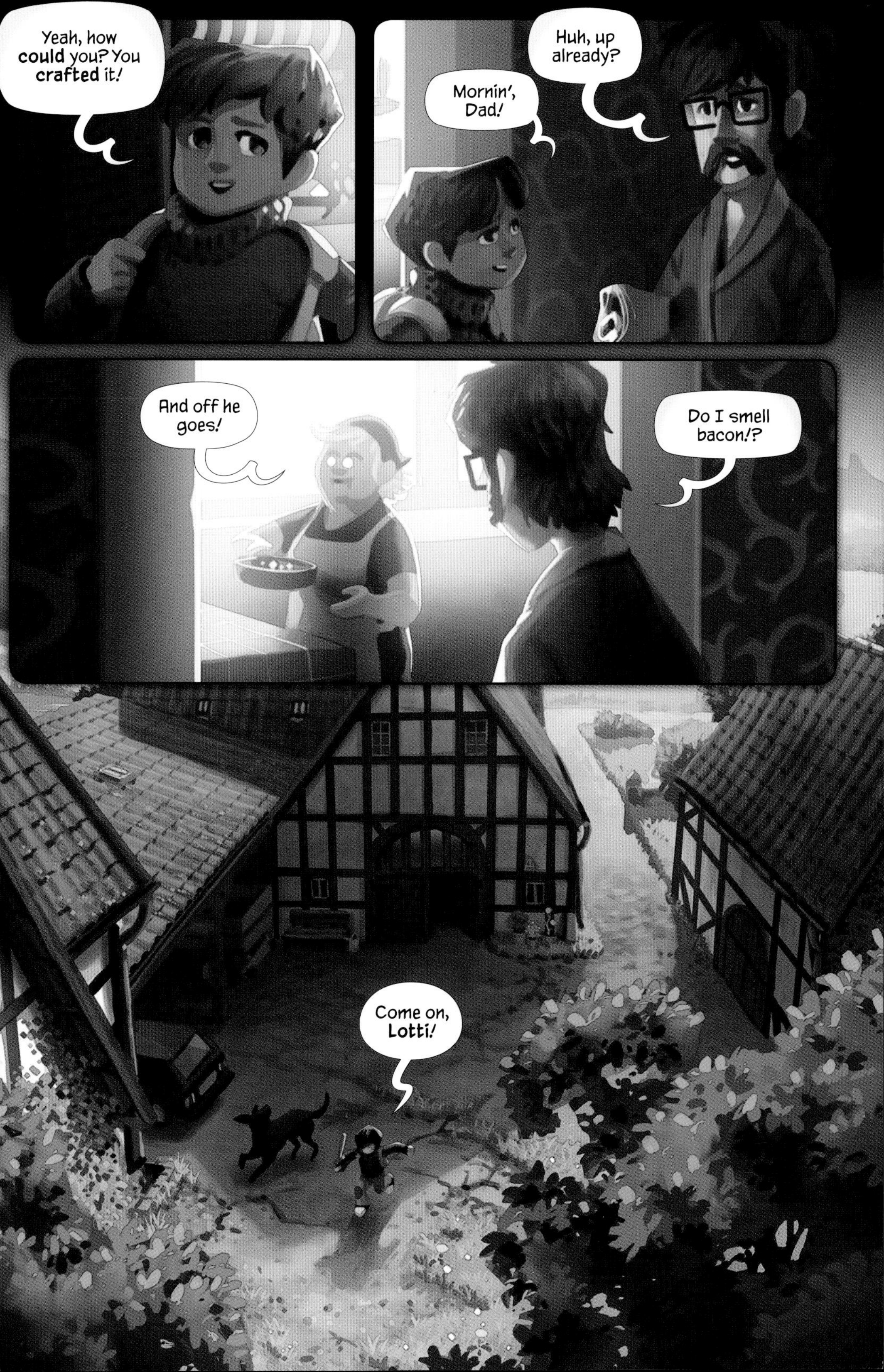
Yeah, how **could** you? You **crafted** it!
Huh, up already?
Mornin', Dad!
And off he goes!
Do I smell bacon!?
Come on, **Lotti**!

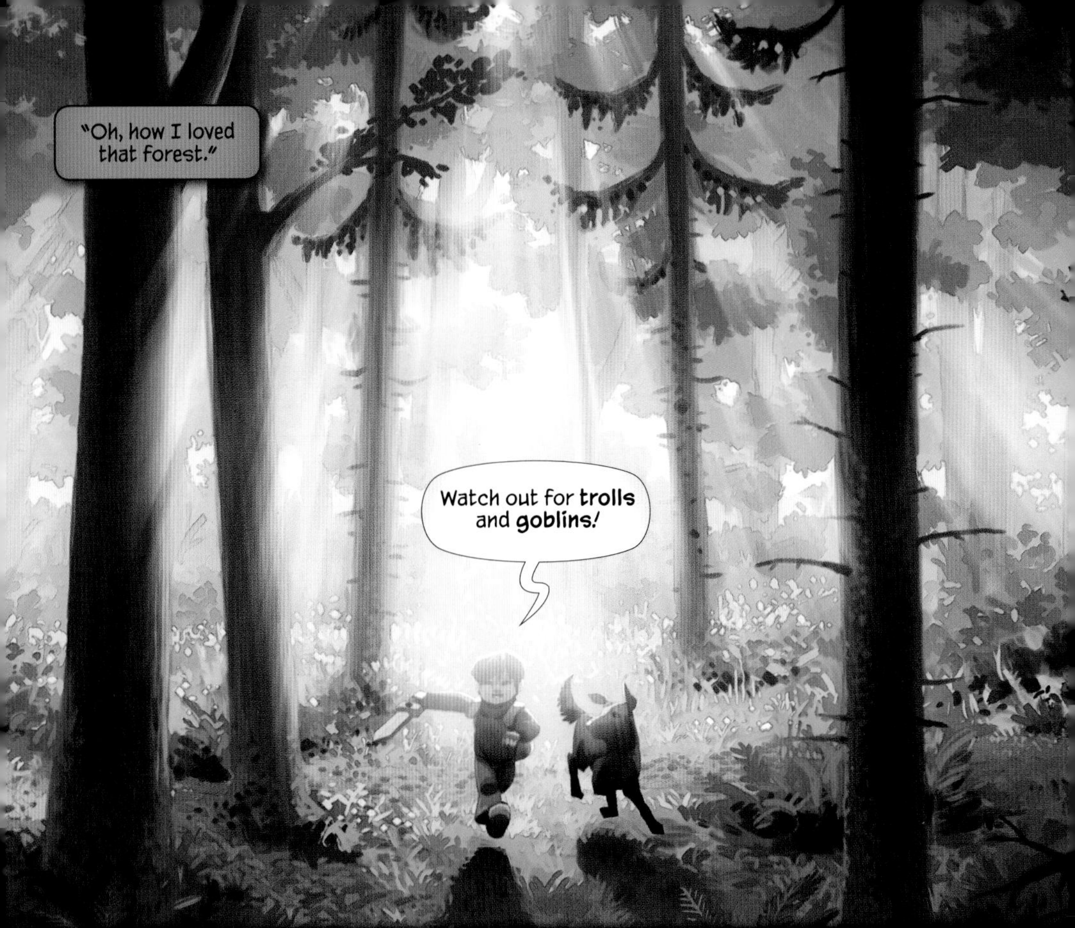
"Oh, how I loved that forest."
Watch out for trolls and goblins!

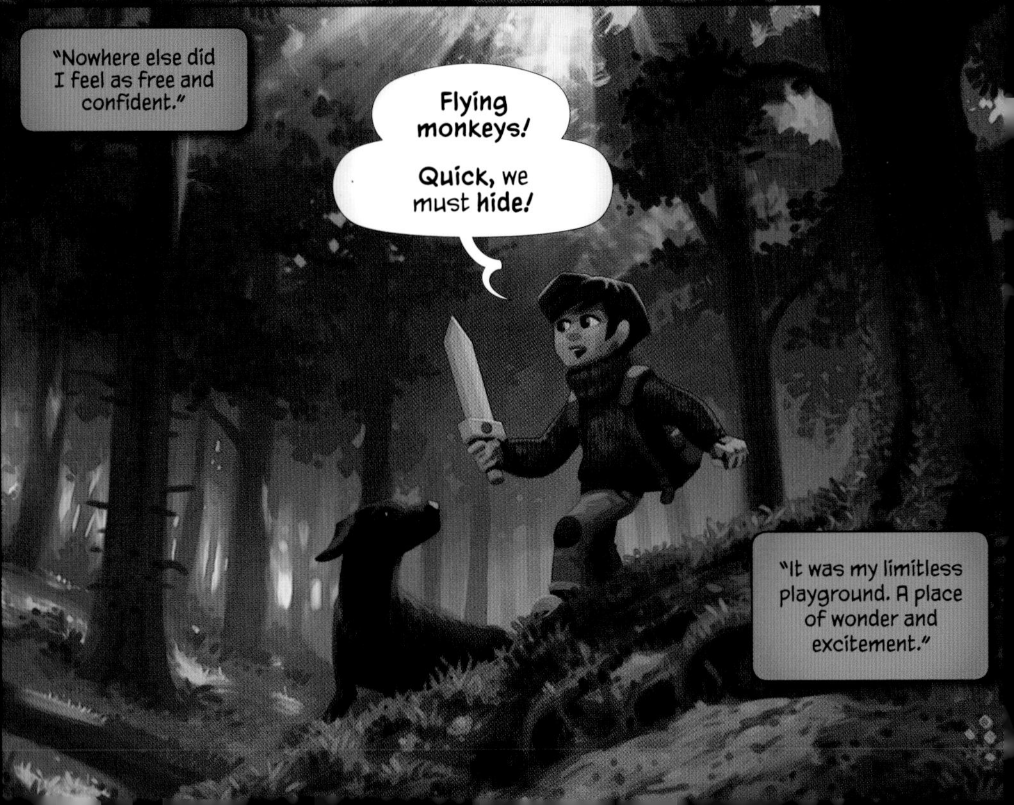
"Nowhere else did I feel as free and confident."
Flying monkeys!
Quick, we must hide!
"It was my limitless playground. A place of wonder and excitement."

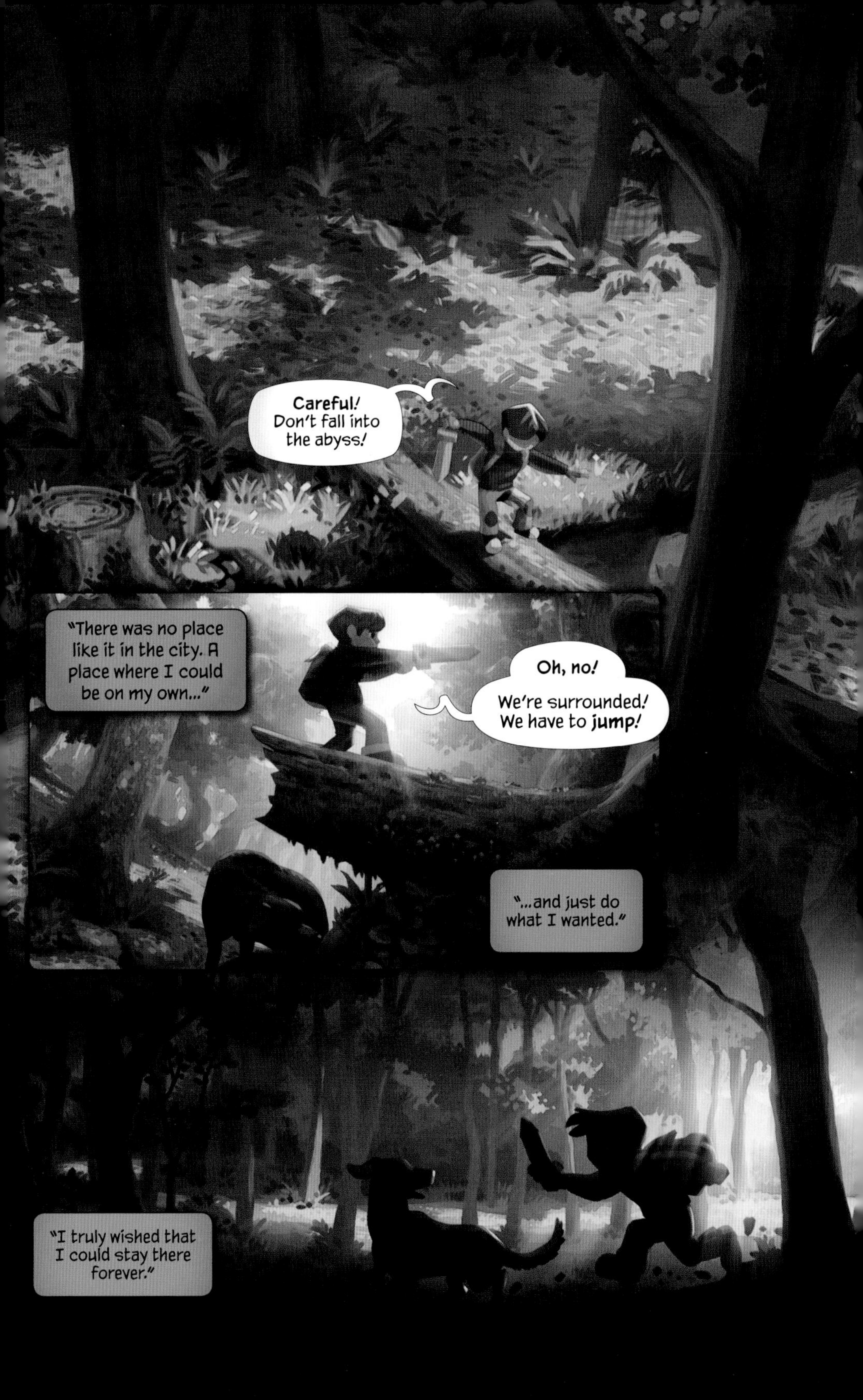
Careful! Don't fall into the abyss!
"There was no place like it in the city. A place where I could be on my own..."
Oh, no!
We're surrounded! We have to jump!
"...and just do what I wanted."
"I truly wished that I could stay there forever."

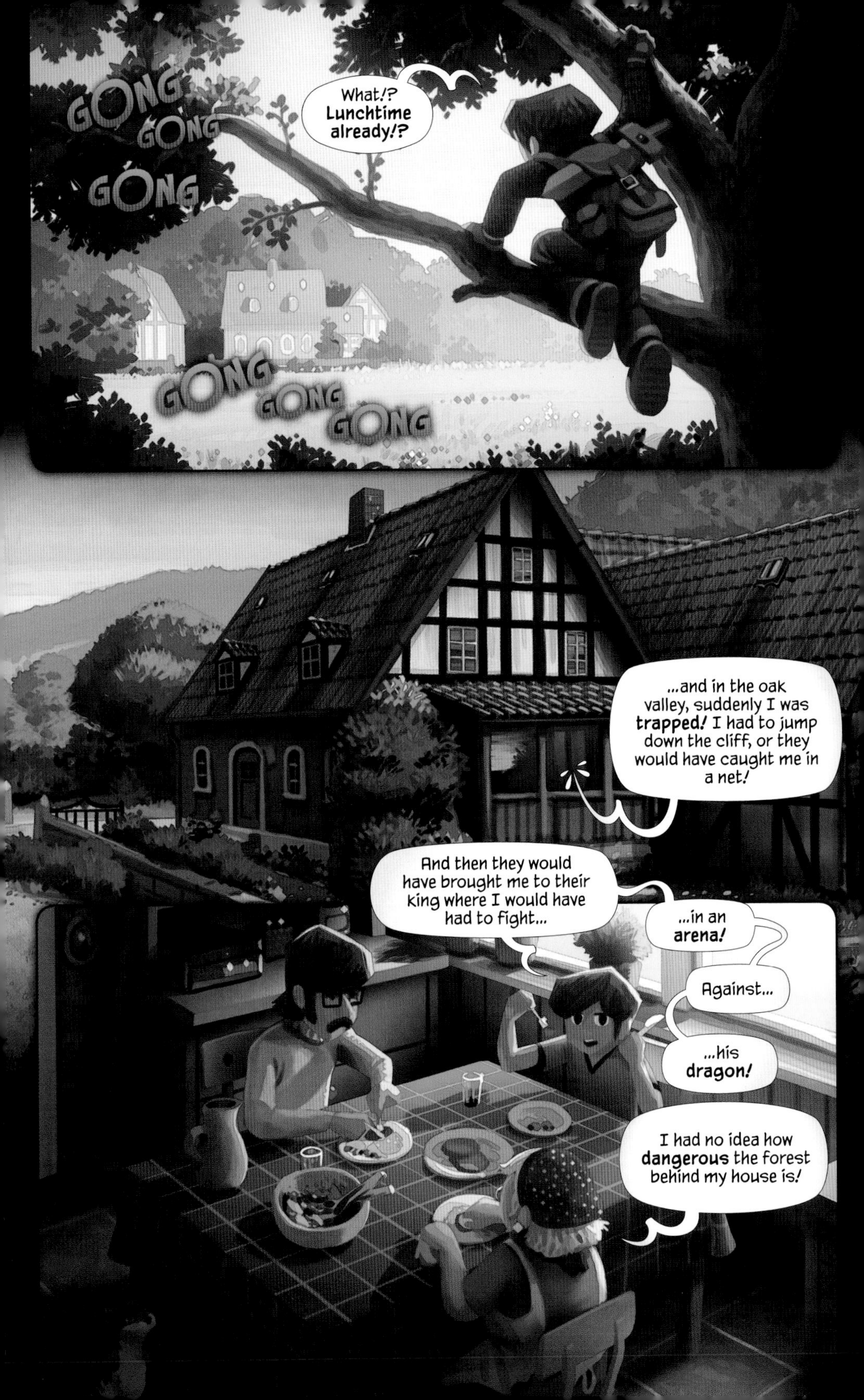
GONG GONG GONG
What!? Lunchtime already!?
GONG GONG GONG
...and in the oak valley, suddenly I was trapped! I had to jump down the cliff, or they would have caught me in a net!
And then they would have brought me to their king where I would have had to fight...
...in an arena!
Against...
...his dragon!
I had no idea how dangerous the forest behind my house is!

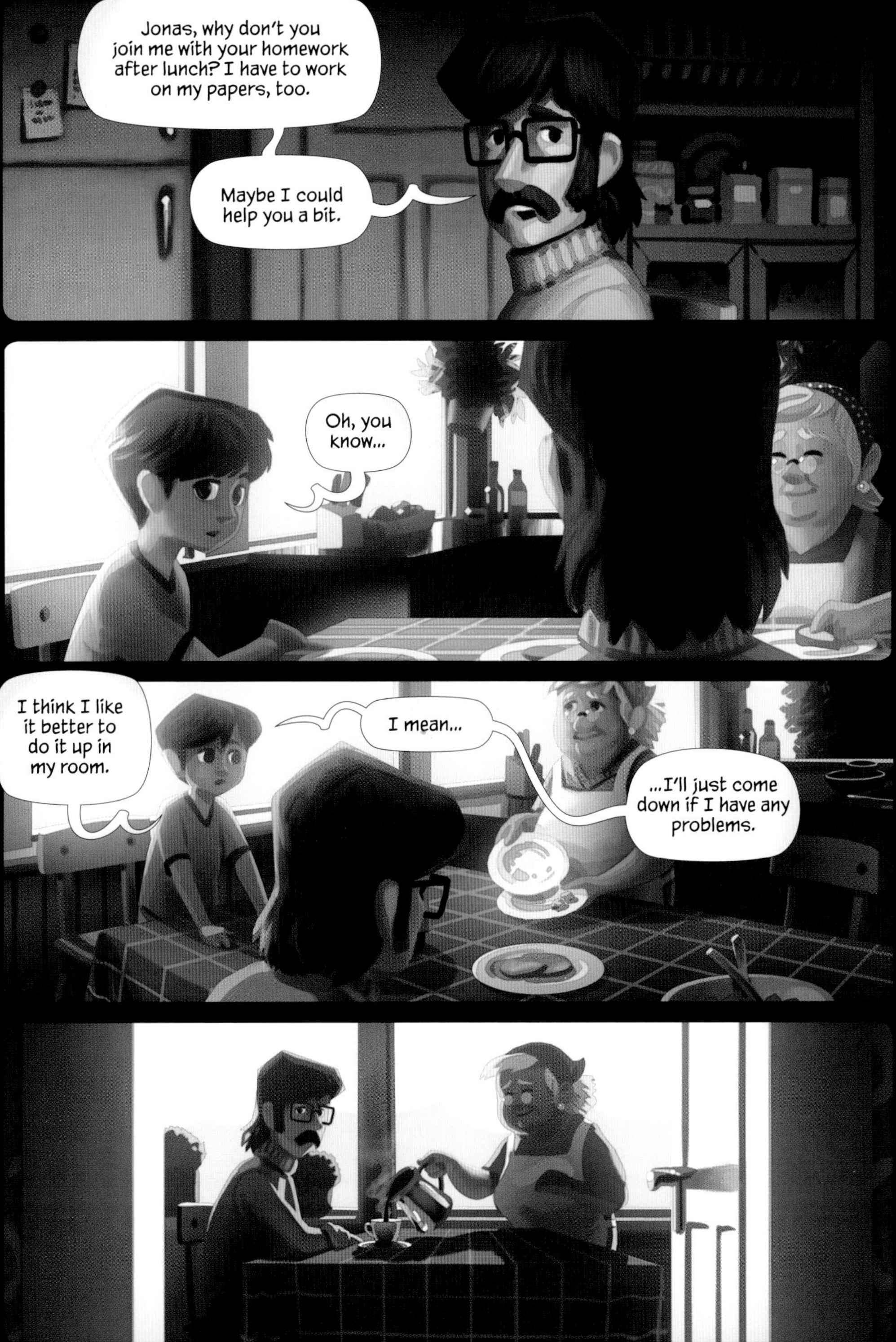
Jonas, why don't you join me with your homework after lunch? I have to work on my papers, too.
Maybe I could help you a bit.
Oh, you know...
I think I like it better to do it up in my room.
I mean...
...I'll just come down if I have any problems.

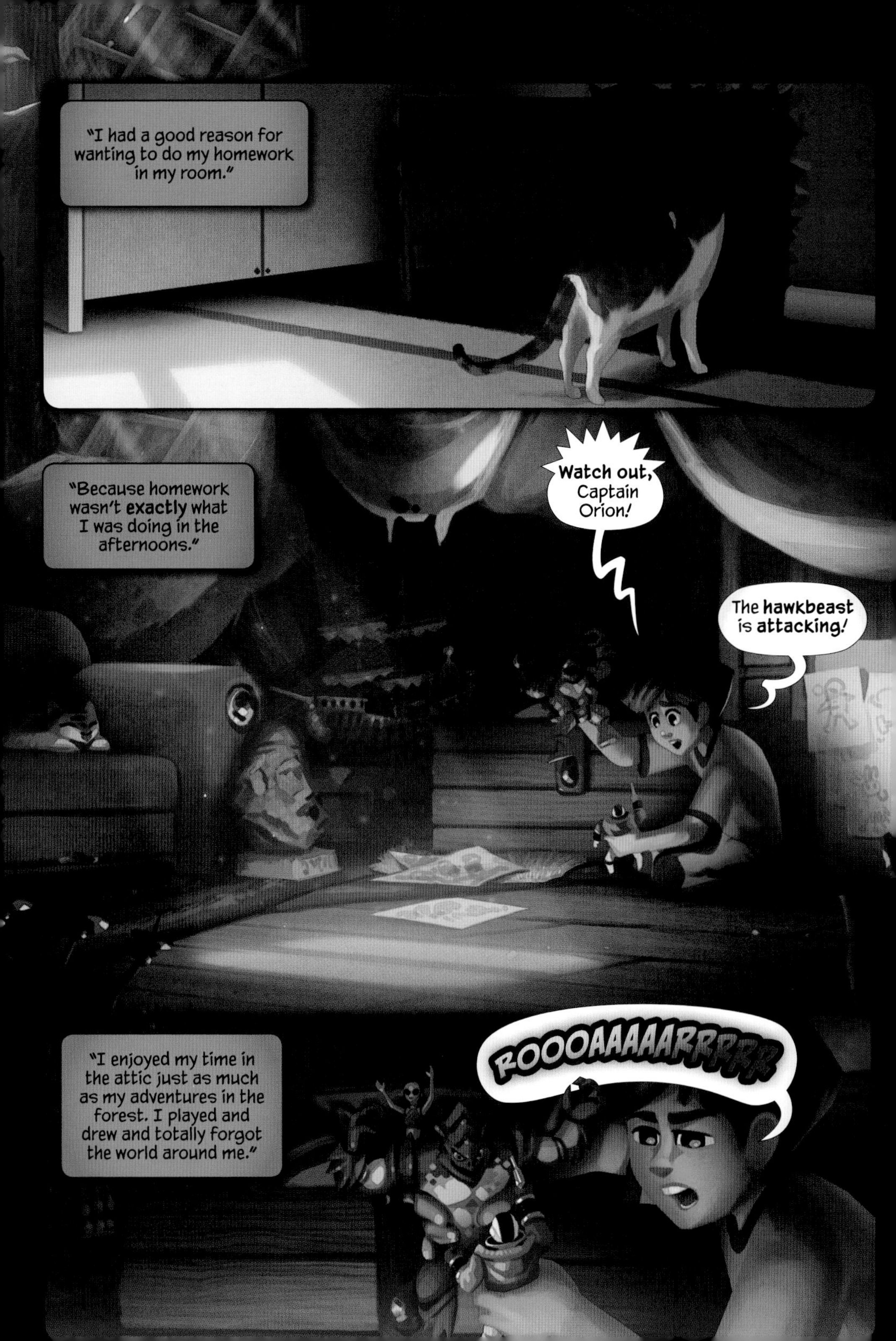
"I had a good reason for wanting to do my homework in my room."
"Because homework wasn't **exactly** what I was doing in the afternoons."
Watch out, Captain Orion!
The **hawkbeast** is **attacking!**
"I enjoyed my time in the attic just as much as my adventures in the forest. I played and drew and totally forgot the world around me."
ROOOAAAAARRRRR

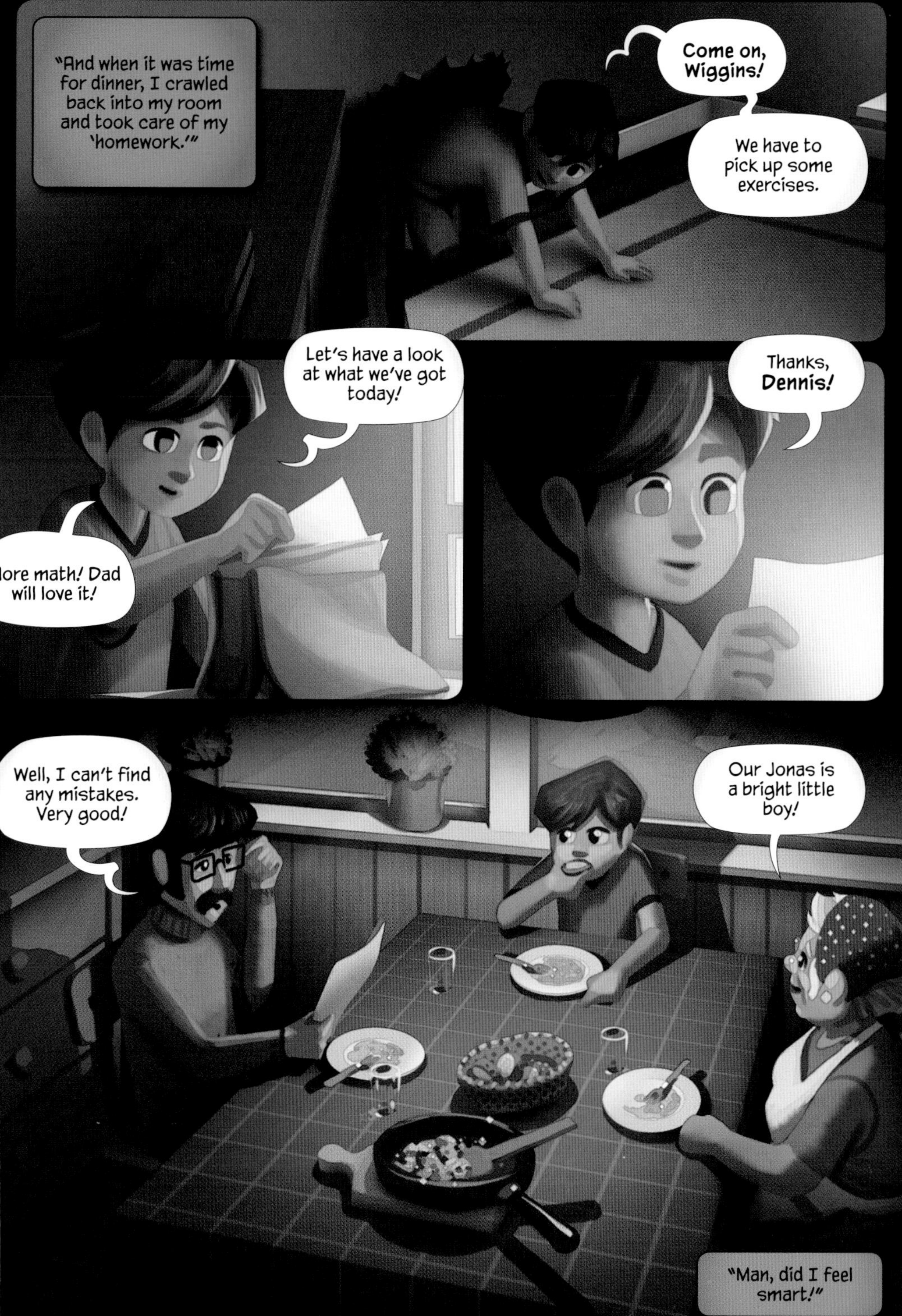
"And when it was time for dinner, I crawled back into my room and took care of my 'homework.'"
Come on, Wiggins!
We have to pick up some exercises.
Let's have a look at what we've got today!
ore math! Dad will love it!
Thanks, Dennis!
Well, I can't find any mistakes. Very good!
Our Jonas is a bright little boy!
"Man, did I feel smart!"

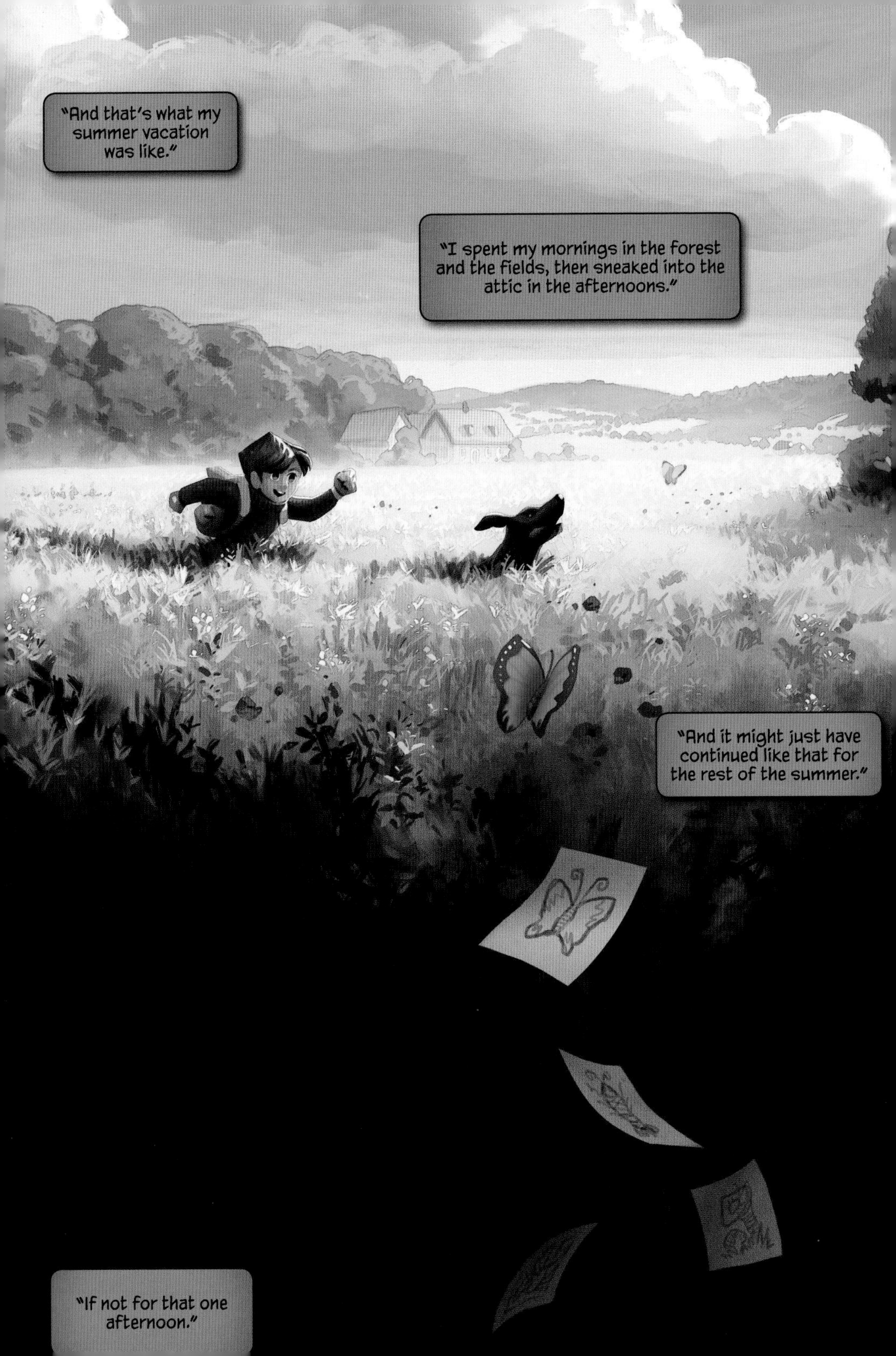
"And that's what my summer vacation was like."
"I spent my mornings in the forest and the fields, then sneaked into the attic in the afternoons."
"And it might just have continued like that for the rest of the summer."
"If not for that one afternoon."

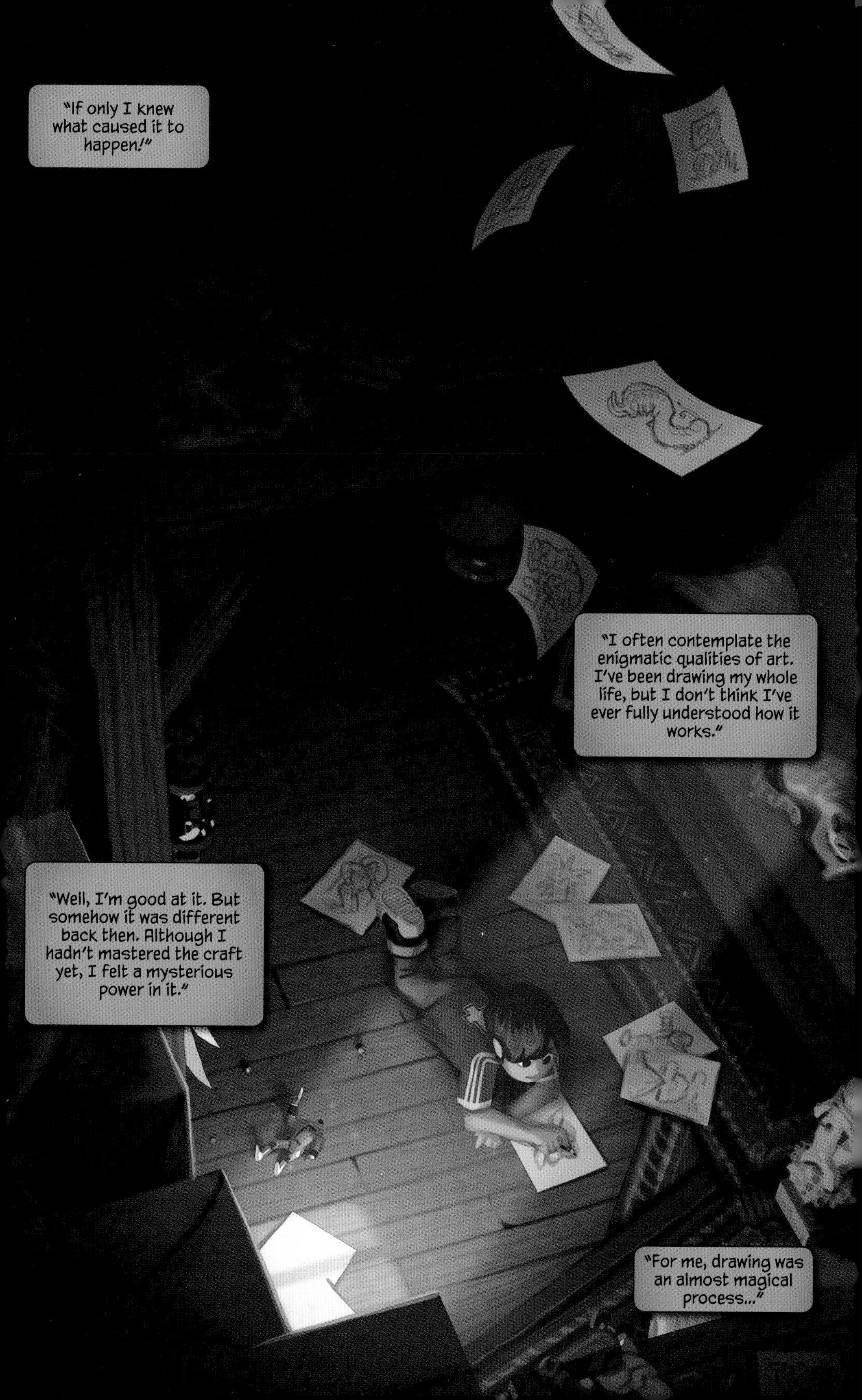
"If only I knew what caused it to happen!"
"I often contemplate the enigmatic qualities of art. I've been drawing my whole life, but I don't think I've ever fully understood how it works."
"Well, I'm good at it. But somehow it was different back then. Although I hadn't mastered the craft yet, I felt a mysterious power in it."
"For me, drawing was an almost magical process..."

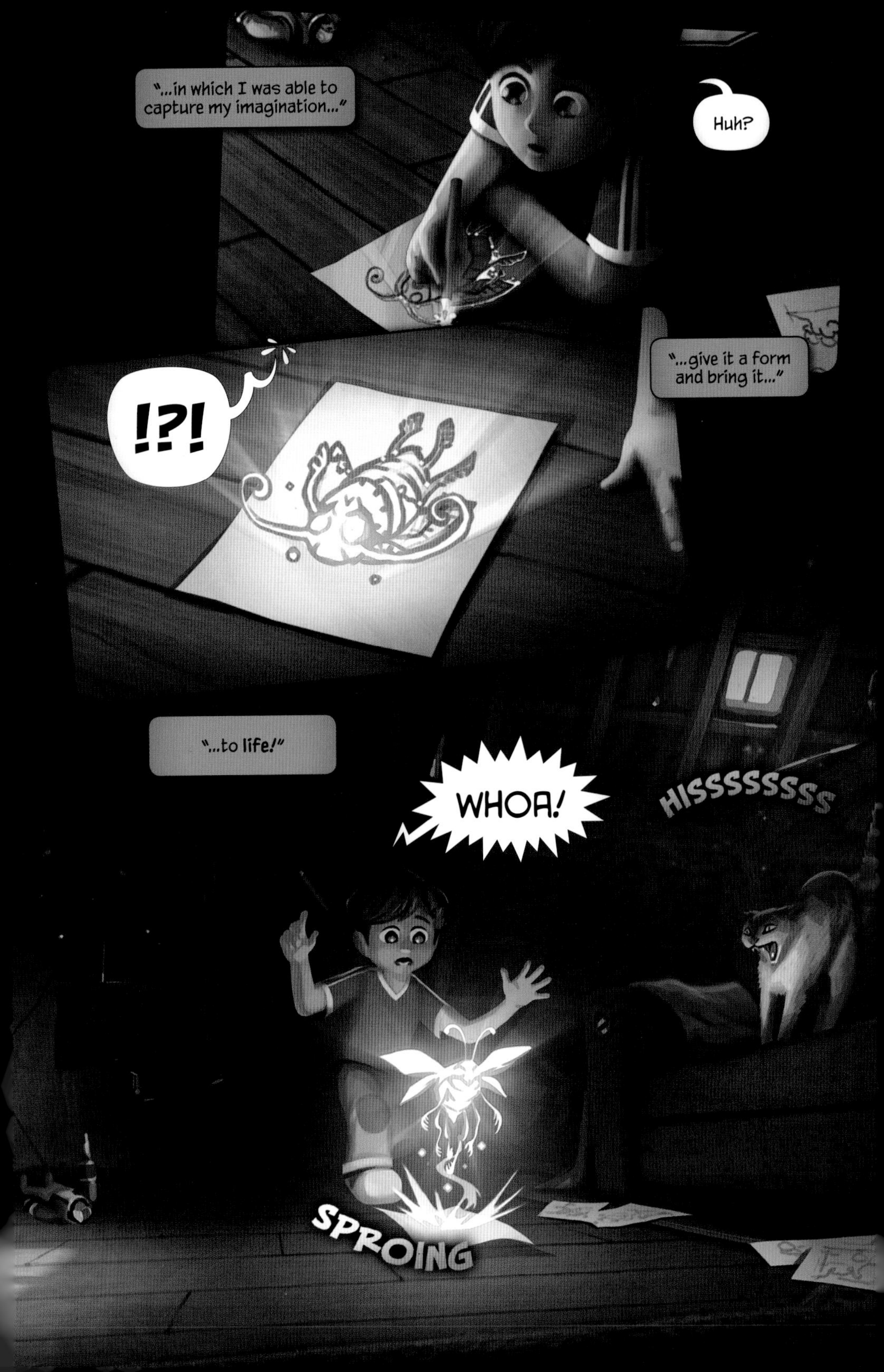
"...in which I was able to capture my imagination..."
Huh?
"...give it a form and bring it..."
!?!
"...to life!"
WHOA!
HISSSSSSSS
SPROING

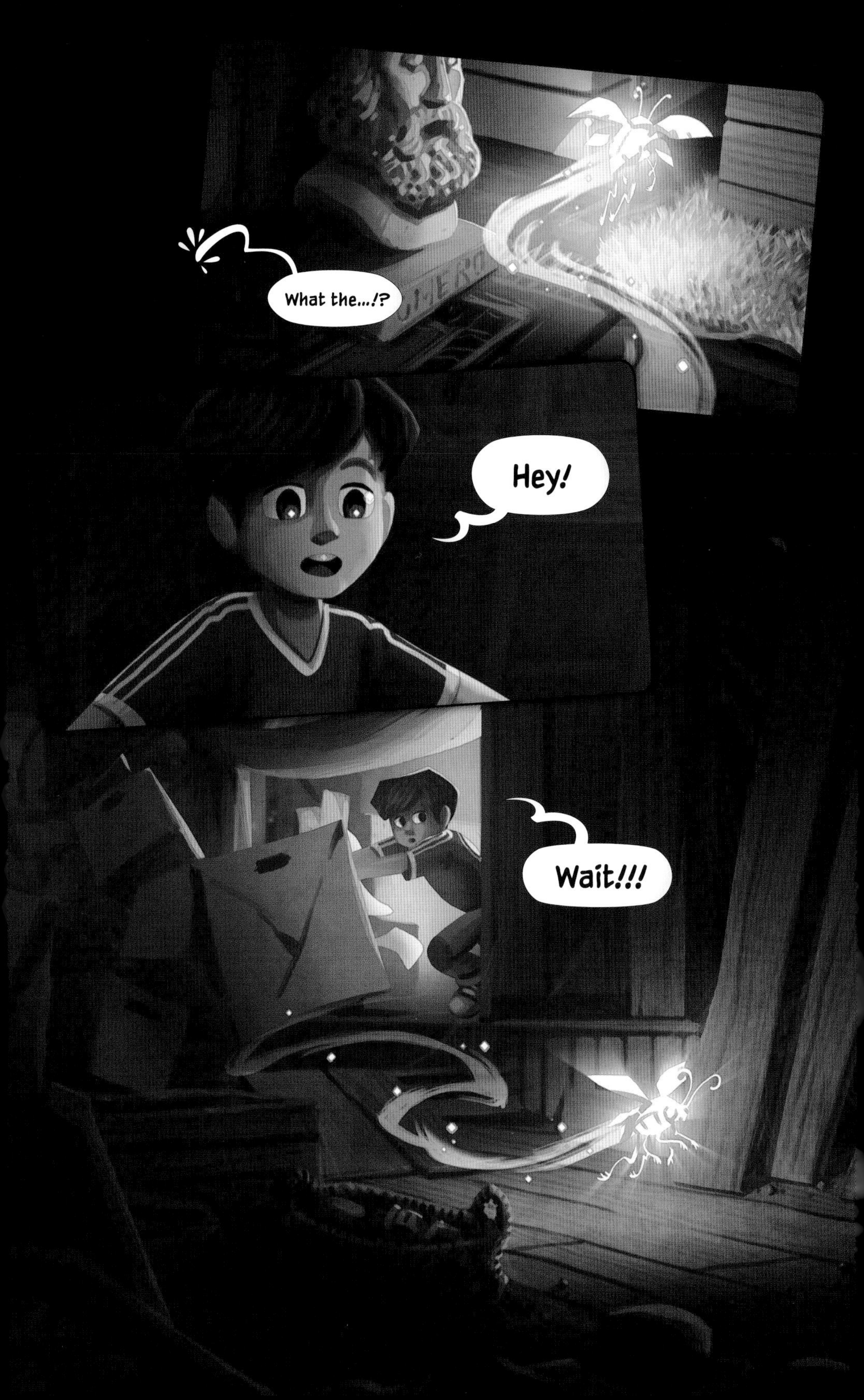

What the...!?
Hey!
Wait!!!

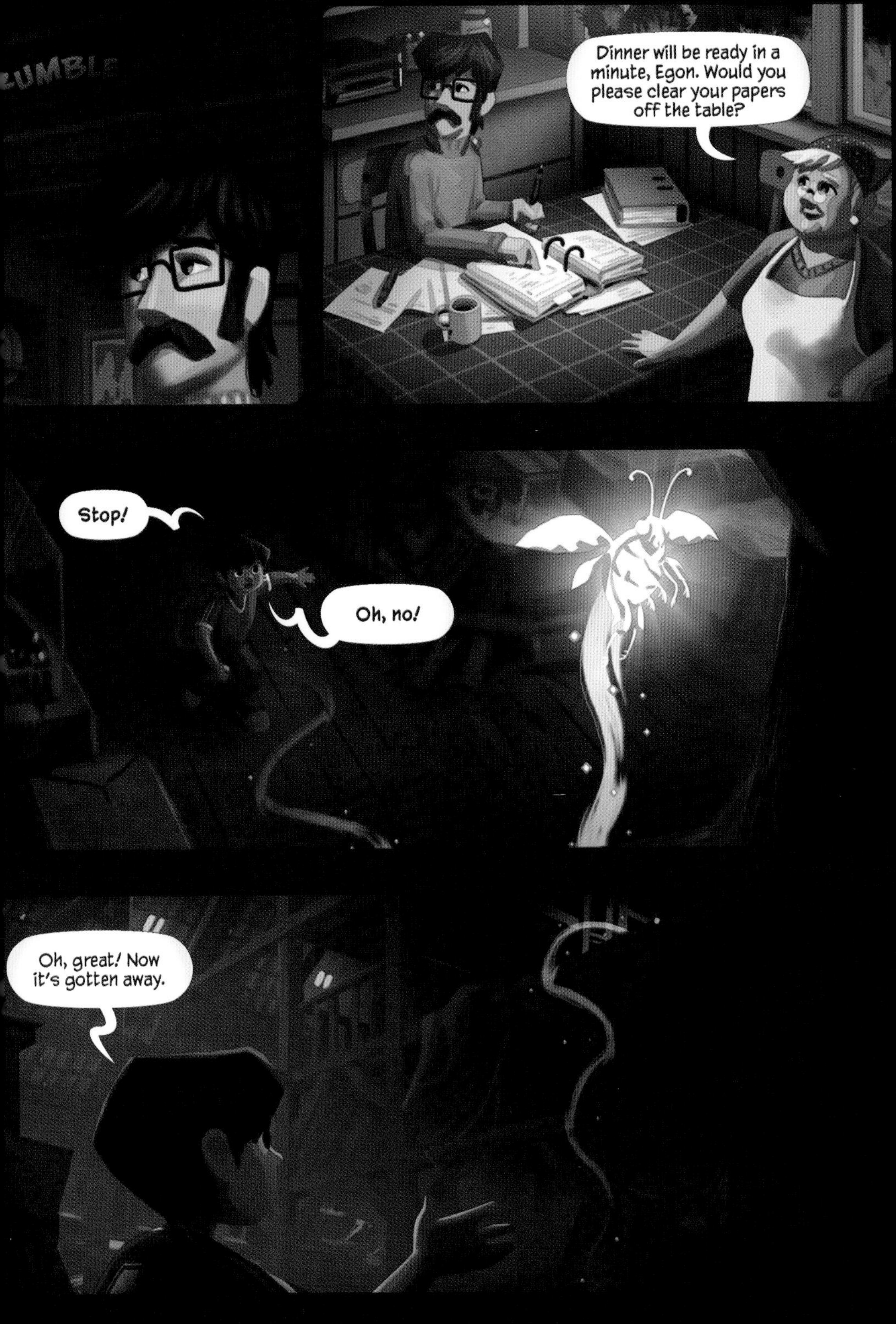
Dinner will be ready in a minute, Egon. Would you please clear your papers off the table?
Stop!
Oh, no!
Oh, great! Now it's gotten away.

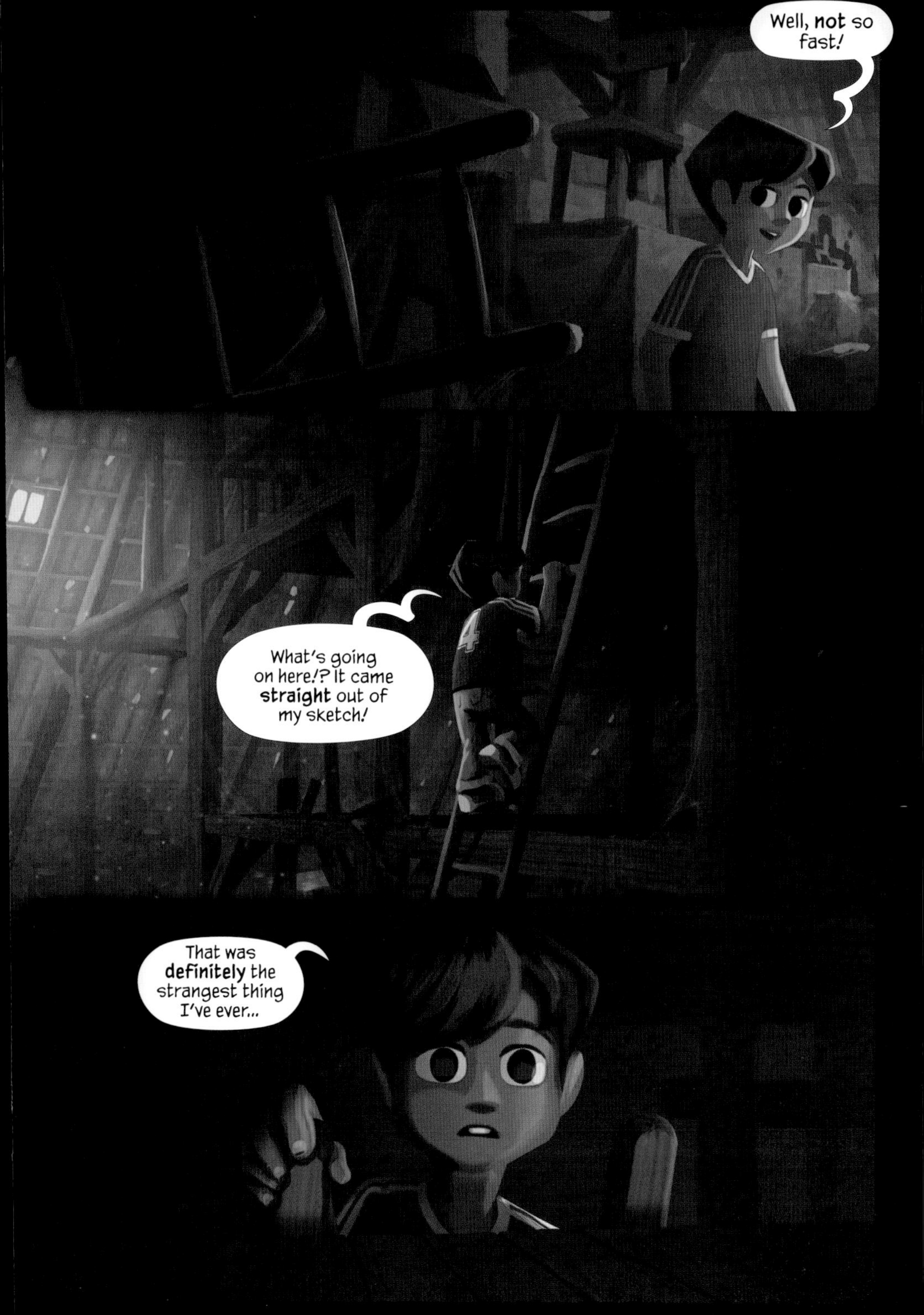
Well, **not** so fast!
What's going on here!? It came **straight** out of my sketch!
That was **definitely** the strangest thing I've ever...

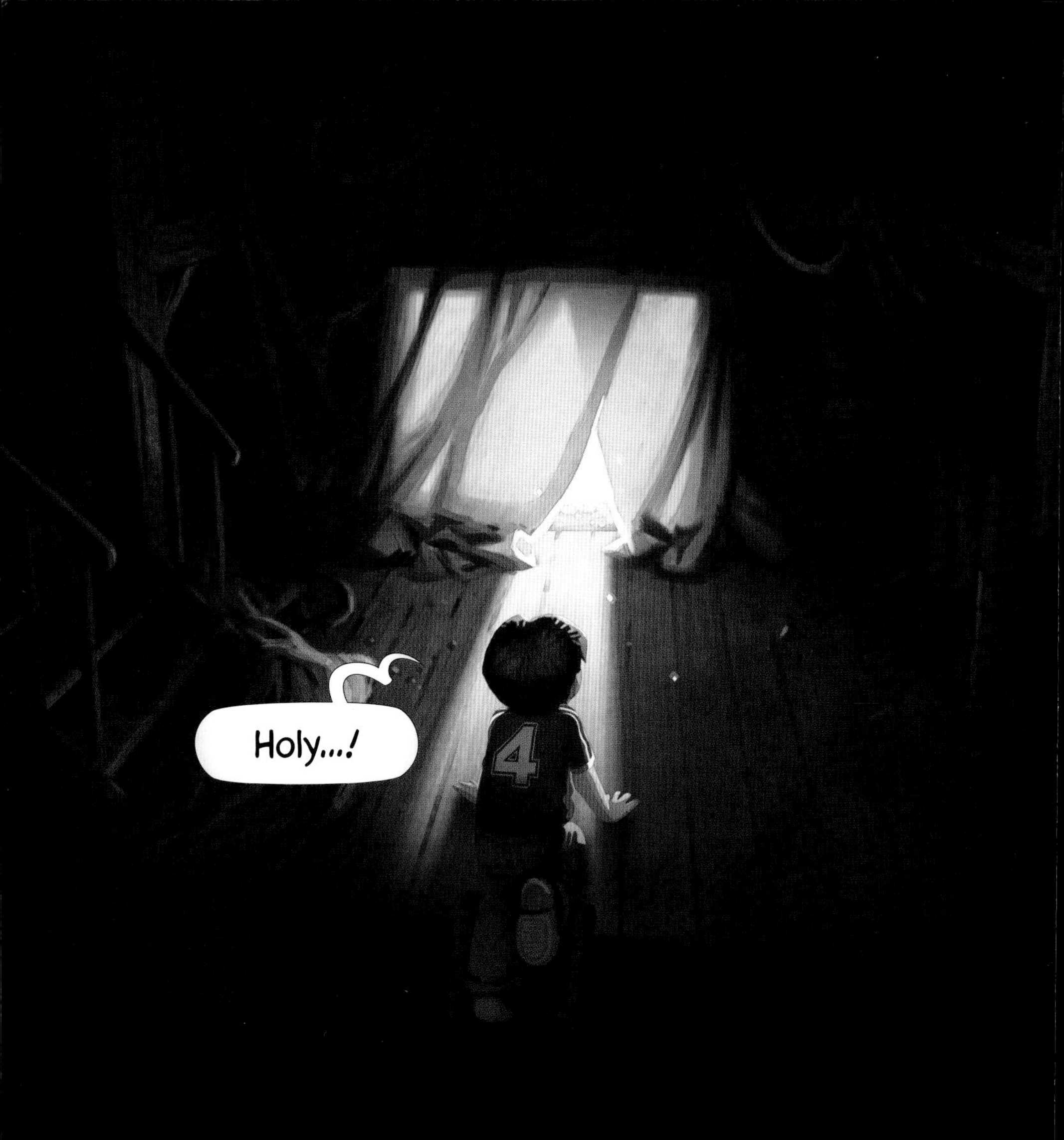
Holy...!

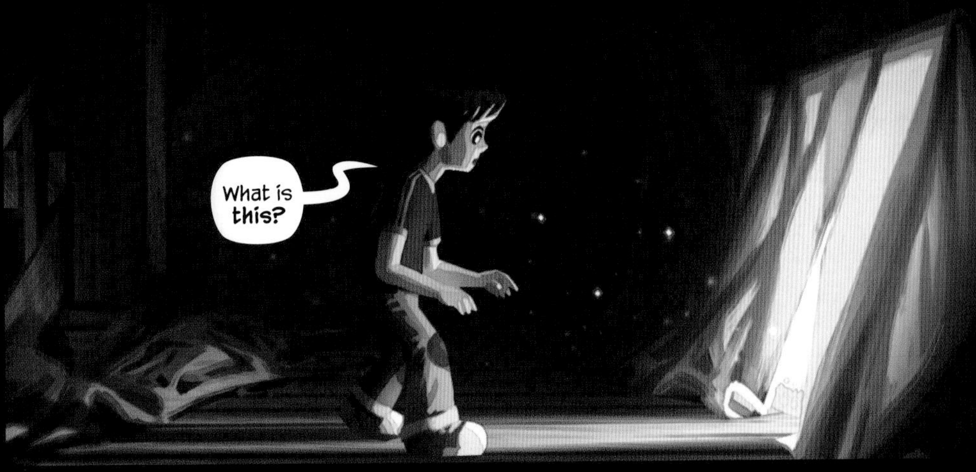
What is this?

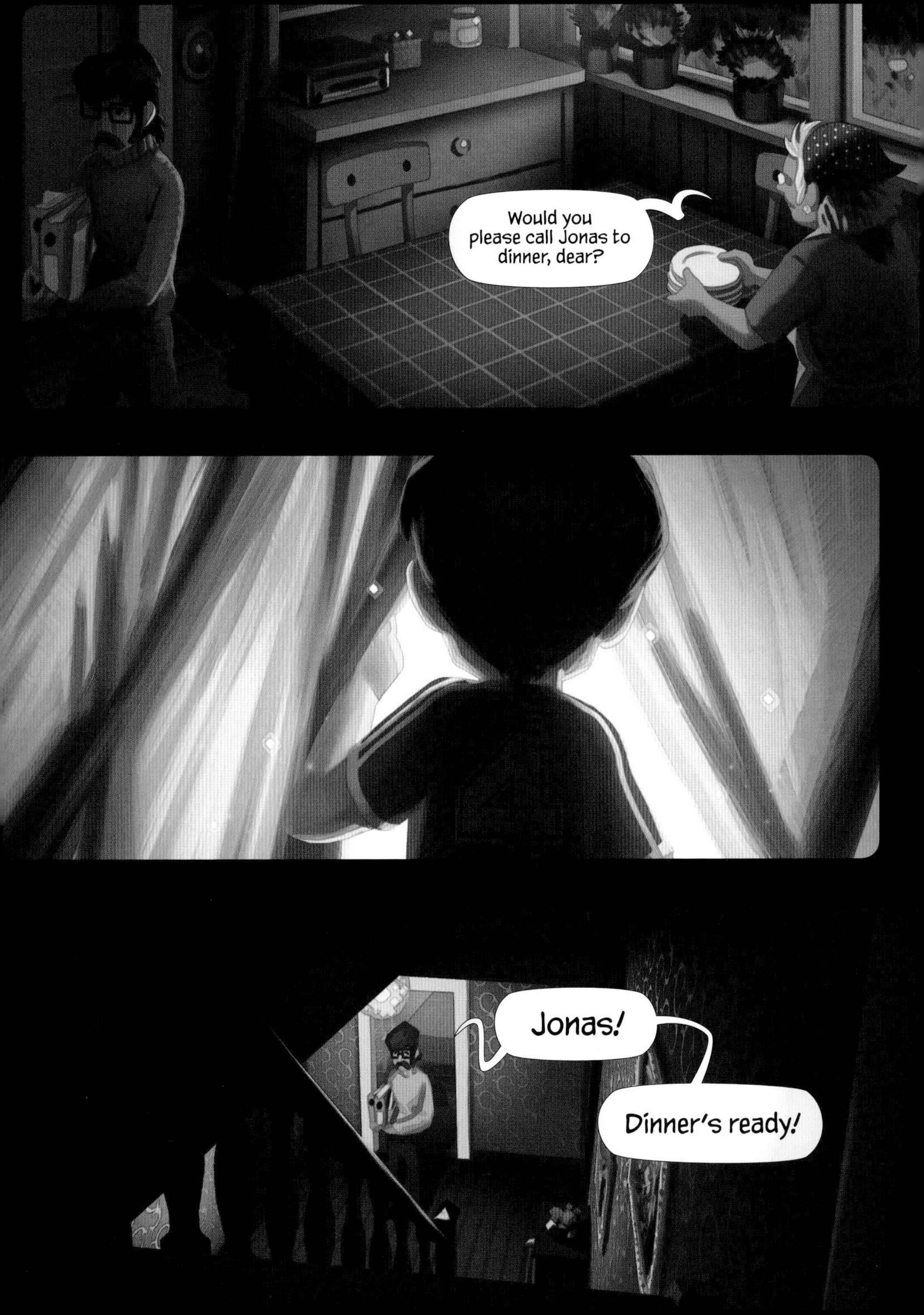
Would you please call Jonas to dinner, dear?
Jonas!
Dinner's ready!

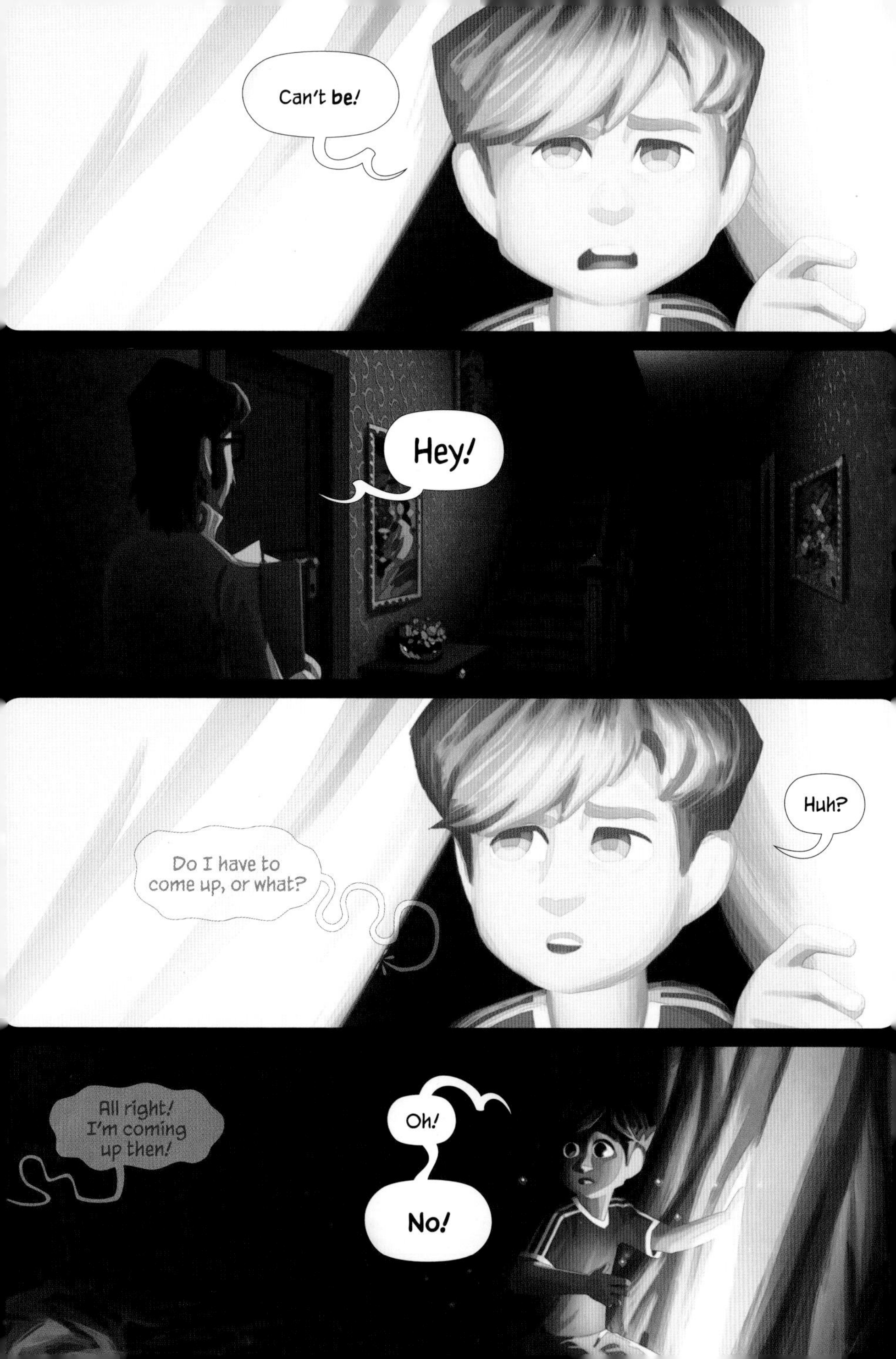
Can't be!
Hey!
Do I have to come up, or what?
Huh?
All right! I'm coming up then!
Oh!
No!

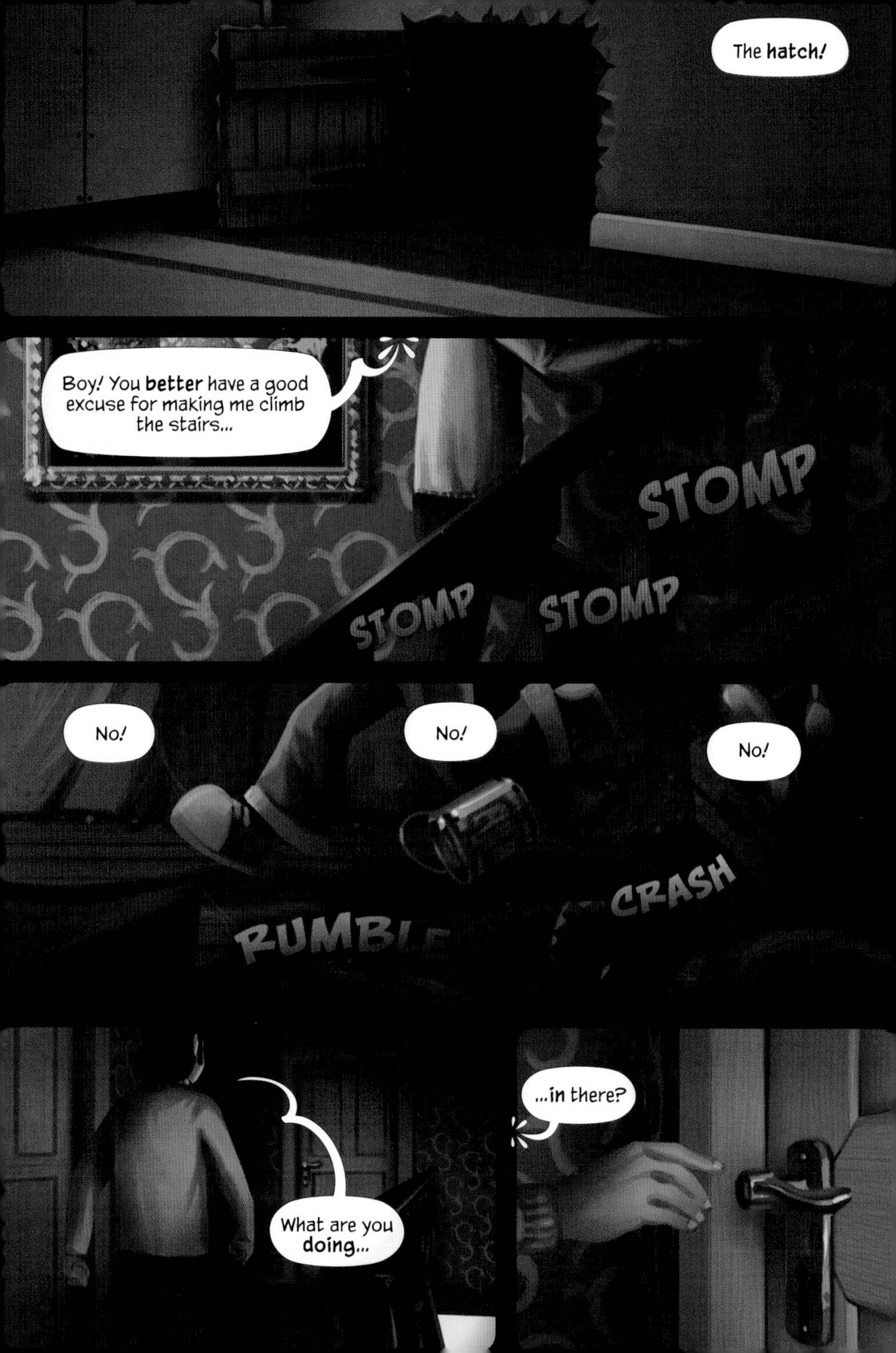
The hatch!
Boy! You better have a good excuse for making me climb the stairs...
STOMP
STOMP
STOMP
No!
No!
No!
RUMBLE
CRASH
What are you doing...
...in there?

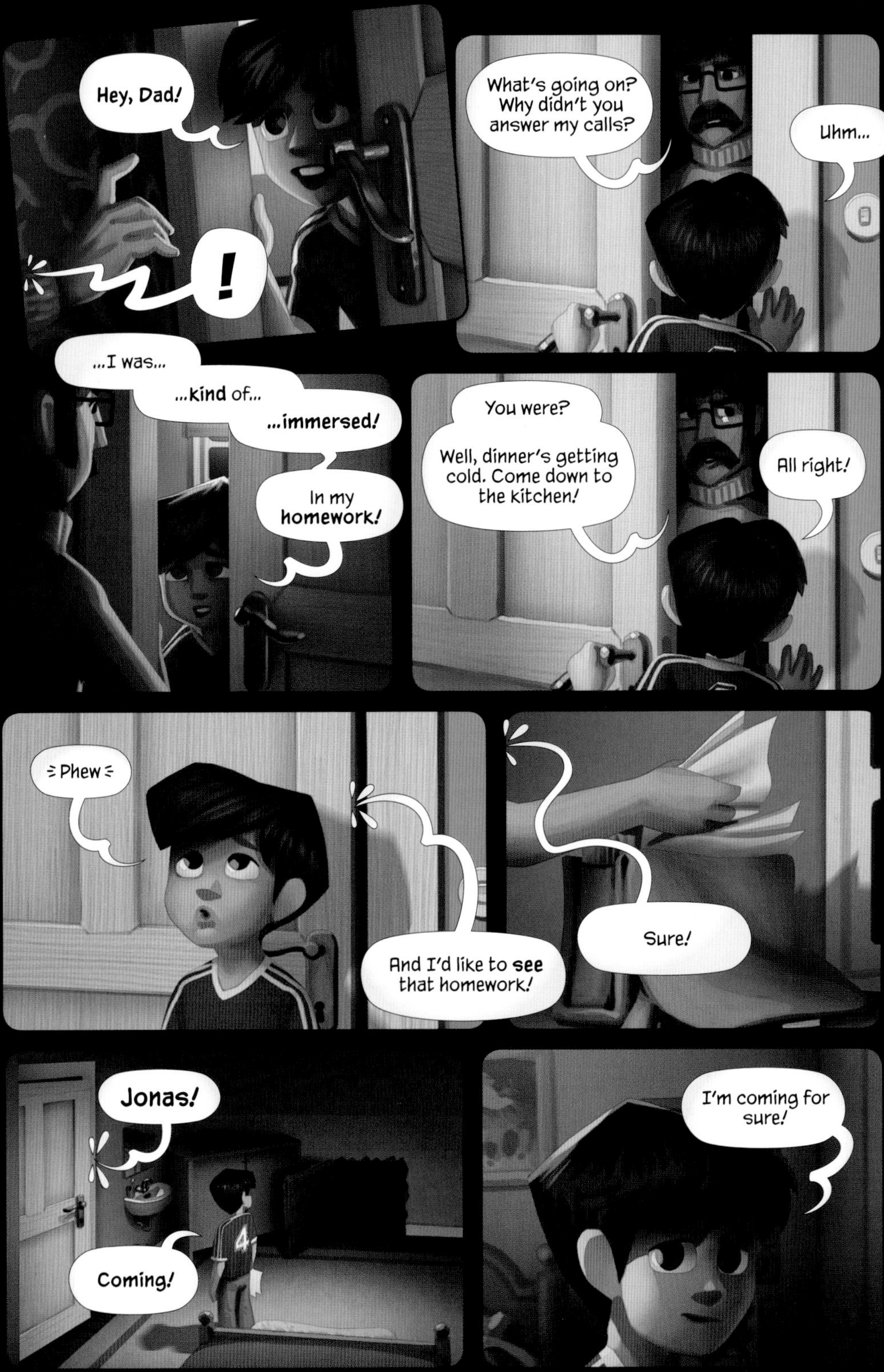
Hey, Dad!
!
What's going on? Why didn't you answer my calls?
Uhm...
...I was...
...kind of...
...immersed!
In my homework!
You were?
Well, dinner's getting cold. Come down to the kitchen!
All right!
Phew
And I'd like to see that homework!
Sure!
Jonas!
Coming!
I'm coming for sure!

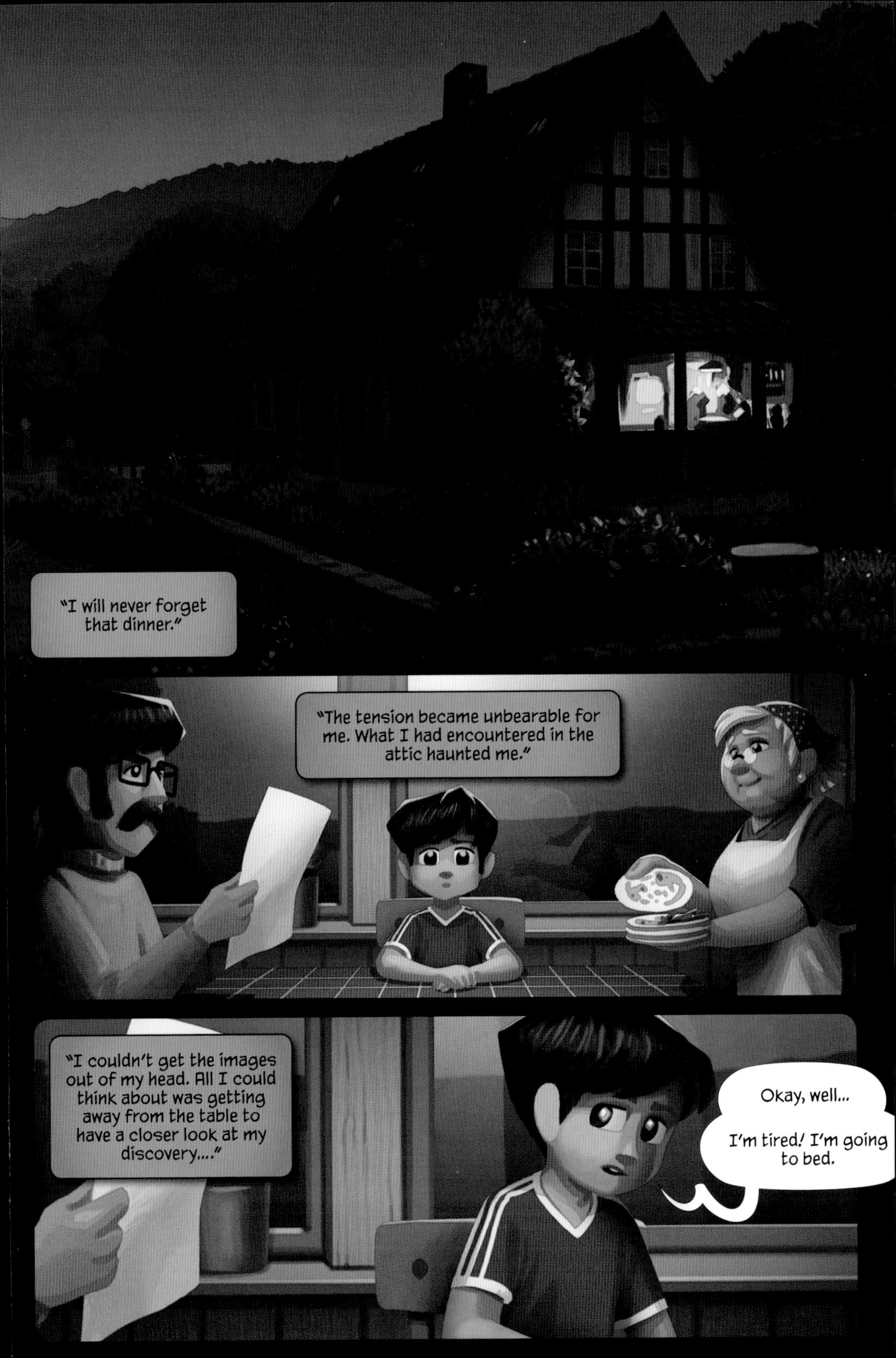
"I will never forget that dinner."
"The tension became unbearable for me. What I had encountered in the attic haunted me."
"I couldn't get the images out of my head. All I could think about was getting away from the table to have a closer look at my discovery...."
Okay, well...
I'm tired! I'm going to bed.

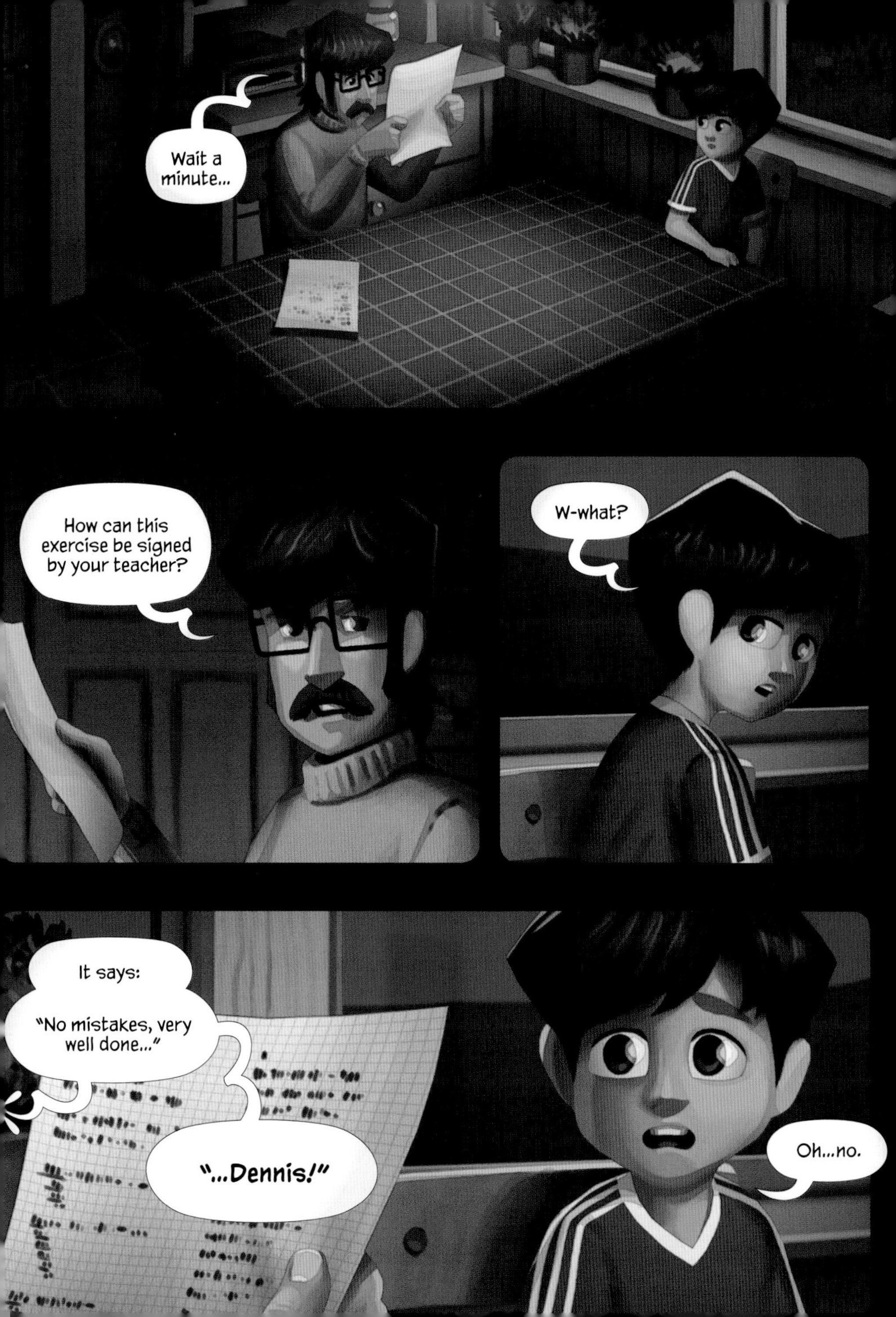
Wait a minute...
How can this exercise be signed by your teacher?
W-what?
It says:
"No mistakes, very well done..."
"...Dennis!"
Oh...no.

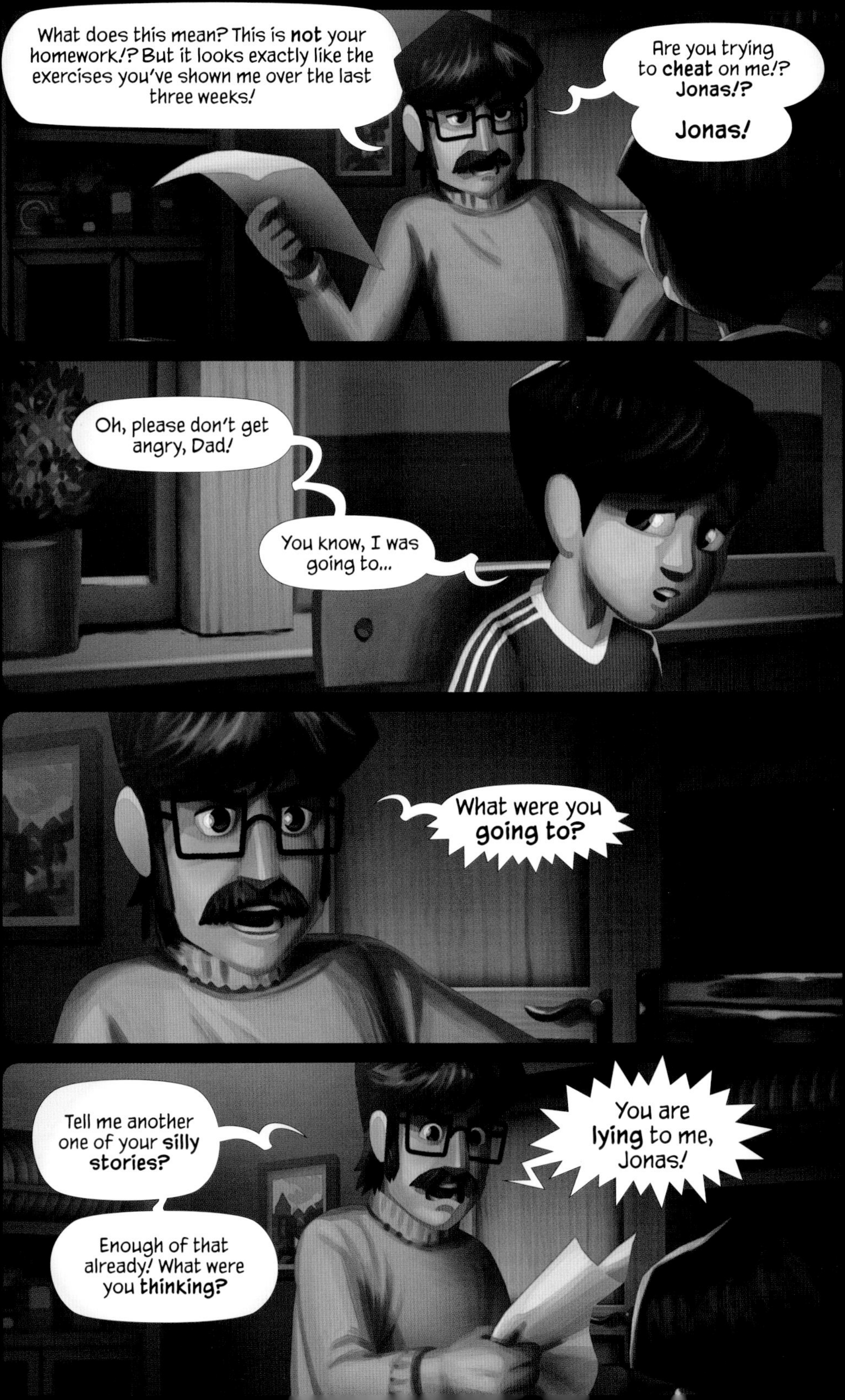
What does this mean? This is **not** your homework!? But it looks exactly like the exercises you've shown me over the last three weeks!
Are you trying to **cheat** on me!? Jonas!?
Jonas!
Oh, please don't get angry, Dad!
You know, I was going to...
What were you **going to?**
Tell me another one of your **silly stories?**
Enough of that already! What were you **thinking?**
You are **lying** to me, Jonas!

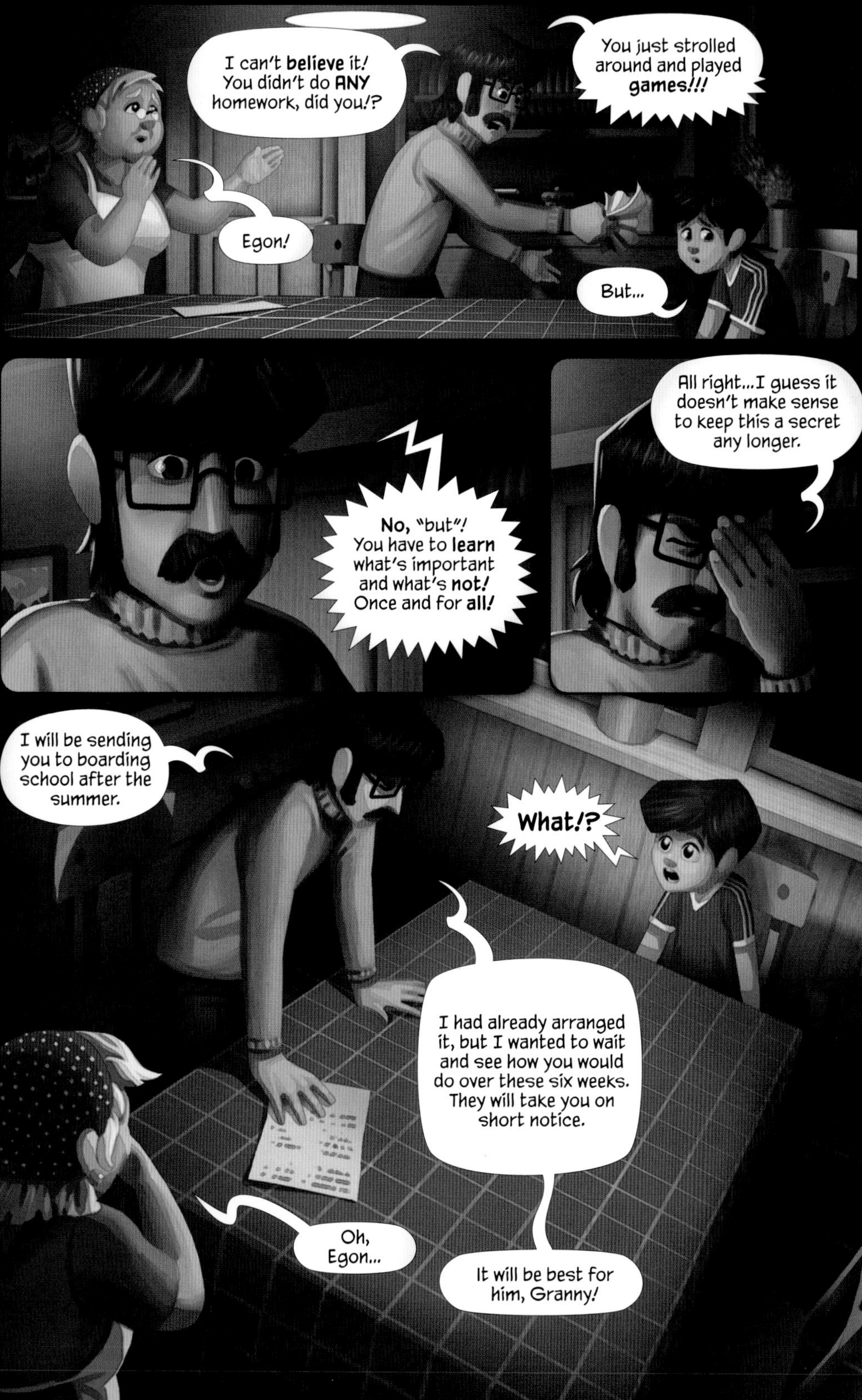
I can't believe it! You didn't do ANY homework, did you!?
You just strolled around and played games!!!
Egon!
But...
No, "but"! You have to learn what's important and what's not! Once and for all!
All right...I guess it doesn't make sense to keep this a secret any longer.
I will be sending you to boarding school after the summer.
What!?
I had already arranged it, but I wanted to wait and see how you would do over these six weeks. They will take you on short notice.
Oh, Egon...
It will be best for him, Granny!

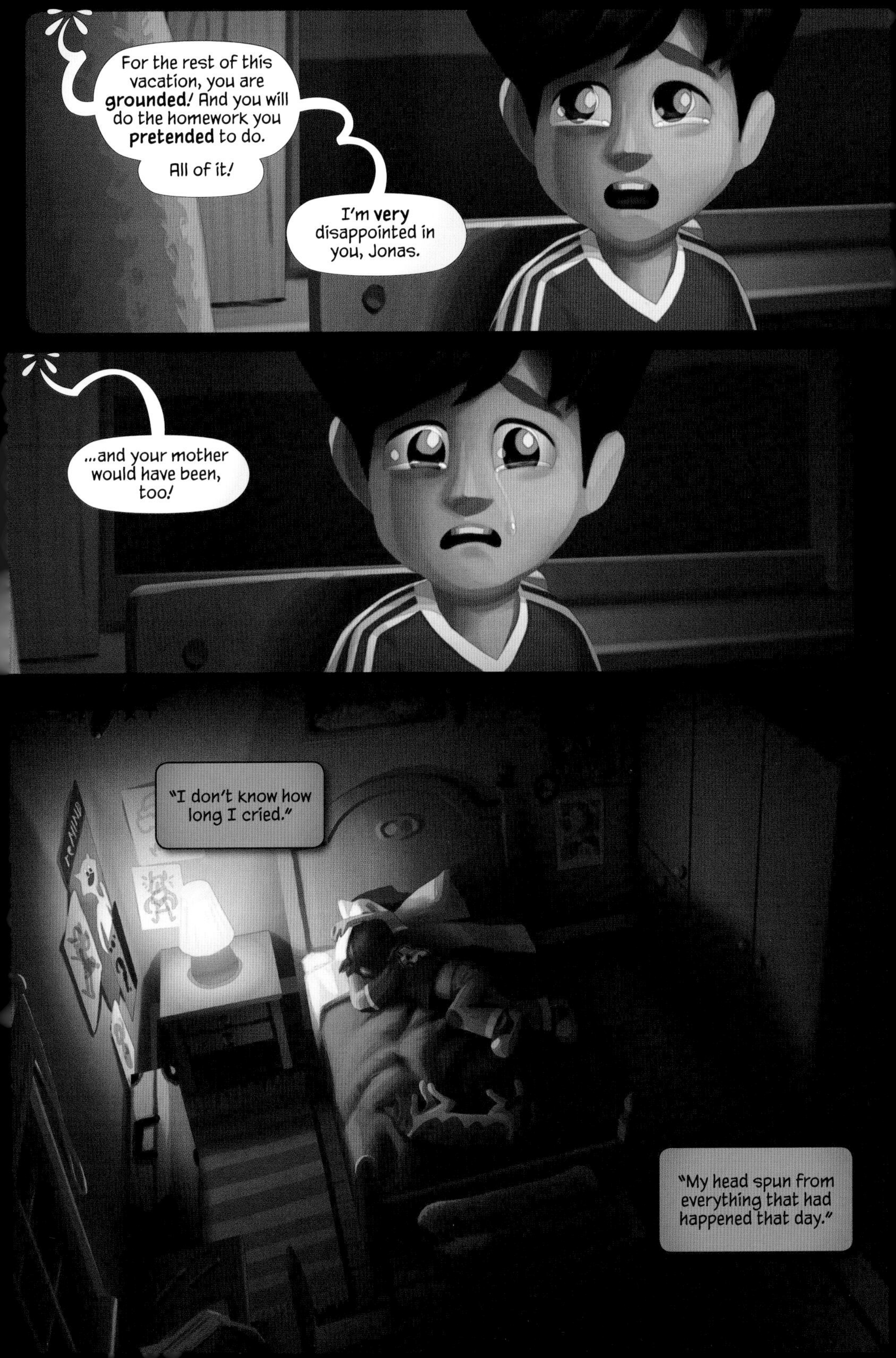
For the rest of this vacation, you are **grounded**! And you will do the homework you **pretended** to do.
All of it!
I'm **very** disappointed in you, Jonas.
...and your mother would have been, too!
"I don't know how long I cried."
"My head spun from everything that had happened that day."

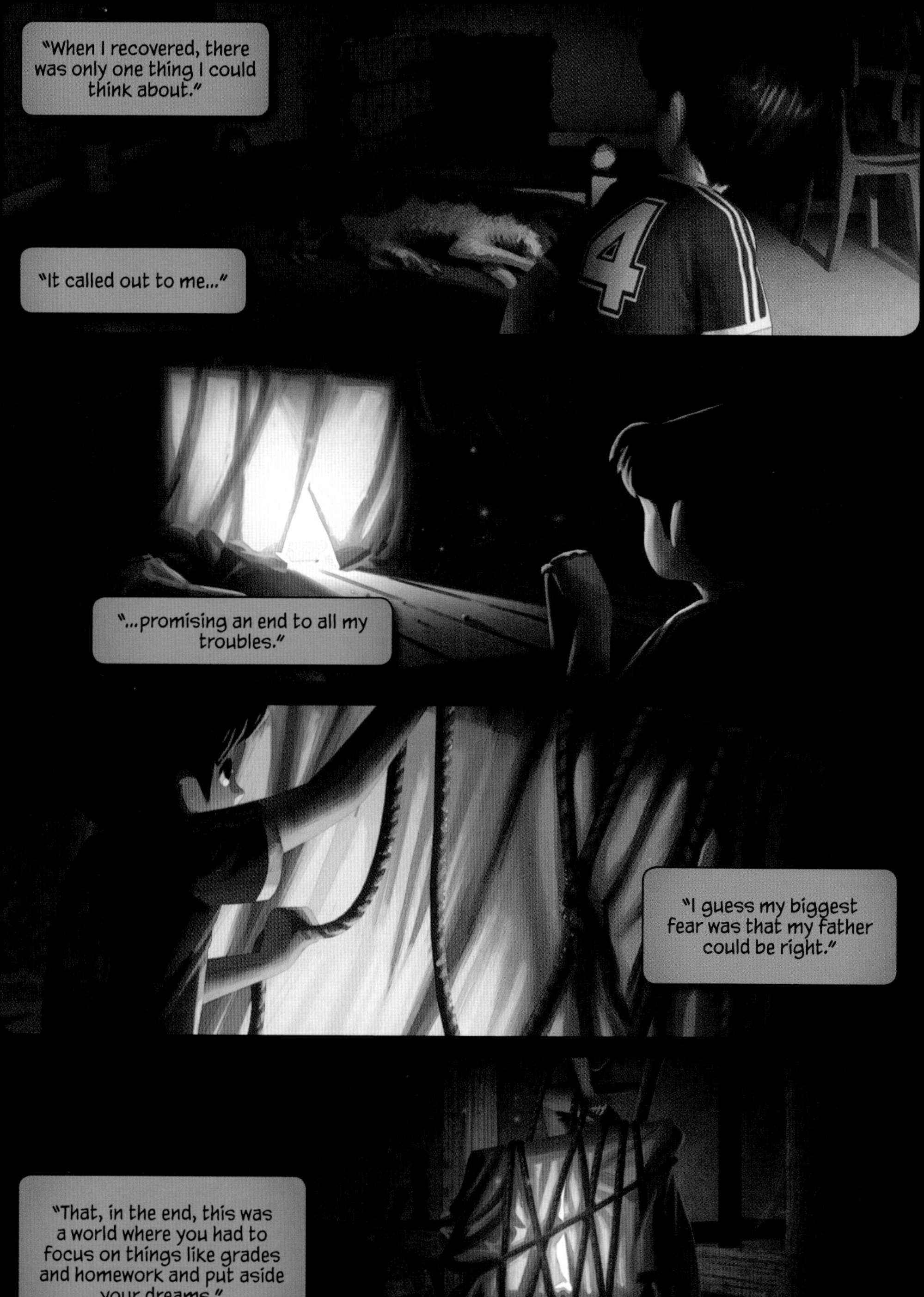
"When I recovered, there was only one thing I could think about."
"It called out to me..."
"...promising an end to all my troubles."
"I guess my biggest fear was that my father could be right."
"That, in the end, this was a world where you had to focus on things like grades and homework and put aside your dreams."

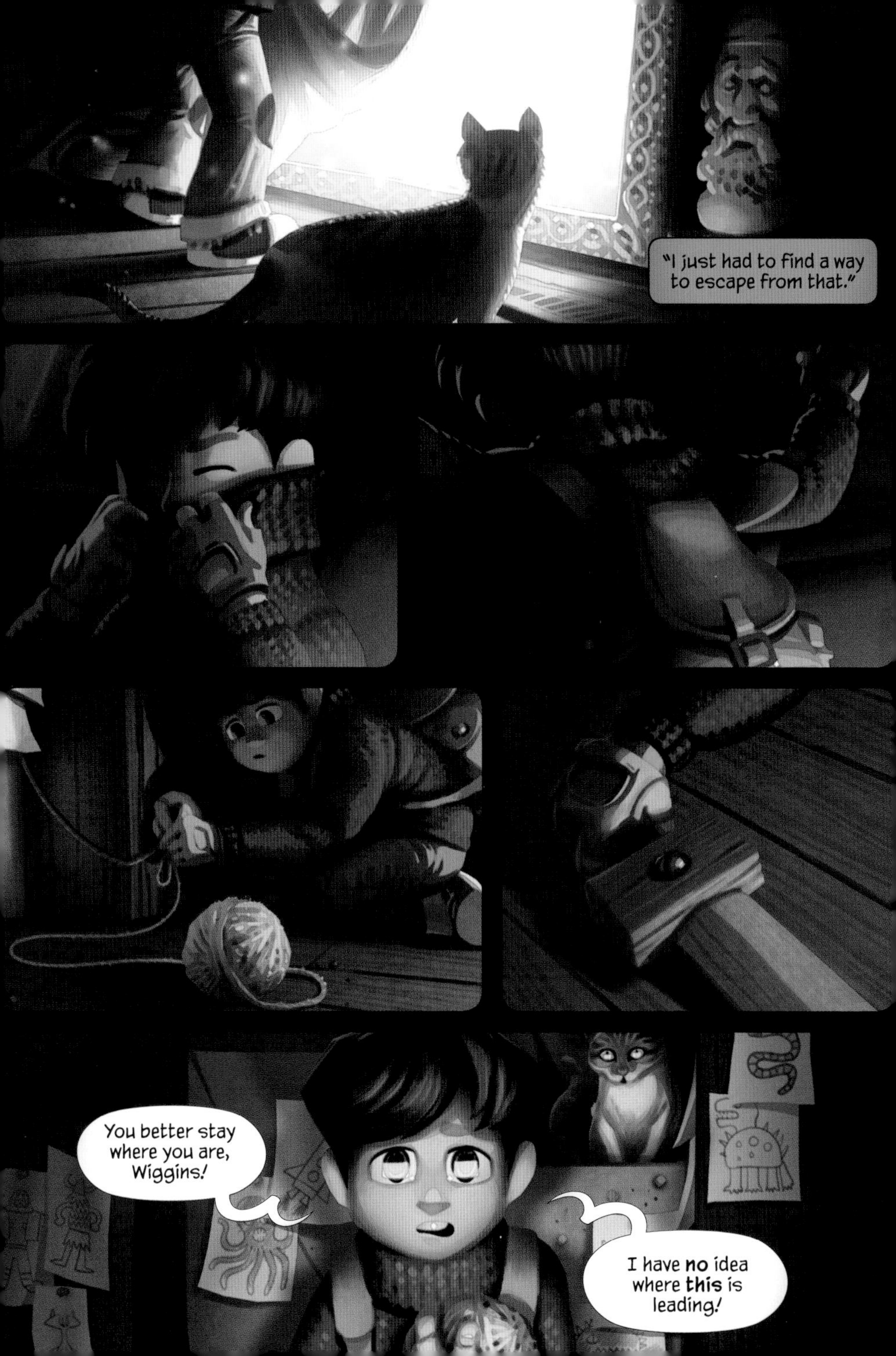
"I just had to find a way to escape from that."
You better stay where you are, Wiggins!
I have **no** idea where **this** is leading!

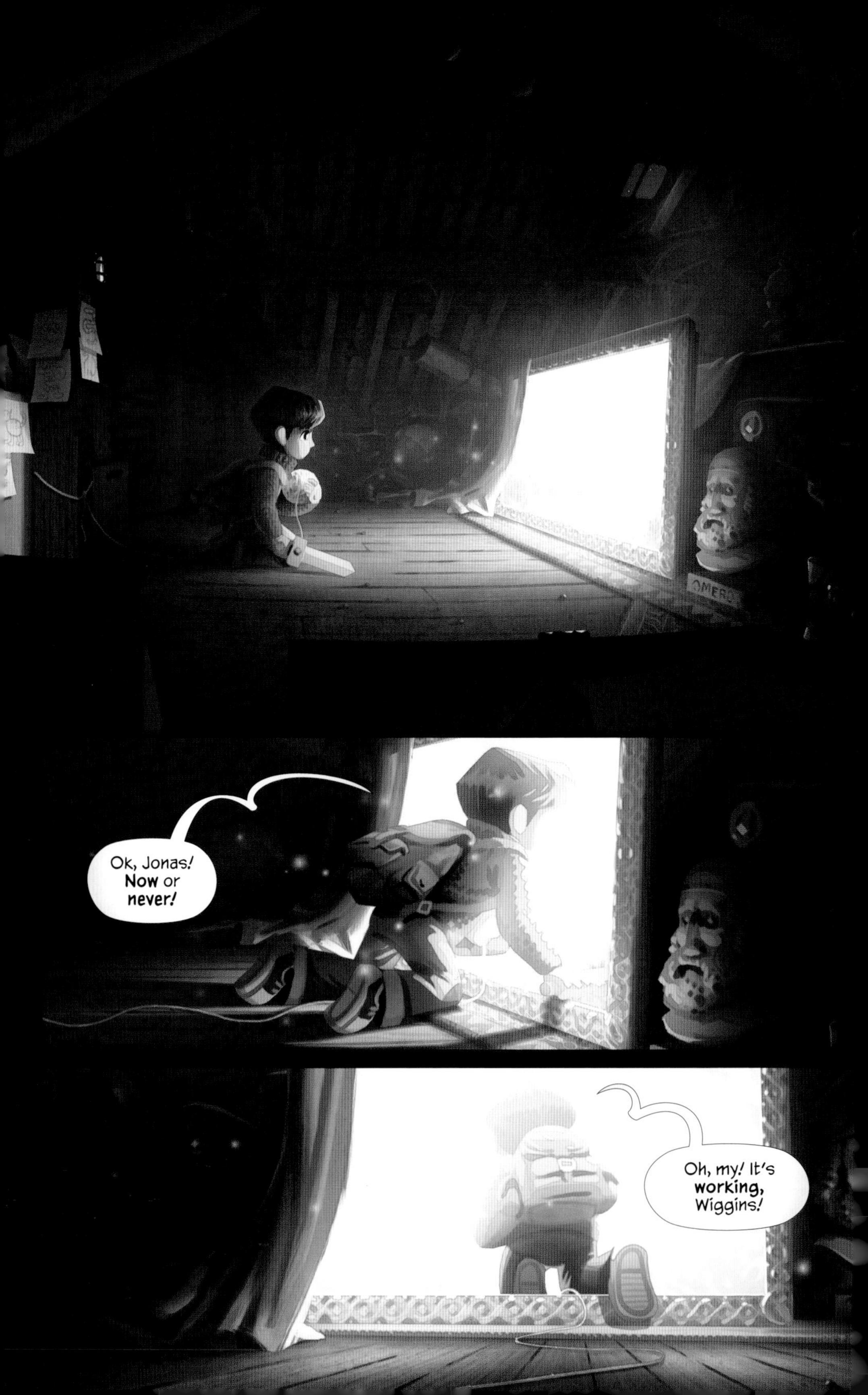
Ok, Jonas! Now or never!
Oh, my! It's working, Wiggins!

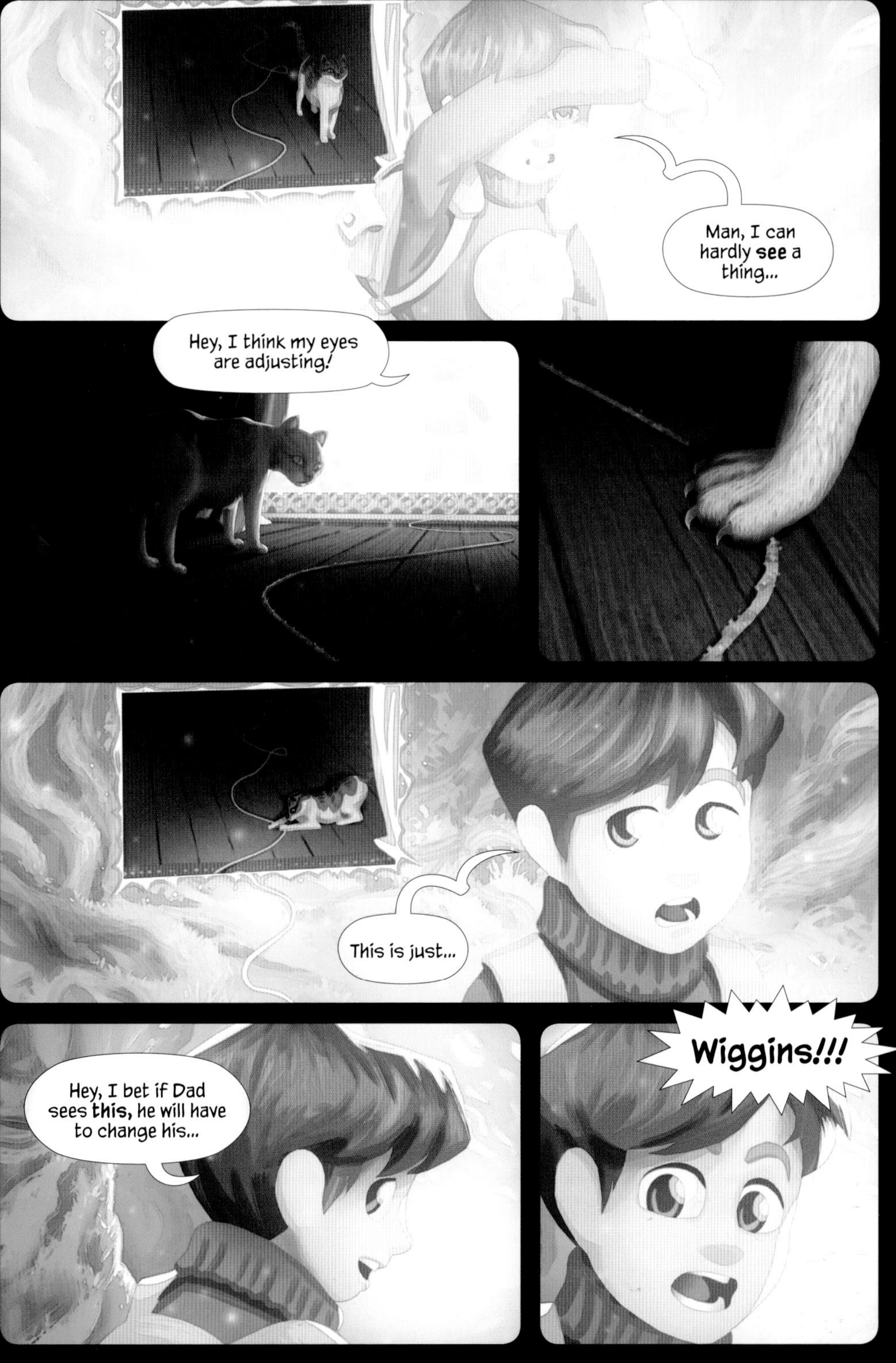
Man, I can hardly **see** a thing...
Hey, I think my eyes are adjusting!
This is just...
Hey, I bet if Dad sees **this,** he will have to change his...
Wiggins!!!

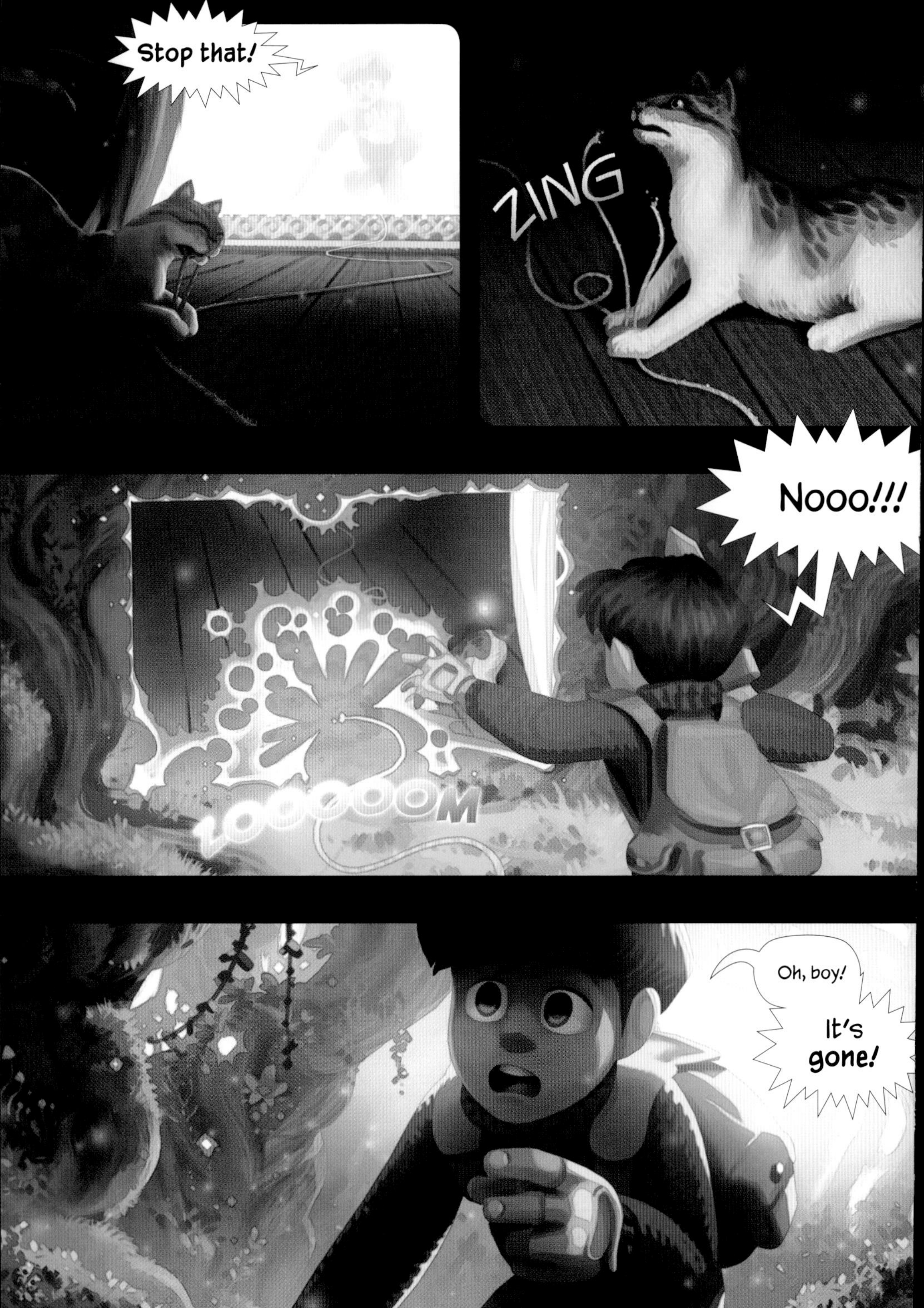
Stop that!
ZING
Nooo!!!
ZOOOOOOM
Oh, boy!
It's gone!

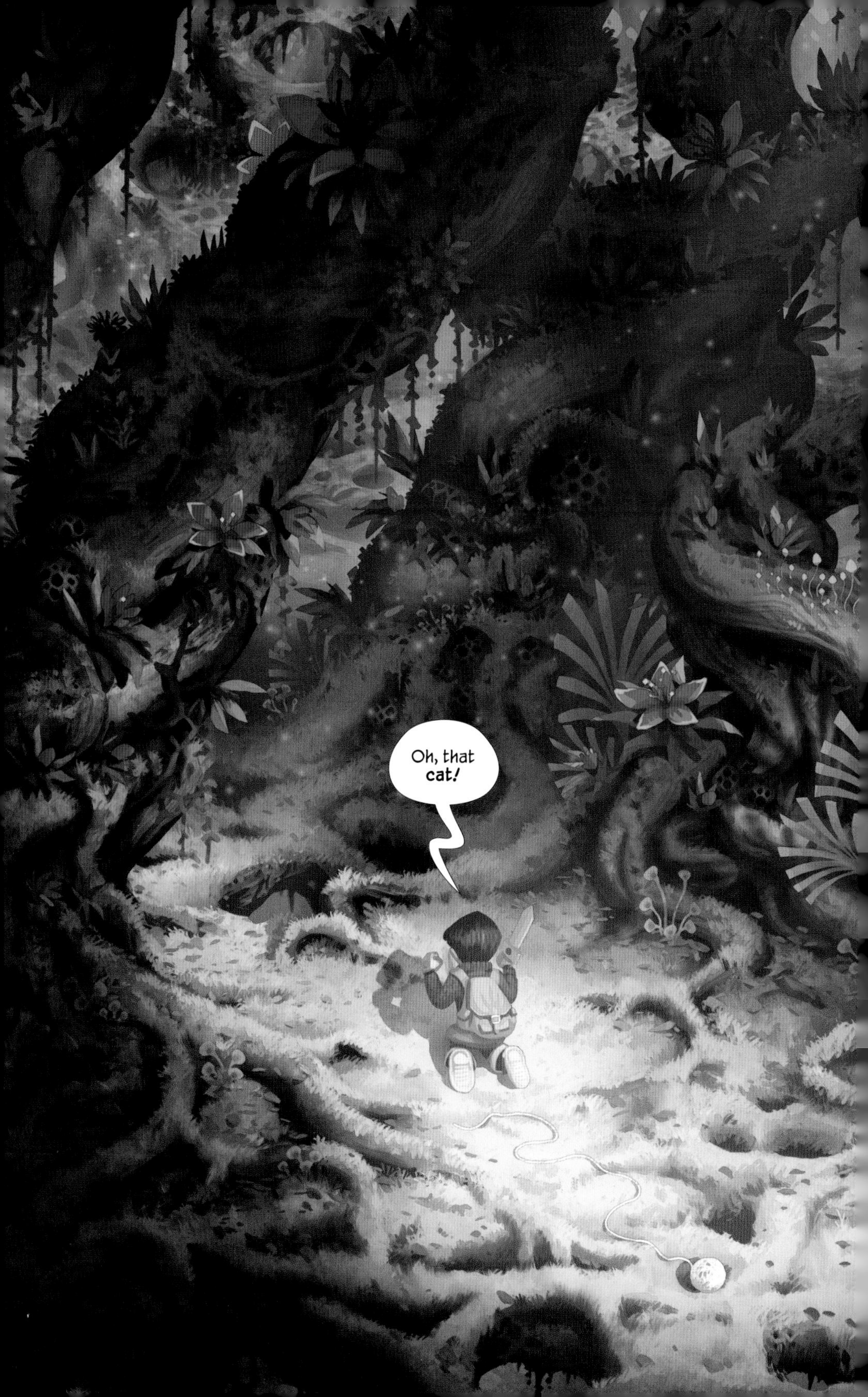
Oh, that cat!

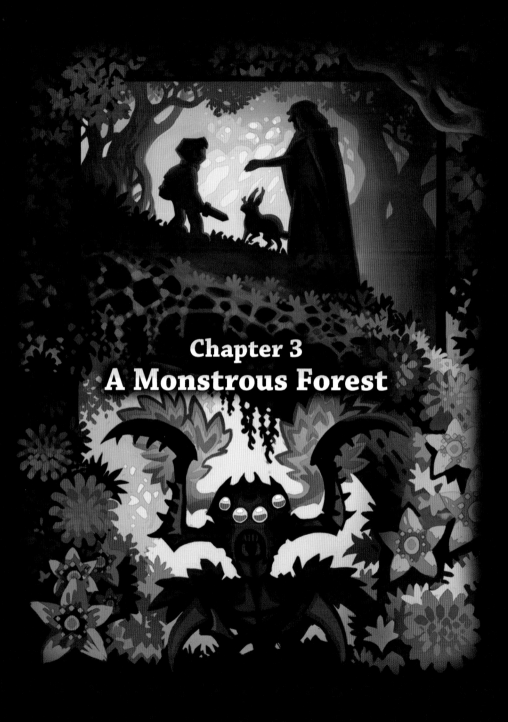

Chapter 3
A Monstrous Forest

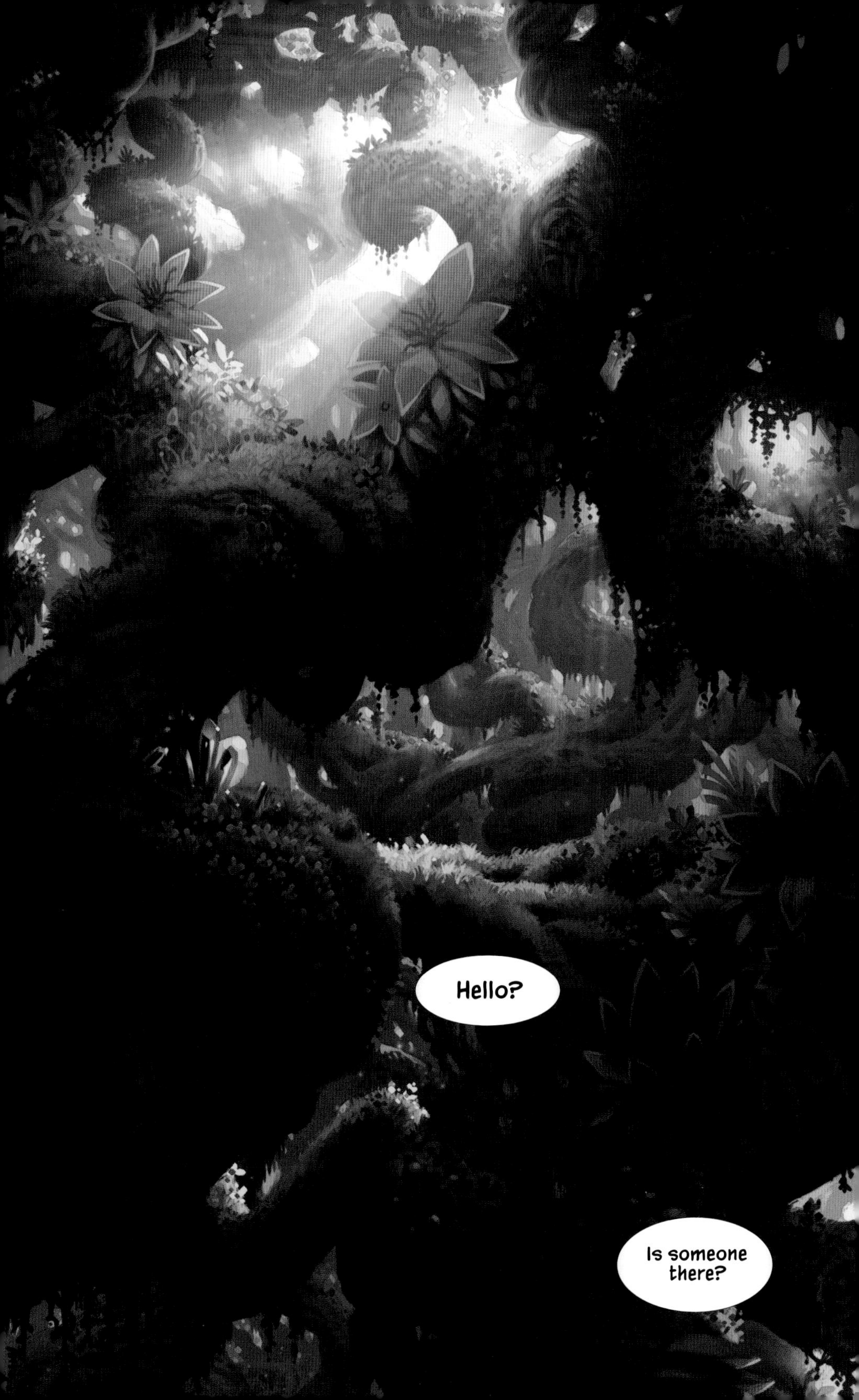
Hello?
Is someone there?

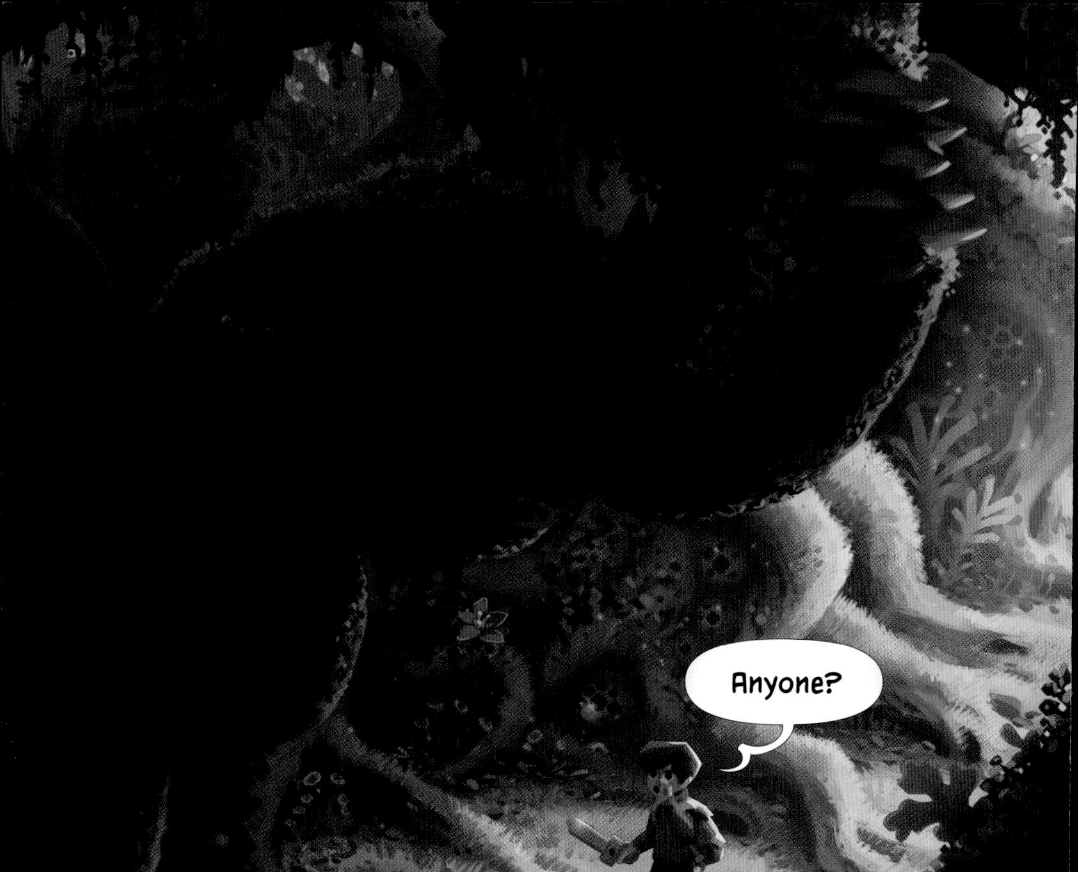
Anyone?

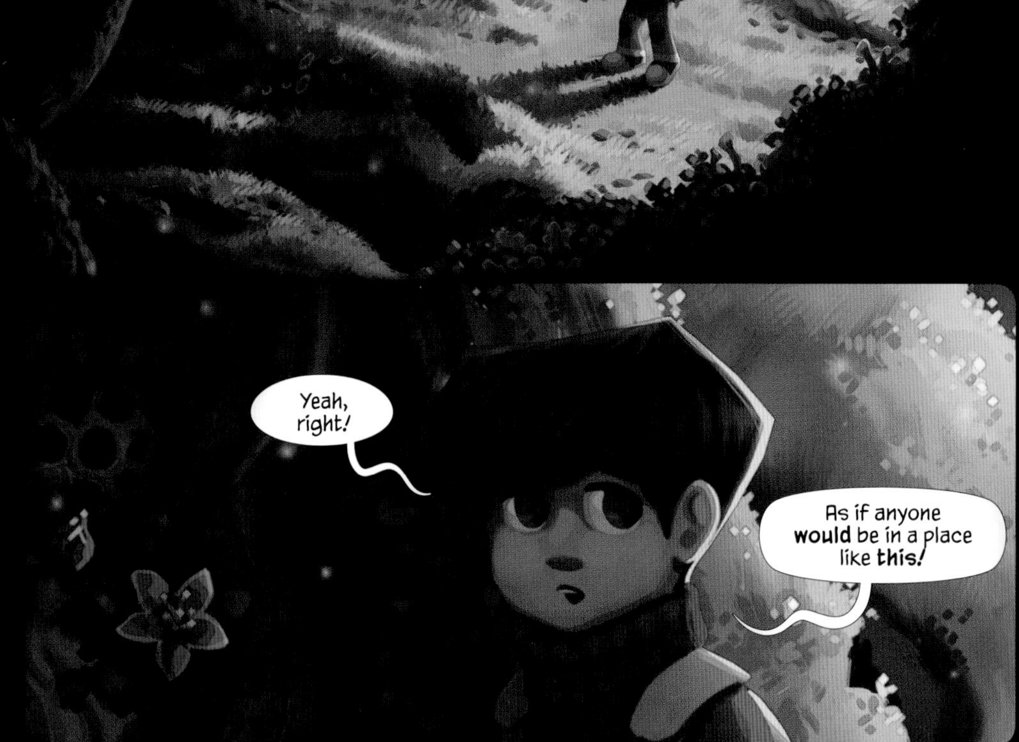
Yeah, right!
As if anyone would be in a place like this!

≝ sigh ≝

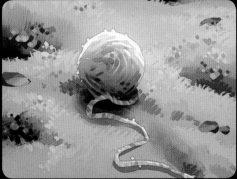

"All around me, the air was filled with unfamiliar noises. But at the same time, the place seemed strangely silent, as though it had held its breath upon my arrival."

Great! I didn't bring **any** food!

"It didn't take long for my initial courage and determination to be replaced by anxiety and regret. This wasn't just one of my imaginary adventures that would conveniently end when Granny called me for lunch."

"This time, I was **really** in trouble."

That was a **stupid** idea, Jonas!

!

BZZZZZZZZZZZ

Hey, I **know** you!

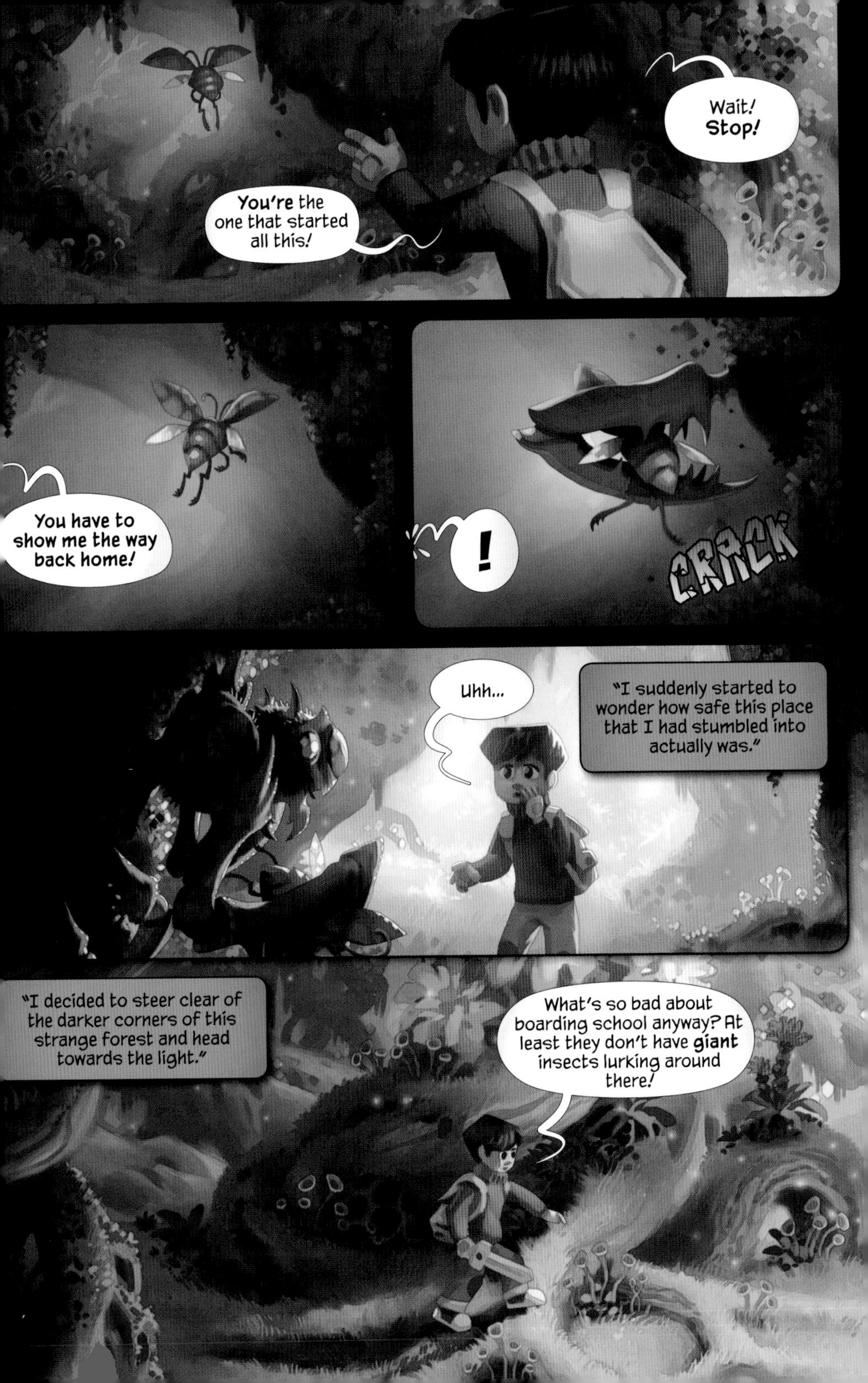
Wait! Stop!
You're the one that started all this!
You have to show me the way back home!
!
CRACK
Uhh...
"I suddenly started to wonder how safe this place that I had stumbled into actually was."
"I decided to steer clear of the darker corners of this strange forest and head towards the light."
What's so bad about boarding school anyway? At least they don't have giant insects lurking around there!

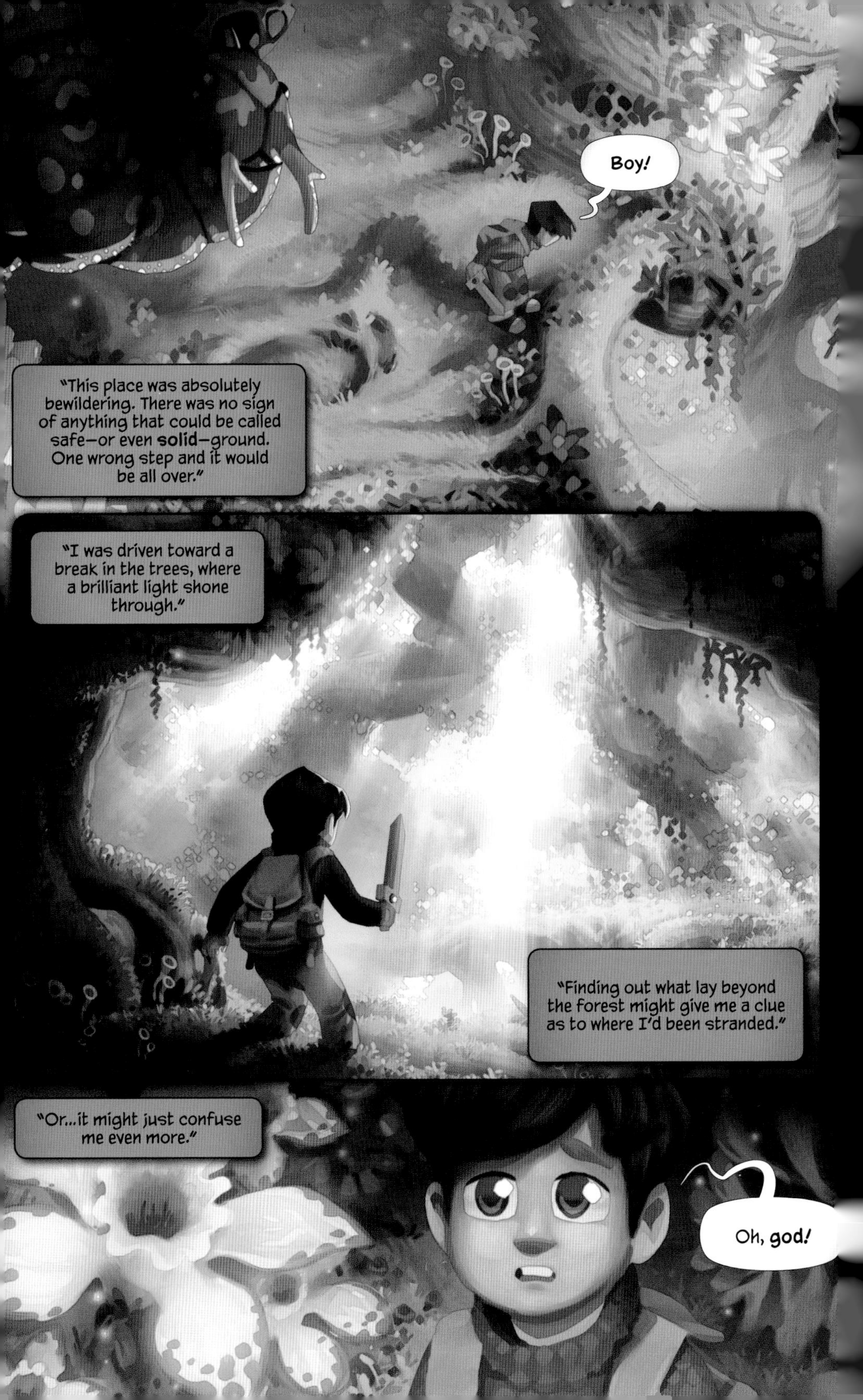

Boy!
"This place was absolutely bewildering. There was no sign of anything that could be called safe—or even **solid**—ground. One wrong step and it would be all over."
"I was driven toward a break in the trees, where a brilliant light shone through."
"Finding out what lay beyond the forest might give me a clue as to where I'd been stranded."
"Or...it might just confuse me even more."
Oh, **god!**

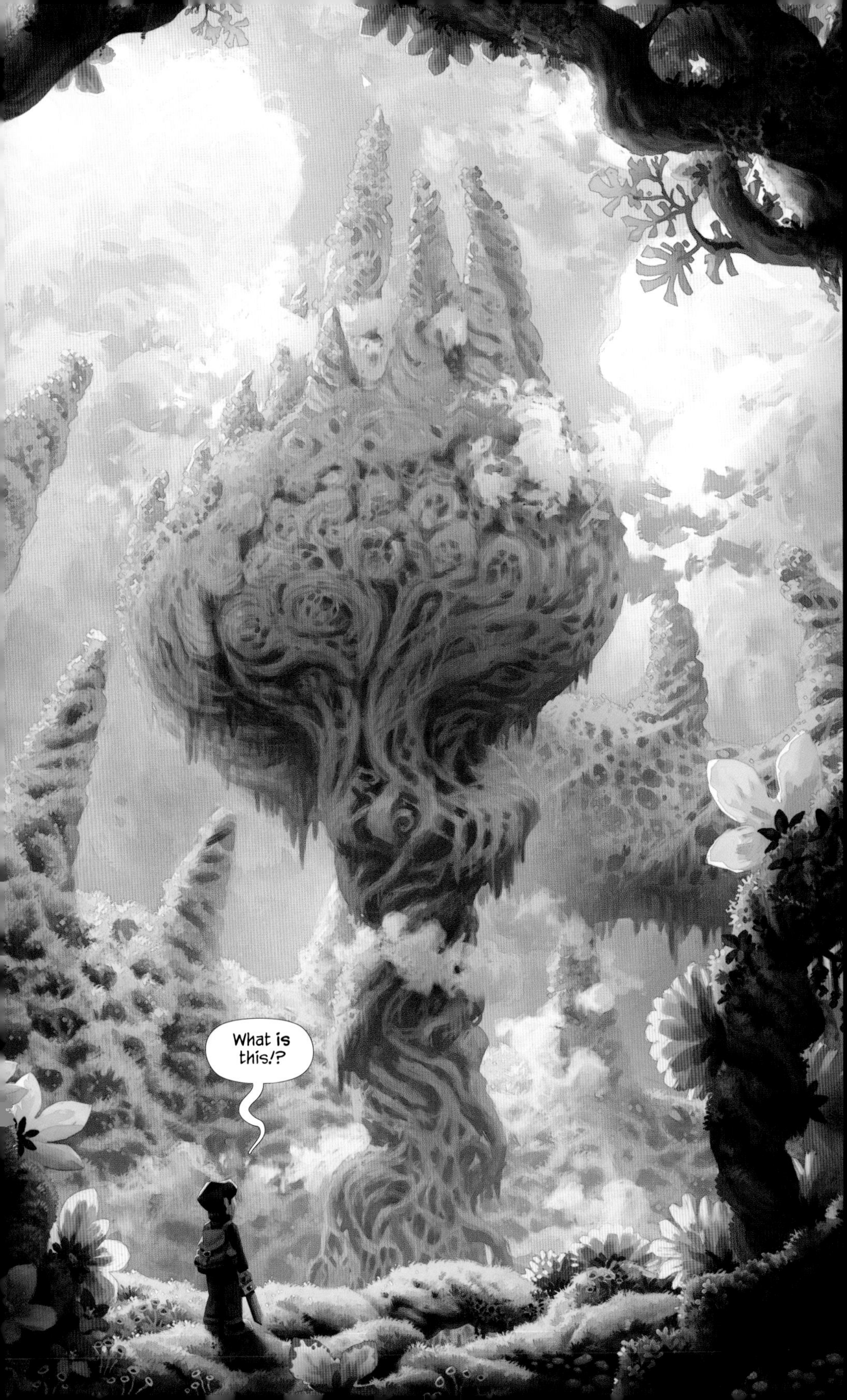
What is this!?

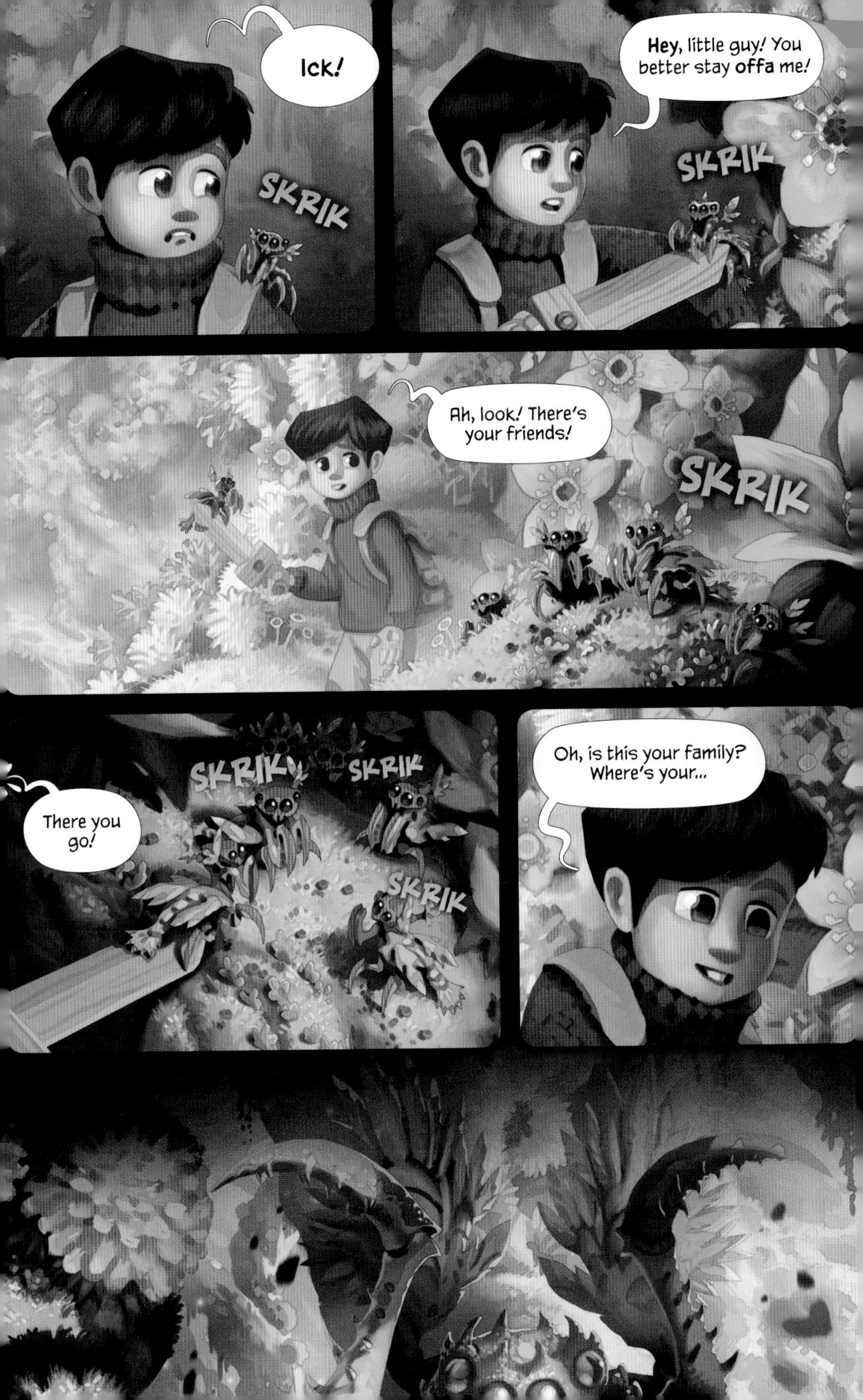
Ick!
SKRIK
Hey, little guy! You better stay offa me!
SKRIK
Ah, look! There's your friends!
SKRIK
SKRIK
SKRIK
There you go!
SKRIK
Oh, is this your family? Where's your...

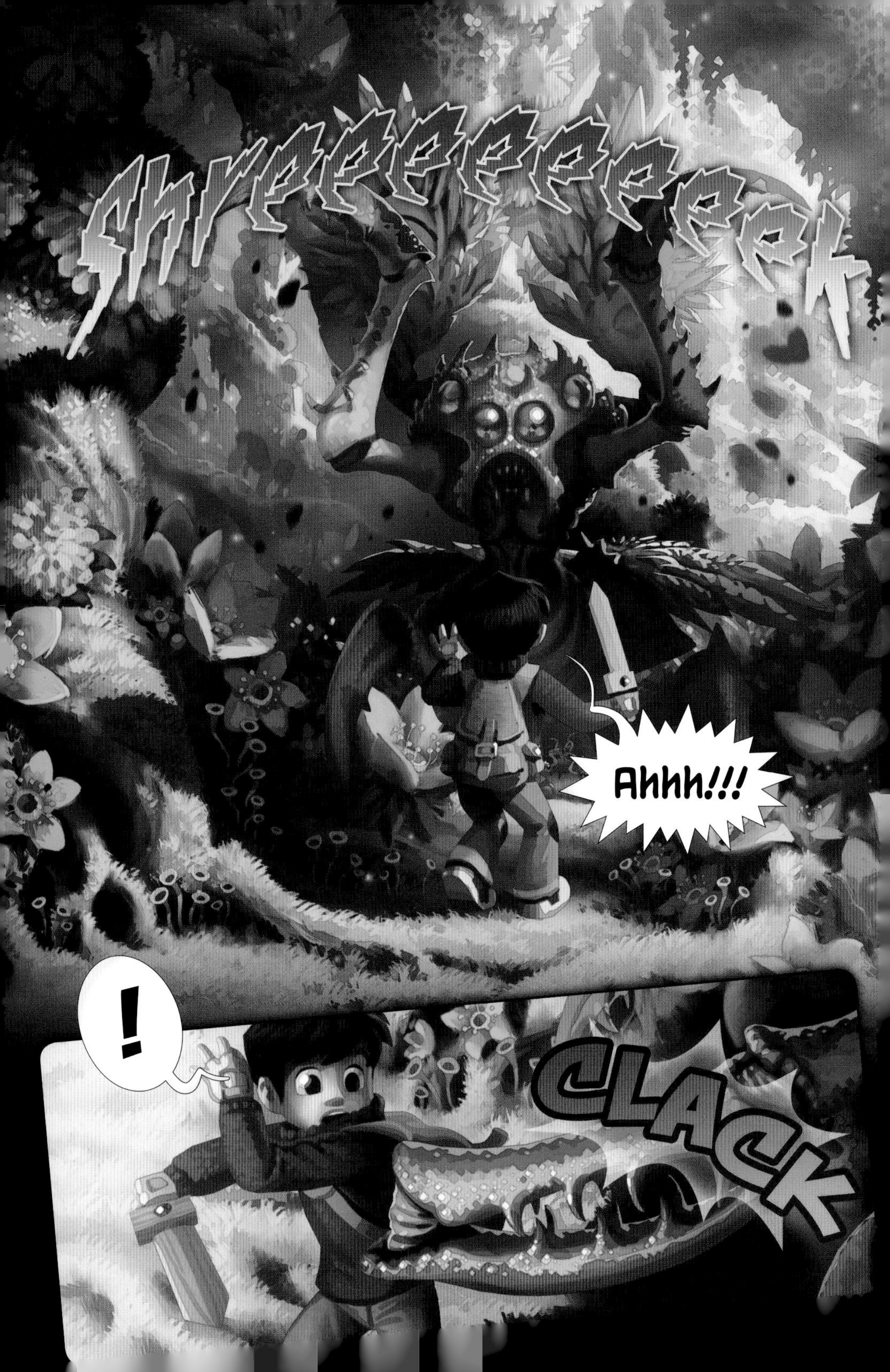
Shreeeeeeeek
Ahhh!!!
!
CLACK

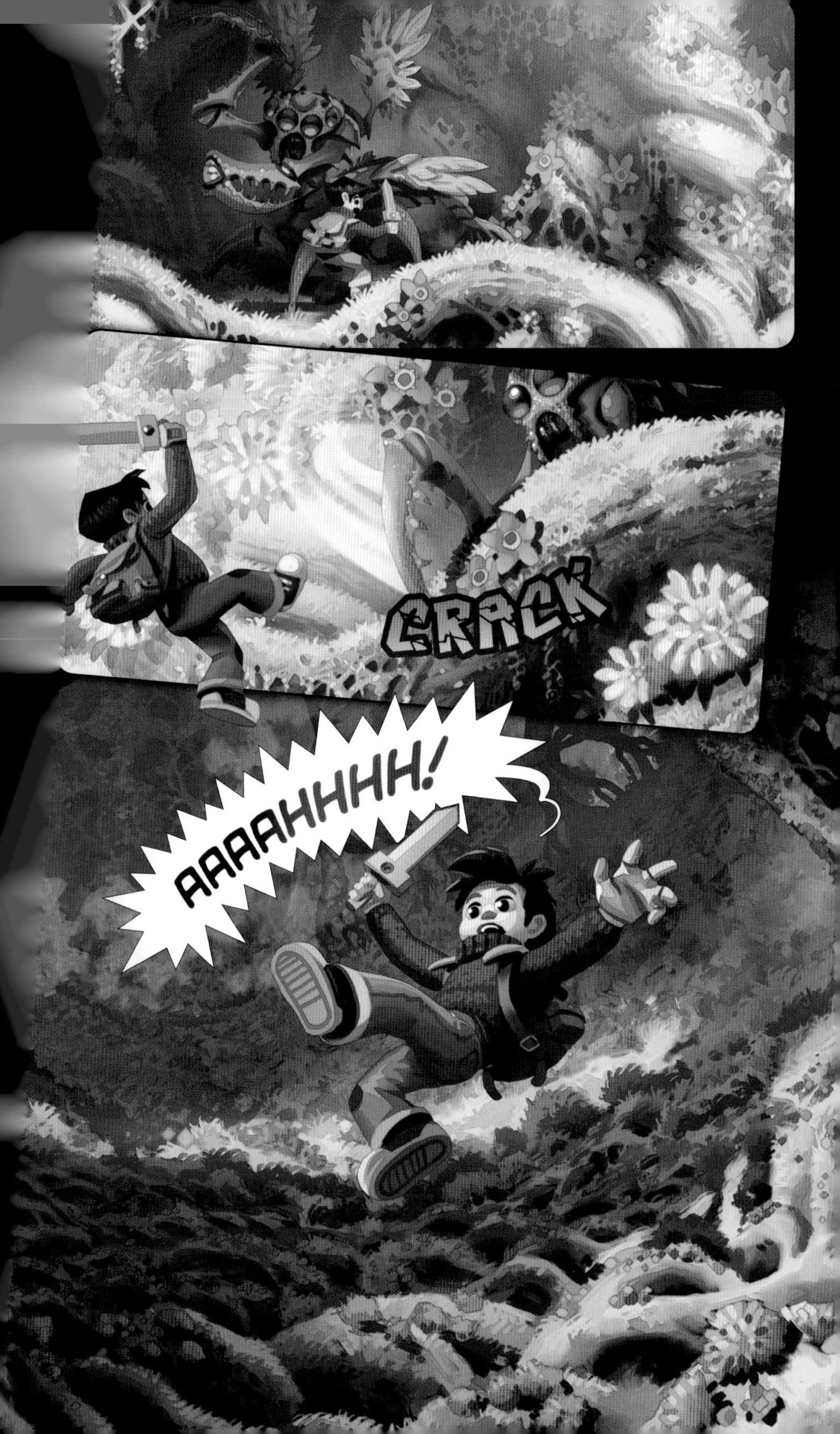
CRRCK
AAAAHHHH!

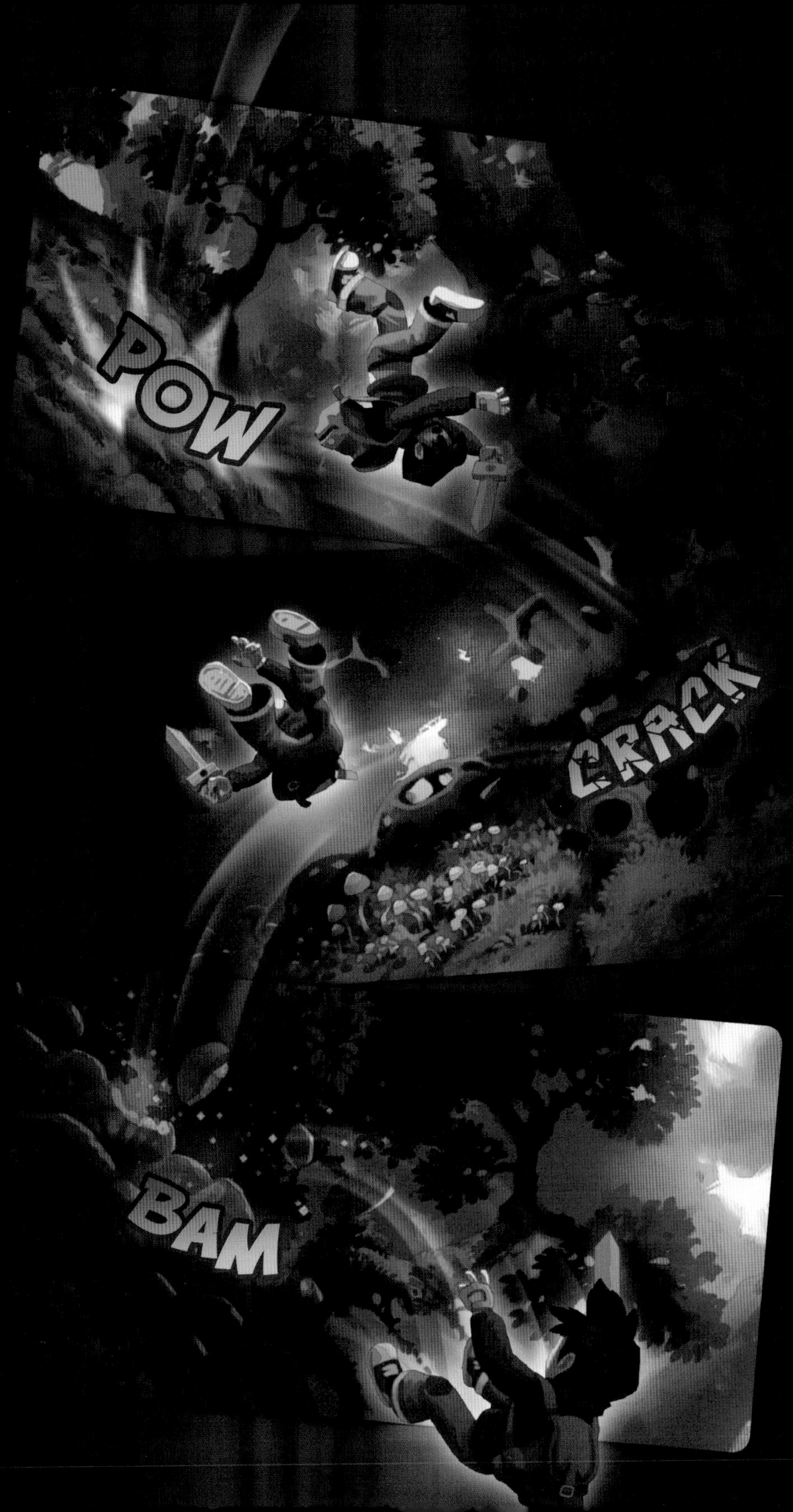
POW
CRACK
BAM

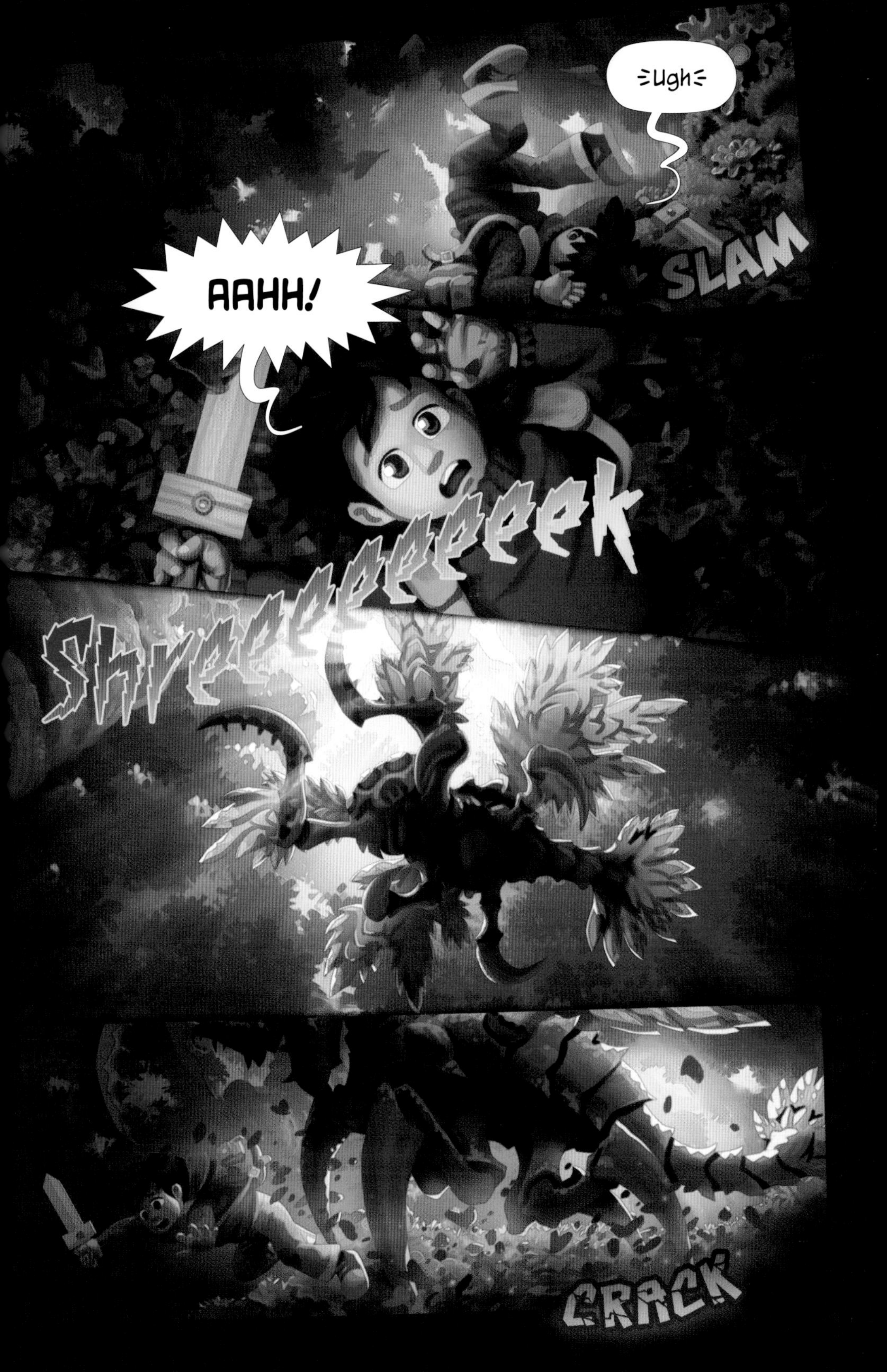
Ugh
SLAM
AAHH!
Shreeeeeeeek
CRACK

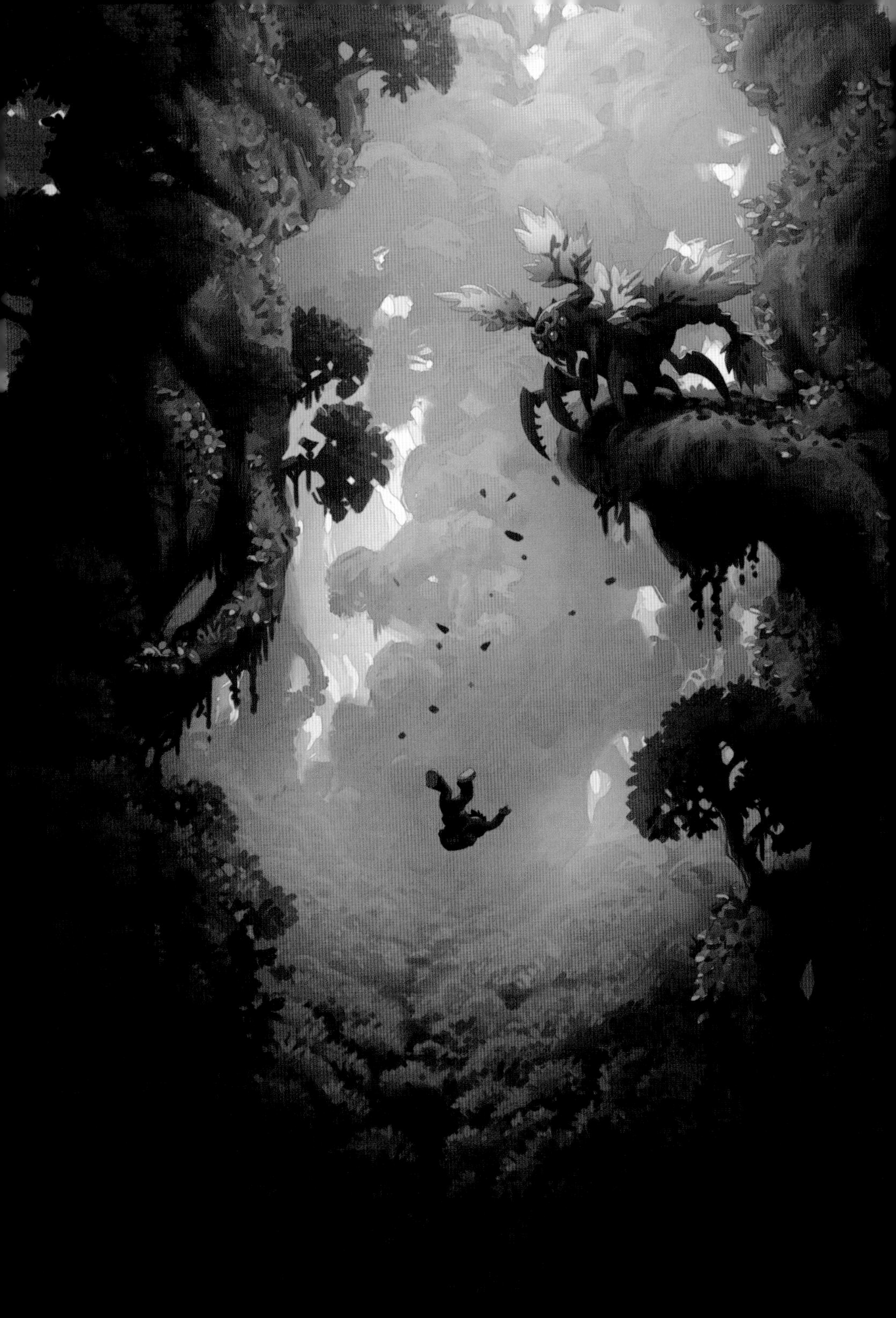

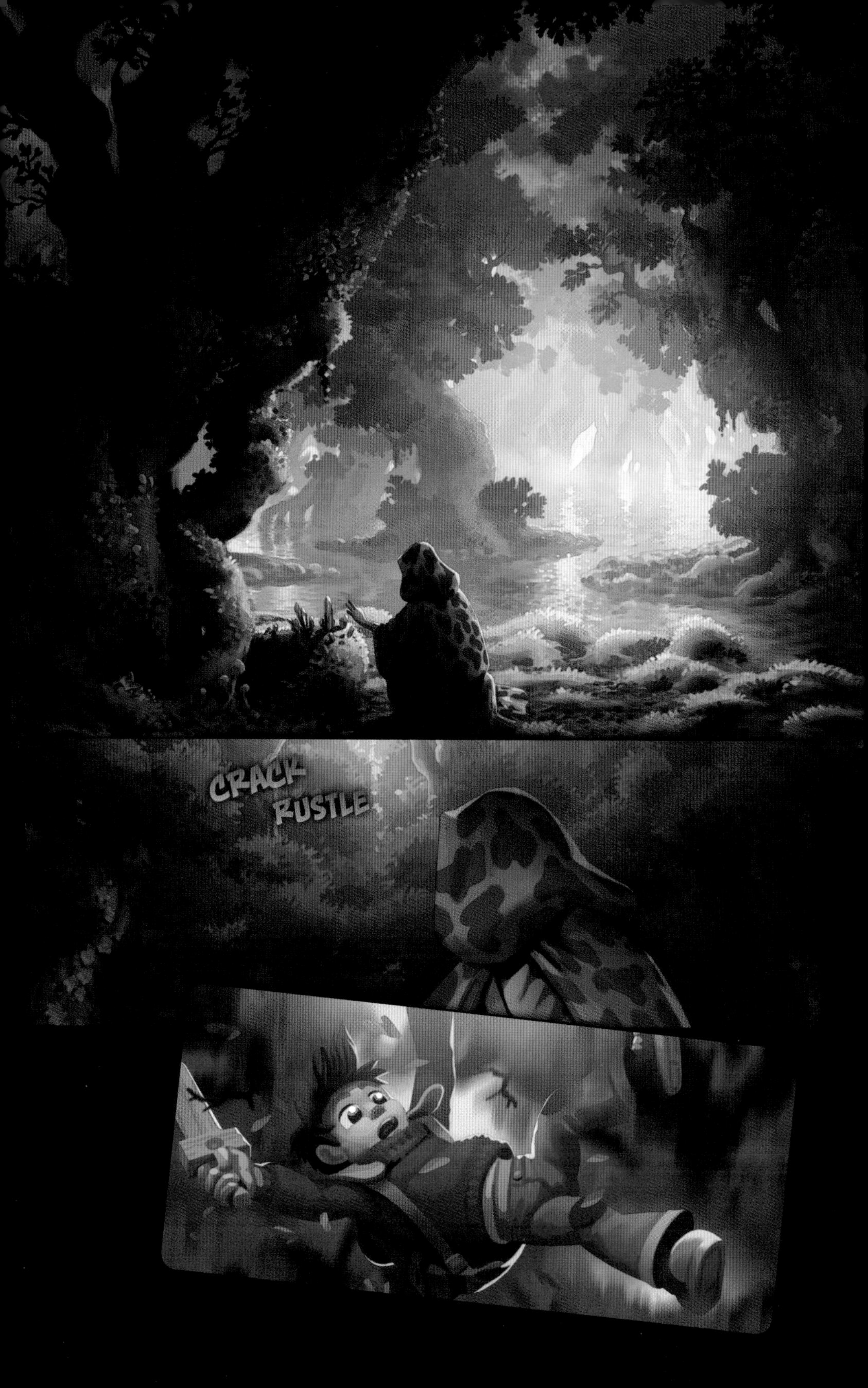
CRACK
RUSTLE

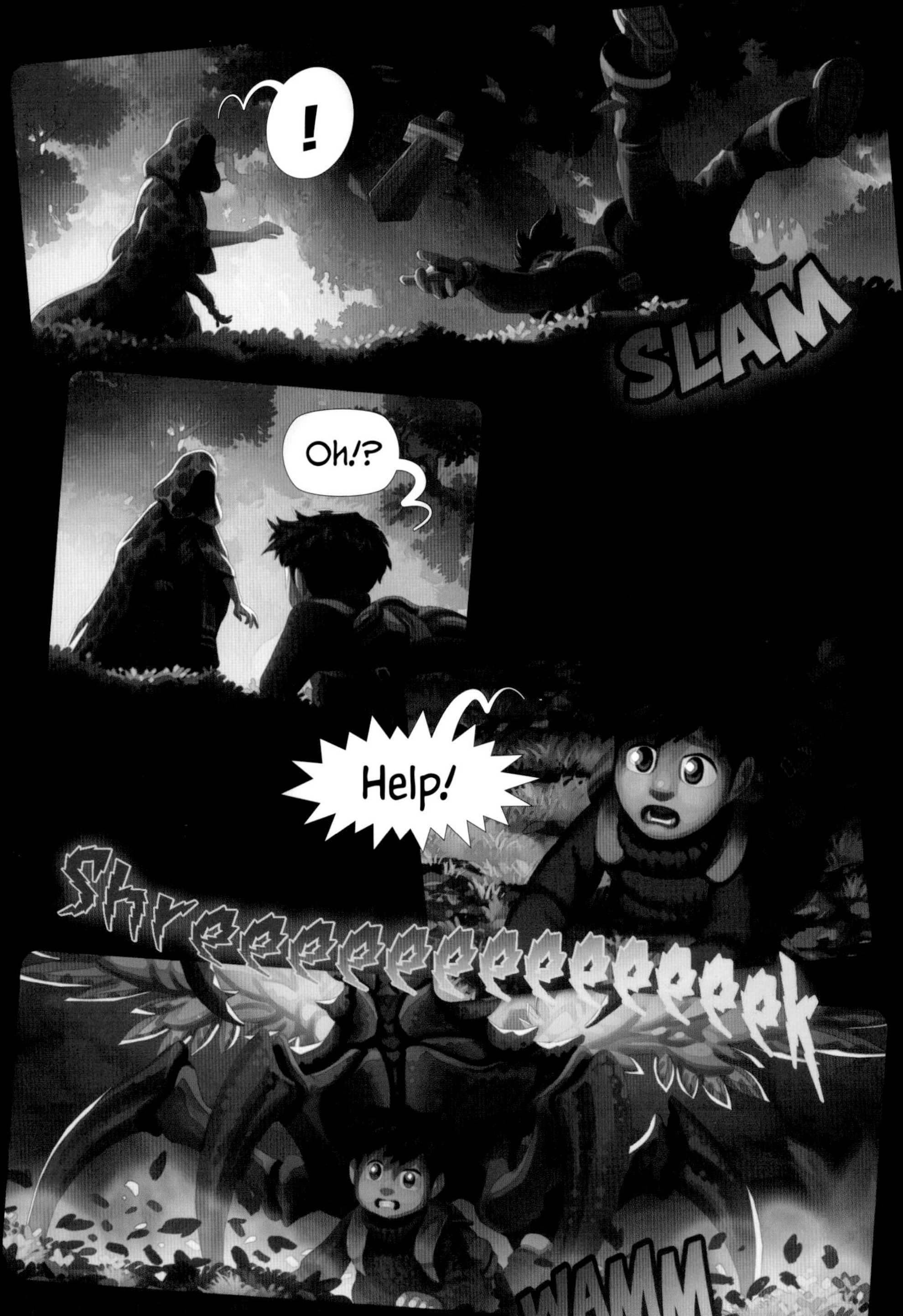
!
SLAM
Oh!?
Help!
Shreeeeeeeeeeeeek
WAMM

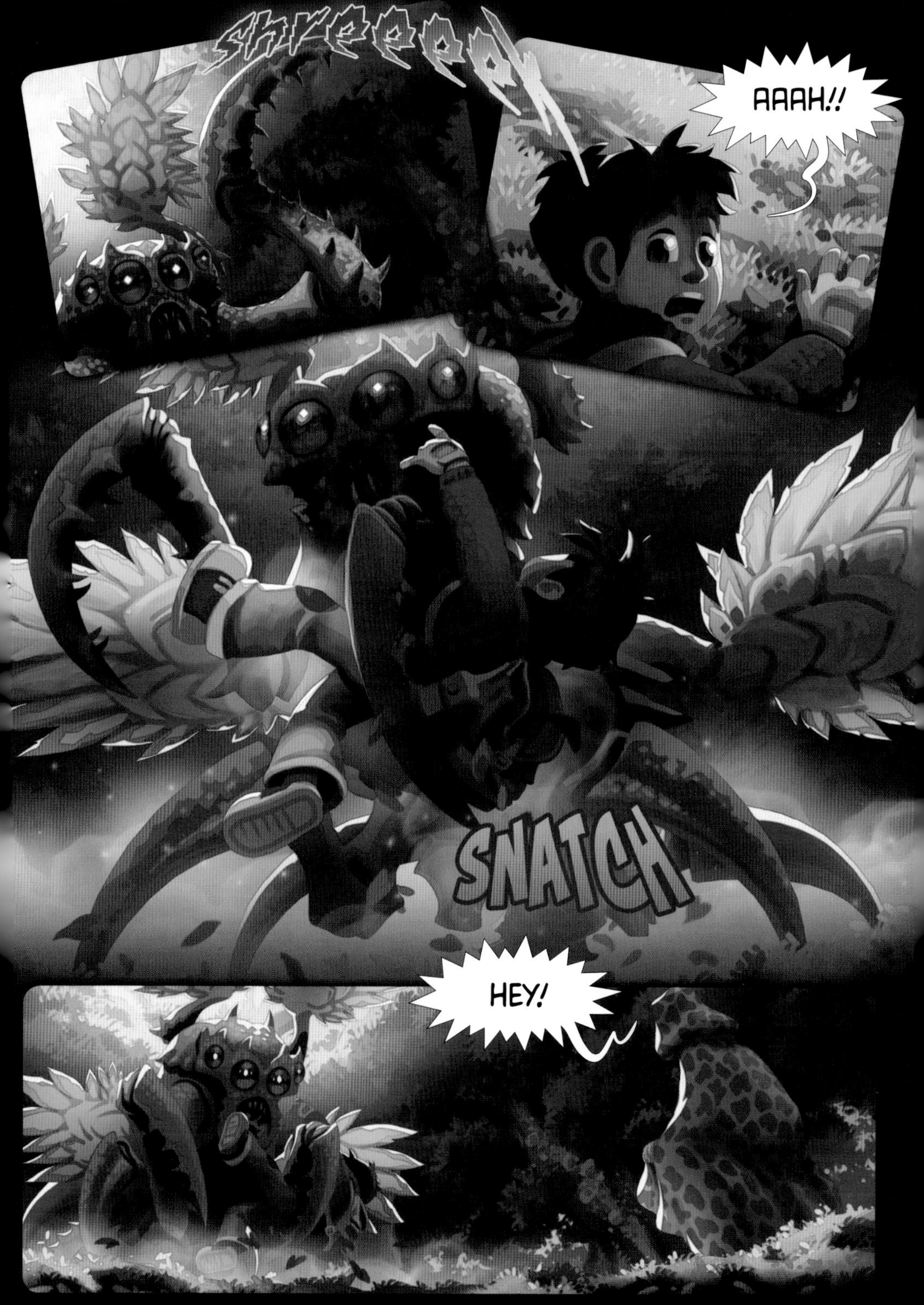
shreeeel
AAAH!!
SNATCH
HEY!

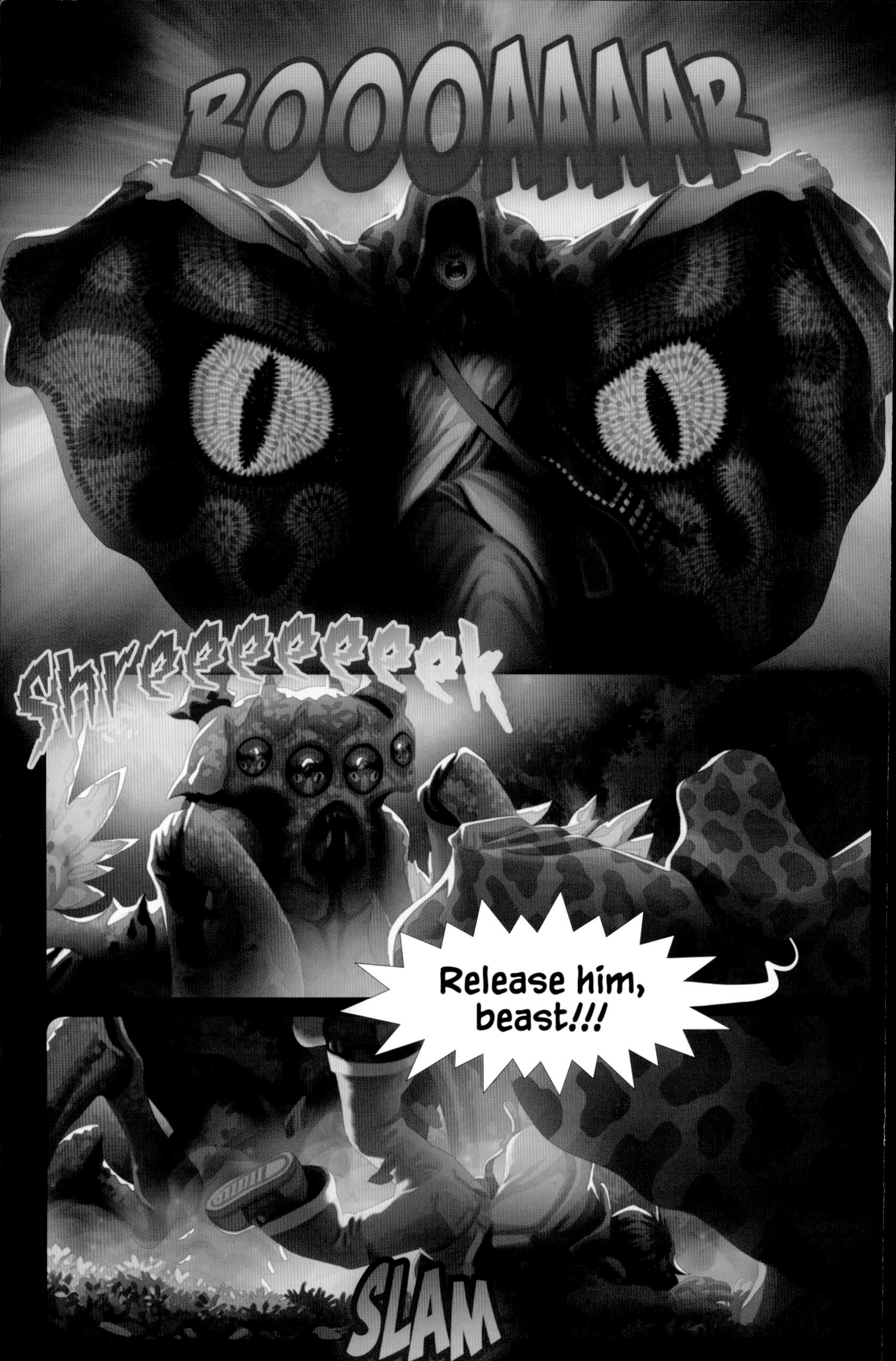
ROOOAAAAR
Shreeeeeeek
Release him, beast!!!
SLAM

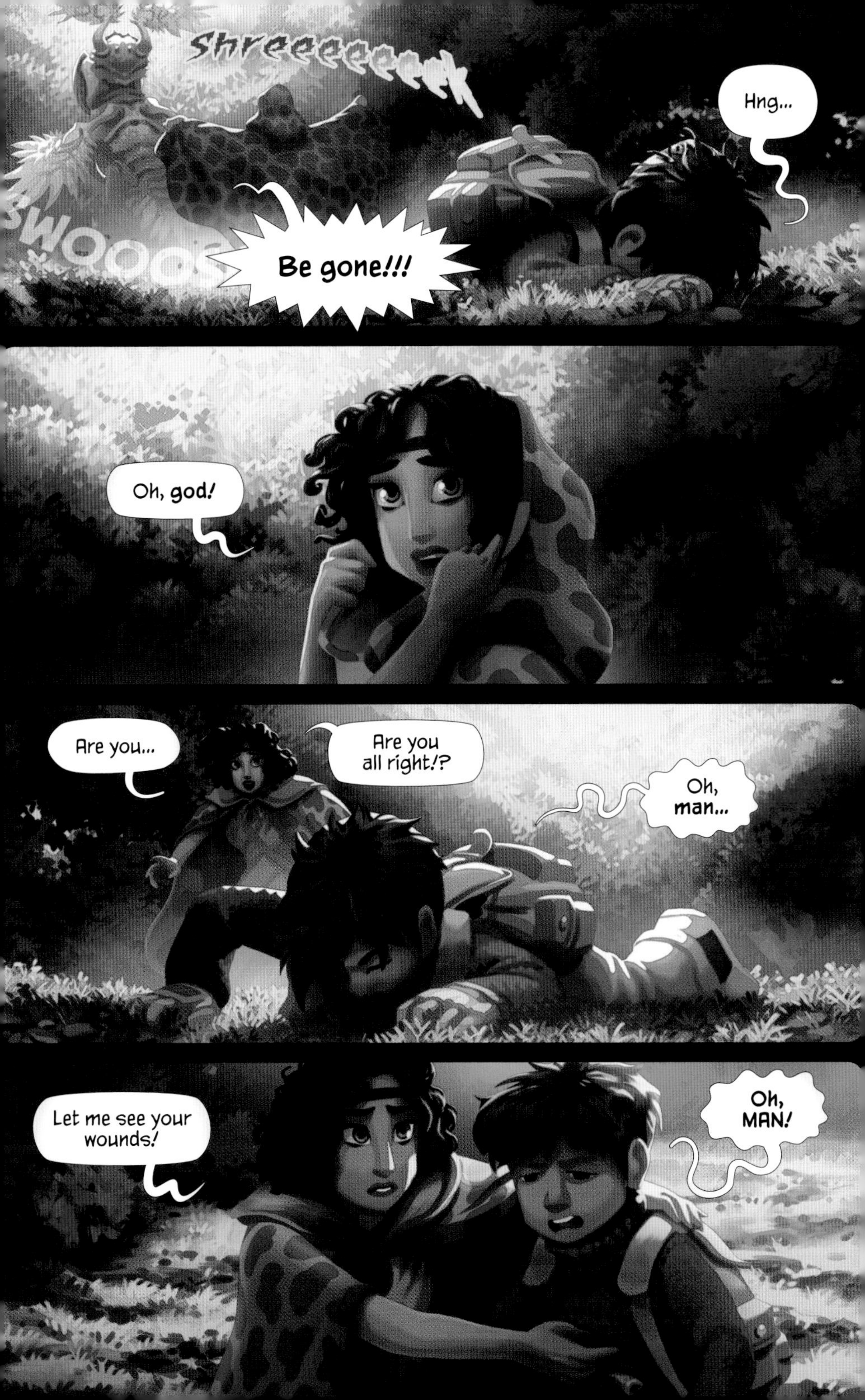
Shreeeeeeek
Hng...
SWOOOS
Be gone!!!
Oh, god!
Are you...
Are you all right!?
Oh, man...
Let me see your wounds!
Oh, MAN!

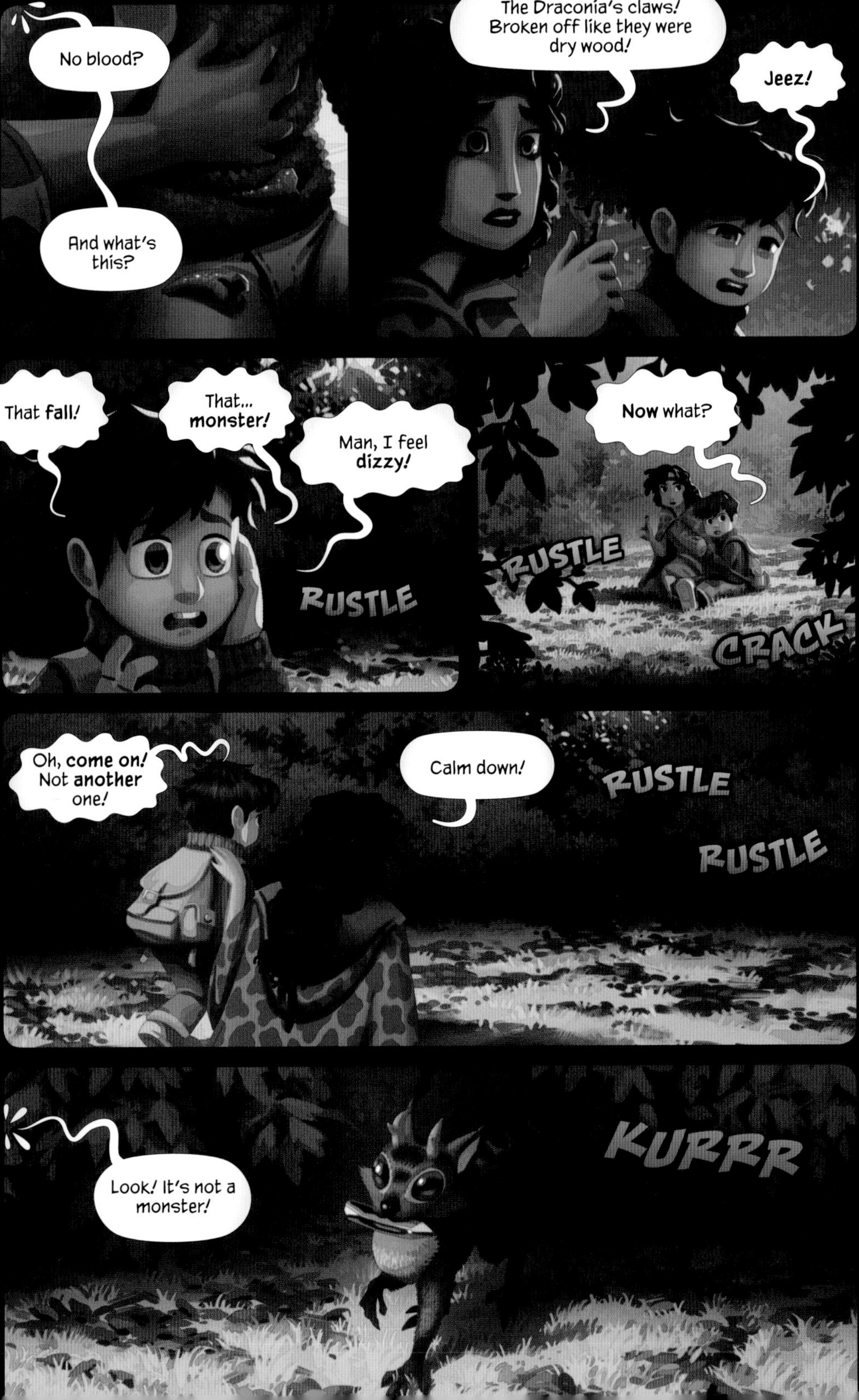
No blood?
And what's this?
The Draconia's claws! Broken off like they were dry wood!
Jeez!
That fall!
That... monster!
Man, I feel dizzy!
RUSTLE
Now what?
RUSTLE
CRACK
Oh, come on! Not another one!
Calm down!
RUSTLE
RUSTLE
KURRR
Look! It's not a monster!

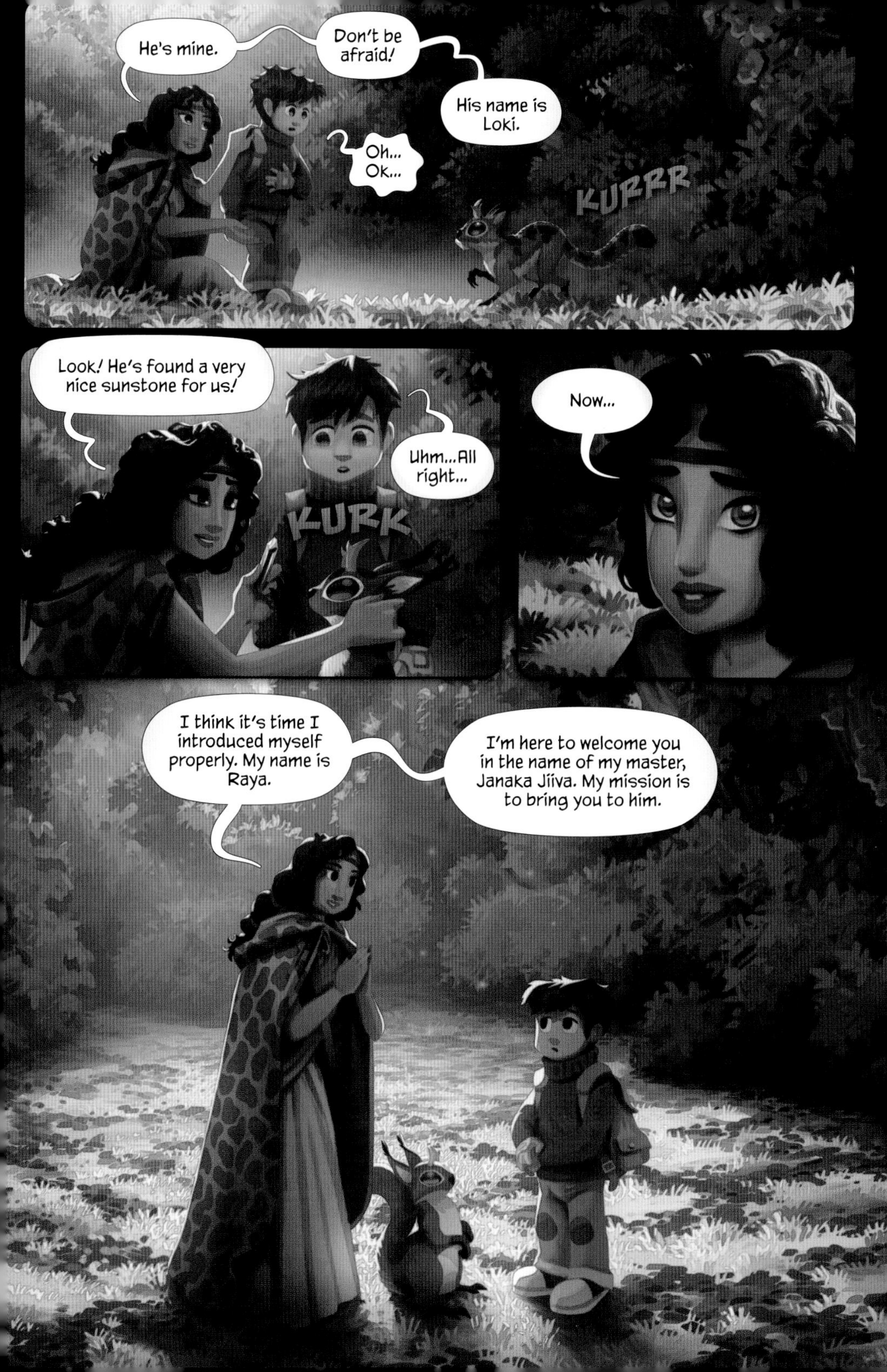

He's mine.
Don't be afraid!
His name is Loki.
Oh... Ok...
KURRR
Look! He's found a very nice sunstone for us!
Uhm...All right...
KURK
Now...
I think it's time I introduced myself properly. My name is Raya.
I'm here to welcome you in the name of my master, Janaka Jiiva. My mission is to bring you to him.

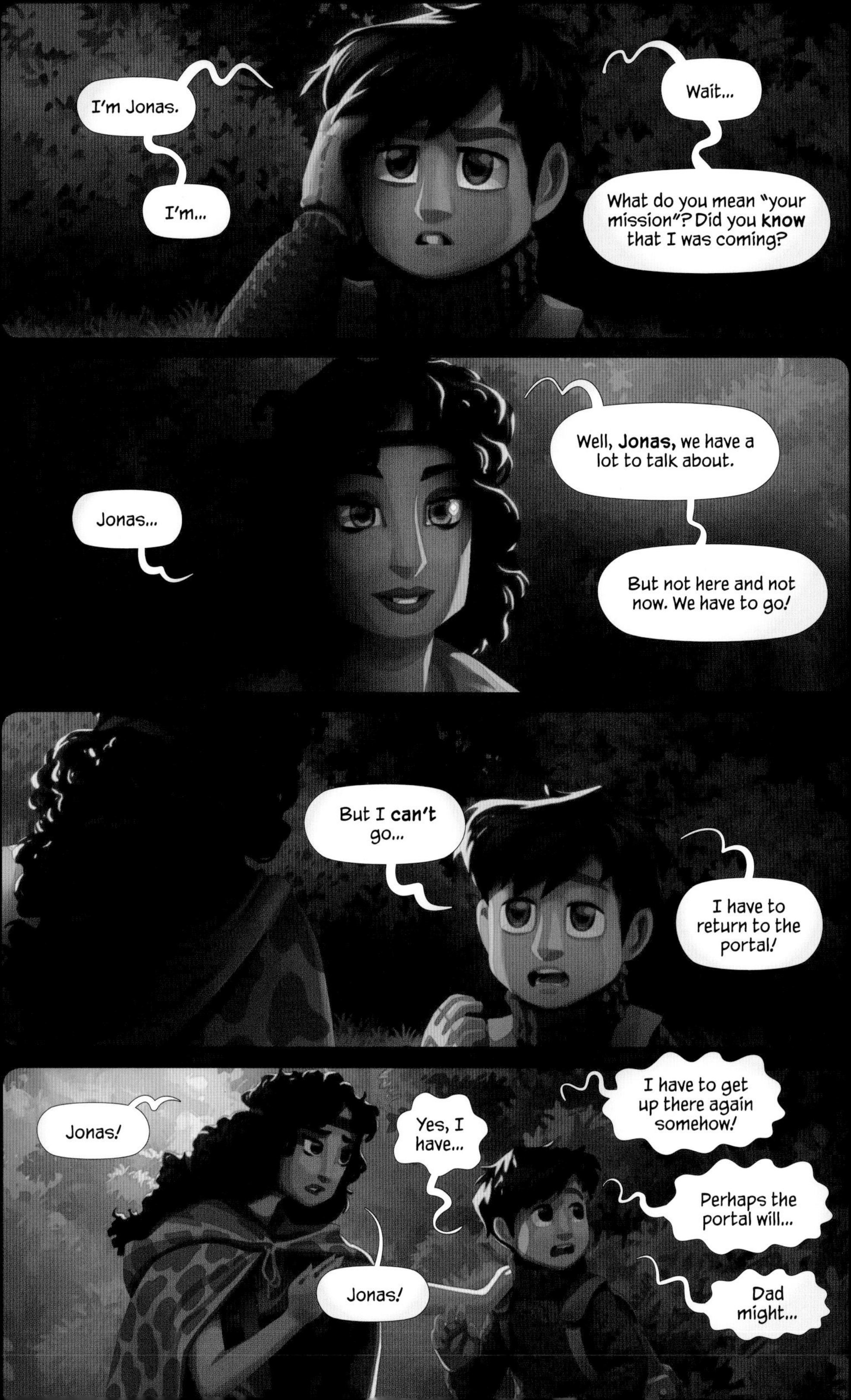
I'm Jonas.
I'm...
Wait...
What do you mean "your mission"? Did you **know** that I was coming?
Jonas...
Well, **Jonas,** we have a lot to talk about.
But not here and not now. We have to go!
But I **can't** go...
I have to return to the portal!
Jonas!
Yes, I have...
I have to get up there again somehow!
Perhaps the portal will...
Jonas!
Dad might...

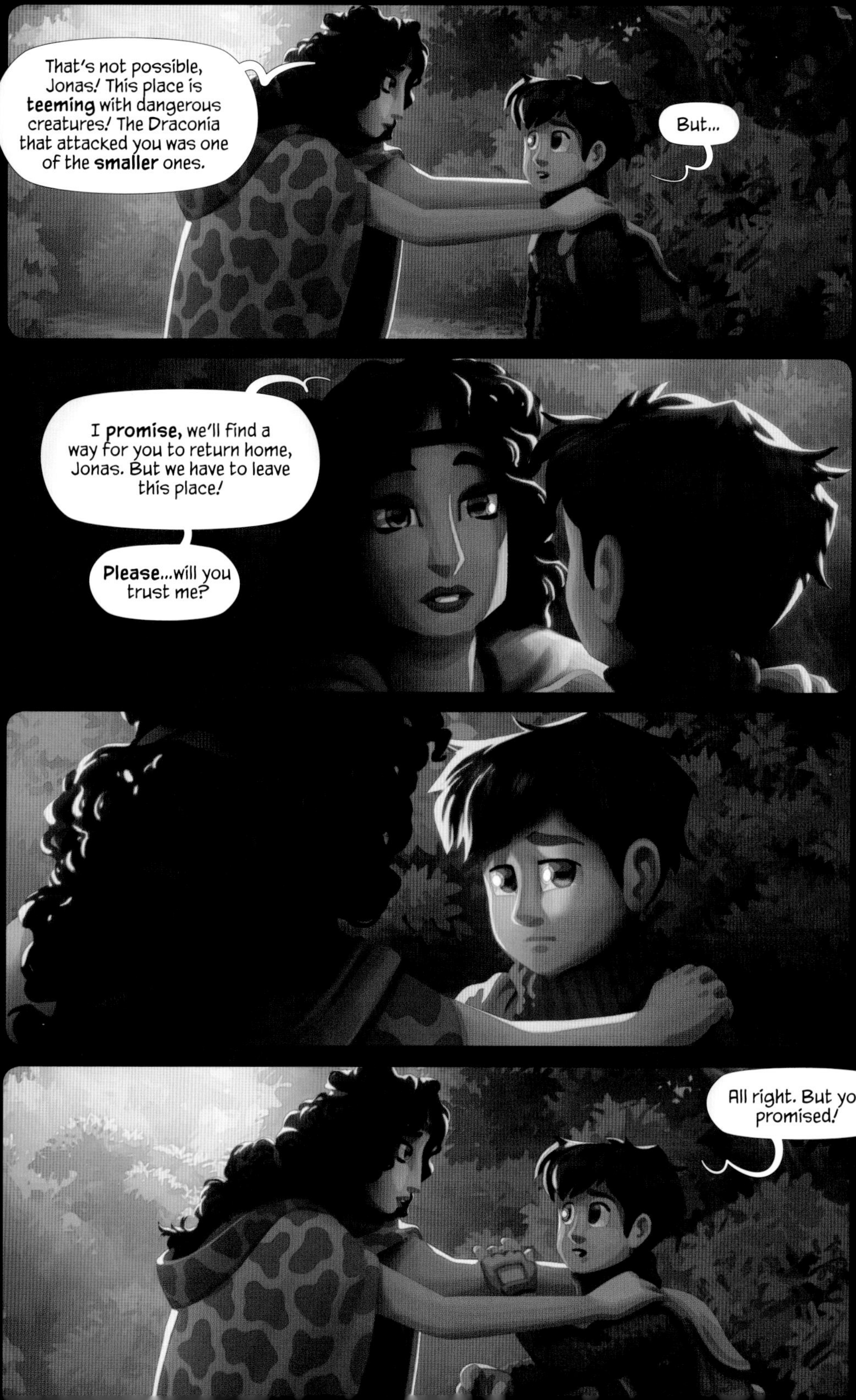
That's not possible, Jonas! This place is teeming with dangerous creatures! The Draconia that attacked you was one of the smaller ones.
But...
I promise, we'll find a way for you to return home, Jonas. But we have to leave this place!
Please...will you trust me?
All right. But you promised!

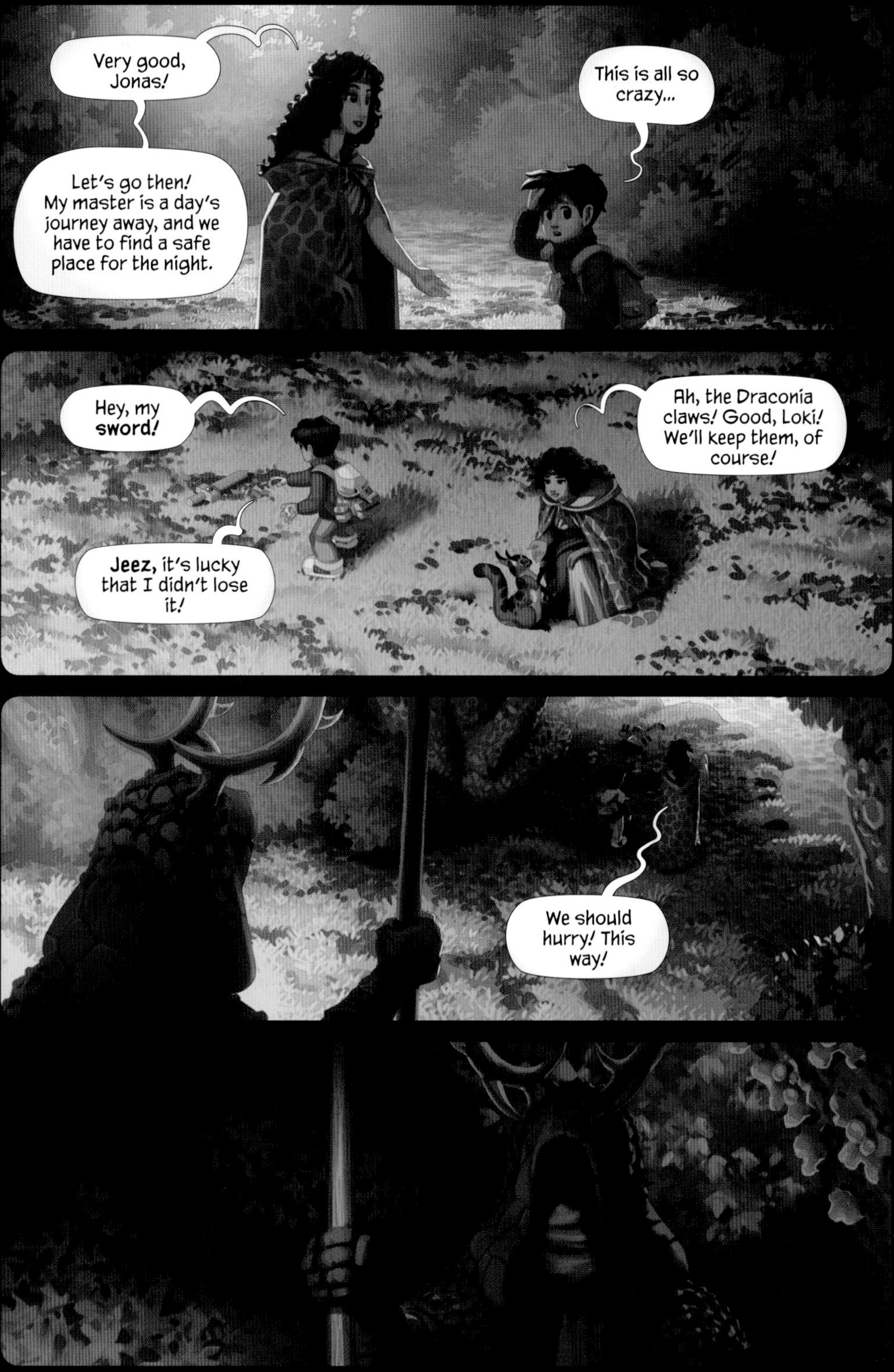
Very good, Jonas!
Let's go then! My master is a day's journey away, and we have to find a safe place for the night.
This is all so crazy...
Hey, my **sword!**
Jeez, it's lucky that I didn't lose it!
Ah, the Draconia claws! Good, Loki! We'll keep them, of course!
We should hurry! This way!

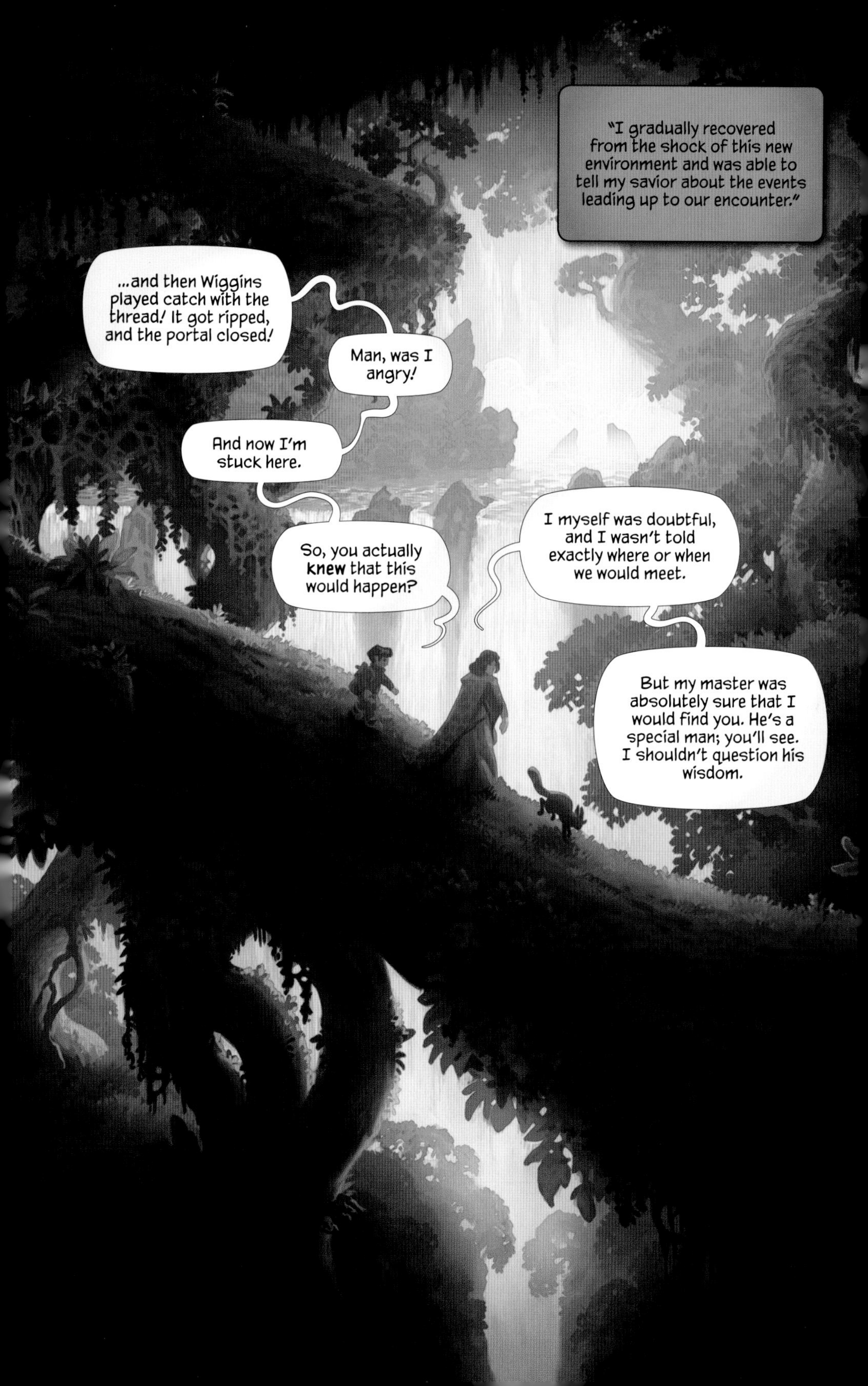
"I gradually recovered from the shock of this new environment and was able to tell my savior about the events leading up to our encounter."
...and then Wiggins played catch with the thread! It got ripped, and the portal closed!
Man, was I angry!
And now I'm stuck here.
So, you actually **knew** that this would happen?
I myself was doubtful, and I wasn't told exactly where or when we would meet.
But my master was absolutely sure that I would find you. He's a special man; you'll see. I shouldn't question his wisdom.

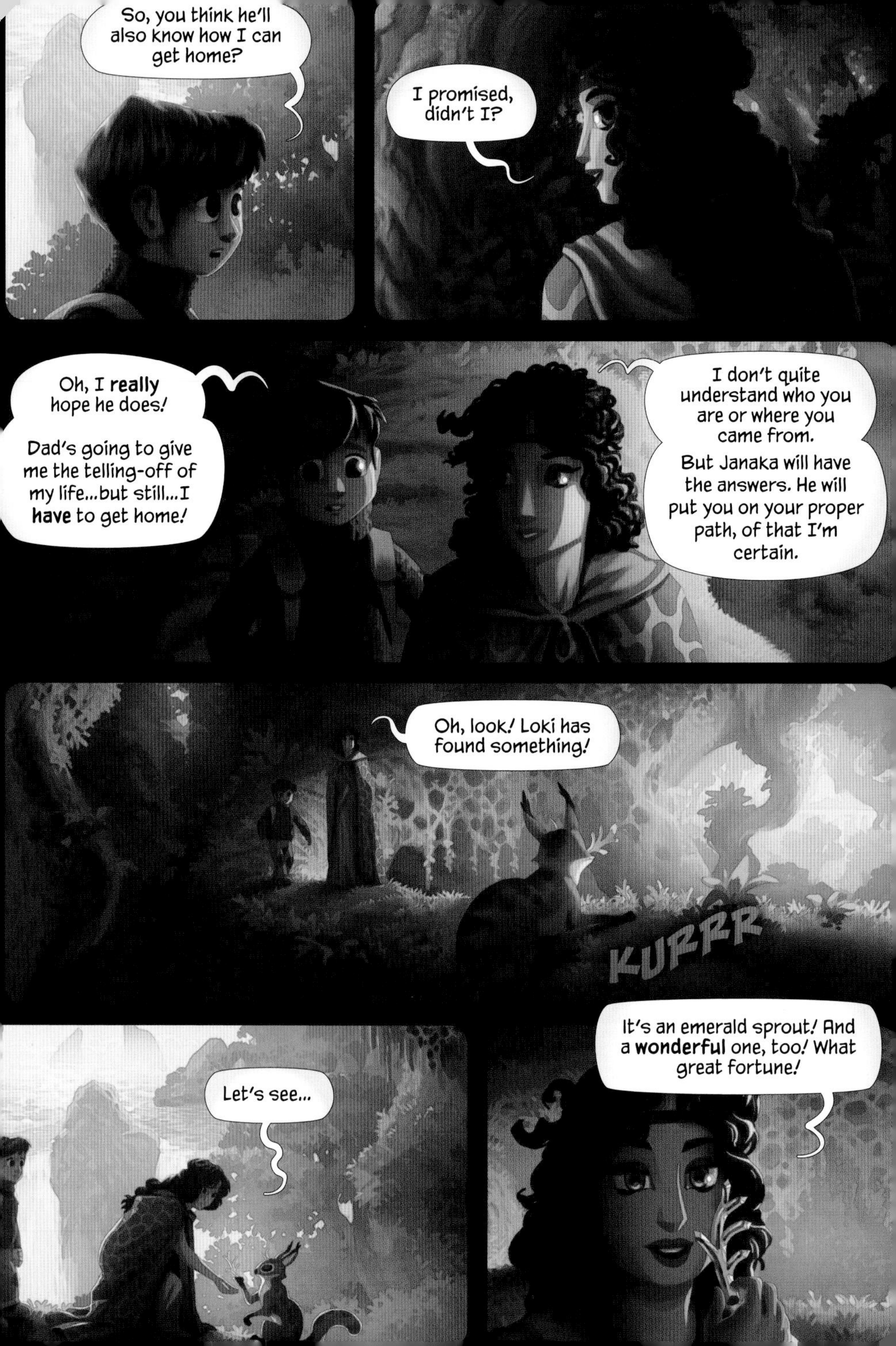
So, you think he'll also know how I can get home?
I promised, didn't I?
Oh, I **really** hope he does!
Dad's going to give me the telling-off of my life...but still...I **have** to get home!
I don't quite understand who you are or where you came from.
But Janaka will have the answers. He will put you on your proper path, of that I'm certain.
Oh, look! Loki has found something!
KURRR
Let's see...
It's an emerald sprout! And a **wonderful** one, too! What great fortune!

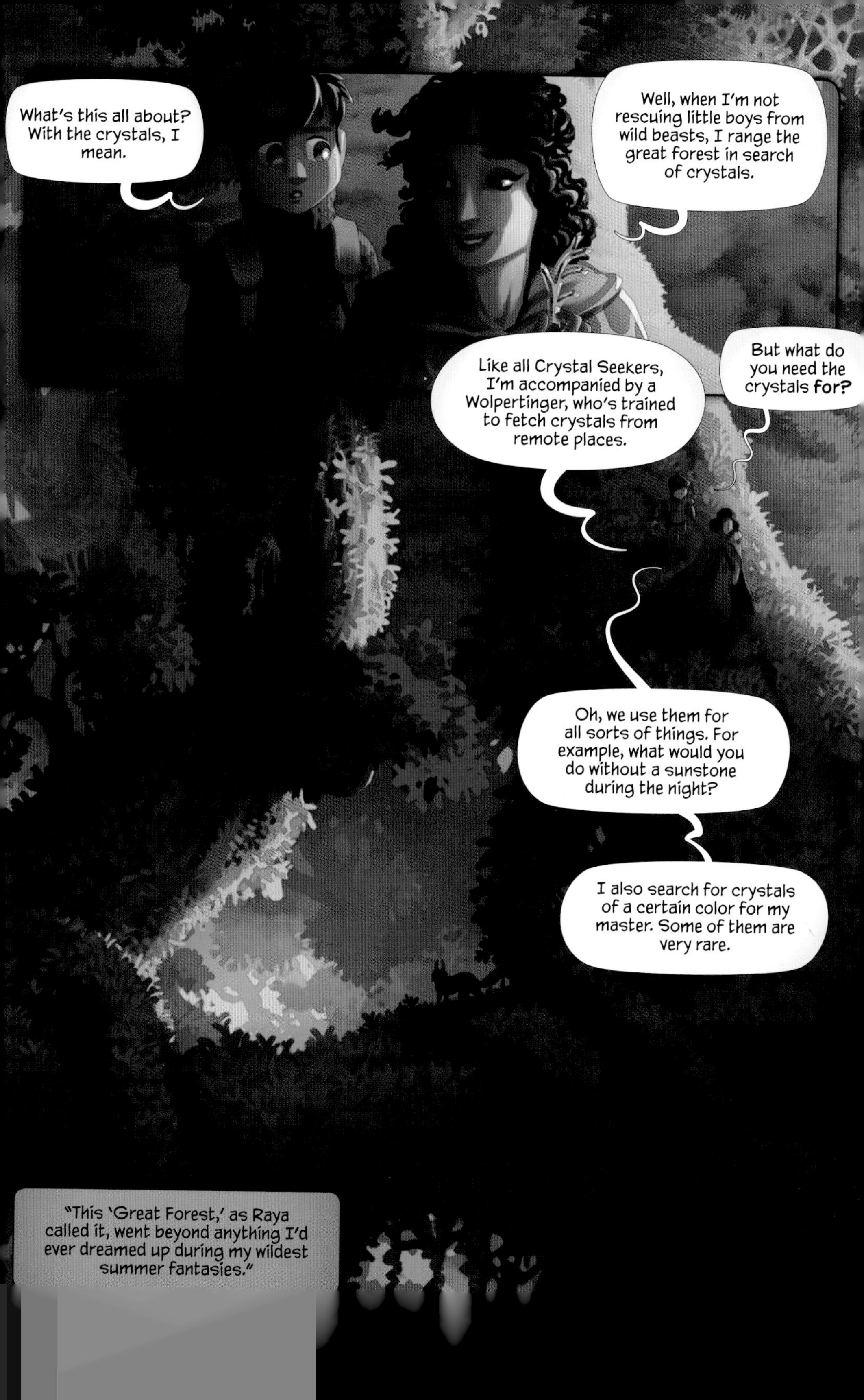
What's this all about? With the crystals, I mean.
Well, when I'm not rescuing little boys from wild beasts, I range the great forest in search of crystals.
Like all Crystal Seekers, I'm accompanied by a Wolpertinger, who's trained to fetch crystals from remote places.
But what do you need the crystals **for?**
Oh, we use them for all sorts of things. For example, what would you do without a sunstone during the night?
I also search for crystals of a certain color for my master. Some of them are very rare.
"This 'Great Forest,' as Raya called it, went beyond anything I'd ever dreamed up during my wildest summer fantasies."

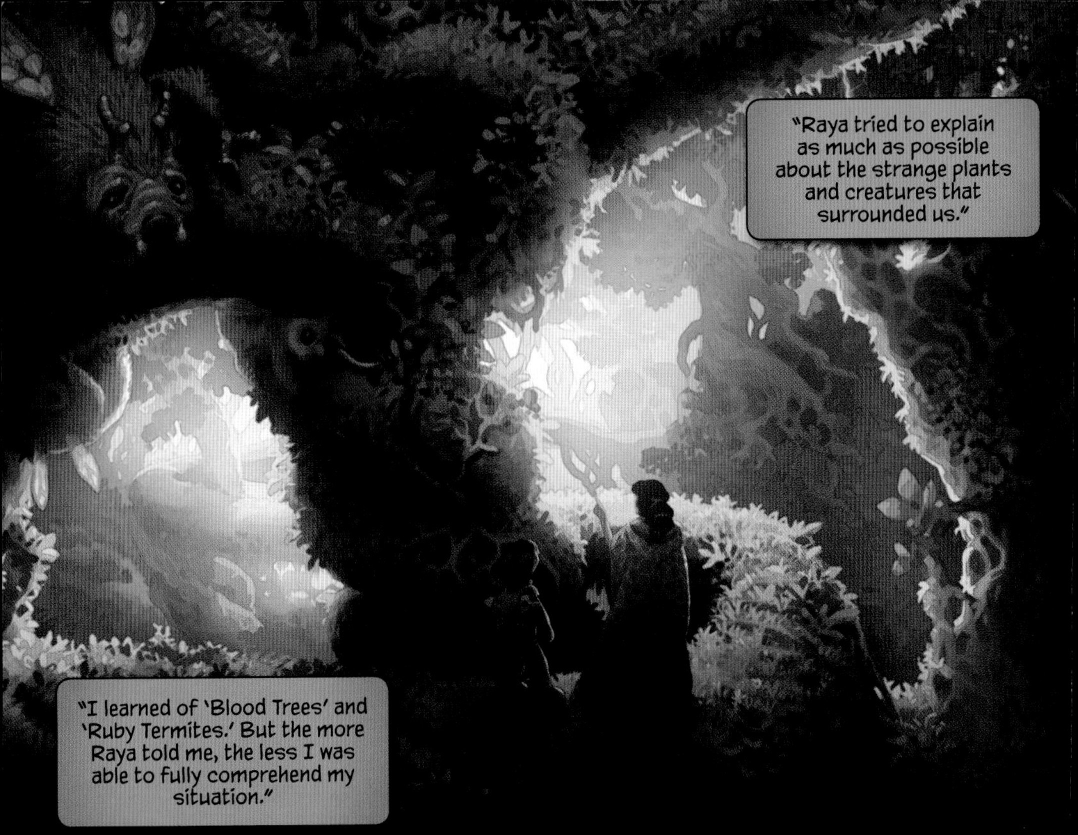
"Raya tried to explain as much as possible about the strange plants and creatures that surrounded us."
"I learned of 'Blood Trees' and 'Ruby Termites.' But the more Raya told me, the less I was able to fully comprehend my situation."

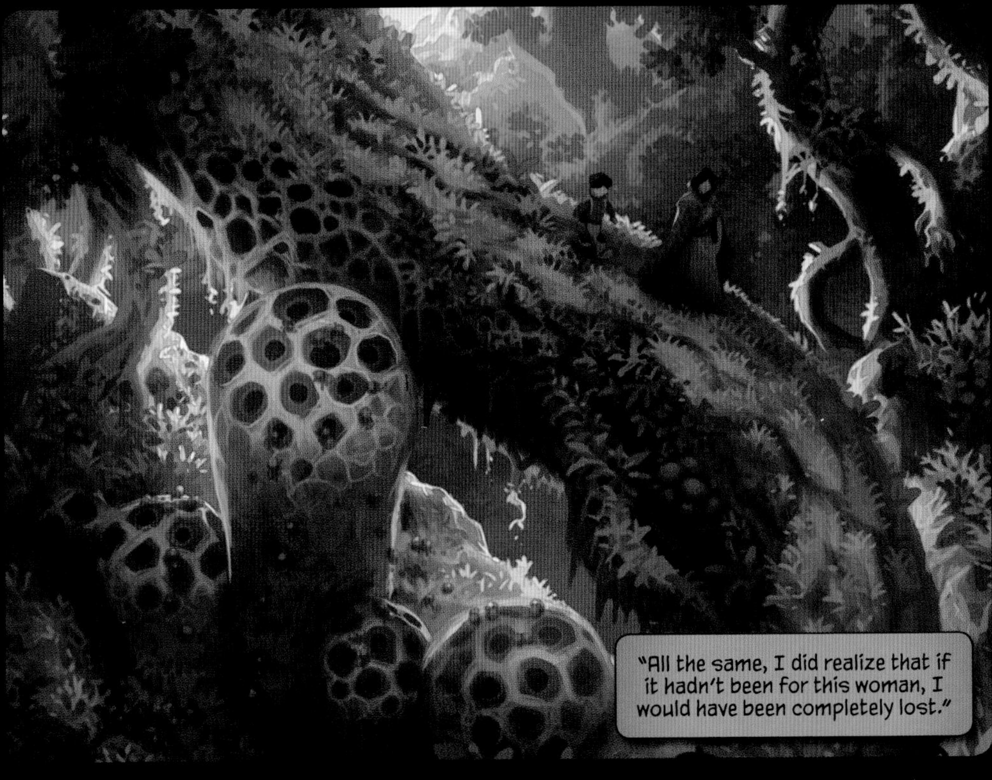
"All the same, I did realize that if it hadn't been for this woman, I would have been completely lost."

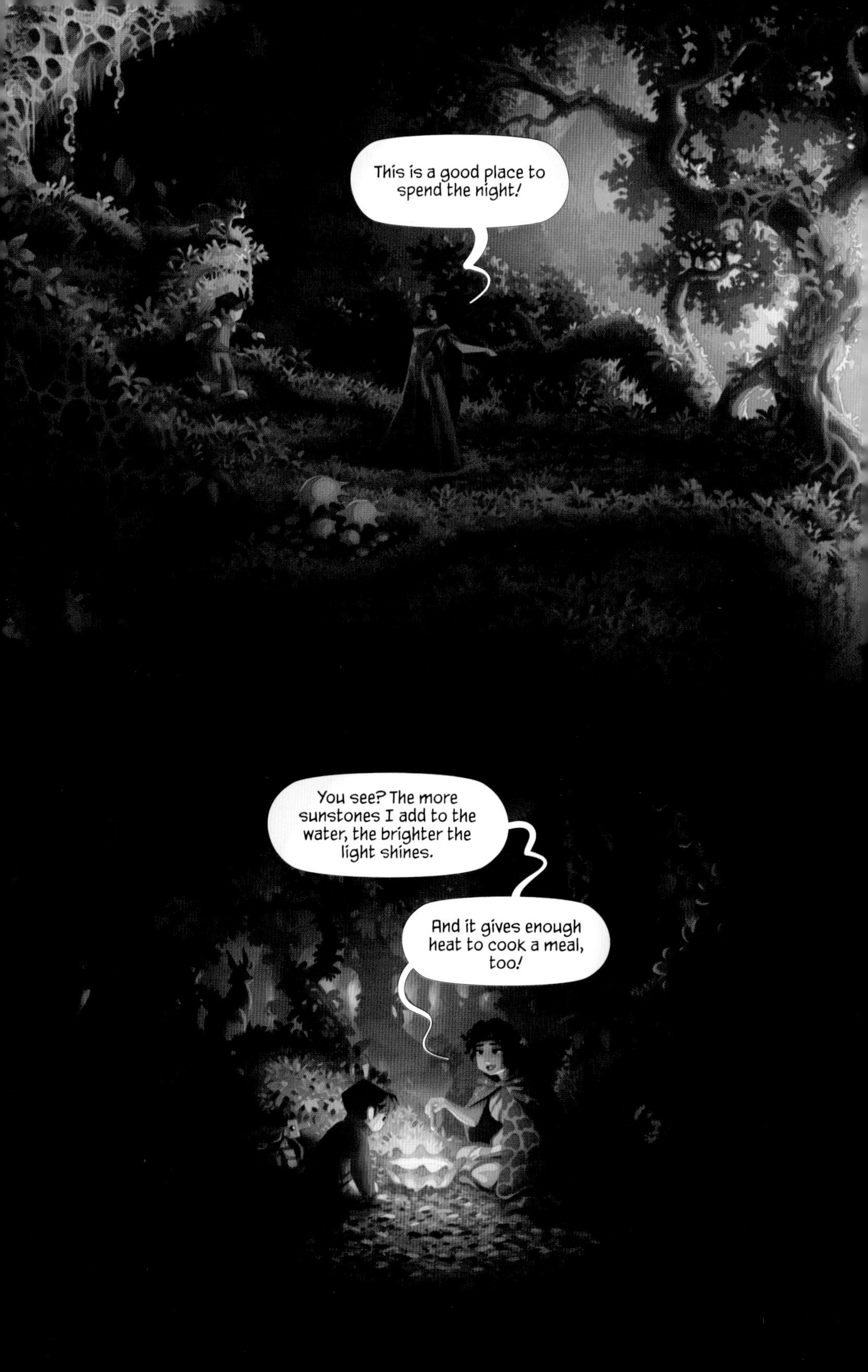
This is a good place to spend the night!
You see? The more sunstones I add to the water, the brighter the light shines.
And it gives enough heat to cook a meal, too!

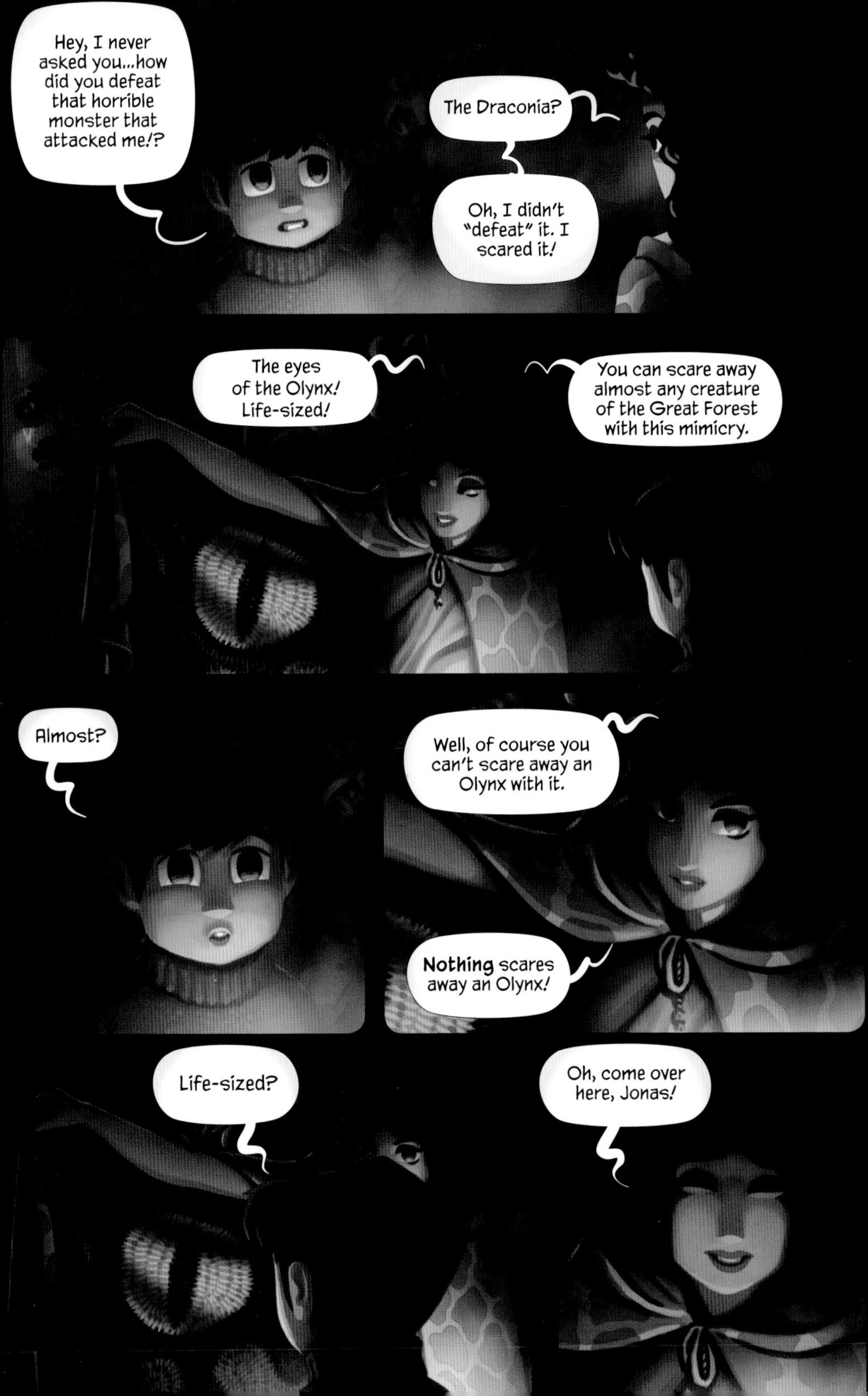
Hey, I never asked you...how did you defeat that horrible monster that attacked me!?
The Draconia?
Oh, I didn't "defeat" it. I scared it!
The eyes of the Olynx! Life-sized!
You can scare away almost any creature of the Great Forest with this mimicry.
Almost?
Well, of course you can't scare away an Olynx with it.
Nothing scares away an Olynx!
Life-sized?
Oh, come over here, Jonas!

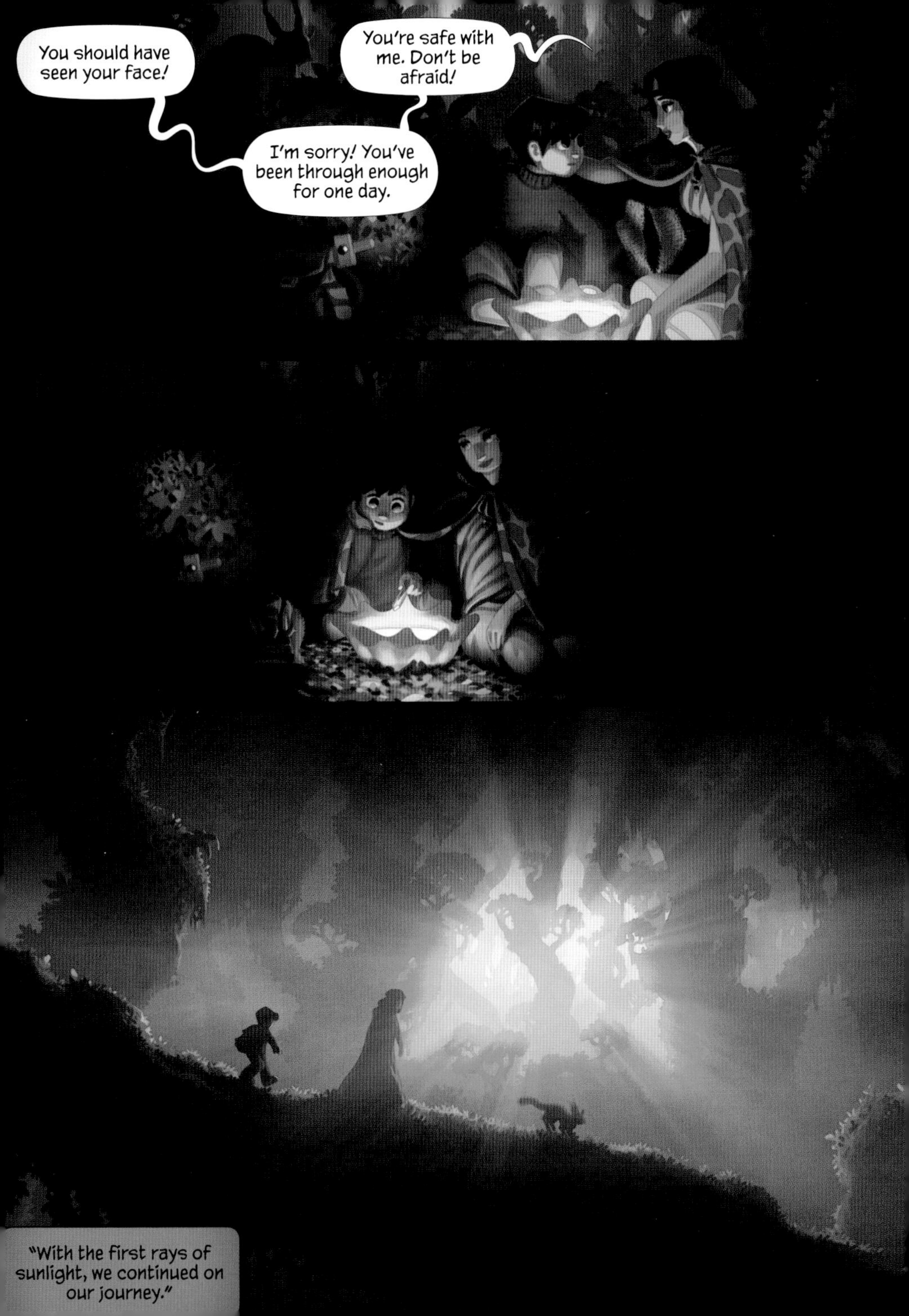
You should have seen your face!
You're safe with me. Don't be afraid!
I'm sorry! You've been through enough for one day.
"With the first rays of sunlight, we continued on our journey."

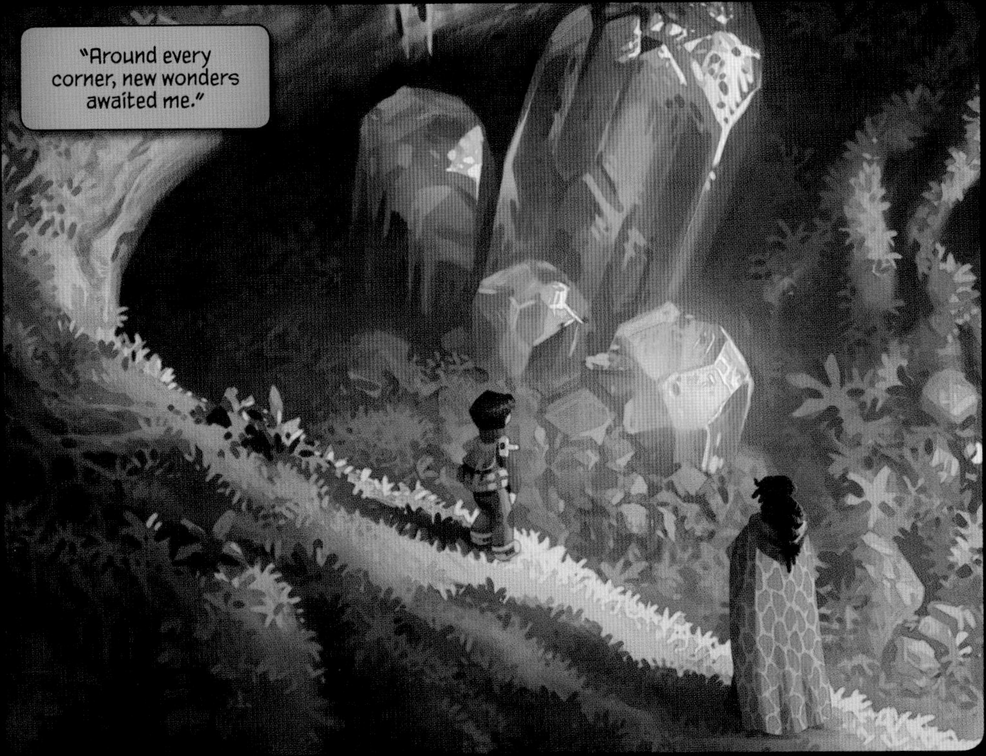
"Around every corner, new wonders awaited me."

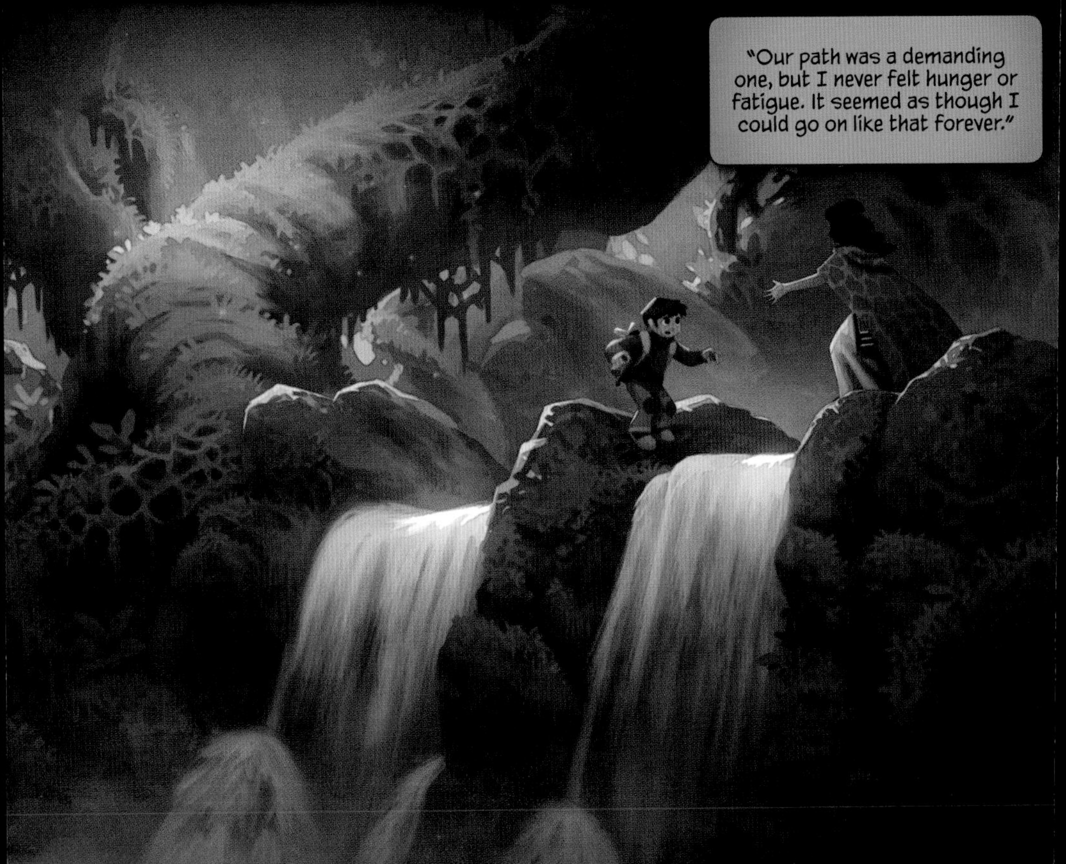
"Our path was a demanding one, but I never felt hunger or fatigue. It seemed as though I could go on like that forever."

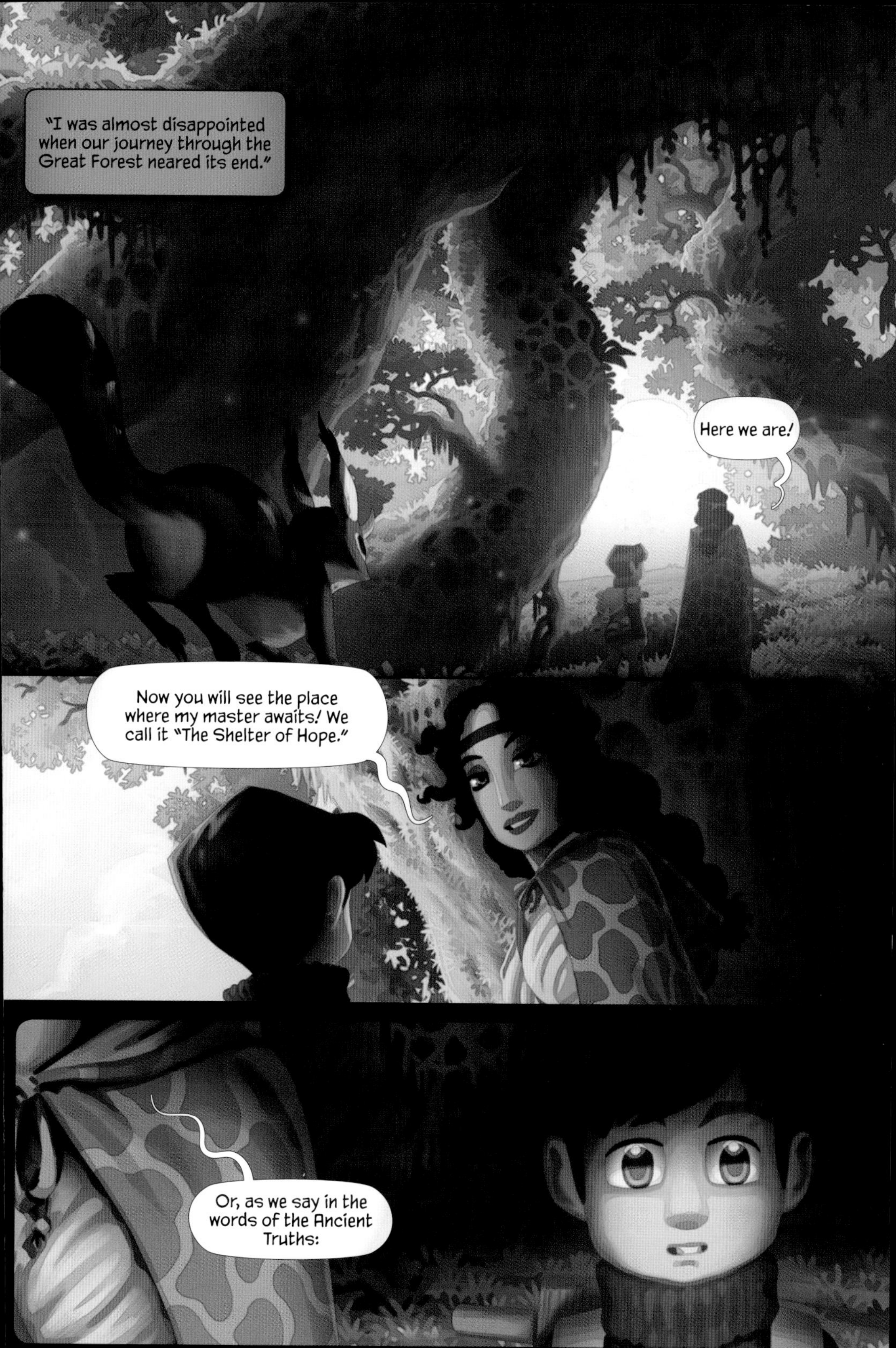
"I was almost disappointed when our journey through the Great Forest neared its end."
Here we are!
Now you will see the place where my master awaits! We call it "The Shelter of Hope."
Or, as we say in the words of the Ancient Truths:

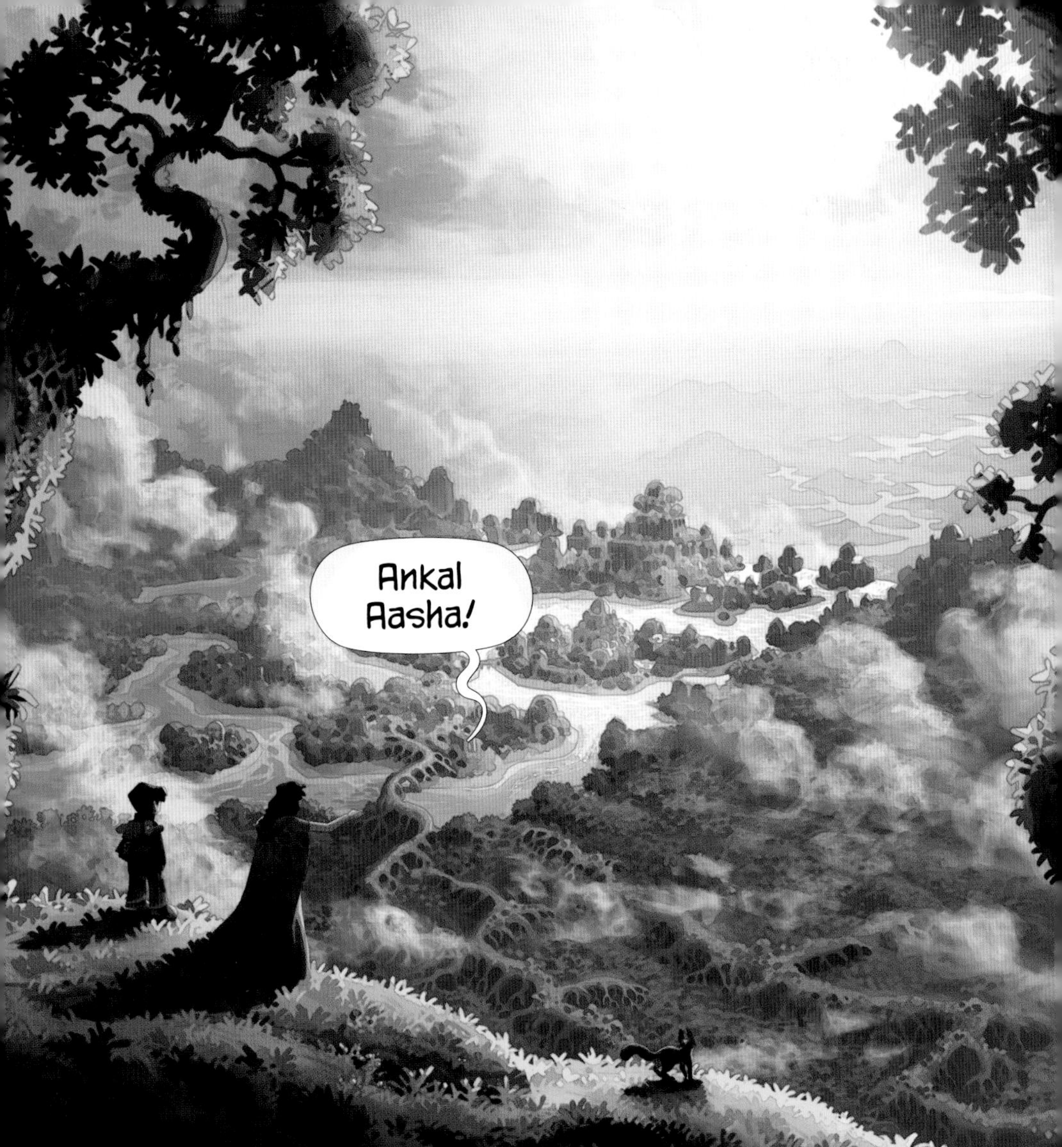
Ankal Aasha!

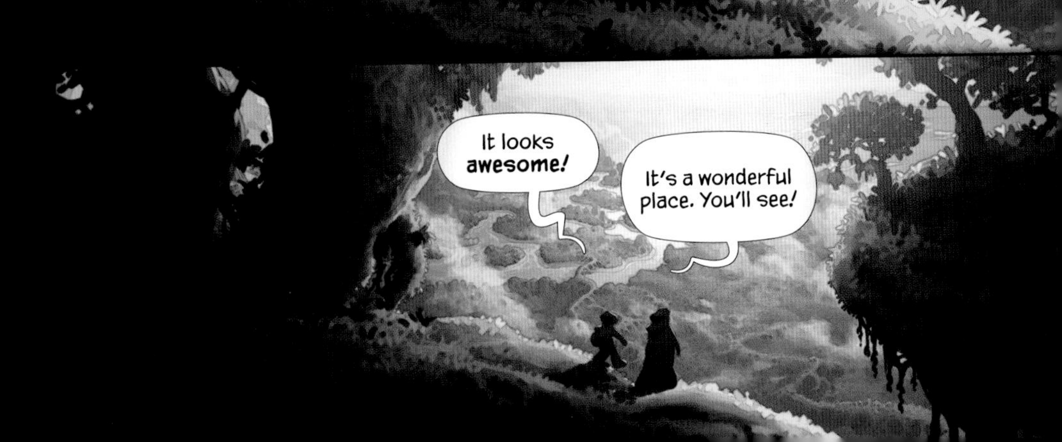
It looks **awesome!**
It's a wonderful place. You'll see!

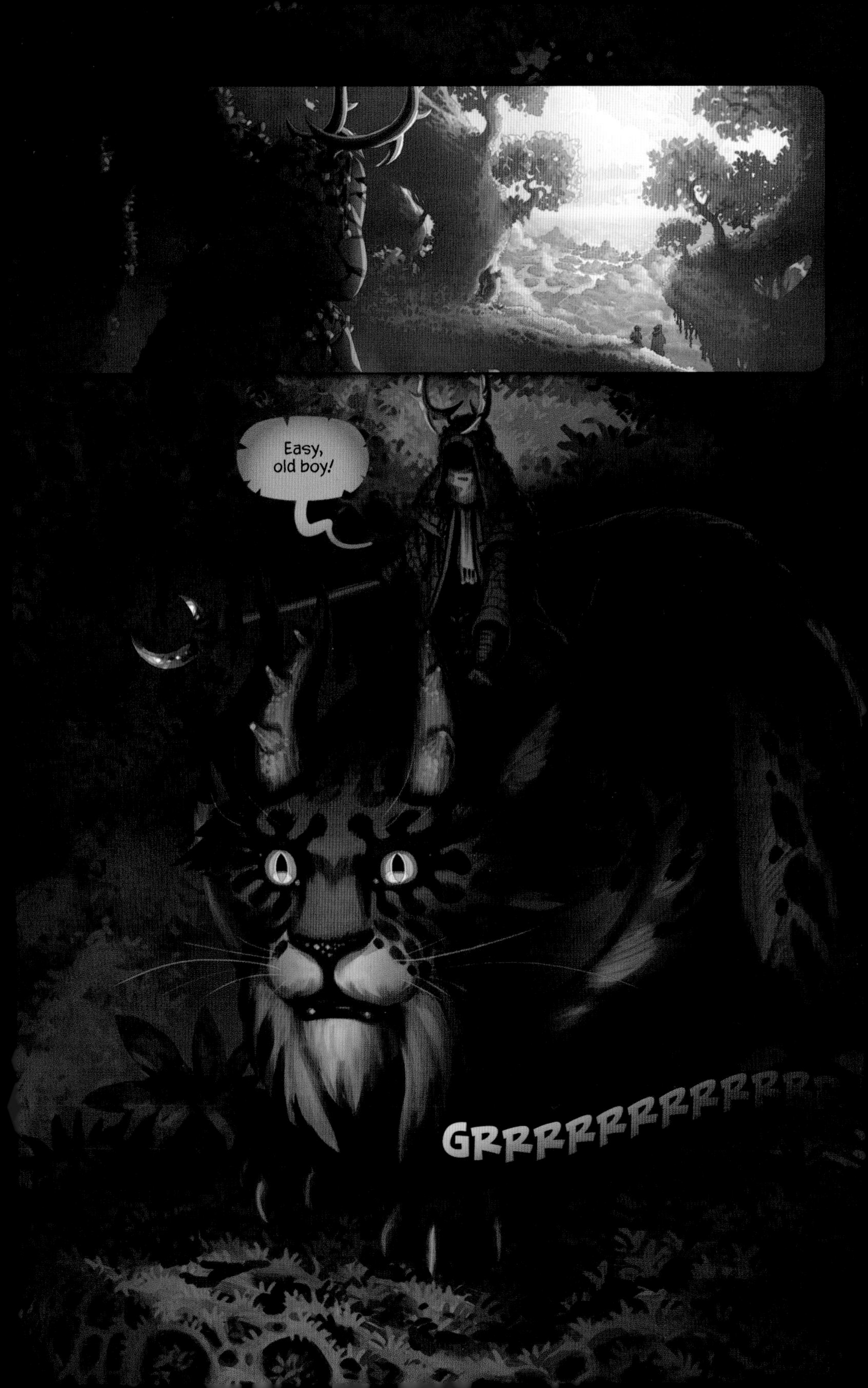
Easy,
old boy!
GRRRRRRRRRR

Behind the Scenes of
The Wormworld Saga

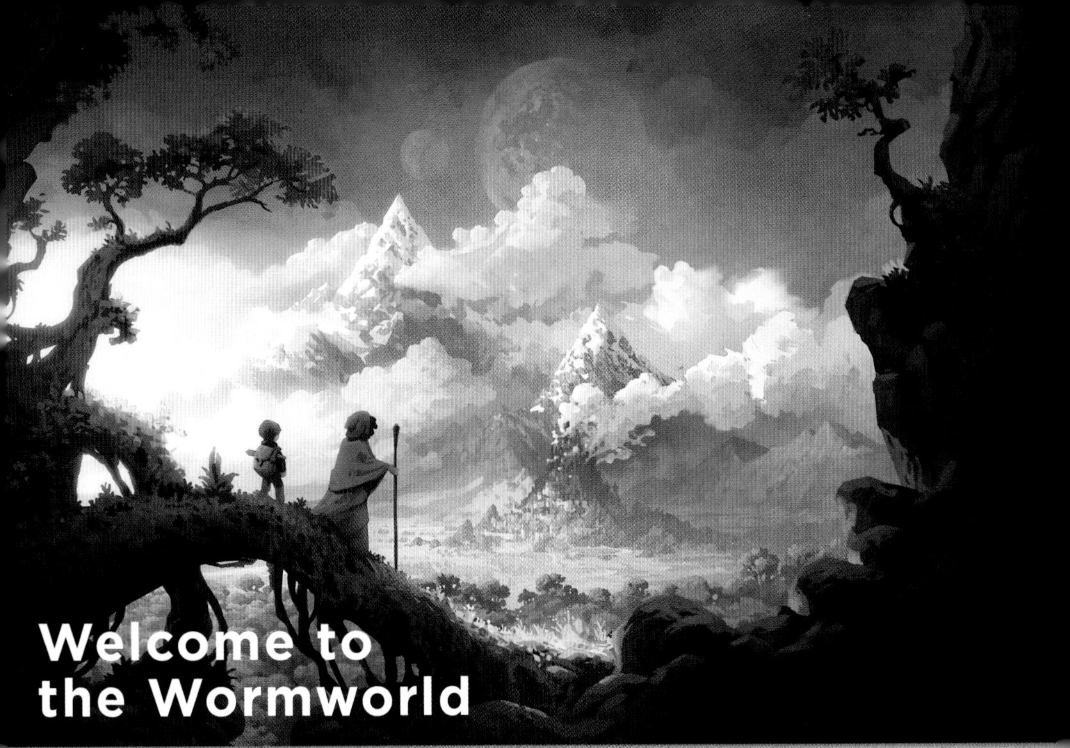

Welcome to the Wormworld

Even the Biggest Journey Starts with a Single Step

When I scribbled my first ideas about a mystical "Great Worm" back in 2003, I had no idea that I was setting foot on an adventurous path that would lead me deeper and deeper into a story that, at some point, would no longer let me turn back. I often get asked how I came up with *The Wormworld Saga*. I can't describe it in any better way than saying that I just stumbled into it somehow. My first step on the path that would later lead to the epic fantasy adventure that is *The Wormworld Saga* was a drawing that I just made up out of the blue.

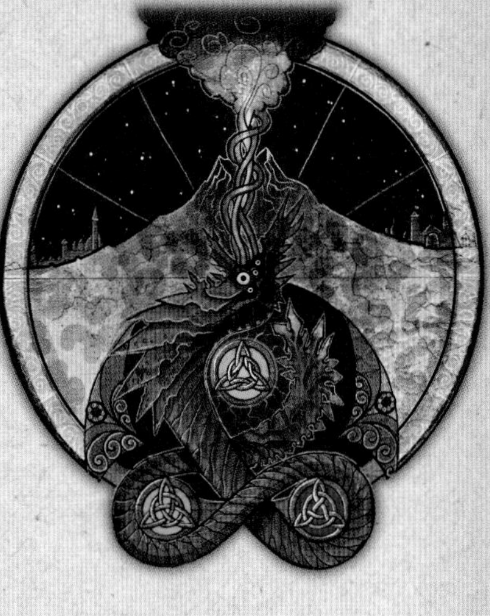

"The Worm Mountain," 2003

The Birth of the Great Worm

By that time, I was heavily influenced by the works of Brian Froud, who created spectacular creatures and set designs for Jim Henson's fantasy films *Labyrinth* and *The Dark Crystal*. When I acquired a copy of the book *The World of the Dark Crystal* (Harry N. Abrams Inc., 2003), I found out that Froud had created a whole mythology around his worlds and creatures. Even though I didn't have a world that actually needed a mythological background yet, I nevertheless started to fantasize about a godlike creature that lay buried inside a mountain, bound by three magical runes. Its fiery tongues reached out of its prison. The whole artwork looked like an illustrated mythology an ancient people came up with to explain the outburst of a volcano. I really didn't put much thought into the backstory of this illustration, and I created it mostly for its decorative value.

However, only two days later I painted another artwork based on the same ideas, and this time the creature got a name. The Great Worm was born.

And maybe that's the whole secret about storytelling. You just have to start at some point and then follow the track to the next idea, and then the next, and so forth. And you have to let time work for you. After having collected these first fragments of a story, I lost track of it and created other things. But the seed was planted, and, unnoticed, it rested in my head, waiting to sprout when the time was right.

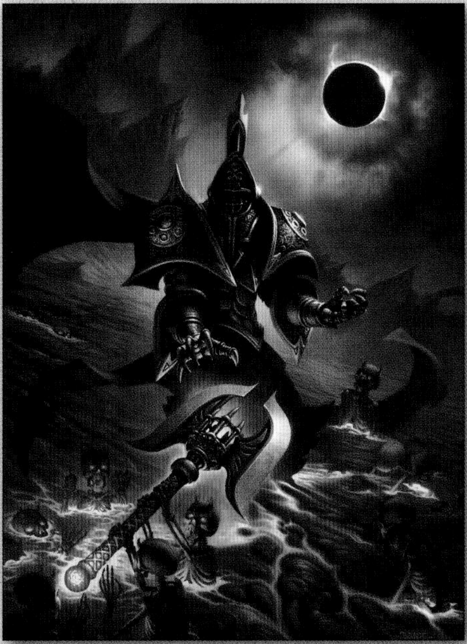

"The Rise of the Firelord," 2005

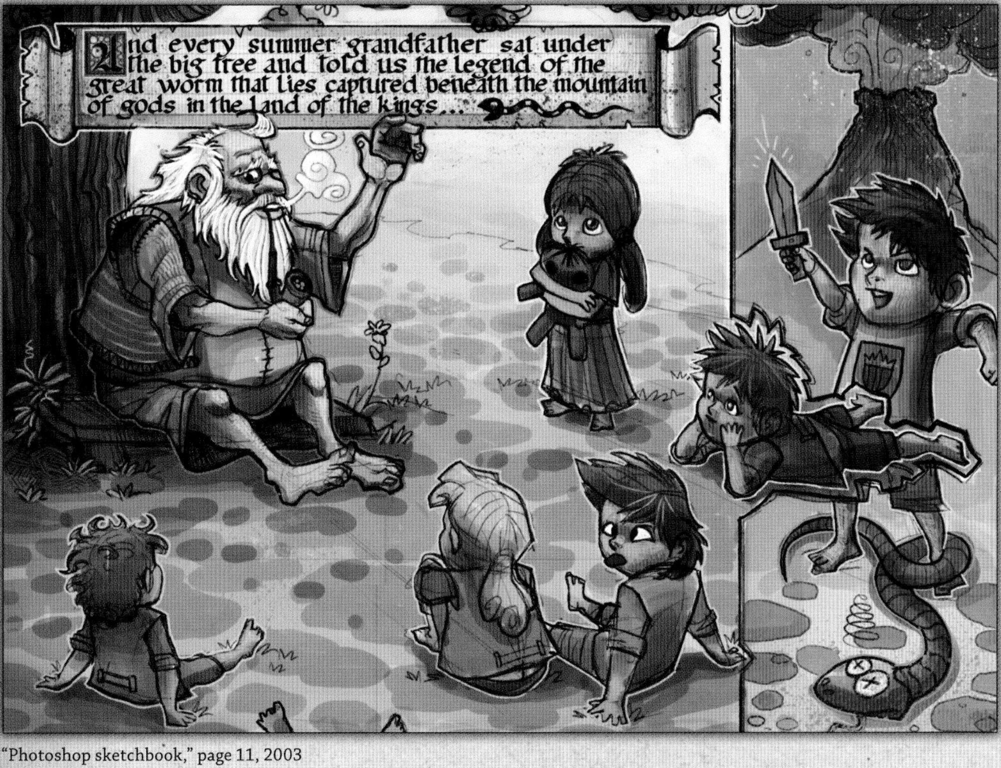
And every summer grandfather sat under the big tree and told us the legend of the great worm that lies captured beneath the mountain of gods in the land of the kings...

"Photoshop sketchbook," page 11, 2003

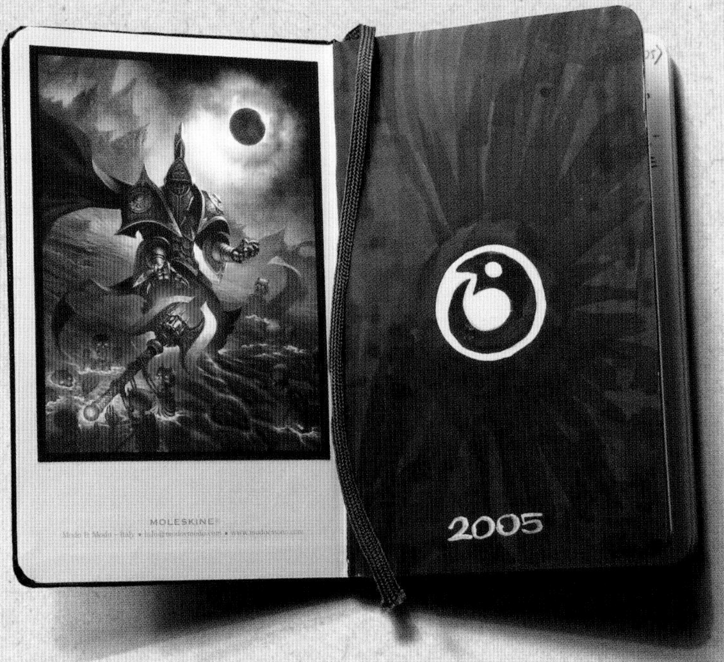
MOLESKINE
2005

The first Wormworld notebook, started in 2005

The Rise of the Firelord

The time was right in 2005. I have no idea what exactly made me pick up the old thread again, but I reencountered a character that I had also painted in 2003 for the first time—the "Fire Knight." Back then, there was actually no connection between the Fire Knight and the legend of the Great Worm, but somehow these two elements clicked together in 2005 like pieces of a big puzzle. I felt that something was building up in my head, and I wanted to start keeping track of it. I started my first notebook—a handy moleskin book that was small enough to carry with me all the time.

Shortly after starting my notebook, I painted "The Rise of the Firelord," and I created a connection between this character and the Great Worm. I imagined the Firelord to be a young prince who suffered from a desperate love and wanted to end his life. He stumbled to the top of the Worm Mountain to throw himself into the fiery abyss. The Great Worm received the prince, but he didn't destroy him. Instead, he clad the poor soul in a magic armor and forced him to do his bidding. The Great Worm was imprisoned, you see, and he needed an agent to prepare his furious return to the world. The painting depicts the moment when the prince rises from the lava streams of the Worm Mountain and claims the "Worm Axe"—the magic weapon that contains the breath of the beast.

From then on, I frequently added new ideas to my notebook. I had a mystic background and a dark villain with an evil mission. All I needed now was a hero to save the world! The grandfather sketch from 2003 already hinted at a young boy to possibly be the hero of the story. In the tradition of classic fantasy stories, I decided that the hero should not be an inhabitant of the fantastic world, but that he should come from our real world and enter the fantasy world under a quest to defeat the Firelord.

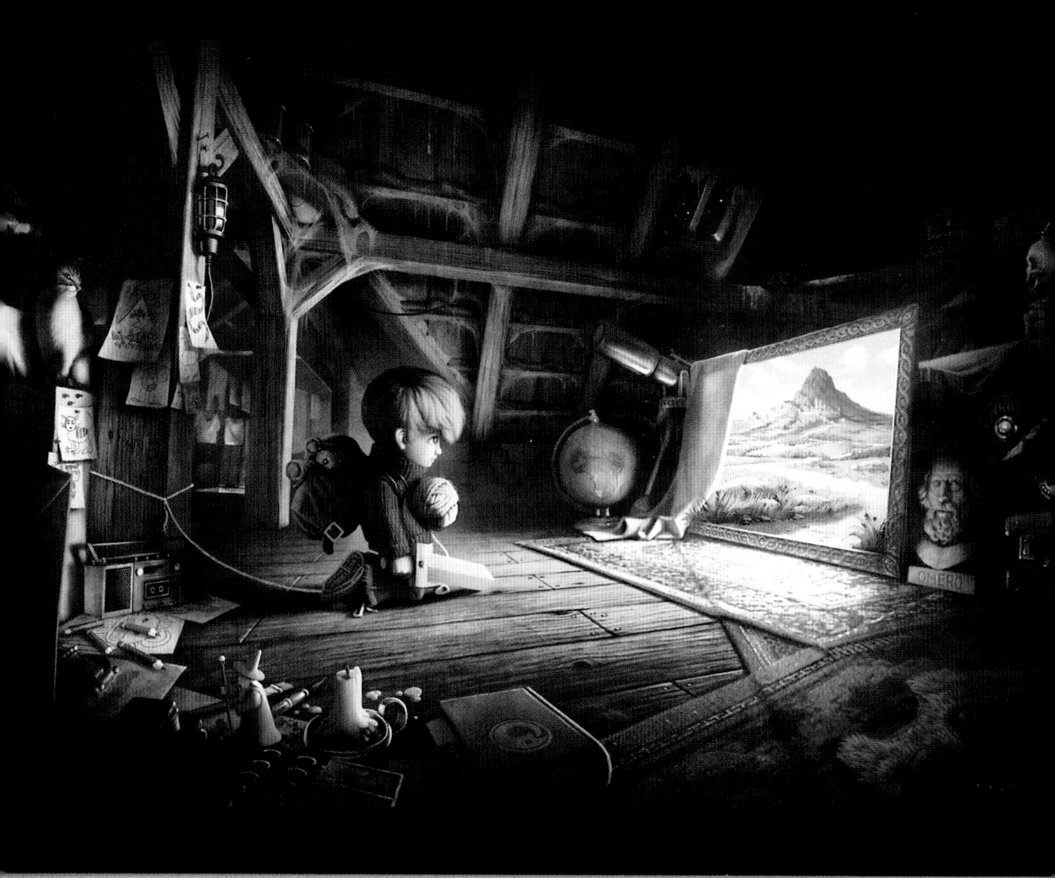

"The Journey Begins," 2006

The Journey Begins

Other popular fantasy worlds were entered through books, mirrors, or wardrobes, just to name a few. Being a painter, I was attracted to the idea of my hero starting his adventure by stepping through a magic painting. In 2006, an international digital art community website started a contest to design an artwork on the theme "The Journey Begins." That was exactly the motivation I needed to put a lot of work into a single illustration. I worked on my entry for the contest in the evenings, and it took me over two months to finish it. But it was well worth the effort—"The Journey Begins" won second place in the contest. Apart from the prizes, it was the overwhelmingly positive feedback, and all the people that became aware of my artwork through the contest, that had the biggest impact on me. I realized that I had created a strong story hook with the little boy in the attic.

And Now What?

On January 6, 2007, I put down a little note in my notebook: "Today I asked myself the question if I should develop this story into a novel." Up until that point, I had just been an illustrator who was collecting ideas for new artwork. And that worked nicely. I accompanied "The Journey Begins" with a second painting that shows the young boy from the attic in a dangerous situation, surrounded by goblins. In "Trapped!," I wanted to show what might wait behind the magic canvas, and I also wanted to try out another visual approach to the story.

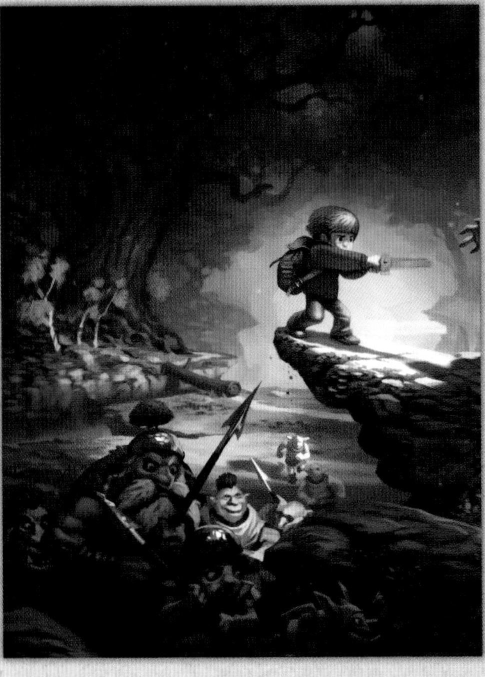

I could have been satisfied with my nice, little backstory: my hero was adventuring through a colorful fantasy world (of which I had even created a map in 2007) and I had a Great Worm, an evil Firelord, and a bunch of goblins to fight against. But, as my note from the beginning of 2007 shows, I had already found that the story had taken on a life of its own. My notebook was full of questions and ideas. I started wondering about what exactly the plan of the Great Worm was. What was the mission of the Firelord? How was it that a young boy from our world was destined to defeat evil in a distant fantasy world? How did this boy find the magic painting anyway? And—most importantly—who painted it? I realized that it was impossible to answer all these questions by merely painting a series of illustrations. In order to tell this story, I had to set foot on a completely new path.

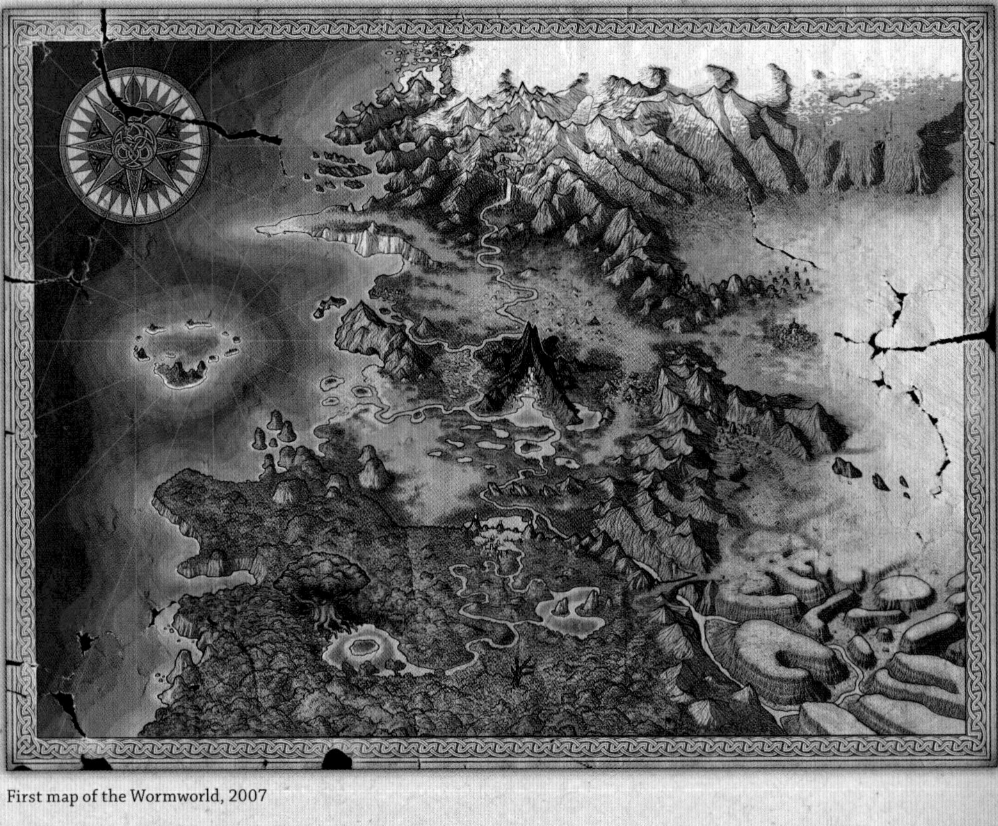

First map of the Wormworld, 2007

The Rebirth of a Graphic Novel Author

Creating a graphic novel wasn't at all the first thing I thought of when I asked myself how to tell the story. My first attempt was to actually write a novel. I started writing little scenes but soon found out that prose was not the right medium for me. My mental image of the story was simply too visual, and I got constantly tangled up in lengthy descriptions of places and atmosphere. I figured out that a good writer would put these things between the lines, but that was not why I had studied painting my whole life. I had to find a more visual medium. Some guys in the online community I was participating in were doing short animations, and I started to research which tools I would need to tell my story in animated form. It soon became very clear that I couldn't tell the story I had in mind by animating it myself—not in the evenings, after a ten-hour day job. It would have been just too much work.

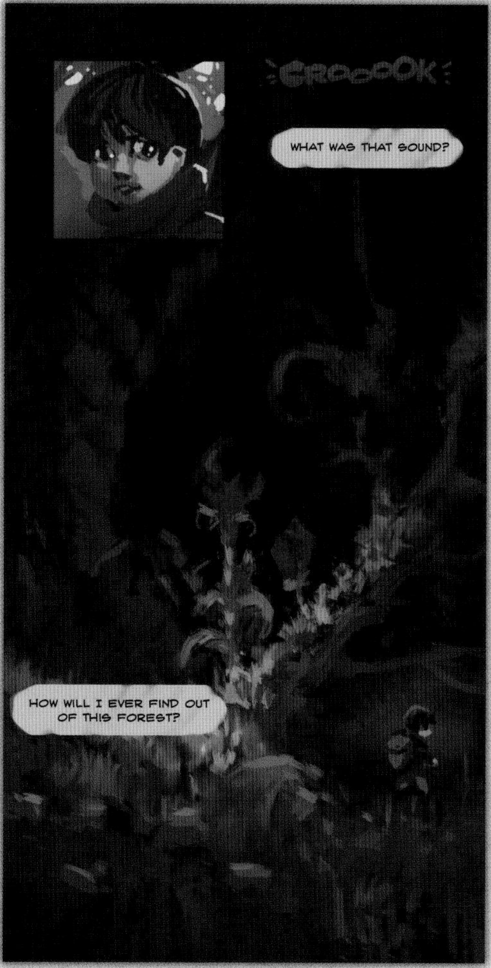
CROOOOK
WHAT WAS THAT SOUND?
HOW WILL I EVER FIND OUT OF THIS FOREST?

Comic experiment for *The Wormworld Saga*, 2009

The ironic thing is that telling my story as a comic should have been my first choice given my personal background. I had created comics as a teenager in school. And I'm not talking about small scribbles on notebook paper. I wrote and illustrated three full-length comic books and sold them as stapled pamphlets in the schoolyard. When I left school, everyone surely expected me to become a comic book artist. But there wasn't what you could have called a comic book industry in Germany. I was lucky to get a job in computer games after I graduated. It was there where I learned to master the tools of a digital artist. While I was working on computer games, I put my focus on concept art and illustration throughout the years. I totally lost the connection to my comic book past. When I put the first word balloons into some of my illustrations, it came to me as a revelation—this was the way to tell my story! After over ten years, I had finally managed to return to my roots.

Digital sculpture of the Wormseal, 2008

The Wormworld Saga as a Digital Graphic Novel and Book

In late 2009, I started my work on *The Wormworld Saga,* a digital graphic novel. I had done research on the comic and graphic novel market, and I figured that the best way to attract an audience would be to publish my work online. I worked on the project in the evenings and on weekends around my day job. I spent nearly three hundred fifty hours creating the first chapter and *The Wormworld Saga* website, and I launched the free online version of the graphic novel on December 25, 2010. The reactions since then have been over- whelming, and my journey since that fateful December day has been a story of its own.

Today I'm working mostly full time on *The Wormworld Saga.* In 2018, with the help of my fans, I was able to create the book that you are, right now, holding in your hands. I'm deeply thankful for that, and hope that you enjoy it as much as I do. The journey has just begun!

Daniel Lieske

From the Sketchbook of Daniel Lieske

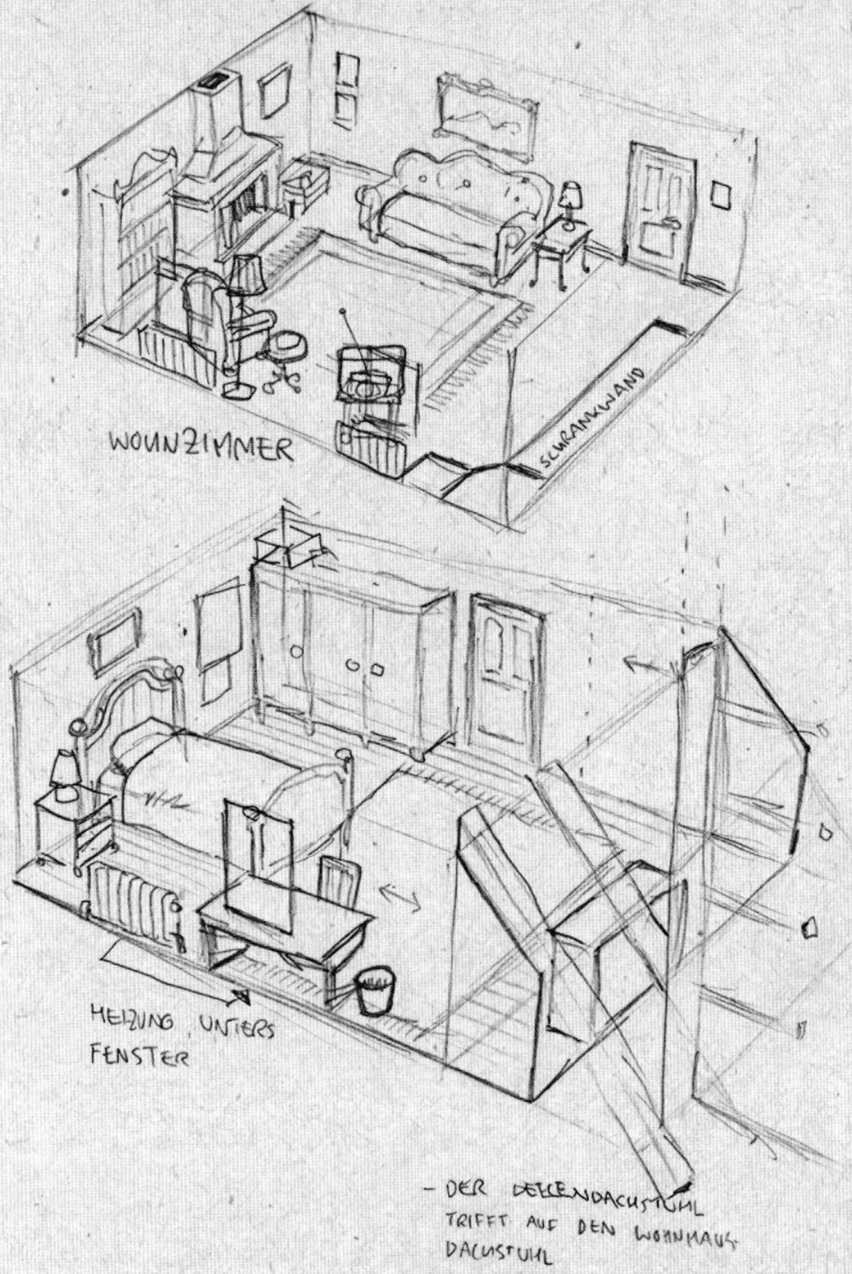
WOHNZIMMER
SCHRANKWAND
HEIZUNG UNTERS
FENSTER
– DER DECKENDACHSTUHL
TRIFFT AUF DEN WOHNHAUS
DACHSTUHL

Notes in Daniel's native German

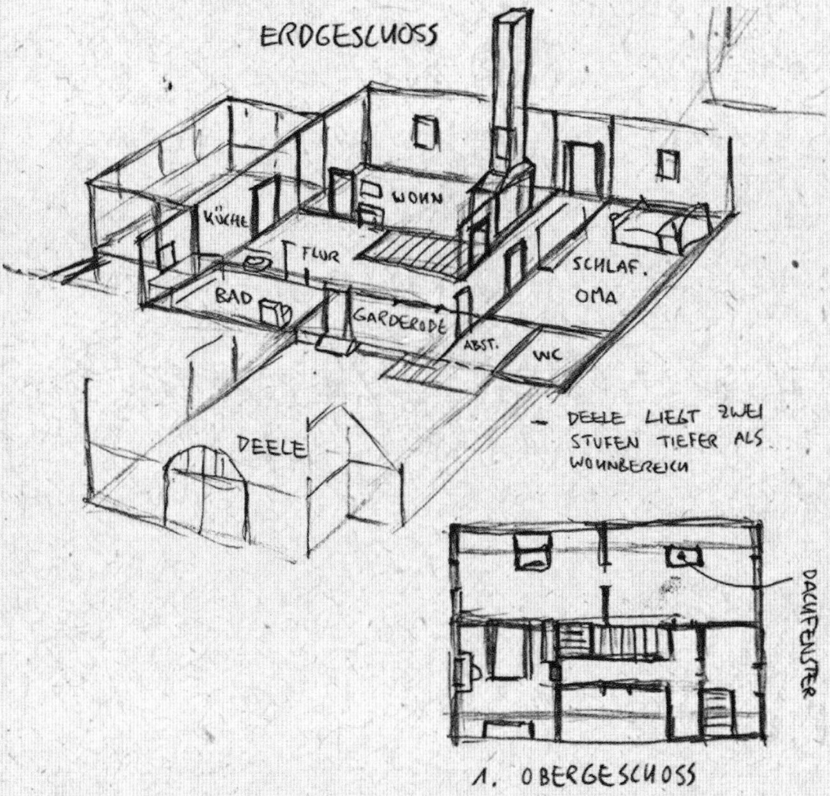
ERDGESCHOSS
KÜCHE
WOHN
FLUR
SCHLAF. OMA
BAD
GARDEROBE
ABST.
WC
DEELE
- DEELE LIEGT ZWEI STUFEN TIEFER ALS WOHNBEREICH
DACHFENSTER
1. OBERGESCHOSS

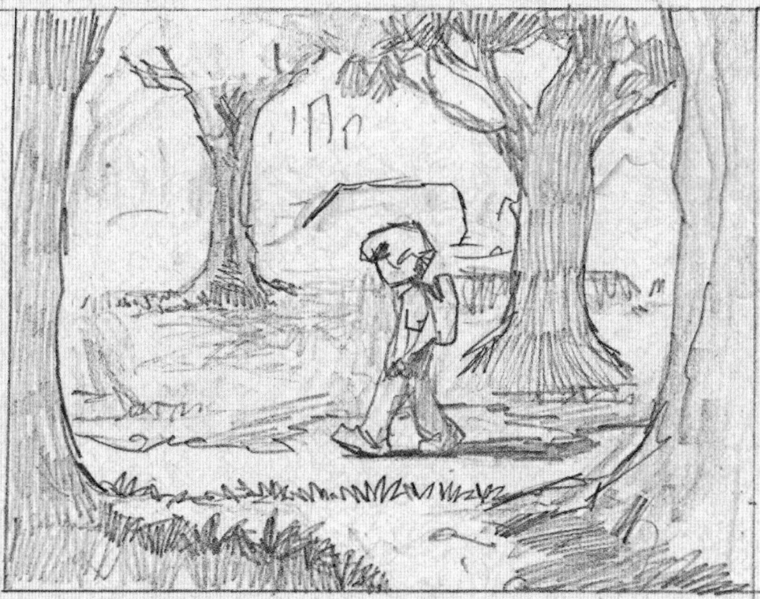

P16 VIELLEICHT ETWAS WEITER RAUS...

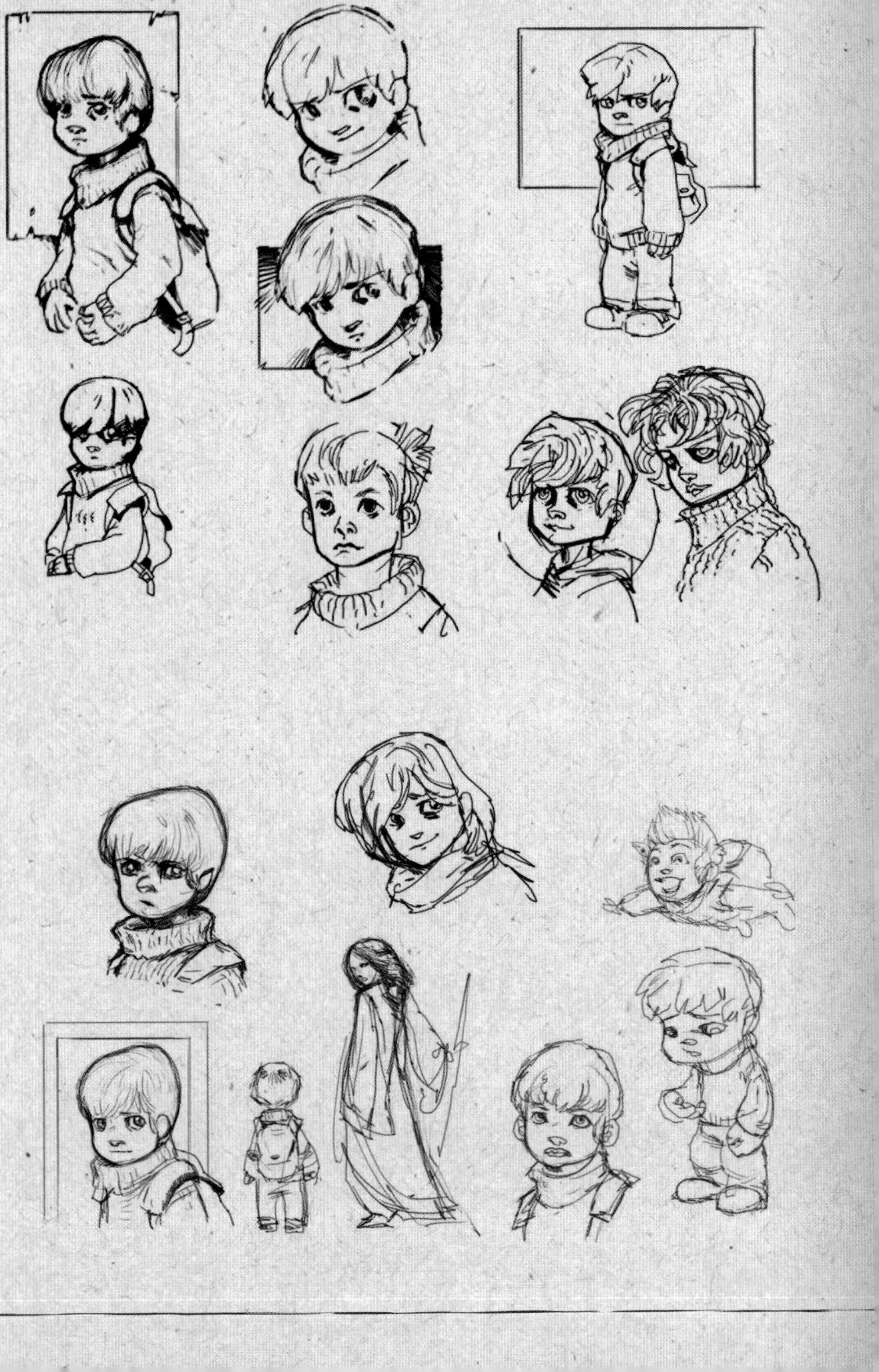

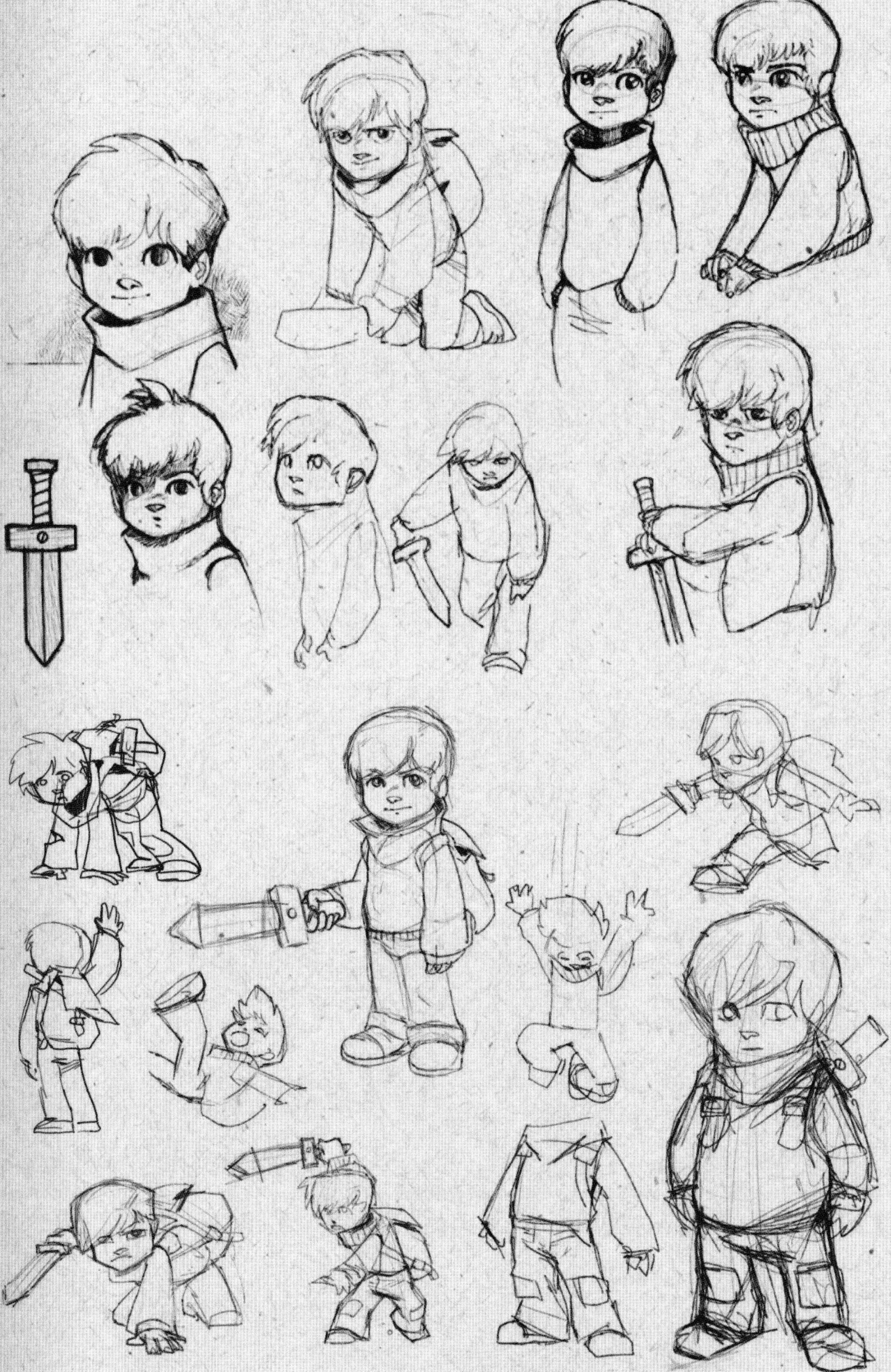

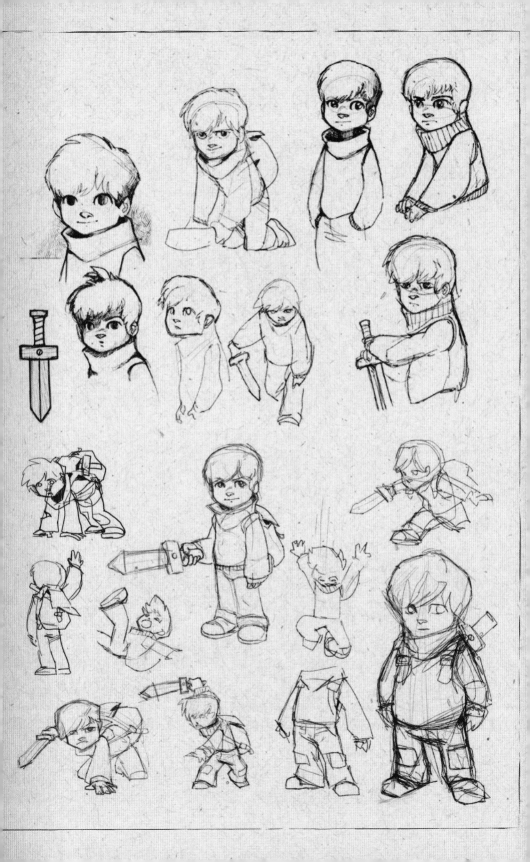

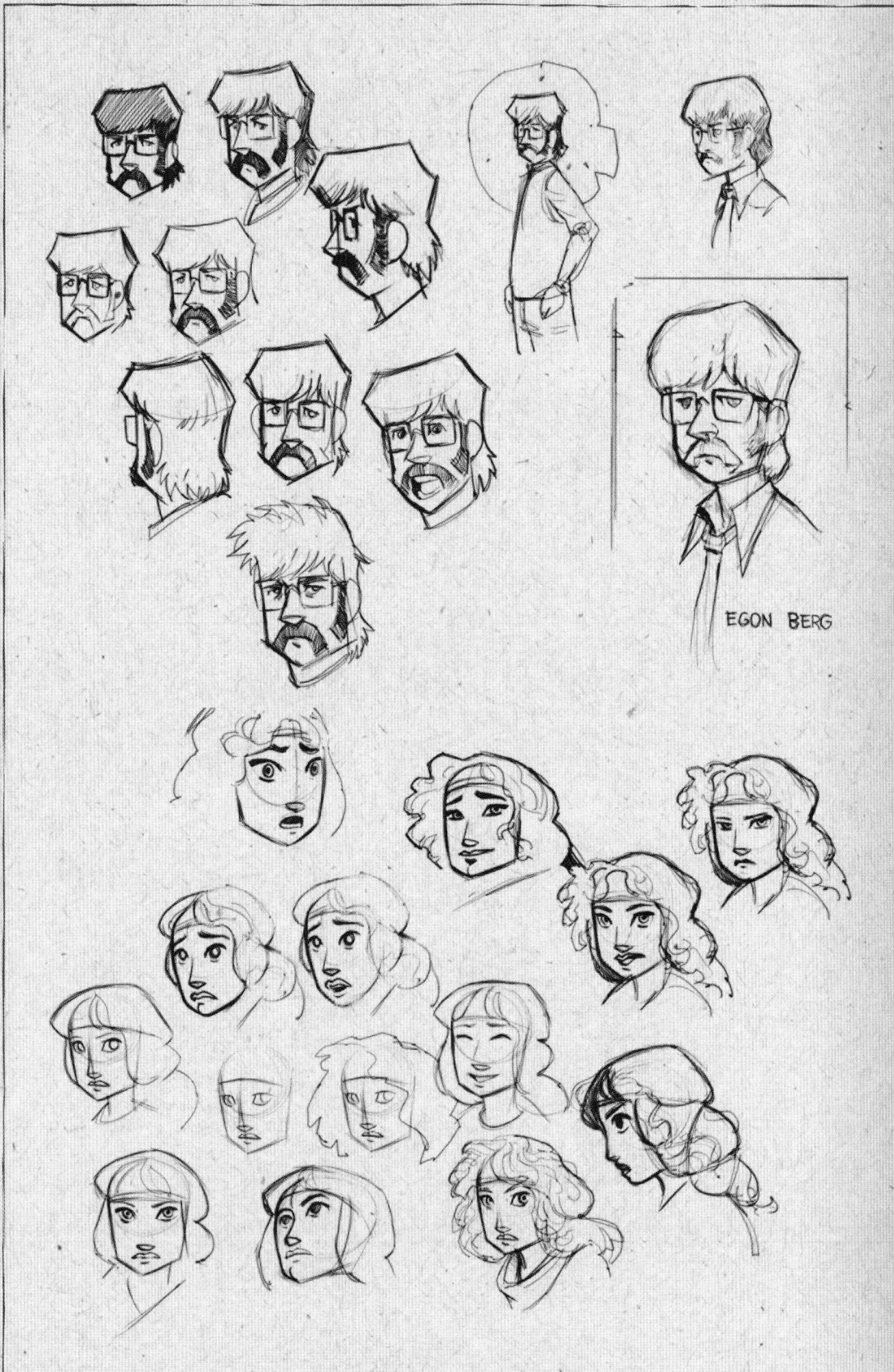
EGON BERG

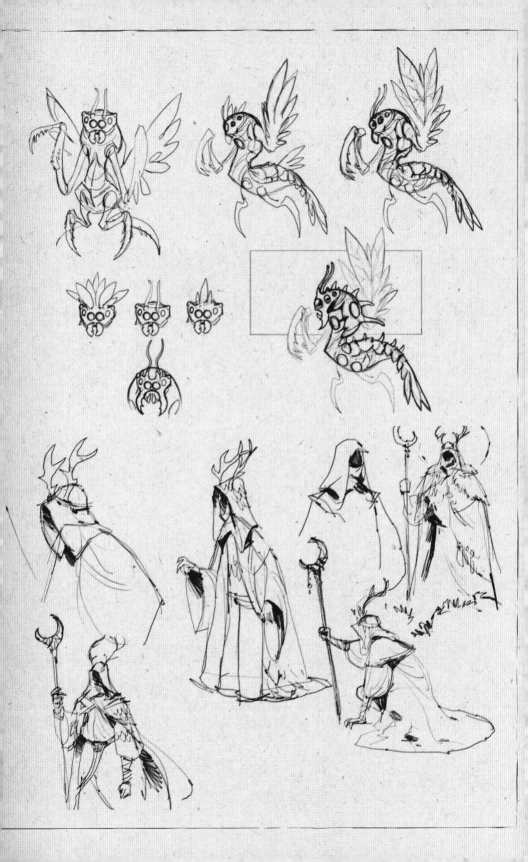

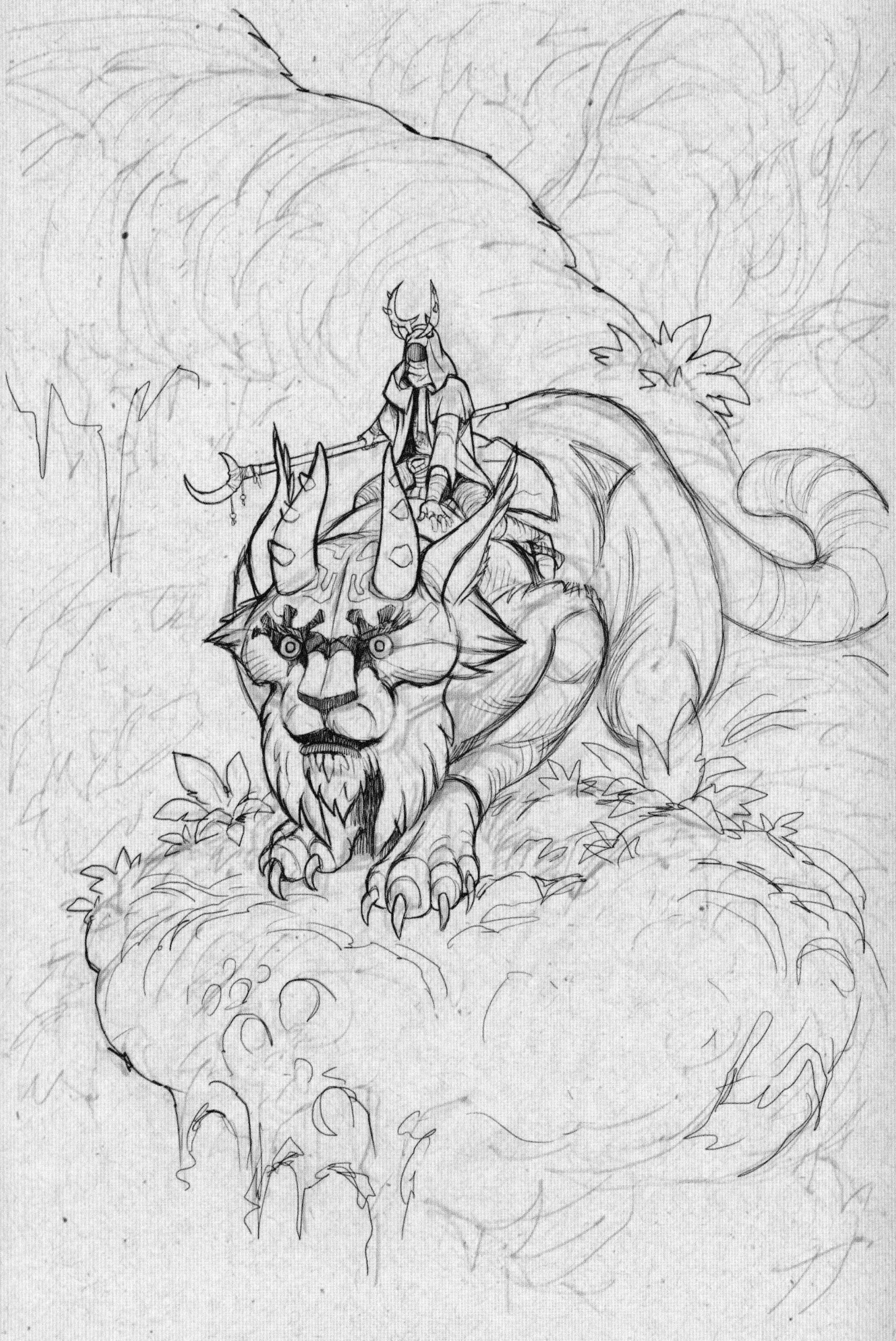

Fan Art Gallery

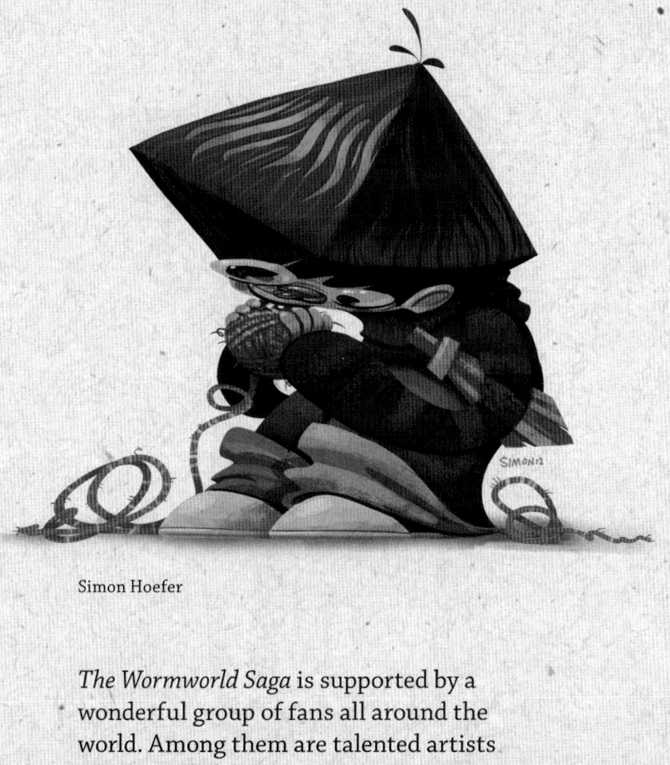
SIMON12

Simon Hoefer

The Wormworld Saga is supported by a wonderful group of fans all around the world. Among them are talented artists who have developed their very own visions around Jonas and his adventures inside the Wormworld. Here, we'd like to present a small selection of the fantastic fan artwork that has been submitted over time, and we'd like to thank all artists for their permissions to share their work with you.

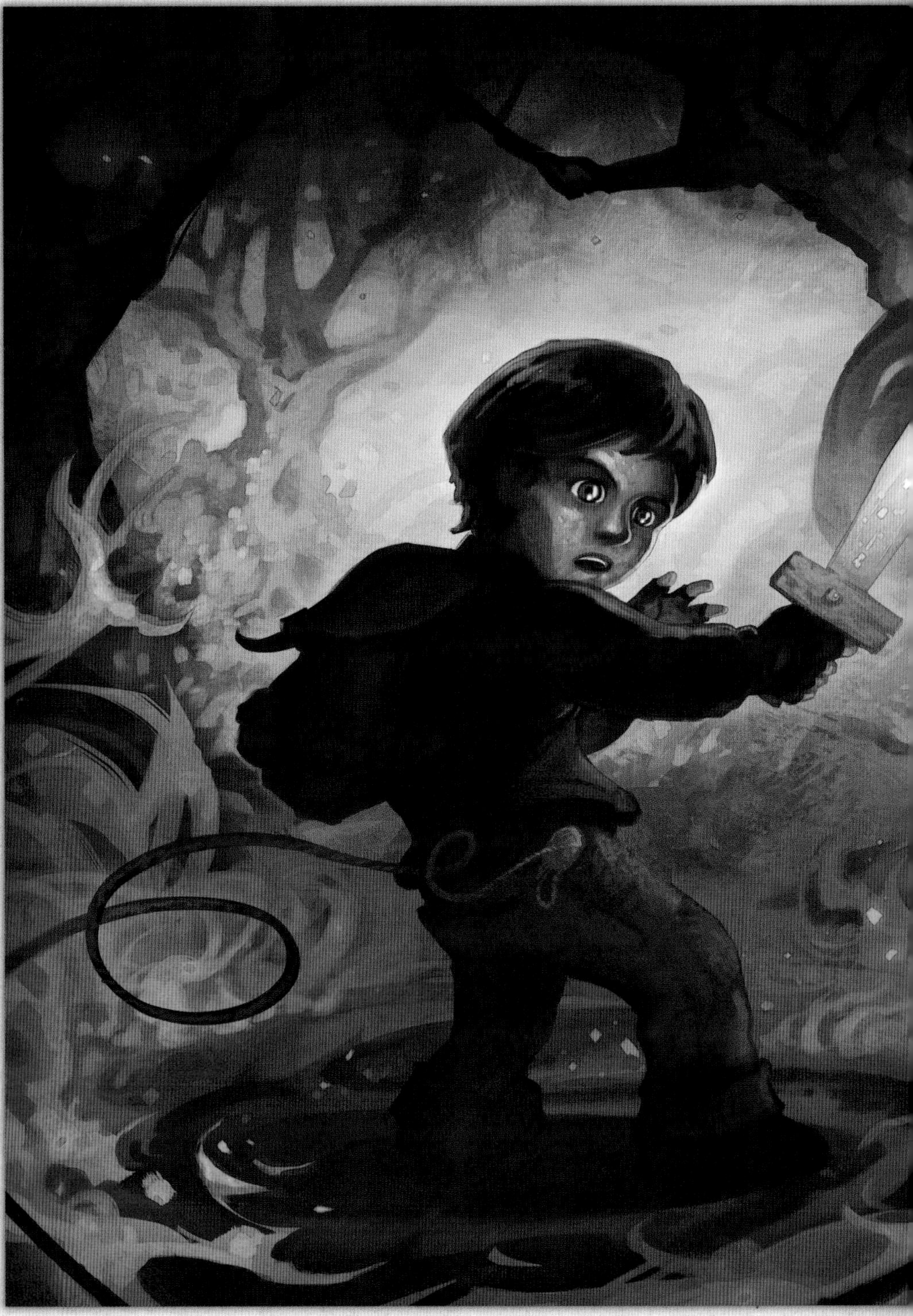
Florian Biege

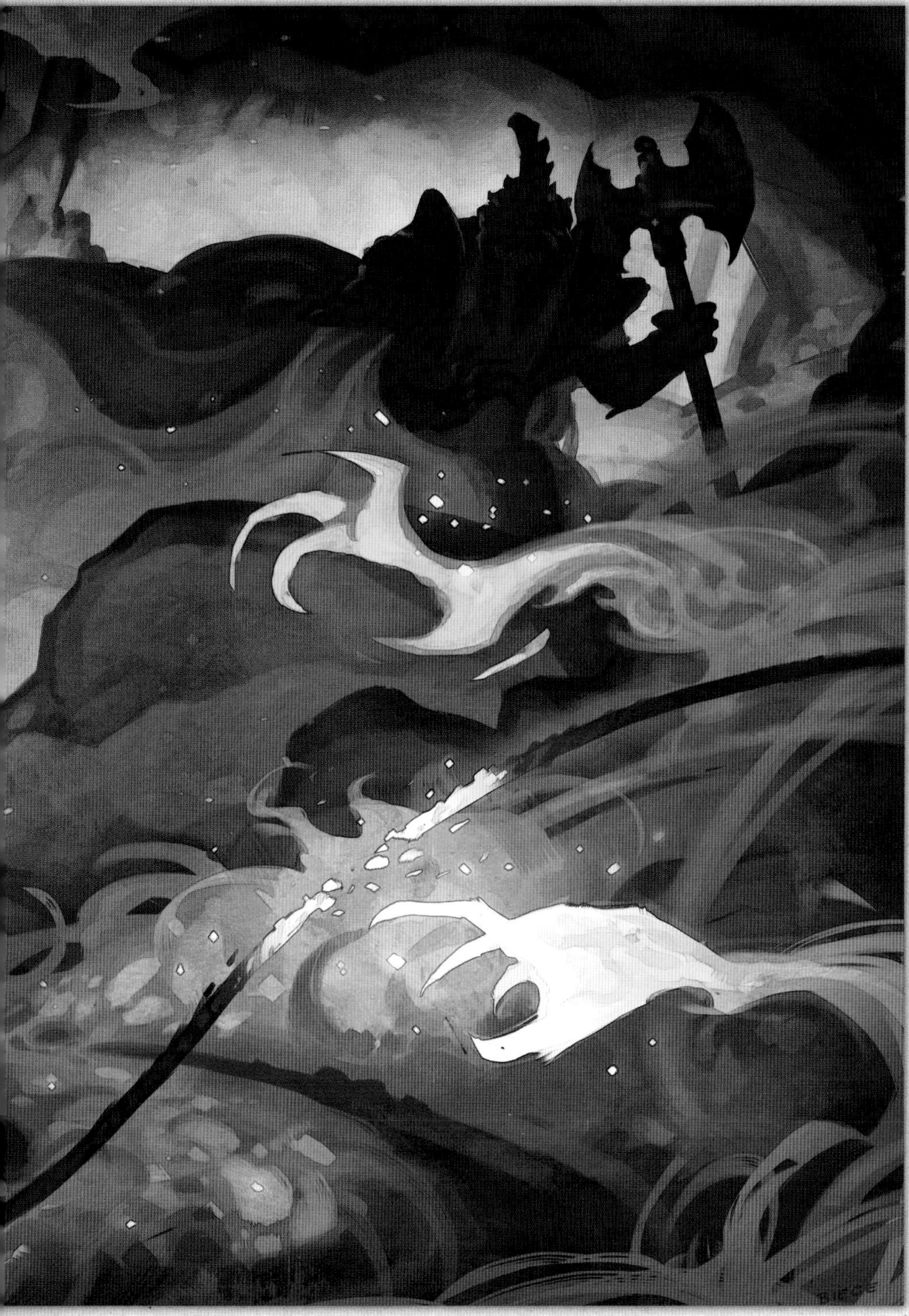

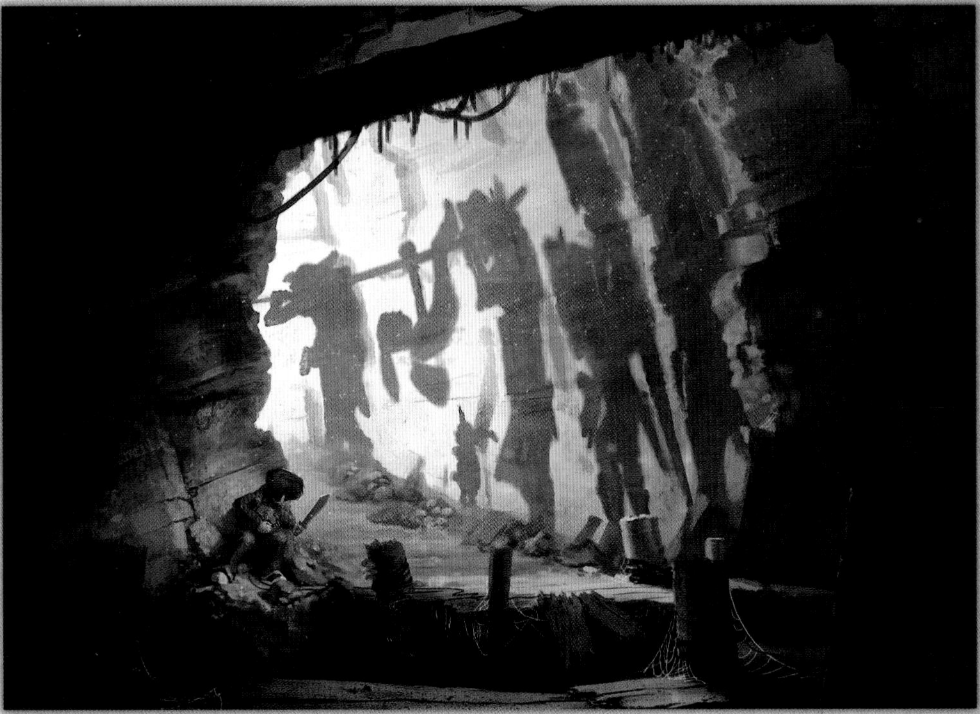

Simon Kopp

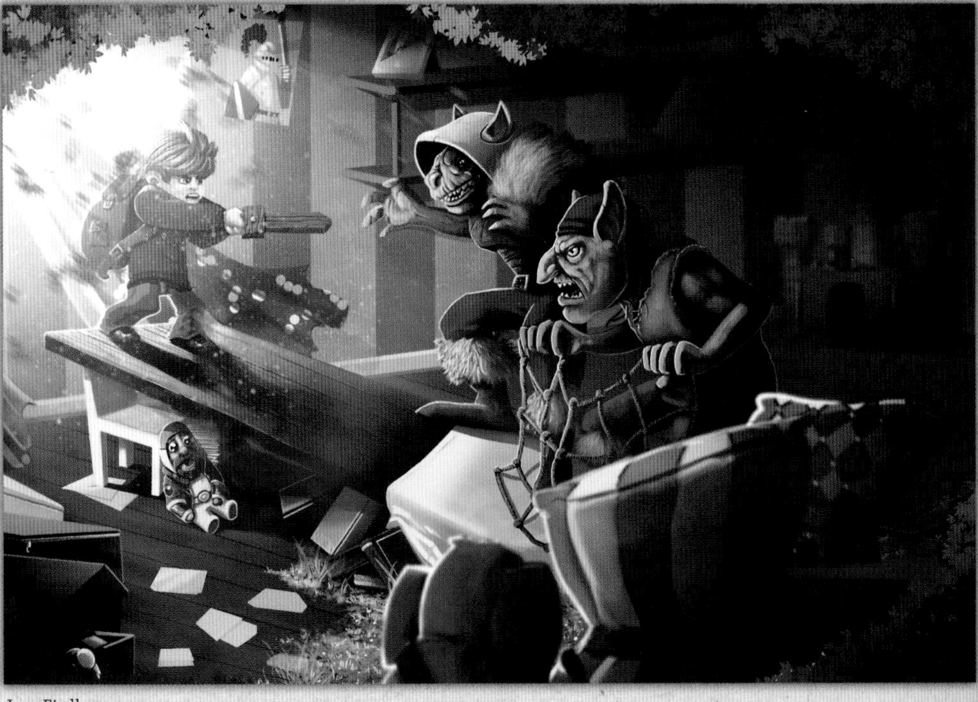

Jens Fiedler

Dirk Wachsmuth

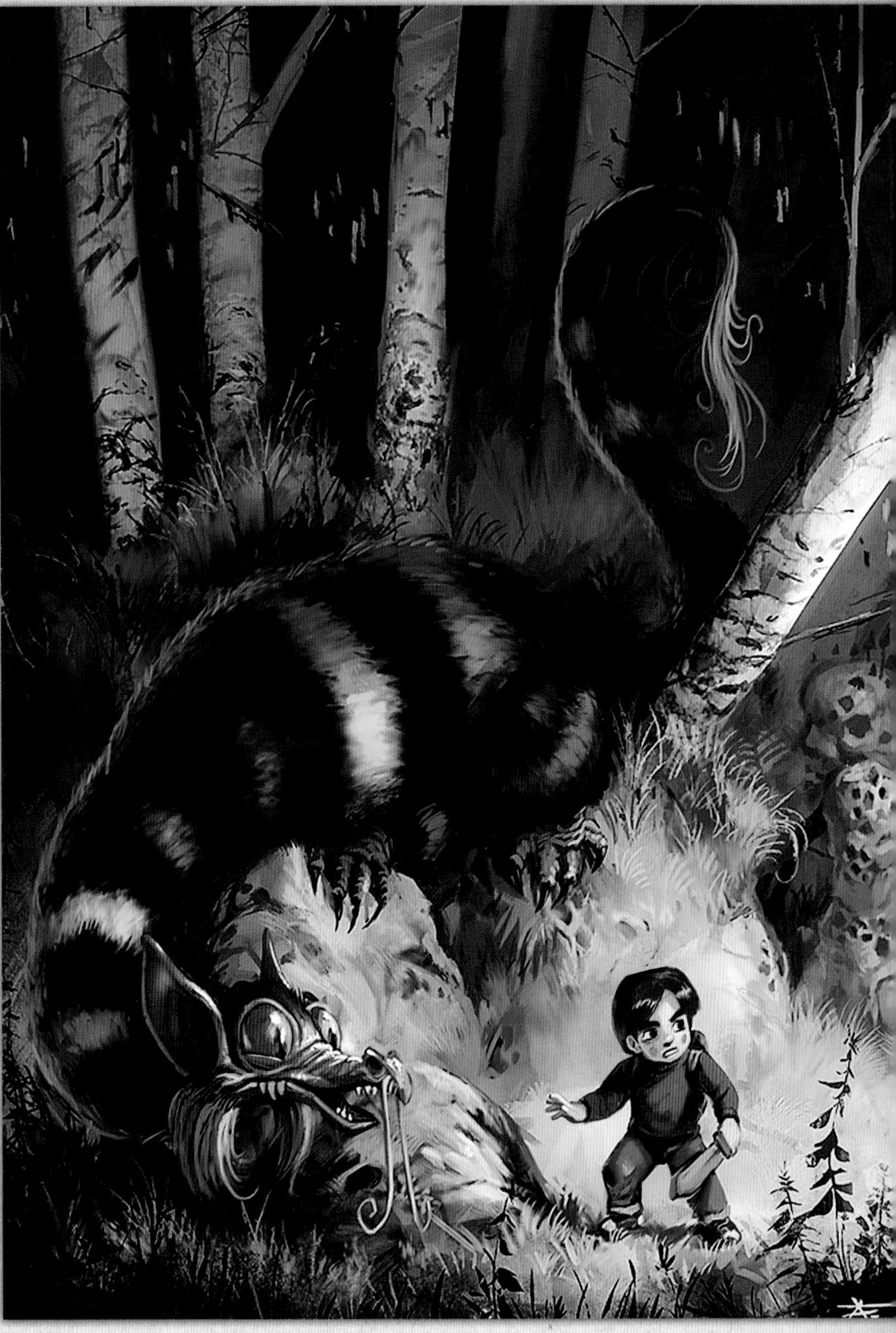

Artur Fast

Sergej Schell

Daniel Lieske

Daniel Lieske was born in 1977 in Bad Rothenfelde, a small town in Germany situated at the edge of the Teutoburger Forest. He began his career as a graphic novel author at a young age by selling his early comic creations in the schoolyard.

After school, he started to work in the computer games industry where he learned to draw and paint digitally. He developed his skills for over ten years before he decided to try his luck as an independent comic creator.

Today he lives with his wife, two sons, and two cats in an old framework house in Warendorf, a small town in northern Germany.

The thought that his work is read and appreciated all around the world still dazzles him.